Peter Carey was born in Bacchus Marsh, Victoria and now lives in New York. He is the author of twelve previous novels, three short story collections and two books on travel. Among other prizes, he has won the Booker Prize twice, the Commonwealth Writers Prize twice and the Miles Franklin Literary Award three times.

www.petercareybooks.com

Further praise for *Amnesia*:

'*Amnesia* yoked Assange-era computer hacking with an Australian political conspiracy from the Seventies, and looks tamer in summary than it proved in practice as its dubious, drunken narrator went further and further off-message with his story.' *Daily Telegraph* Books of the Year

'Linking the Assange and Snowden affairs with the UK crown's coup against the Australian government in 1975, Peter Carey's *Amnesia* is a completely original political novel.' Mark Lawson, *Guardian* Books of the Year

'Behind this dazzle of diversity, persisting themes can be discer⌐   ons, fugitives, misfits. Another is anger at political skulduggery: in particular, covert American machinations in Australia. In his new novel, *Amnesia*, they coalesce. Often rumbustiously funny, it has an almost Dickensian zest for colourful characters. Scenes of the cyber-underworld and its bizarre obsessives buzz with fascination . . . Metaphorical vitality pulses through Carey's prose: Australia's natural beauty – "stern khaki bush slashed with verticals in pink and white and grey . . . impasto yellow limestone glowing ecstatically in the morning sun" – is as sensuously celebrated as the treacheries and lies he sees infesting the country are scathingly portrayed.' Peter Kemp, *Sunday Times*

'It is the story of WikiLeaks as if transmogrified by Dickens and turned into a thrilling fable for our post-Edward Snowden era.' Luke Harding, *Guardian*

'I couldn't believe I was so caught by the throat by a story about "malware" and cyberspace and sabotage . . . but it's also about a dark stain of political history, about a mother and daughter, about power and brutality, about being young and furious . . . I thought Felix Moore in all his humanness, messiness and determination, was a masterpiece of character-making.' Hermione Lee

'Carey has twice won the Booker price for his excavations of Australian history . . . *Amnesia* carries that forward into this century, while providing a sharp riposte to those who say fiction can't cope with the cyber age . . . But he has written an intriguing version of a history about which we British know shamefully little.' *The Times*

'*Amnesia* . . . is for the most part vital, funny and humane . . . Carey's loving depiction of Australian landscapes, and especially the birdlife that inhabits them, suggests realms unfettered by our own paltry concerns. It is a sobering but optimistic reminder worthy of a terrific book.' *Independent on Sunday*

'Carey says a great deal in an entertaining, provocative novel, weighty with polemical intent, yet he never forgets to tell a story that is as large as life and as exuberantly complicated, and, as regards setting the record straight, long overdue. If fiction can summon the now, this novel has.' Eileen Battersby, *Irish Times*

'*Amnesia* is exhilaratingly suffused with Carey's wild prodigality of invention . . . *Amnesia* glitters with nervy verbal inventiveness and pungent characterisation. Carey conjures the longings and anxieties of his wayward teenage idealists with the same pathos and precision with which he depicts the pains and disillusions of middle age.' Jane Shilling, *Evening Standard*

Amnesia

PETER CAREY

FABER & FABER

First published in 2014
by Faber & Faber Limited
Bloomsbury House
74–77 Great Russell Street
London WC1B 3DA
This paperback edition first published in 2015

Typeset by Faber & Faber Ltd
Printed in England by CPI Group (UK) Ltd, Croydon, CR0 4YY

'Chuck E's In Love' words & music by Rickie Lee Jones © 1978, 1979,
Chrysalis One Music & Easy Money Music. All rights administered by
BMG Rights Management (US) LLC. International Copyright Secured.
All rights reserved. Reprinted by permission of Hal Leonard Corporation.

A CIP record for this book
is available from the British Library

ISBN 978-0-571-31122-4

FSC
www.fsc.org
MIX
Paper from
responsible sources
FSC® C101712

2 4 6 8 10 9 7 5 3 1

For Frances Coady

PART ONE

It was a spring evening in Washington DC; a chilly autumn morning in Melbourne; it was exactly 22.00 Greenwich Mean Time when a worm entered the computerised control systems of countless Australian prisons and released the locks in many other places of incarceration, some of which the hacker could not have known existed. Because Australian prison security was, in the year 2010, mostly designed and sold by American corporations the worm immediately infected 117 US federal correctional facilities, 1700 prisons, and over 3000 county jails. Wherever it went, it travelled underground, in darkness, like a bushfire burning in the roots of trees. Reaching its destinations it announced itself: THE CORPORATION IS UNDER OUR CONTROL. THE ANGEL DECLARES YOU FREE.

This message and others more elaborate were read, in English, by warders in Texas, contractors in Afghanistan, Kurdistan, in immigrant detention camps in Australia, in Woomera, black sites in the Kimberley, secret centres of rendition at the American 'signals facility' near Alice Springs. Sometimes prisoners escaped. Sometimes they were shot and killed. Bewildered Afghans and Filipinos, an Indonesian teenager wounded by gunfire, a British Muslim dying of dehydration, all these previously unknown individuals were seen on public television, wandering on outback roads.

The security monitors in Sydney's Villawood facility read: THE ANGEL OF THE LORD BY NIGHT OPENED THE PRISON DOORS, AND BROUGHT THEM FORTH. My former colleagues asked, what does this language tell us about the perpetrator?

I didn't give a toss. I was grateful for a story big enough to push me off the front pages where I had already suffered PANTS ON FIRE. I was spending my days in the Supreme Court of New South Wales paying Nigel Willis QC $500 an hour so I could be sued for defamation. Nigel's 'billable hours' continued to accrue well past the stage when it became clear that he was a fuckwit and I didn't have a chance in hell, but cheer up mate: he was betting 3:2 on a successful appeal. That my barrister also owned a racehorse was not the point.

Meanwhile there was not much for me to do but read the papers. FEDS NOW SAY ANGEL IS AN AUSSIE WORM.

'Would the defendant like to tell the court why he is reading a newspaper.'

'I am a journalist, m'lud. It is my trade.'

Attention was then brought to the state of my tweed jacket. Ha-ha, m'lud. When the court had had its joke, we adjourned for lunch and I, being unaccompanied on that particular day, took my famously shambolic self across to the botanic gardens where I read the *Daily Telegraph*. Down by the rose gardens amongst the horseshit fertiliser, I learned that the terrorist who had been 'obviously' a male Christian fundamentalist had now become the daughter of a Melbourne actress. The traitor appeared very pale and much younger than her thirty years. Dick Connolly got the photo credit but his editor had photoshopped her for in real life she would turn out to be a solid little thing whose legs were strong and sturdy, not at all like the waif in the *Telegraph*. She was from Coburg, in the north of Melbourne, a flat, forgotten industrial suburb coincidentally once the site of Pentridge Prison. She came to her own arraignment in a black hoodie, slouching, presumably to hide the fact that our first homegrown terrorist had a beautiful face.

Angel was her handle. Gaby was her name in what I have learned is 'meat world'. She was charged as Gabrielle Baillieux and I had known her parents long ago – her mother was the actress Celine Baillieux, her father Sando Quinn, a Labor member of parliament.

I returned to my own court depressed, not by the outcome of my case, which was preordained, but by the realisation that my life in journalism was being destroyed at the time I might have expected my moment in the sun.

I had published several books, fifty features, a thousand columns, mainly concerned with the traumatic injury done to my country by our American allies in 1975. While my colleagues leapt to the conclusion that the hacker was concerned simply with freeing boat people from Australian custody, I took the same view as our American allies, that this was an attack on the United States. It was clear to me, straight away, that the events of 1975 had been a first act in this tragedy and that the Angel Worm was a retaliation. If Washington was right, this was the story I had spent my life preparing for. If the 'events of 1975' seem confusing or enigmatic to you, then that is exactly my point. They are all part of 'The Great Amnesia'. More TC.

In court, I listened as my publisher got a belting from the judge and I saw his face when he finally understood he could not even sell my book as remaindered.

'Pulp?' he said.

'Including that copy in your hand.'

Damages were awarded against me for $120,000. Was I insured or not insured? I did not know.

The crowd outside the court was as happy as a hanging day.

'Feels, Feels,' the News International guy shouted. 'Look this way. Felix.'

That was Kev Dawson, a cautious little prick who made his living rewriting press releases.

'Look this way Feels.'

'What do you think about the verdict, Feels?'

What I thought was: our sole remaining left-wing journalist had been pissed on from a mighty height. And what was my crime? Repeating press releases? No, I had reported a rumour. In the world of grown-ups a rumour is as much a 'fact' as smoke. To omit the smoke is to fail to communicate the threat in the landscape.

In the Supreme Court of New South Wales this was defamation.

'What next, Felix?'

Rob a bank? Shoot myself? Certainly, no-one would give me the Angel story although I was better equipped (*Wired* magazine take note) to write it than any of the clever children who would be hired to do the job. But I was, as the judge had been pleased to point out, no longer employable in 'your former trade'. I had been a leader writer, a columnist, a so-called investigative reporter. I had inhabited the Canberra Press Gallery where my 'rumours' had a little power. I think Alan Ramsey may have even liked me. For a short period in the mid-seventies, I was host of *Drivetime Radio* on the ABC.

I was an aging breadwinner with a ridiculous mortgage. I had therefore been a screenwriter and a weekend novelist. I had written both history and political satire, thrillers, investigative crime. The screen adaptation of my novel *Barbie and the Deadheads* was workshopped at Robert Redford's Sundance Institute.

But through this, even while bowing and scraping to get 'seed money' from the Australian Film Commission, I remained a socialist and a servant of the truth. I had been sued ninety-eight times before they brought me down with this one, and along the way I had exposed the deeds of Kerry Packer and Rupert Murdoch (both Old Geelong Grammarians, btw) always a very dangerous occupation for a family man, and apparently terrifying for those who rely on him for succour. As the doors of the mainstream media closed to anyone unworldly enough to write the truth, I still published 'Lo-tech Blog', a newsletter printed on acid paper which was read by the entire Canberra Press Gallery and all of parliament besides. Don't ask how we paid our electricity bill.

I worked as a journalist in a country where the flow of information was controlled by three corporations. Their ability to manipulate the 'truth' made the right to vote largely meaningless, but I was a journalist. I did my best. In 'Lo-tech Blog', I revealed the Australian press's cowardly reporting of the government lies about the refugees aboard the ill-fated *Oolong*.

'I can't comprehend how genuine refugees would throw their children overboard,' said our Prime Minister.

Once again, like 1975, here was a lie of Goebbelsesque immensity. The fourth estate made a whole country believe the refugees were animals and swine. Many think so still.

Yet the refugees belonged here. They would have been at home with the best of us. We have a history of courage and endurance, of inventiveness in the face of isolation and mortal threat. At the same time, alas, we have displayed this awful level of cowardice, brown-nosing, criminality, mediocrity and nest-feathering.

I was overweight and out of breath but I was proud to be sued, reviled, scorned, to be called a loser by the rewriters of press releases. I took comfort from it, which was just as well because there was comfort nowhere else. As would be confirmed in the weeks ahead, none of my old mates were going to rescue me from the slow soul-destroying grind of unemployment.

2

A five-star hotel might seem an unwise venue for a bedraggled outcast to lick his wounds but the Wentworth was favoured by my old mate Woody 'Wodonga' Townes. My dearest friends all exhibit a passionate love of talk and drink, but of this often distinguished crowd it was Woody Townes who had the grit and guts. He had attended court every day although he had had to fly seven hundred kilometres from Melbourne. Any fight I had, he was always by my side. And when I had endured the whacking from the press I found him where I knew he would be, where he had waited on almost every gruesome afternoon, with his meaty body jammed into a small velvet chair in the so-called Garden Court. The moment he spotted me he began pouring champagne with his left hand. It was a distinctive pose: the heavy animal leg crossed against his shiny thigh, the right elbow held high to ward off the attentions of an eager waiter.

I considered my loyal friend's exposed white calves, his remarkable belt, his thick neck, the high colour in his cheeks and I thought, not for the first time, that it is Melbourne's talent to produce these extraordinary eighteenth-century figures. In a more contested space, life would compress them, but down south, at the Paris end of Collins Street, there was nothing to stop him expanding to occupy the frame. He was a Gillray engraving – indulgence, opinion, power.

By profession my mate was a 'property developer' and I presumed he must be sometimes involved in the questionable dealings of his caste. My wife thought him a repulsive creature, but she never gave herself a chance to know him. He was both a rich man and a courageous soldier of the left. He was a reliable patron of unpopular causes and (although he was possibly tone deaf) Chairman of the South Bank Opera Company. He financially supported at least two atonal composers who would otherwise have had to teach high school. He had also bankrolled my own ill-fated play. Woody's language could be abusive. He did occasionally spoil his philanthropy by demanding repayment via small services, but he could be relied upon to physically and legally confront injustice. In a time when the Australian Labor Party was becoming filled with white-collar careerists straight from university, Woody was old-school – he did not fear the consequences of belief.

'Fuck them all,' he said, and ground the champagne bottle down into the ice. That would be pretty much the content of our conversation, and three bottles later, after several rounds of fancy nibbles, he called for the bill, paid from a roll of fifties, got me into a taxi and gave me a Cabcharge voucher to sign at the other end.

'No surrender,' he said, or words to that effect.

It was only a short drive across the Anzac Bridge to our house at Rozelle. Here the best part of my life awaited me, my wife, two daughters, but – in the narrow passageway of our slightly damp terrace house, there stood, by poisonous chance, five cardboard cartons of my book, maliciously delivered that very afternoon.

Were these for me to pulp myself?

Was this not hilarious, that my puce-faced publisher, with his big house in Pymble, had gone to the trouble and expense of having boxes sent to my humble door? I was laughing so much I barely managed to carry this burden through the house. Apparently my daughters saw me and cared so little for my distress that they went straight up to watch the Kardashians. Claire must have been there somewhere, but I didn't see her yet. I was much more occupied with enacting the court order.

I could never light a barbecue. I had no manual skills at all. It was my athletic Claire who handled the electric drill, not me.

Naturally I overcompensated with the firelighters. Did I really enclose a free firelighter in every book? Was that a joke? How would I know? It was not necessarily self-pitying and pathetic that I set my own books on fire, but it was certainly stupid or at least ill-informed to add a litre of petrol to those feeble flames. I was unprepared for the violent force, the great whoosh that lifted off my eyebrows and caught the lower limbs of our beloved jacaranda.

As the flames crawled from the branches to the second-floor extension, I should – people never cease insisting – have picked up the garden hose and put it out. Fine, but these dear friends did not see what I saw. I made my judgement. I chose human life before real estate. I rushed up the stairs and snatched the audience from the Kardashians. Yes, my babies were teenagers. Yes, they resisted, but here was no time for explanation and I had no choice but treat them roughly. Apparently I smelled 'like a cross between a pub and a lawnmower'. I rushed them out into the street and left them screaming.

I don't know what happened then, but somehow the next-door copywriter stole my girls and the Balmain fire brigade were soon pushing me aside, dragging their filthy hoses down our hall and Claire, my wife, my comfort, my lover, my friend was waiting for me.

The next bit should remain private from our kids. But I will never forget exactly what was said.

3

Claire was clever, kind and funny. She slept with her nose just above the sheets like a little possum. She woke up smiling. She stripped a century of paint from the balustrades and waxed and oiled them until they glowed. She climbed on the roof during lightning storms to remove the leaves from the overflowing gutters. She canvassed door to door for the Leichhardt by-election. She was a Japanese-trained potter whose work was collected by museums but there was never a night when I came home from Canberra or Melbourne or a union pub in Sussex Street that she was not waiting to hear what had happened.

She was commonly regarded as a perfect mother while I was known to have been unfaithful or at least to have attempted it. I was said to be continually drunk and impatient with decent people whose politics I did not like. I was allegedly unemployable. It was thought I was a communist who did not have the intelligence to see that he had become historically irrelevant.

All day Claire ripped her strong square hands with gritty clay, from which human sacrifice she extracted long necks and tiny kissing lips. She cooked like the farmer's daughter that she was, leg of lamb, baked vegetables, proper gravy. But each night she devoured the life that I brought home. My darling was what is commonly called a political junkie – awful term – but I delivered what she wanted most. We had fun, for years and years. Yes, I developed a Canberra belly and was ashamed to jog. She, as everyone remarked, stayed neat and trim. She wore jeans and windcheaters and sneakers and cut her hair herself, eschewing 'sexy' legs and teetering fuck-me heels. After the fire I learned that certain mates had wondered if she might be gay. Idiots. None of them had the slightest clue about our love life. We were tender maniacs in ways known only to ourselves. If not for debt we would be in bed today.

Some people are good at debt. We were bad at it, and only discovered it in the way people who get seasick learn of their weakness when the ship has left the shore. We were a journalist and a potter thinking they could send their kids to an expensive private school. You get the joke.

Earlier I described how I abandoned these children on the footpath. Abandoned? For God's sake, they were almost at the end of their investment curve. To listen to their conversation you would never dream that their parents were both third-generation socialists. Did they even remember their father toasting crumpets in the smoky fire? Can they hear their mother's lovely voice sing 'Moreton Bay'?

> *I've been a prisoner at Port Macquarie*
> *At Norfolk Island and Emu Plains*
> *At Castle Hill and cursed Toongabbie*
> *At all those settlements I've worked in chains*
> *But of all places of condemnation*
> *And penal stations of New South Wales*
> *Of Moreton Bay I have found no equal*
> *Excessive tyranny each day prevails*

She sang that to our little girls? You bet she did.

We had made the awful mistake of sending the girls to school with the children of our enemies. We thought we were saving Fiona from dyslexia. In fact we were wrecking her family by putting it under a financial strain it could not withstand. I would never once, not for a second, have thought to call Claire timid. How could I know that debt would make her so afraid? We got a line of credit for $50,000 and every time I acted like myself she hated it. She had loved me for those qualities before: I mean, my almost genetic need to take risk, to stand on principle, to poke the bully in the eye. I could not compromise, even when I was – so often – physically afraid. A sword hung over the marriage bed and I did not see it. I refused compromises she privately thought a father was morally obliged to make.

And of course the girls had not the least idea of what was at stake. If they paid attention to a newspaper it was only the Life and Style section. I doubt they had read a single one of my words, and had no notion of my work and life. They had never seen the evidence that might have justified my absences. If I allowed Claire's bond to be the strongest it was because I saw how much she wanted them to be 'my daughters'. Only once I bought them clothing (T-shirts, that's all). Then I learned that this was not my job and I should never try again.

Before this final defamation suit, Claire had been the pillion passenger who closed her eyes and hung on tight but the Supreme Court's finding was the final straw. When she heard the size of the damages, she quite collapsed.

As a child she had seen the family farm taken by the bank. Was it that? Was it something else? In any case, she did not believe my assurance that 'everything will be OK' because Woody had flown up from Melbourne for the court case. He had promised nothing. She was correct to say this, but she could not grasp that this was exactly the sort of situation when you could rely on Woody. Claire could not grasp his influence. She did not care that he had saved me from my burning car. All she could see was that his father had been a slumlord and a thug.

Nor did she trust Nigel QC because she believed, correctly, that he was the prosecutor's friend. I told her that did not matter. I was right. If only she had trusted me, I would have got back on the bike and taken her hurtling through the bends at a hundred and fifty kilometres an hour. I would have won the appeal. I would have sorted out the legal costs, and we would have celebrated as we had celebrated many times before.

'Everything will be OK,' I said, and it was dreadful to see the fury in her eyes.

4

I was from a small town in Victoria, but I had thought of gorgeous wicked Sydney as my home for fifteen years. Yet once I was cast out of Denison Street, Rozelle, I saw I had no home at all. I was pushed up into the heartless traffic of Victoria Road and across the vertiginous Anzac Bridge. I had to admit my mates had all abandoned me. Darling Harbour was below. All of that bright chaotic city lay before me. I had no mobile phone. I had no bed. I was reduced to ringing doorbells in the eastern suburbs. I cannot go into the details of my reception, but so reluctantly was I given refuge that I felt compelled to refuse my host's coffee in the morning. I certainly would not crawl on my belly to ask to use his phone.

I spent the day at Martin Place, at the post office, searching the Sydney phone books and getting change at the counter.

'Do I know you? You were on TV last night?'

'That's me, mate.'

This clerk was a pale red-headed fellow with no bum and his sleeves rolled up to show his biceps. He slowly counted out my phone money.

'Felix,' he said.

'Yes, mate.'

'You're a wanker, mate.'

I took my money down the far end and crouched in

the gloom, trying to find someone to take my call. I had expected my colleagues might enjoy a gossip, but they were clearly nervous of what I was going to ask of them. So many people 'stepped away' from their desks at the same time, they must have made a conga line, from Pyrmont to Ultimo, from Fairfax to the Australian Broadcasting Corporation.

I left Martin Place and walked under the gloomy Moreton Bay figs in Hyde Park, down along William Street, past Westfield Tower, an ugly building once occupied by the most exhilarating mix of power, almost forgotten figures such as Gough Whitlam, Neville Wran, Harry Miller before and after his spell in Cessnock jail.

Dusk came early and I really had no heart to test another friendship so I ended up at the inevitable: the Bourbon and Beefsteak in King's Cross. Why did we always love the B&B? It was an awful place, owned by an American called Bernie Houghton. We all knew that Houghton was an arms dealer with an uncontested CIA affiliation. That never stopped us going to eat there late at night, and even when we discovered Bernie was a partner in Nugan Hand, the same CIA bank that helped finance the events of 1975, we continued to go to drink at the Bourbon and Beefsteak.

My wife said I was a romantic, that the B&B was my idea of noir, with prostitutes and tourists, bludgers and transvestites, well-connected criminals and murdering policemen. She may not have been completely wrong.

It was not dark yet and I got a breezy table near the street from which vantage point I soon saw – approximately forty-five minutes after my arrival – our dinged-up Subaru rise from the street and mount the footpath. Did I cower?

Oh probably. But I did not dive under the table no matter what your friends have told you. In fact my wife was carrying nothing more frightening than a plastic bag which would later turn out to contain a mobile phone, a charger, a framed photo of my daughters, and my complete signed set, all six volumes, of Manning Clark's much loved *History of Australia*.

The photograph was on the top. It gave me hope. If I had seen my treasured Manning Clarks I would have known this was the coup de grâce, but in my foolish optimism I thought, sweet girl, she knows my life is built upon my family. She came straight at my table. I thought, thank God, I would have died to lose her.

'They cut the jacaranda down this morning.'

She had such a pretty face but her eyes were red-rimmed and her mouth was straight as a knife. What was I to say? Sit down?

'Call Woody,' she said, attempting to hand over the carry bag.

I grabbed at her. She said not to touch her. The charger fell to the floor. By the time I had discovered the Manning Clarks, she was gone.

And who would ever feel sorry for me? Had I not risked my family's life?

But even then I was an optimist. Woody wanted me to call him and I knew exactly why. He had talked to Claire. He knew I was in the doghouse. Naturally he would find me a place to stay. I called immediately and he picked up.

'You're in the shit.'

'I am.'

'Where are you now?'

'Where else? The B&B.'

'Fucking Bernie,' he laughed.

'I thought he was dead.'

'Yes mate.' His tone became weirdly serious and I thought, of course Woody would know Bernie Houghton, and probably Frank Nugan too. There were stranger friendships in this town. Shoot me for saying it, but Sydney, our dense dark city, is really very small.

'I've got something for you,' he said. I thought, thank God. I could not bear to go begging for a bed.

'You're a mate,' I said.

'You're going to have to get your arse down here.'

'Where's here?'

'Melbourne.'

'Why Melbourne?'

'Jesus, don't argue with me Feels. I'm about to save your life again. Why Melbourne? Jeez. Don't be offensive.'

'Thank you,' I said. 'I appreciate everything you've done.'

Of course Melbourne was where he owned most property, where he would most easily find an empty flat for me. I should be very, very grateful.

'You want this or not?'

'Yes, I want it.'

'Then I'll see you tomorrow in my office. I'll take you to lunch at Moroni's like the old days.'

I could have charged the flight to our joint credit card, but truly, I had seen Claire's face. It was Thursday night, late night shopping. I took a cab to the distinguished book dealer on Oxford Street where I offered my Manning Clarks. Each one was signed 'To Felix with respect.' I argued that they were association copies.

'The association being?'

I was not one of Manning's many worshippers, but I liked him and he was unfailingly amused by me. 'He is Manning Clark,' I said. 'I am Felix Moore.'

The bookseller showed no particular reaction, although he did spend an awfully long time staring at the spine of Volume I. He was a gentle, diplomatic young man. He did not call me a wanker or argue about the plunging value of my name. Rather, he indicated, quite correctly, that Vol. I was associated with red wine and biro and Vol. V was foxed. He offered two hundred in the manner of his caste, giving me my books back as if to say, don't even try to haggle. Of course I took the money and it turned out just enough: $112 for the ticket, $60 for a shitty room I found nearby in Surry Hills.

Sad and sorry on my slippery motel sheets I called my wife.

To my delight she took my call.

'If you do this one more time,' she said, 'I'll have your phone cut off.'

5

Before exhausting the last of the birdshit deposits which were the source of its fabulous wealth, before going into business as a detention facility for asylum seekers, the nation state of Nauru destroyed two landmark buildings in Collins Street and erected a 52-floor octagonal monument to its own ineptitude and corruption.

Who would want to have an office on this site? My mate of course.

'If I applied your standards, Feels, I'd be sleeping on the beach. Also,' he said, revealing his true Melbourne heart, 'the last time I looked, you lived in Sydney.'

Woody had his office on the fiftieth floor and here he liked to swing back and forth in his fancy chair and gaze up at the violent scudding clouds and down on Parliament House and out to his developments at Docklands. He could see all the way south to St Kilda and north-east to Collingwood and all that rising damp he had inherited when his father was shot to death.

That murder was not a subject I ever raised with Woody. His personal history resided in the world of 'it is said'. It is said that he was a stellar student at Melbourne High. It is said he had wanted to be a literature professor. It is said he had no choice but to pick up his father's revolver. It is said that he continued that habit long after he employed others to collect his rents. I know this last is true because he once persuaded me to go to the beautiful old Florentino restaurant to pick up 'something' he had stupidly left behind. He didn't say it was a pistol but I noted the blanched face of the unerringly polite Raymond Tsindos when he presented me with a shoebox marked 'Mr Townes'. Outside, on Bourke Street, by the window of that famous bookshop, I lifted the lid. I never told him what I saw.

It is not common for people in Melbourne to carry guns. Indeed it is a criminal offence. So it may seem odd that, rather than stain his good name, my friend's idiosyncrasy brought a certain frisson to his reputation. Patron of the arts, collector of first editions, street fighter, champion of the left, also, of course, most of all, a property developer. In a different society Woody Townes would have been a player in nothing grander than a city council, but in our dry sclerophyll country his species nests very high indeed.

'I'm going to save your arse, young Felix.'

'That's very noble of you, mate.'

He stared at me and I, like a drunk who realises he has caused offence, was confused and hurt and dared not look away. This was not Woody in the Wentworth but Woody in his office. My mate had scary moments.

'Thanks for this,' I said.

'Ah, comrade,' he sighed, 'you know I am not noble.'

'In your fashion, mate.'

'You thought you were fucked,' he said. 'You were up shit creek again.'

'Pretty much, yes.'

'Now you're going to be top dog.'

Oh fuck, I thought, as I sat down opposite him, he is

offering me one of his disgusting penthouses on the Yarra. It would be impossible to refuse.

'Just a place to stay till I get started.'

'But what would you possibly start on? Workwise.'

'Jeez. I've just arrived.'

'Maybe you'll be working sooner than you think. You know who the Angel's mother is?'

'Yes. And so do you.'

He raised his big eyebrows, grinning, withholding.

'You've been in touch with her,' I suggested.

'Mate, I've never stopped being in touch with Celine.'

The innuendo was not prettily expressed, but I wanted to believe what he was hinting at. 'You got me a gig?'

'You write *the* bloody story, mate. Exclusive. Felix Moore. The defendant won't talk to anyone but you.'

'Bullshit.'

'I bailed her. Five hundred k,' Woody said, as if he'd purchased a Dobell portrait. I did not judge him for his vulgarity. I admired him. Who else in Australia would have stepped up in his place? 'While you were packing shit in the park in Sydney, I was on the phone. I bailed the bloody Angel before the US could touch her. What about that? She's yours.' He was grinning at me like a wide-mouthed frog. I didn't have to tell him I was already on her side.

'And she wants me to write her story? That's what you're saying.'

'Mate, she never heard of you.'

I didn't believe him for a second, and in any case I did not care.

'No newspaper's going to run this,' I said.

Wodonga threw his sandwich in the bin and I recalled I had heard his stomach had been stapled and that when you ate with him at Florentino he would vomit discreetly into his handkerchief. He sat more formally now, his awful elephantine hands clasped gently above his stomach.

'Book,' he said. 'Big advance. You can lose your court appeal and pay your damages and still buy Claire a sexy nightie. The contract is being written now. But if you don't want the job, just say so.'

As it turned out the money was terrific, although his company would own the copyright and I would have no royalty, ever, and no recourse if my name was, without consultation, removed from the title page. Nor did he tell me that he did not control the source at all. For many weeks I would be tormented by the subject's unavailability. If he had warned me? It would not have changed a thing. I saw myself accept a fat brown envelope that I imagined contained a paperback. Woody said it was $10,000 and I did not even count.

'A good-faith deposit,' he said. 'Buy yourself a suit.'

'Fair enough,' I said, thinking, fuck the suit, I can pay the school bills.

Woody slipped into his jacket and took a dainty umbrella from his drawer.

'You're going to write about a traitor,' he said, watching me stuff the envelope into my jacket. 'Being the mug you are, you will fall in love with her. The only problem is: she will most likely be put to death.' I was about to remind him that Australia had no death penalty but he retreated to a private bathroom in the office and peed so long and loud I knew he was showing off his prostate operation.

'I've got the table at Moroni's,' he said when he emerged. 'Do you need a comb?'

'Certainly not.'

I did not need a comb to gain admittance to Moroni's. I had eaten there a hundred times, with Gough Whitlam, John Cain – that is, a Prime Minister and a State Premier whose speech I had once rewritten in that very restaurant, assisted, it might be added, by Moroni's lethal grappa.

The maître d' was named Abramo. He was always the same, like a benign James Joyce with perfect vision. Abramo had good reasons to be fond of me as he shortly demonstrated by ignoring Wodonga and warmly welcoming my slovenly self. He showed me to a corner table where there sat an unusual individual. First, she was a woman, the only one in all the hushed besuited room. She was wearing a charcoal silk Shanghai Tang jacket with a brick-red lining and her haircut was a million-dollar job, by which I mean short and simple and sustained by strong, almost springy, silver hair. I was wrong about her age, and so would you have been. She had all those looks that come from great cheekbones, the sort of structured beauty a hundred years of Gauloises could not corrode.

As I approached she stood to shake my hand. She said her name but I did not catch it. I assumed she was the publisher.

'Felix Moore,' I said. I heard Woody groan. He could not believe I didn't recognise the famous face.

'Felix,' she said. 'It's Celine.'

I began to speak but could not end the sentence. The traitor's mother leaned across and kissed me on both burning cheeks.

6

It was not simply a famous face I failed to recognise. We had known each other for years and years. Celine and I had been two of 347 freshmen at Monash University. There had been no second- or third- or fourth-year students. Indeed there had not been a Monash University the year before. The so-called 'campus' was a raw construction site twenty kilometres east of Moroni's. There were acres of hot shadeless car park across which a young woman walked in stiletto heels.

This Celine was a vision, like the redhead on the Redhead matches box. She was in no way like the woman at the table in Moroni's. She was much taller, fuller breasted. She had flouncing skirts, gorgeous bouncing fair hair.

The woman at Moroni's was famous. Her lips were full but also pale, carved in soapstone. The nineteen-year-old had a violently red mouth and was dramatically 'accessorised' by what we might now call her 'posse', a very dangerous-looking collection of young men who I immediately decided would have to be my friends. There was a beatnik, a poet, a queeny boy, a sort of Hell's Angel, and finally her lover, Sandy Quinn, an older man in a linen jacket who certainly had not come from high school. It would be years before I learned a trade union was paying him to go to university. I did not notice any sadness in his eyes. I saw his beard, sun-bleached, trim and sculpted to his jaw. I took his silence to be both powerful and judgemental.

'I was a total dork,' I told her, and this was true.

'He was very cute,' she said to Woody.

'So he was a randy little dog,' said Woody. 'Cop a feels.'

This caused a silence. I thought of my tumescent adventure with her father's photograph. Abramo filled my glass.

I had been short and scruffy with the nasal vowels I had learned in Bacchus Marsh. My hair was short and less clean than it might have been. I did not have the requisite sloppy sweater. Celine's gang had been at first amused, then appalled, then made completely rat-faced by my presumption – that I was fit to be their friend. They said things which would have made a lesser person run away and cry.

But I was the son of a man who would stand in a muddy potato paddock all afternoon if that was what it took to sell a Ford. Those were my genetics.

Celine never thought me cute. But she saw my will, which was well in advance of my other attractions and was therefore dazzling. One afternoon in Springvale she told me I would be the only one of all of them who would make something of my life. Now she was about to make her own prediction come true. She would give me sole access to her outlaw daughter. So watch me, I thought, watch me do the rest.

The waiters had surely seen my recent humiliation on television and I was pleased they would now be witnesses to this redemption, those tall private men with white aprons and elegant grey moustaches. Now they saw the queen of stage and screen kiss me on my raddled cheek.

'To Felix,' she said and clinked my glass.

'I am in disgrace,' I said, referring of course to PANTS ON FIRE, but also, in my own way, underlining my outcast character which could never really be acceptable. I did not reveal that I had information about her life that she herself was unaware of, but I most definitely hinted, in my subtle way, that an honourable writer needs to be a scorpion as well. A writer serves the story. He dare not weigh the private consequences.

'It is not you who are in disgrace,' she said. 'You shamed them, as usual.' And I recalled that very particular fire in her grey eyes, her characteristic arousal at the prospect of a little danger.

'You might have lost the case but you made them look as corrupt and venal as they are.'

Yes, I had fought the good fight all my life but I had also become an awful creature along the way.

7

The beginning of the academic year had been stinking hot. The rain fell in buckets and the steam rose off the lawn where I had recently stood beside my father while the Chancellor of Monash University delivered his opening address. I was the first member of my family to get past the lower reaches of high school. I had no conscious knowledge of why I had chosen a university with no cloisters, no quadrangles, no suck-up colleges, no private school boys with their Triumph TR3s. Instead I had chosen the sea of mud that had been a market garden, where the footpaths were not yet paved, where the campus was surrounded by light industry and the cream brick homes of those who worked beneath those sawtoothed roofs. My choice was not political. I had no politics I was aware of.

This was three years before the Gulf of Tonkin, three years before conscription for Vietnam, seven years before the Monash Labor Club invented revolution, which would involve – I was given this message personally – being put against a wall and shot.

We students walked on narrow paths, single file like cows on their way to milking. We returned to landladies whose husbands were fitters and turners but were introduced as engineers. We were barbarians to our hosts to whom we delivered our Monash mud (PLEASE REMOVE YOUR

28

SHOES) and splashing urine (PLEASE LIFT THE SEAT).

I am not sure that Celine's high heels were muddy as she later claimed, but there is no doubt she had peed standing at the urinal. Everybody mentioned it. I was impressed by Sando's crumpled linen jacket and did not know enough to buy my own clothes second-hand. I tried too hard, most likely. I listened to everything they said. As a result I got the train from Clayton into Flinders Street and found, not without some difficulty, both *Ulysses* and *The Cantos* of Ezra Pound. I carried these heavy volumes back to the suburban bedroom I shared with a chemistry student from Wonthaggi. There was just one desk. When that was occupied I read lying down or wrote whilst kneeling at my bed. I shoplifted an expensive commentary on *Ulysses* and made margin notes on the significance of 'Agenbite of inwit', for instance. 'Inwit' should have been 'inwyt'. Did Sandy know James Joyce couldn't spell? Did he understand that 'U.P.:up' was meant to suggest urination and erection? I kneeled. I annotated. I stored away my ammunition. Beyond the sad lace curtains, parallel with my bed, was a grey wood-paling fence. One kilometre away, the electric train line was also parallel. In a long black cape, Barry Humphries stalked the streets.

It should have been obvious that I was not suited to engineering, but my father's ambition was to see me established as Shire Engineer of Bacchus Marsh. He bought me an expensive slide rule which I never learned to use. I faked my physics experiments, working back from the correct value of *g* which I still recall as 980 cm per sec per sec.

I had no idea that I was on the path to catastrophic failure. Indeed, anything seemed possible. Celine's friends were drama majors, psychologists, political philosophers and poets. They discussed Description, Narration, Exposition, Argumentation. Had I been capable, I would have faked this too, but all I had to offer them were some controversial facts: Agenbite of inwit. U.P.:up.

My clever father never had a need to develop a treatise or present an abstract. Nor had this skill been required of me at high school up in Ballarat. I had sat my matriculation confident I was a whiz at chemistry and mathematics, but I arrived in Celine's magic circle with four plain passes and no clue as to how to play their game. They were reading Frantz Fanon, Simone de Beauvoir, Alfred Jarry. Any radical thought I might offer – that there might be no God for instance – was tedious to them, and they seemed embarrassed I should mention it. I was staggered that, while they had not known each other previously, they seemed to be continuing a conversation which they had started years before. They all knew rhinoceros was a play.

More than once they told me to piss off, but I had chosen them, and I would stay until they saw my worth.

The motorcyclist rarely spoke to me. Sandy Quinn had the habit of smiling while I talked. Years later he would tell me he had been anxious on my behalf and had only smiled to give me some support.

Celine's body could not have been at all as I imagined it but she would always be a physical actor who could make you believe her waist was smaller and her legs longer than in real life. She was not as clever as I thought she was. Sometimes she was cold to me, other times quite tender. Once she mussed up my hair in public, and perhaps she was as much on my side as she later claimed, but she was always, unfailingly, relentlessly amused to see me run to fetch the balls thrown by the poet. The poet had a long square-shouldered body and a freckled face that might have been bland if you could not see that he was, in his very quiet brown-eyed way, capable of absolutely anything.

'*Catcher in the Rye*,' the poet said mildly. 'You said you read it, but you didn't, did you? Not really.' His manner was so agreeable. It was hard to believe he was tormenting me.

The leather boy had his head down rolling cigarettes, one after the other, lining them up on the table edge then tucking in their hairy ends.

'Not really, no.'

The poet had a smile like someone sucking on a match. 'Too American I suppose?'

'Stop it Andrew,' said Sandy. 'Enough.'

'So Felix,' Andrew persisted, 'it's Patrick White for you and Salinger Go Home?'

I had not read Patrick White either. 'Sometimes that's necessary,' I said.

'So, with literature, you are Australia first.'

It was time to take this idea and run with it.

'For me it's the Battle of Brisbane,' I said, 'every bloody day, mate.'

The leather boy snorted through his nose, but of course not even Sandy had heard of the Battle of Brisbane.

'There was no *battle* of Brisbane,' he said. 'You must mean the Brisbane *Line*. We were ready to give the Japs everything north of Brisbane.'

'No, Sandra.'

Even now I am ashamed I spoke to him like that. I was

too defended to even glimpse his extraordinary capacity for empathy. I called him Sandra and it was as if a starling spat at him. He smiled wanly. 'I think you'll find the Japs bombed Darwin and Broome in 1942,' he said.

I was a scrappy little fellow and I thought I was being condescended to. 'It was not a battle *with* the Japs,' I said. 'The Americans were in Brisbane,' I said. 'Brisbane was MacArthur's headquarters. So you tell me, Sandy, what was the other garrison in Brisbane in 1942?'

'Australian obviously,' he said, and cocked his head at me. Fuck you, I thought. You're wrong.

'Australian soldiers fought the Americans in the streets of Brisbane,' I said. 'It is known as the Battle of Brisbane.'

It took a lot of nerve for me to let the silence last.

'OK,' he said.

'No. It was censored. The only reason I know is that my old man lost half his hand to an American shotgun.'

Celine caught my eye and I didn't know if I should be pleased or nervous. It was my uncle not my father who had the flipper hand. I waited. She poured sugar from the glass dispenser and pushed it into a heap. In this action, as in so many, she managed to generate a certain heat, an expectation that she would do something wild and dangerous and we would be condemned to simply sit and watch. She emptied the ashtray on top of the sugar and planted matches there. Then she glared at me and I understood I had offended her, and all this compressed and coded malice was for me.

'What would you know about the bloody Battle of Brisbane?'

'I think I answered that already, love.'

'Love bullshit. What crap.'

I knew my cheeks were burning.

'Stop smirking you big baby,' she said. 'You can't even find it in a book.'

'I think Mr Moore may be thinking about the Brisbane *Line*,' said Sandy.

Celine snatched away her lover's cigarette and threw it on the floor.

'No, pom-pom, he is not confused.'

Seeing how the poet enjoyed this revelation of a secret name, I recognised one more competitor. He helped himself to one of the motorcyclist's beautiful hand-tailored cigarettes. 'So what was the Battle of Brisbane?' he asked me.

'It was about sex,' Celine answered. 'The stupid Australians were jealous of the Yanks. The only people in the world who want to help us, and so they shoot them because they like Australian girls.'

'A brawl.'

'No, a bloody *battle*. It lasted two days, with guns. And it was *really* stupid because those Americans were the ones who went off to New Guinea to fight the Japanese there.'

'There were no Yanks in New Guinea,' said the motorcyclist. 'None, baby, none.'

'Bullshit, baby,' said Celine. 'My father was there, baby, baby.'

'I meant Americans.'

'My father was American, baby. He bloody died there,' and she was crying, standing, turning away from the group. 'Come on Titch,' she said to me, and took my arm.

She was crying, and I was callow enough to be overjoyed. She was sobbing, but I had won. I had stood my ground.

33

Thus the previously unthinkable circumstance developed where Sandy and his car were banished and I was invited to walk Celine Baillieux to the bus on Ferntree Gully Road.

8

Contemplating the cracked blackened portraits of colonial no-ones on Moroni's gloomy walls, I recalled that Sir Robert Menzies was one of two prime ministers who 'owned' this corner table. Paul Keating was the other. Of course Keating was NOT A MELBOURNE PERSON, but he always looked at home in Moroni's, his strangely delicate pale face peering out of the same chiaroscuro which soaked up his dark tailored suits. It was here, at this corner table where I now sat with Celine and Woody Townes, that the Prime Minister's wife – I mean Annita Keating – had spoken so passionately about the 'thread counts' of her sheets. This was probably a safe conversation in New York or Washington or even Sydney, but in our puritanical socialist certainties we were offended by thread counts. Or perhaps we did not know what thread counts were.

The menu in Moroni's had not changed since 1970, the year of the Vietnam Moratorium, when we marched outside the windows, behind the great Jim Cairns ('The responsibility for violence will rest squarely with him' – *The Age*). There were a hundred thousand of us including me with my celebrated banner FUCK THE RICH. Four months later I was first taken to Moroni's and disturbed the genteel weather with my exploding hair.

Veal chop.

Osso bucco.

Rum baba.

Same then. Same now. There could be no other only half-serious Italian restaurant in the world that served such plastic bread.

While Abramo filled my glass assiduously I watched, in the high tilted mirror on the western side, a certain 'hard man' from the Trades Hall Council being entertained by a class enemy. He would not catch my shit-stirring eye.

Woody offered San Pellegrino but those bleak bleached paddocks where my dad sold Fords, the loveless rock-and-rabbit farms of Anakie, now produced this flinty straw-coloured Chenin Blanc as complex as a Vouvray. Who would have dreamed it possible?

'I'm fine with the wine,' I said. 'Talk to me.'

Celine had one of those faces we adore on screen – thoughts and feelings passing like shadows, leaving one not wiser, but drawn in. She looked at my wine longer than was polite.

Forty-nine years ago she and I had set off up to Ferntree Gully Road and finished at her mother's home in Springvale. Later we found ourselves working together in the Deputy Prime Minister's office, but the last time I had seen her was at a Christmas party, breastfeeding her baby girl.

Now she produced a yellow legal pad and with this simple action made herself a lawyer.

As always, I declined to take notes. Silence fell while my glass was filled again.

'I need unlimited access.'

Celine glanced at Woody. Woody turned to me. 'All you want mate, she's yours. That's why you've got the moolah.'

'Do you call her Gaby or Gabrielle?'

'Both.'

'She is in Melbourne?'

'Need-to-know basis, mate.'

Woody. What a prat!

'She has agreed to all this?' I asked Celine. 'To speak to me at length and on the record?'

'Mate,' said Woody, 'don't make problems where there are none.'

Moroni's famous whiting arrived, but Celine did not touch her cutlery. 'Before we rush ahead so merrily,' she said, 'can we deal with this crap about extradition? She's an Australian citizen for Christ's sake. Why do the Americans think everything's to do with them?'

'She opened hundreds of their jails.'

'She didn't mean to, obviously. And we cannot extradite her to a country with the death penalty,' Celine told me. 'You have daughters,' she insisted. Surely you can imagine how I feel.'

'Felix's job,' Woody said, and Celine cut him off.

'What did your great barrister say to you? You told me. They cannot extradite her to a country with the death penalty.'

Woody laid his meaty hand upon her slender wrist. 'If she actually intended to attack America, that's a political act. That's a good thing. Once we prove it was a political act she cannot be extradited. Felix is the man to pitch that story. He can do it standing on his head.'

'Will you listen to what I've told you? She is a gutsy kid, but she could not have done what she is charged with. I love her, but she isn't all that bright.'

'Sando is her father,' I said. 'She's got two very brainy parents.'

'Actually, I got B's and C's. And Gaby never finished high school which is why she had such shitty jobs at IBM. She is incapable of doing what the charge sheet says she did. That is how we should be fighting this,' she said to Woody. 'Let them give her exams. She'll fail them. She's got the B-C gene. She's innocent.'

'Fair enough,' I said. 'But I do believe she has confessed?'

'She can confess all she likes.'

'She bragged she was going destroy twelve corporations. She named them. The Koch brothers are on her to-do list.'

'Actually, her mad supporters did that for her. They go on chat rooms and make up all sorts of shit. They project. They invent. They write her lesbian love letters. They're nuts, and God help you if you speak out against them. They'll destroy you.'

'Felix's role,' Woody began again and this time Celine let him finish. 'His role will be to properly educate the Australian public who are naturally inclined to believe the Americans are over-reaching again. Once Felix writes the story, she'll be Gaby from Coburg. She won't lose any points for pissing off the Yanks. No-one will want to hand her over.'

'She didn't mean to hurt them,' Celine said.

'Australianise her, mate,' Woody said. 'Gaby from Coburg. Fair dinkum. Blood is thicker than water.'

'Please fire me,' I asked Celine. 'You know I'll do this because I need the money.'

'Why on earth would we fire you?'

To be true, I thought. To be decent. Because clearly I'm

being used. Because I know things about you, Celine, I would have to reveal. I couldn't help myself.

'They could just grab her,' she said, 'off the street. Like they grabbed what's-his-name in Rome.'

'In Milan. Please take your deposit back,' I said to Woody. 'Put it in your legal fund. I'm a journalist. I can't do PR. What are you sniggering about?'

'What sort of mug would ask you to do publicity?'

'We have to try everything,' Celine said. 'We have to celebrate her real life without hysteria.'

'Your job is to save an extraordinary human being,' Woody said. 'I want to impress that on you, mate.'

His little elephant eyes had become so moist and sentimental that I had to look away. 'I'm not the right person,' I told Celine. But at the same time I ordered a grappa, and even while Woody tried to catch my eye, I continued to insist that I was not the man to do the job. I then learned that, legally speaking, I had accepted the deal when I accepted the envelope of cash. I also accepted a second grappa. I negotiated a prescription for Dexedrine, a MacBook Pro, a Cabcharge account and, finally, a place to live until my wife forgave me for being myself.

9

Neither Celine nor Woody had said I was to live in Eureka
Tower and yet their silence as we entered Melbourne's tallest
building seemed to confirm that this would be my home.
Passing the fiftieth floor, my ears popped. As we continued
skywards, I experienced a pleasurable murmuring in my
neck, a very particular excitement which arrives, inevitably,
when one is cast into a decadent situation without it being
in any way one's fault.

The lift door opened on giddy walls of glass.

'You're scared of heights.' The bastard laughed. He was
my friend, yes, but he would not let me grab his forearm
for support.

The lift door closed and I was imprisoned.

'You know I get vertigo.'

Celine certainly did. There had been an episode at
Monash when she had me climbing the scaffolding of the
Menzies Building. She put great store in courage in those
days. Now I was unmanned again she would not even
catch my eye.

Woody strolled to the windows from where he observed
me as I stabilised myself on the kitchen counter. 'Don't be a
girl,' he said. 'Come on out here.'

Celine had now disappeared and I understood that she
was intimately acquainted with this apartment. I once more
had that feeling, common back in those Monash days, of

being outside the sexual inner circle, of not knowing what was going on.

'Kitty, kitty,' Woody called me, tapping his keys against the glass.

'Bathroom,' I demanded.

Only when the dunny door slammed behind me did I see I was locked up with the very view I was seeking to avoid.

Who would ever dream of such a thing? A toilet with a wall of glass.

'You can shit all over Melbourne,' he called. 'That should suit you, mate. You've been doing that for years.'

'Let me out.'

'Door's not locked.'

I flushed then emerged to find him by a grand piano, leaning back against the plate glass, ankles crossed, a vaudeville joke that would only pay off when he plummeted to his death. Of course he had a bottle and the corkscrew. He took the Vosne-Romanée between the wool press of his thighs and slowly withdrew its long French cork. 'Cellar Pro constant-temperature wine cellar,' he said. 'Valet service. Cleaner comes twice a week – just throw your undies in the basket. The devil took Jesus into a high place,' he said. 'Get used to it.'

Claire would be in heaven here, seated at this Steinway. I locked the thought away.

The great Wodonga had splashed some wine as he filled the glasses, and he now attended to the spill with a large white handkerchief.

'Château Valium,' he offered.

I accepted the gift and sunk to the piano stool. Celine

called. Then Woody seemed to be discussing my bed sheets with her. By the third glass I was able to raise my eyes. Then, of course, we were to leave.

'Here's your key mate. When you lose it, the concierge will let you in.'

Then we were all safely back in the elevator and a moment later on the earth where I was introduced to Bruce the concierge who had 'read your book'. Bruce gave Woody a package which Woody handed on to me. It was my new iPhone and MacBook, all set up, he claimed. I was not at all suspicious.

Celine kissed both my cheeks. Was she leaving? Woody punched me on the arm and shepherded me to the lift and then, once more, I was alone, being sent back to the place of terror.

If you have never had vertigo it is likely you will have no sympathy for me and I will only make the situation worse by confessing what I did. By day's end, however, I was piss-faced drunk, sitting cross-legged by the windows. The sun was low over the water-bound fingers of container terminals behind which, somewhere in the drowning dark, lay those drear volcanic plains and my childhood home in Bacchus Marsh. The east, in comparison was a vault of gold, threaded by the Yarra River. My wineglass was a murder scene, besmirched with the brutal sediment of Château Valium. I pressed my nose against the window.

Out there eastwards, not too far, seventeen kilometres perhaps, lying dead and buried like a gangster beneath the Monash Freeway, was the place where I had once planned to kiss Celine.

Her father was American. He died. In her distress she had chosen me from all the others to walk her to the bus. I honestly tried to ask about her father but we were, as she reminded me, walking to the bus not going to confession. What then? We crossed the car park and started up the gravel road. I asked her if she had heard of Ornette Coleman.

'Oh Felix, don't be boring.'

But of course I was boring. I was a wet-feathered thing just fallen from his nest. What grade are you in? Have you heard of this? Have you heard of that? 'Do you have a record player?' I asked.

She considered me, smiling so frankly that I knew my virginity was naked in the light.

'Do you like me Felix?'

I had been aroused beyond hope by the occasional brush from her pleated skirt. Now I found a stone and threw it further up the road. 'I don't know you yet.'

She held her thick fair hair up from her eyes and studied me so insistently that my cheeks took fire. 'Why did I ask you to walk me to the bus? What did you think? That I wanted to cry on your shoulder? What went through your head?'

Sex went through my head. I had thought I would play her side two, track three, *Una Muy Bonita*. For days I had had the album in my bag. All I needed was a stereo. I would tell her she was Una Muy Bonita. I would kiss her if I could.

'I don't know.'

'Obviously,' she said, 'it's the Battle of Brisbane.'

Then it seemed I was following her inside a pub. That's

what being eighteen was like, learning that walking to the bus meant going to the Notting Hill Hotel, also called the Vicarage or Nott.

I have known famous Monash graduates, all men, get dewy-eyed about the Nott and its licensee, Kath Byer, but on that day I noticed only that Celine's skirt had a dangerous flounce to it and she chose an isolated table where she carefully arranged her Ronson lighter and a pack of black Sobranies, as exotic in their way as women's underwear. She bit the cellophane with her straight white teeth. The black cigarettes had gold tips. I had not known such things existed in the world.

'I was conceived in Brisbane,' she said as she placed a Sobranie in her mouth. 'You're blushing.'

'I'm not.'

'You're very sweet, Felix. Would you please loan me a whisky lime and soda? I really will pay you back.'

I had intended to show her Ornette Coleman when I returned, but it took a good while to clear up the misunderstanding about my age, and by the time I had the drinks in hand she had spread an untidy collection of photographs and clippings across the table. What these were she did not explain. She took her drink and pushed her chair back so I might easily examine her display: a small Kodak print showing a white and willowy American soldier standing beside a palm tree. There was one clipping that had been pressed and folded as flat as a violet in a scrapbook. There were bigger prints, all soldiers, clearly Americans. The Melbourne *Herald* had stamped a number on the back of some of the larger glossy prints but the biggest had been cut from *Life* magazine, leaving scalloped nail-scissor marks along one side. Two of the subjects wore bib and braces, three uniforms, and the entire tribe had fair hair and good teeth. All but the grey-haired matriarch enthroned in a bentwood chair with an exceptionally long-barrelled rifle across her knees.

'He wasn't a hero. He didn't die in New Guinea,' she said. 'That was the bullshit she raised me on. Now she says it was the Battle of Brisbane. Why would she say that to me now, like she has saved it up all my life, and used it to punish me the first time I stay out all night?'

She had stayed out all night with who?

'Did you hear me?'

'What?'

'My father died in a bar-room brawl.'

'It was a battle,' I said. 'Two Americans did get killed.'

'Then my father was one of them.'

'Then he was the victim of a crime. The military police killed them.'

'Yes, but she's a liar. Why would she tell me New Guinea all those years. I never needed a hero, just a father of some kind, but the more you look at it the more he vanishes.' She crumpled her Sobranie. 'I can't tell Sandy any of this.'

I thought, she slept with him.

'Never,' she said. 'It would ruin my life.' She spat on her hand and held it out.

Her nails were bright vermilion. There was a gold bangle around her slender suntanned wrist. It did not take a lot to arouse me. Our hands slid together, skin and spit on skin.

'Who'd want to marry the daughter of a madwoman?'

'The right man will understand,' I said, but she did not see the point that I was making.

'You think I'm exaggerating. Look at these photographs.'

'I looked already.'

She moved her chair closer. 'Look again.'

'For what?'

'Don't play silly buggers.' Her hair brushed my cheek.

'One of them's your father, right?' I said, but all these men had in common was fair hair and American uniforms.

'What if I told you I was raised to believe they were the same man?' She held my eyes. It was unbearable. 'All my life. What do you say to that?'

'I don't know.'

Whatever pheromones were in the air she did not seem to notice. 'Thank you Felix, that's very diplomatic of you, but if you're brought up to see a thing a certain way you just see it. It wasn't until she came out with that Battle of Brisbane I took the frames off the wall to look at them. I had an awful hangover. I was in no shape to see anything very much, but when she saw what I was doing she went really nuts. I saw her face. Then I understood how terrified she was. So I carried the whole lot into my room and locked her out and I took them all out of their frames, and found pictures hidden behind pictures. She was crying and knocking on my door.'

'What did she say?'

'I don't care. I'm never going to talk to her again.'

Did she mean that literally? I didn't take it to be so, but then, as we both agreed, I did not know Celine. I never would.

'Can you imagine what my mother's done to her only child? Why would she punish me like that?'

46

Well, I also had a missing parent whose absence from my life was a source of constant pain. My mother had gone, that's all I knew. My father could not speak of her without crying. I did not think he was mad or we were strange but I kept my secret folded tight and locked away and I had no intention of revealing it to Celine Baillieux.

But I finally listened to her with authentic interest. I learned to see the house in Springvale from whose backyard her peculiar mother ran a taxi service. The house was like its neighbours, cream brick, triple-fronted, the sort of place we saw in our Melbourne minds when we heard Pete Seeger sing about little boxes made of ticky tacky. Who would have known that it contained, in its plastic-wrapped front room, its dark passages, its neon kitchen and dining room, an obsessive memorial to a fallen American who was known as 'Dad'? There were, besides the seven framed photographs, odd artifacts like cowry shells and a faded pink tram ticket and a Purple Heart, framed and hung beside the certificate that declared the kitchen the registered offices of the taxi company.

The pretty girl needed me, not handsome Sandy Quinn whose heart was clearly not big enough to hold her pain. Of course Sandy's life business would be to hold the pain of others, but in my ignorance I thought myself the better man. Celine stroked my arm. She touched my hair. I judged it would be OK to kiss her just behind the ear.

'Quit it,' she cried suddenly.

I reached to touch her cheek but she slapped my hand away.

'You're a baby. I can't believe I've chosen you to tell,' and suddenly there were fat tears and eyeliner and mascara everywhere and two gents were curious to know if I was 'bothering the lady'.

'No,' the lady said, 'go away you bloody oicks.'

'It's all right, mate,' I told them both.

'Yes mate,' she sneered at me when her rescuers retreated. 'It's all right, mate, baby.' She pushed her untouched drink towards me, and then she began to sob.

'I'm pretty screwed up,' she said.

She rocked forward in her chair and then she leaned a little further, with her face all wet, kissed me, softly, all ash and whisky, with mascara cheeks, she kissed me very slowly on the lips.

'You've a lovely kind face,' she said. 'I'm pleased I chose you to tell.'

I thought, I will solve this puzzle for her. I lifted her chin – smeared blue eyeliner, iridescent like abalone shell – and I kissed her, at last, not understanding the role I had been cast in.

10

How was Gaby going to reach me? If she encrypted her email how in the hell would I decrypt it? Forget what I said about *Wired* magazine. I had no preparation for this modern world.

As the days passed my vertigo gave way to a general unease, something worse than the fatty biliousness caused by takeaway food. I was queasy. I was impatient. I abused the delicate MacBook as I had once hammered my Olivetti Valentine (until I snapped a character straight off the type bar.) Already, in Eureka Tower, my keyboard had developed bright white stress marks on the 'f' and 't'.

I peered and pecked on Google and LexisNexis where my subject was a teenager of interest to the police, a schoolgirl, totally enclosed in a yellow Hazchem suit, arrested for interfering with chemical effluent.

I traced one of her former teachers at R.F. Mackenzie Community School. Her name was Crystal, for God's sake. She was an activist. A progressive. We spent a lot of time on the telephone while she explained that R.F. Mackenzie had been an almost perfect place for a clever radical to go to school. It was hard to divert her. She talked mournfully about a whole chain of inner-city schools, East Brunswick through to Bell Street High School, to Moreland, where progressive teachers had once been able to make a difference. She remembered Gaby Baillieux had a boyfriend but she forgot his name. She knew Gaby had Samoan friends but then decided this was 'private information'. She was more informative about all the smart left-wing teachers who had been sucked out of classrooms and swallowed up by the Education Department once Labor came back to power.

Through the Samoan Methodist Church in Coburg, I tracked down Gaby's friend Solosolo. Solosolo was now living out in Sunshine where her sister, a big girl, had been stabbed, just before I called. Yes, Solosolo played with Gaby in the Bell Street High girls' soccer team. She prayed for her. She had to go.

Gabrielle Baillieux disappeared from my screen until I found her in a fossilised blog: she was twenty-two, a technical solutions engineer at IBM. Three years later a Gaby Baillieux was charged with trespass and causing wilful damage to a government facility near Alice Springs.

Of course IBM fired her. They must have. Two years ago a Gaby Baillieux had been appointed as a project engineer at a game startup in South Melbourne. The company still existed, but they refused to talk to me. I found her credit rating: Fair. She had not married. She had owned no property and had not given birth.

I found no evidence of hacking or any other criminal or political activity. I began to wonder if her mother might be correct, that she was innocent. Perhaps it just meant that she was very, very skilled. I really hoped so. I wanted her to exist.

I called Sando at his electoral office in Coburg and he told me to go and fuck myself. Fair enough. I belly-flopped into the shallow end of computer crime, an online world of Tor and bitcoins. I made many notes, understood nothing, and stopped short, thank God, of entering the dark web without protection.

I studied the extradition treaty between Australia and the US and learned that everything Woody had said was true, but, really, so what? Everything we knew from life suggested that America would do what it liked and Australia would behave like the client state it always was.

I saw Sando on CNN, poor bugger, his looks gone, his hair worn down with worry and divorce. Due to his strange mustard-coloured coat the Labor MP had an unfortunate Eastern European appearance. The *Washington Post* had already written that Gaby was a product of the 'Culture of Envy', which was their nod to the Socialist Left faction of the Australian Labor Party.

Sando told CNN he hadn't seen his daughter in many years, he could not remember when.

Still, Mr Quinn, if you had to choose between betraying your country or your daughter?

It was clear Sando wished to cry. I turned away from him and put my nose against the window and realised that it had become my comfort, the cool glass in the middle of the night.

I slept badly.

I would lie in bed imagining the apartment was full of people only to discover that it was nothing but the television where, at any hour, one could see the same old footage of the Angel and hear, again, the American politicians who did not seem to understand she was not their citizen and therefore could not be their traitor any more than she could be their patriot. The House Majority Leader found it politically necessary to call for her execution.

It was in the midst of this swelling hysteria, with dawn breaking over the Dandenong Ranges, that I learned that her pompous barrister had obtained his first adjournment. There had been a late night news conference outside the court where Gaby hesitated and glanced timidly at her bewigged QC who patted her familiarly, the creep.

Now, I thought, my wait is over. This woman needs me. Then a day passed, then another, then one more. I woke todiscover bottles and pizza cartons and cold French fries littered over my quilt.

My first thought was that Woody had got legless and trashed his own apartment. This was not a rash conclusion. I had been drunk with him many times and had witnessed a whole spectrum of behaviour that went from hiding raw prawns inside a motel's hollow curtain rods to sharing the logic of a real estate development that would cost him $30 million. He could be rude, crude and sentimental, but throughout it all he had been my protector, never embarrassed to be an admirer or a servant to a higher cause.

I had been pleased but not at all surprised when he came to sit with me in court each day. I cannot describe the comfort. That was how we had been together all our lives. He was, he said so often, 'a fan'. It was only when my attention moved beyond the shocking debris on my bed, when I read the notes sellotaped around the bedroom wall, that I understood there had been a tectonic shift in our relationship. My fan was now my boss.

YOU ARE PAID TO WRITE, NOT EAT YOUR-SELF TO DEATH.

He awaited me at breakfast, dressed like a patron Pope in a carmine jogging suit, twin white stripes down each side. My computer was on his generous lap and he was opening my files which contained all sorts of shit he had no business reading. The secrets of Celine's mad mother and the imaginary father were not the worst of it.

'It's only notes, mate.'

'I can't publish your fucking notes,' he cried. 'I want whole pages with proper spelling and punctuation. Australianise her, for Christ's sake. Please, Feels. Be a sport.'

I said I would prefer him not to read my files.

For reply he slammed the MacBook shut and threw it on the table top.

'Do you think we control the duration of the discovery process? How long will it take? Five months? A year? If there is going to be an extradition request we need your book in the stores by the time it happens. You saw her on TV? You think she's cute, right? You got a hard-on just watching her. But listen to me, she's on the spectrum. She's scary. She does not respond normally.'

'I need background. That's what you've been reading on my laptop. Background notes.'

'*My* laptop,' he corrected. 'It's foreground I'm paying for, mate. That's what we need. Do what you always do. Did you really go to the war in Bougainville? No. Was the piece impeccable? Absolutely. You're a genius. Make it up, and most of all make the bitch loveable, all right?'

'She won't be like that, Woody. Remarkable people never are.'

'Come on, Feels. Who's the big sook who sat with you in court and smelled your socks all day? Who applauded when you told the court that there was no such thing as objective journalism?'

'That was not a defence of making things up.'

'Extrapolate, isn't that how you explained it? Be intuitive. You want some useful advice? Don't make this story all about yourself. That's what pisses people off. That's why they don't like you. That is why you are always in the shit. No offence.'

This was hurtful, and yet the very peculiar thing about the history of patrons is how often the most ignorant and barbaric amongst them have shaped great works of art. Only because of this offensive speech did I finally glimpse what my book might really be.

'And for Chrissakes go and buy some clothes.'

'I am waiting for her to make contact.'

'You think you can dress like this for your interviews? What if you end up on TV? Get decent. Buy clean socks too. Go. I'll wait here until you come back.'

So it was, strolling across the Swanston Street bridge for the first time in forty years, I found myself swimming in the giddiness of time, knowing exactly where I was and having no idea at all. I chose to go to Henry Bucks by way of Flinders Street, in order that I might pass the embalmed corpse of *The Herald* building (where I had once been so firmly edited). The bitter wind drove lolly papers past its shuttered doors.

I sometimes dream of the Herald as it was so long ago: the marble and terrazzo, oak panels, the whistling thumping vacuum tubes above your head. There are always bizarre copy boys and copy girls with carbon-paper smudges on their cheeks. People come and go in pursuit of unimaginable business. Some walk directly to the banks of clunking lifts. Men in hats rush past the front desk and through a swinging door.

The first time I entered this holy place I was carrying all Celine's putative fathers in a manila envelope. It was my strongly held conviction that one of them would turn out to be real. I explained my general purpose to the receptionist who clearly did not take me seriously.

I waited. I missed my physics lecture. Then physical chemistry. As the clock struck eleven, an hour when Professor R.D. Brown could be relied upon to wipe the blackboard clear of his gnomic equations, I saw a snazzy-suited fellow with a ramrod back charge through the swinging door. This, although I did not yet know his name or rank, was Captain Stackpole. Captain Stackpole thought he knew me. Clearly, I answered a description. He pointed a finger at me and raised an inquiring eyebrow.

'Thomas Ryder?'

I stood. It was enough.

'Follow me,' he said, returning through the swinging door with me at his heels. I was afraid. I followed him deeper, down stairs, up stairs, along corridors, into the office where I saw his name written very clearly on his door.

What could he do to me?

Captain Stackpole was a short man, very trim, and brisk. He had a dimpled chin and a military moustache and an RSL badge in his brown lapel. He indicated a chair but I could not waste a moment and displayed the photographs of Celine's various fathers.

'What's this?'

'I need to see the photo editor.'

'The librarian?'

'I don't know.'

'Don't know?' He whacked his pipe against his ashtray. 'You're Thomas Ryder.'

'I'm Felix Moore, sir.'

'You said you were Thomas Ryder.'

'No.'

'No?'

'No, Captain Stackpole.'

He stared at me belligerently. He reached for the telephone. I thought, oh shit. He changed his mind. 'This place is a bloody circus,' he said and shoved my pictures back at me and grabbed my arm and marched me down some stairs and along a hallway to a door with a tacked-on paper sign that read ABBOT.

Inside was a large room like my dad's spare-parts department: grey steel with regularly drilled holes stretching from floor to ceiling, deep shelves about a metre apart stacked with what I would now call archival boxes, patchy brown or straw colour, each corner protected by metal tips.

Captain Stackpole led me down different aisles or avenues, bawling out Miss Abbot's name.

I turned a corner and there she was, the librarian of *The Herald*, riding on the top rung of a wheeled loft ladder, propelling herself forward with her white-gloved hands. Even perched so high, it was clear she had a lot of waist and long straight legs.

'Herr Steckenpoo,' she cried, descending.

In the year of the bouffant her black hair was radical, not just for being short and shaped, but in anticipating the fashions of the years to come. She was handsome, with high cheekbones and the jawline of a heroine. All this was eroticised by her narrowed eyes, which, in their present puffy state, suggested very bad behaviour.

'Cobber,' she said to me, holding out her hand which revealed, beneath the curatorial white glove, the inflexibility of a prosthetic.

'Miss Abbot, might you assist this young fellow?'

'Captain Steckopopo, your servant.'

'You are asking for it, Miss Abbot.'

'Yes, but not from you. What can I do for you, cobber?' asked Miss Abbot and left Captain Stackpole to make his own arrangements.

'Let's have a deck at what you've got.' She had a lovely reckless coordinated walk and if her bum was not small it was not corseted and therefore lovely to behold.

She settled herself at a long high work bench. Her thighs were generous and her ankles nicely turned.

I turned over the manila envelope and she briskly emptied the contents onto her desk. 'Give me a squiz.' With her left hand (which, being ungloved, was slender and long-fingered) she began to sort the images into different categories.

'One of these men is my dad,' I said. 'I don't know which one.'

'You couldn't just ask your dad himself?'

I did not lie, but she clearly saw my grief.

'Ah, so.' Miss Abbot had an active bright intelligence which was not contradicted by her puffy eyes.

'Can you help me?'

She lightly touched my upper arm.

'No-one better, cobber. I'm your man.'

Celine's pictures were in five piles. The first consisted of the prints I judged to have been already purchased from *The Herald*. Miss Abbot recorded the pencilled numbers on their verso sides.

'Stand by,' she said and I listened to the ladder wheels moving amongst the stacks. Then silence. Then she was back with the names of all the four soldiers and the date and place where they had been photographed.

I thought, I am a genius. I am going to win. I am going to ask Celine to the Purple Eye Jazz Club next Friday night.

Miss Abbot took a blank sheet of paper and drew a grid. She made notes of all of the photos but one, a yellowed cutting, which she slid back in the envelope.

'What about that one?'

'It's not your dad.'

'Why?'

'The Yanks were mostly lovely,' she said. 'You can't say that in Melbourne without being called a tart, but they were gentlemen. You had a very handsome daddy whichever one he is.'

This father, here, had appeared in *The Argus* between 1942 and 1946. That one was in *The Age* after 1943. This here was definitely *Life* magazine and the Melbourne public library had bound volumes so I must go there straight away. As the Yanks were in the war so bloody late, there were only two hundred issues to check.

I was looking at a cheeky GI offering an apple to a grinning girl. I was wondering if they did 'it'. Miss Abbott rested her left hand on my wrist. 'Don't be hard on your mum,' she said.

'OK.'

'Cobber, you're not listening. We all thought we were

58

going to die. Everyone did a lot of stupid things. If your mum slipped up, you must forgive her. She doesn't know you're doing this, does she? Your mum.'

'Not really.'

She searched my face and I did not know how to respond. She removed a large white envelope from her lower drawer and extracted a 10"x8" glossy black and white print. It was the sort of picture I had seen before: the liberation of a European city, an American tank, crowded with soldiers and a very pretty girl with tangled jet-black hair. The girl was a photographer. She had two big cameras slung around her neck. She waved both arms in triumph. Beside her was a handsome GI with a wolfish grin who, I realised with a shock, had both his hands upon her breasts.

'You get it.'

'Yes,' I said, but only as she slipped the photograph away did I understand that this stunning girl photographer had become Miss Abbot.

'Be nice to your mum,' she said. 'It was a different time.'

When she had finished with her sheet of paper she tucked it back with all Celine's photographs.

'Do you know where the public library is? Of course you don't.'

So she led me out and up the stairs and through the newsroom and into the foyer past the receptionist with the hairsprayed bouffant and then she walked with me two blocks to the corner of Swanston Street.

'Walk that way,' she said. 'The library is on the corner of La Trobe Street, on the right. You can go and see Phar Lap when you're finished. You know who Phar Lap was?'

'A horse that died.'

'Yes, a horse that died. Do you smoke, cobber?'

I said I did and she gave me a Craven "A" and lit it for me.

'Come back and see me,' she told me as I tried hard not to cough. 'Come and tell me which hunk is which.'

She kissed me then, rather strangely, directly on the lips.

I should have been in lectures, but there was no contest in my mind. So I walked up towards the library carrying the burning Craven "A". There was a hot north wind, and you could smell the smoke of bushfires amongst the traffic.

I was high and happy, triumphant in my quest, and then quite suddenly, as I crossed Bourke Street, unspeakably sad.

It was a puzzle then, but I know what caused it now: the tears in my eyes were precipitated by the flavour of lipstick on my mouth, the taste of my mother perfectly preserved. Gone, empty, then as now as I go to Henry Bucks to buy my suit.

11

I returned with my gorgeous silk and cashmere suit still not understanding that I had signed a contract with a property developer and not a publisher. I was not yet accustomed to thinking of Woody as my boss. I had told him to wait for me, and he had completely failed to follow my instructions. I pinged him off a pissy email.

It took only a minute for me to discover that he had locked his temperature-controlled wine cellar and left nothing but a can of Foster's in the fridge.

When I discovered he had been into my computer again I wrote him another email. I said this was not on. If I had been his surgeon would he expect to help me wield the knife?

He still had not answered my first communication but I could not work like this. I opened an account on Dropbox and hid the icon and transferred all my files where he couldn't read them anymore. That's how naive I was. Are you sure you wish to delete the file named Angel from your hard drive? Yes, yes, yes again. Cop that, young Harry, as my father would have said.

My source was too important to talk to me just yet? I forgave her. There was plenty to get on with. Woody's Dexedrine was past its use-by date and therefore tasted like Fruit Tingles on my tongue. He wants me to write intuitively, I thought. I can do much better than that. I already had parts of the story that no-one else could know. This book would be truer than my patron could have dreamed.

By the time dusk settled on Marvellous Melbourne, Wodonga had still not replied to my emails and I did not give a shit. I was buzzed. I worked all that night, all the next day. When it was dark again I thought it sensible to stop before I had a heart attack. Coming off speed is awful. I already felt the tears in my throat. All my buried past turned sticky, cloying like spoiled velvet, dead roses. I took one Valium and two Temazepam and lay down on the bed with my laptop held like an X-ray machine against my chest.

Just two hours later I woke to find hail driving against the windows at ninety kilometres an hour. The *Age* archive will tell you about that morning, people all over Melbourne were woken by a roar of ice, but behind the laminations of Eureka Tower, it was so quiet I could easily hear the voices in the other room.

It was almost three o'clock in the morning. In the open kitchen I found Celine barefoot, smoking, sipping whisky, making a mess with files and papers on the countertop. She had dumped two cardboard boxes on the stove and it was surprising to see such a fit, pared-down person carried her accumulated life like a bag lady – sun-bleached papers, cartons with sides collapsed, guts naked to the air.

'Hello,' I said.

She frowned.

Was she cool towards me or simply tired? Why were her feet bare?

The Great Wodonga was settled at my desk, fleshy

enough for Lucian Freud, his huge thighs pressing against the limits of his tailor, hunched over the laptop which had obviously been removed from my embrace like a teddy bear from a sleeping child.

'The scribe,' he said sarcastically. So they were reading my work again, and of course they had suffered the fate of all snoops – they were upset by what they had discovered.

'So where's my source?' I demanded. 'Is it true you can't deliver her?' This was what you might call a tactical diversion and I was pleased to see how it changed the mood.

Woody returned the computer. Celine said no, no, no, but I must understand the difficulties. We were all on the same side. I must rest. I must sleep. I must wait until Monday, although that was Easter Monday, so it would probably be a few more days before I got face time.

Woody yawned and stood. I thought, he's going home to his photogenic new family, but instead he stretched himself out on his four-metre-long 'designer' sofa. Then Celine joined him and there they were, not touching, but close enough for electricity. They had 'stayed in touch' all right. Was she fucking the brute? Was this why Wodonga had taken on the cause? His big head was like a mallee root and his feet were ugly, even in his socks. But her feet – dear Jesus, they were just as astonishing as they had been, so many years ago, on a blue candlewick bedspread in Springvale. And of course she was one of those beauties who age like precious fabric, rubbed and rinsed, day after day, year after year so the reds become pink and the blues turn almost white.

Out in the dark world the hail was surely melting, and the hulls of massive clouds were sailing eastwards from the plains, presumably passing over the 'secure location' where Gabrielle Baillieux wore a tracker anklet.

What would be a secure location? I wondered, imagining a slender ankle not so far away.

Woody sighed. His eyes were dull and clouded. I thought, he is really pissed off with something I have written. When he spoke he sounded nasty. 'Can I give you some advice, mate?'

'We all have to wait for Gaby,' Celine interrupted anxiously. 'Even me. The supporters need to approve of us.'

'So Gaby won't see *you*?'

'Lay off, Felix,' Woody snarled.

But it was not him I was addressing: 'Your daughter won't see *you*,' I said. 'That's it, isn't it, Celine? Woody's paid for her and now she won't even talk to you.'

Woody narrowed his eyes but I was still too high for caution. 'If you guys can't deliver Gaby, there is nothing here for me to do.'

Why did I lie like that? I don't know. To stir him up? To take control? In any case, it had been a bad idea. He shivered like a horse. I recognised the symptoms. In a minute he would stamp his foot. This would be a bad event, I knew already. Even before he made a firearm of his hand, I understood.

Then here it was, the five-fingered pistol, pointed directly at my head. It was clearly time for Felix Moore to say goodnight.

12

In the morning there was no sign of Woody but I found Celine standing over the busy printer, pale as a corpse, dressed as she had been the night before. Her hair was like dry grass where wild animals have slept. She wearily considered me from behind large dark glasses.

Anyone else would have known that these sunglasses hid a blackened eye. Not me. 'Are we going to the beach?' I reached for them and she slapped my hand away.

Anyone with half a brain would have known he had hit her. What I noticed was that she was intent on stealing my pages. 'Then just give me back that bag,' I said.

'I need to read what you've done.'

I kept my temper. I stayed silent as she carried my writing to the bathroom. I waited for the shower but heard only the lock and then the hair dryer. I made coffee and calmly set out bowls, milk and cornflakes and a very short time later a freshly coiffed Celine was standing at the counter studying my offering from behind her shades. She had been sleeping with him, I was almost certain. He had always been a brute with women.

'Felix,' she said at last. 'You were far sweeter than you remember. You were eighteen years old. You were so full of life. Why would you betray me now?'

So I had revealed her mad mother in a draft. Could she have read that? I would fix it. There was no cause for this hysteria. 'Don't go, Celine. I won't betray you.'

'You won't mean to. Stay clear of Woody.'

'You're upset. Give me back my pages.'

'Yes I'm fucking UPSET. You've no idea what you've got yourself involved with. Don't you get it: he's playing the other side.'

But that was the one thing you could not say about Woody. He had been at my side during the dark nights of November 1975. He had coached me in my role for *Drivetime Radio* and when disaster struck he carried me to safety. He was incapable of playing for the other side.

'I dragged you into this,' she said. 'Now the game has changed.'

I planned to rescue my pages but somehow she tricked me. 'I'll just be a moment,' she said. A second later the lift pinged and my pages were gone. As they descended in the dark, the rising sun raked the banks of the Yarra and made a mirror of the yellow office tower. It was then I remembered how Woody had pointed his imaginary pistol. I had glimpsed that private passionate creature, the son of the murdered man. My friend's neck, his lips, his big sloping shoulders suggested a sexual underworld I had always chosen not to see, but this morning I recalled his first wife's testimony in the divorce court. It was the first time it occurred to me that she might have told the truth.

It was a cold-skied Melbourne day and the blackwood wattles were blooming in the hills. As Flinders Street station turned to gold, I composed a careful email to Wodonga Townes wherein I regretted any distress I may have caused him, or Celine. I didn't know what I had done, but I was sorry. I did not hold back. I confessed to being both blind and careless. I had no idea how true that was. I could only assume, I wrote, that they had stumbled on my last few weeks' work, which would seem less grotesque when it was understood I had written it off my face on his Dexedrine. I crawled. I admitted to an ugly excess of ambition, the desire to make the story 'rich' and 'complex'. My own good sense, I explained, had already lead me to conclude that much of the information was too personal. As for my overexcited interpretation of the daughter's relationship with the mother, I had been out of line.

This was the general sort of abject letter I have had reason to compose many times before. I grovelled in my usual style. Once again I said I was an awful creature.

I sent the email and showered. Then I dressed in my new clothes which I expected to amuse my old fan on his return. It was a ludicrously expensive shirt and I was struggling with the unexpected cufflinks when I heard the knocking. I had not known there was a door to rap on, but I found it finally, in an unused laundry. If there was a light switch, I could not see it. There was not even a spy hole.

'Who's that?'

'Felix?' It was a male voice, breathless.

'Who's that?'

'Jesus Felix, it's George. I'm knackered.'

What George? I knew no George. Whoever it was, he could walk back down and see the concierge. But then, of course, I wondered, was this what I was waiting for? The door had one of those brass security latches and I placed the hasp firmly over the hook and cracked the door.

I saw an unpleasant green shirt and, for a moment, a hairy arm. A gilt-edged card slid into the narrow crack. I thought, wedding invitation. Indeed I may have been correct, but the invitation's purpose, in this context, was to flip the latch. Then all hell broke loose. I was rushed by a wide fellow with thinning hair and sweaty beard.

'No,' I shrieked.

I dropped my cufflinks. I took a mop and poked his gut. He ripped my weapon from me and broke it across his big bare knee and came at me with its lethal end. I stood on the cufflink and cut my foot.

'Don't hurt me.'

'You stupid cunt, no-one's going to hurt you.'

I had retreated to the living room. There were sharp knives in the kitchen, but of course he would have taken them away from me.

DISGRACED JOURNALIST STABBED TO DEATH.

'For fuck's sake. Calm down. I'm here to take you to her. Don't you have a notebook or something?'

I pulled the cufflink from my foot. I took a pen and chequebook and shoved them in my pocket. I backed towards the Steinway. 'Her?'

'Nice place,' he said. 'Does he really have eight parking spaces?'

I asked him who he was working for but he had different matters on his mind.

'I'm not going to walk down ninety flights,' he said. 'Can we get into the car park directly from the lift?'

'I don't know who you are.'

'I told you, I'm George. I'd have thought you'd remember me. George Olson. From Cottles Bridge.'

'It's thirty years since I was in Cottles Bridge.'

'I'm not here to have a natter, mate. Give me the fucking key to the fucking lift.'

But you did not need a key to leave, and I soon found myself riding down with the intruder who smelled like old cleaning rags, BO, cigarettes, depression. This was not the sort of contact I had expected.

'Are you taking me to meet a certain young lady?'

'That's right, mate. I'm going to have to hide you on the way out, OK mate?'

'At a secure location, let's say.'

'That's right.'

I had no choice but trust him. I listened as he explained that he must put a blanket over me, 'like a budgie in its cage'. I was more excited than afraid. I would meet the Angel without her mother's help. I would shake her hand. The blanket had a certain logic. That is, we were just five minutes from the CIA's great bum boys, ASIO, the Australian secret service on St Kilda Road. That was only one of about six state and corporate 'entities' I could imagine watching me. When we entered the car park I was relieved to see, waiting right outside the lift, a thirty-year-old Holden sedan with powdery paintwork.

'Are you a potter?' I asked him but he was busy opening the boot, sorting through an unappetising tangle of crocheted rugs and quilts. He selected an unsavoury lemon-coloured blanket and held it up as if for size.

'OK?' he asked. I had no time to answer because he wrapped the blanket round my head.

'Don't panic.'

I was mainly worried about my suit. 'How long do I need to keep it on?'

'Just till we get going.'

And with that the bastard picked me up. It was then, in his fierce embrace, I knew I had been kidnapped. I screamed with fright.

'Shut up,' he cried and dumped me in the boot.

You work for property developers this is what they do to you.

13

I was a complete idiot. I would die now, because I could not acknowledge what was clearly true, which I had always known, that my greatest admirer was capable of anything.

How pathetic that I had got myself entangled in his love affairs. I did not even know what my offence was, or why Celine should be so afraid, but I would die without my decent law-abiding daughters knowing I was something better than a drunken arsonist. They would never see me in a decent suit. They would not imagine how I loved them or what I had suffered, nor imagine these smells inside this airless coffin, wet burlap and mould, the odour of real Melbourne crime. My father once traded in a Holden and discovered £10,000 hidden in its doors. Being a Holden, the door had filled with water and all the money turned to pulp which smelled like this exactly. I could not breathe. I found a tyre lever and began to beat the boot lid. The car slowed, accelerated violently, then pulled off the road. I heard the driver's door open and slam shut.

A key entered the lock. The lid cracked open. I saw a slice of my kidnapper's bright red lips.

'I can't breathe.'

'If you hit my car again,' he spoke with chilling deliberation, 'I'll tear your fucking throat out. Do you understand that? Can you hear me?'

'Yes.'

'What the fuck got into you? Are you mad?'

'I can't breathe.'

'Here.' He pushed a paper bag through the gap.

'What's this?'

By the time I understood what was in the bag, we were on a freeway and I knew I was a dead man. Vodka, to help me through my execution. It would be a western suburbs murder but committed in the east, a nail gun, probably, on sale at Mitre 10 at Thomastown, six-inch nails inside my skull.

What would you have done? I had Woody's number on speed dial but when I called he had his phone turned off. We all used to laugh about Woody. We used to say that the Big Fella knew where the bodies were buried. Now I drank his vodka and prayed the exhaust fumes might have me dead before we reached my destination. Then I dialled again.

My kidnapper drove on and on and I must have called Woody's number twenty times. Then we left the freeway and then – an hour from Moroni's – we were off the sealed road and were bumping along one of those dirt tracks which had once allowed me to pretend that I had escaped suburbia. I should have called my daughters but I would have cried. They could never know what a dirt road used to signify. They had grown up city kids. They would laugh to think of their father even chopping wood.

I wondered if he would stop to buy the nail gun or if he already had it. The road was so rough I wished it would knock me out. I phoned Woody one more time.

'Hi Felix, where are you?'

'In a car.'

He laughed, sadistic bastard.

'Woody, I didn't mean to be hurtful about Celine.'

Long silence.

'That's the last thing I wanted to do.'

Another pause before he spoke. 'Didn't sound like that last night.'

'I am an appalling creature.'

'Felix, don't say another word. You've been making that grovelling speech for thirty years.'

'You're right, mate.'

'Did it ever occur to you that I might go public with that *Drivetime Radio* event?'

'What part?'

'The chickenshit part.'

'Oh, mate, you wouldn't.'

He would though, the bastard. He had my moral cowardice in the bank and he would be a hard man if he had to. He could destroy my left-wing reputation in a heartbeat.

'I'm thinking I'm not suited to this project, Woody.'

'You're not trying to renege are you?'

'I can give you the money back.'

'Feels, you signed the fucking contract.'

Jesus. 'You still want me to write it?'

'Why would I put up with you otherwise?'

I could not ask him, why am I still in a car boot? 'I'm up for it, mate,' I said. So long as you want to continue, mate. I really wanted to continue in every sense.

Was he laughing? It wasn't clear. 'That's good,' he said. 'We don't want misunderstandings.'

'Just one thing.'

'Got to go, mate. We're taking off.'

'Woody, is there something you need to cancel?'

But he was gone, and when I called Celine I got her voicemail. I had never used a GPS before but this was a brand-new iPhone and it told me we were just past Eltham where Claire and I began our family. Long weekends of planting tiny trees, station wagons all coated with yellow dust, the smell of wattle, and that pungent blackcurrant smell from the deep gullies of the bush, all the rural beatniks from Eltham and Cottles Bridge sniffing at each other's bums. In those years I worked the police beat in the city and came back home to this non-suburbia, mudbrick houses, slate floors. You got an excessive amount of adultery in the so-called 'extended community' but not a lot of murdered men. Eltham was rutting ground but not much worse.

I dialled Woody. He was gone. I was sweating in private places. The car was pulling to a stop. I drained the awful vodka and took the tyre lever in my hand so, when the lid was lifted, I was crouched inside, my back in agony, my calves both cramped.

'Oh Felix!' The kidnapper relieved me of the lever as he helped me out one hand beneath my arm. He threw the lever back into the boot.

'You remember a piece of arse named Skye Olson?'

'You're her husband.'

'I'm her son you twat.'

He spat at my feet and climbed back behind the wheel. I remembered a little boy with a curled lip and big black accusing eyes.

'What now?' I asked.

'I'm off home mate.'

'What about me?'

It was an open invitation for him to tell me I could fuck myself. Instead he pointed up the hill where two pale tyre tracks were interrupted by the evidence of a vigorous four-wheel drive engagement.

14

Forty-five kilometres from the Melbourne GPO, I crossed a narrow creek and came upon a burned-out jeep with wild blackberries growing through its broken eyes and imagined every possibility at once, not only Woody's enforcers but also Angel's angry 'supporters' waiting to grill a reporter from 'the mainstream media'.

I was not a brave man. I never said I was. Two rutted wheel tracks had once continued up the hill but now they were swallowed by wattles and all the regrowth that follows fire. It looked like Eltham in the 1950s when tracks like these led to the homes of communists and free lovers and artists and bullshitters of all varieties. Beyond the fallen fence there was a stand of peeling paperbarks, no path other than that indicated by a piece of blue rope that might mean something if you knew. Children had left dirty drawings on the tattered white bark, broken crayons on the ground. Why did this seem sinister? Beyond these melaleucas was a rise on which stood a stand of slender white-barked eucalypts. From here one looked down on a sea of creeper which had colonised a long flat tin roof and a cedar pergola. Sensing a surprise might be dangerous to my health I called, 'Coo-ee.'

A woman said hello. And I saw what I expected although, honestly, who could have anticipated the gorgeous white pyjamas or Monet's broken light. My suit was like nothing

I had ever owned. It had the faintest hint of indigo hidden in its charcoal, like a crow's feather reflecting the sky. As I descended the rocky steps I was alive to every sense and colour. My hair thrilled on my neck.

'Felix Moore,' I called.

'I know who you are,' said Celine Baillieux.

I thought, fuck you. 'It was you who kidnapped me? You locked me in a fucking coffin.'

'That was not the plan,' she said and she was monstrous in her injury, the whole of her lower left eyelid both black and purple, swollen, shocking, inflamed and ugly like baboon sex. She slid open a slick glass door and I followed her. She paused. She turned. And slapped me, twice. I saw sparks. My ear went dull. 'You cunt,' she said.

For what? I had already been punished, tortured even. I realised my lovely suit jacket was torn, revealing stuffing like a sofa at an auction. Onward I tottered, entering a baronial room with a brick floor and heavy beams and long dark refectory table whose surface was awash with that pearl-white manuscript. My assailant walked to the big slate-floored kitchen and filled a glass with water, then again, then again. Her back was to me, but as the tap turned on and off I could hear mad rage knocking in the pipes.

'If I'd got into your manuscript before I came up here, I would have left you to deal with your psycho mate.'

She thrust her ruined face at me.

'You're a dreadful person,' she said.

'No.'

'Have you always been like this?'

I was innocent. I had not laid a hand on her. But what came to my mind was the helicopter that had clipped the top of Sydney's Westpac building and killed the pilot who I knew. I was sent down to Bondi Junction to ask the widow for a photograph of the dead man. I was twenty-one years old. The journos at the gate laughed at me for even trying. The widow wasn't speaking, but I was already Felix Moore. I had my will. I knocked on the front door. A boy opened it, almost my age. I said I knew how he felt. I had lost my own father last week. I said the *Sun-Herald* made me come and do it and I needed the job to support my mum. For this I got asked inside. I was given a photograph. His mother kissed me. Yes I was a dreadful person. It had been my trade for years. But this — that I had discovered the trauma of Celine's birth and not revealed it to her? Honestly, that did not seem as bad, although I certainly did not say that now. Instead, I apologised. I confessed that I had been infatuated with her. She had run away from home. She had been so frail. I could not bear to hurt her anymore. This, and other stuff, was true.

'You're a fantasist.'

'Not at all.'

'You're a creep.'

I wasn't really a creep. I was a good person. I had been secretly in love with her. I had lost her to another man. Now was not the time for that discussion. 'You've got the only copy in the universe,' I said. 'Tell Woody to check the Mac. I deleted everything.'

'You'd as likely chop your hand off.'

'This is all there is.'

'You're a liar. But why would you think you could write this in the first place? How could you be such an authority of my mother's home? I wasn't even born. You were never there. What makes you think you can write about her?'

'Show me what you read.'

'825 Stanley Street, Woolloongabba,' she said, and thrust my stuff back at me. 'The house isn't even there anymore. They put a highway through it. Everyone is dead.'

15

The greatest virtue of 825 Stanley Street, Woolloongabba, I had written, was the trams which rattled past the front door and thence across the Brisbane River where, if you took care with your appearance, no-one would know where you had come from. Without these trams Celine Baillieux could not have been born.

Celine's grandmother – who died at the beginning of our first year at Monash – was 'tall and skinny as a rake'. She 'never had a sick day in her life'. She had a son and husband fighting overseas. She took in boarders, but she was always broke. She was a Methodist. During the Depression she fed her family by stealing her neighbours' potatoes in the middle of the night. She had all the good manners and principles she could afford and when the women of Australia were instructed to welcome the 'Yanks' into their homes, when they learned it was their daughters' patriotic duty to be 'Victory Belles', in those few short months before she understood exactly what this meant, she communicated to the authorities that she would be very happy to entertain some officers, except no Jews.

Her gratitude to the Americans was well based. The Japanese had bombed Pearl Harbor, invaded Thailand, and the Philippines, seized Guam, marched into Burma and landed on the beach in British Borneo. Soon they would bomb the port of Darwin, then Broome, then what?

They bayoneted men tied to trees, they raped and chopped off heads. They were headed for Brisbane and the British 'could not do a bloody thing about it' except run for home. As for 'our own boys', they were in Egypt in their bargain-basement uniforms, trying to save the Poms.

In these first days, Celine's grandmother was grateful to the Americans with all her heart, plus, of course, sugar and cigarette rationing did not apply to GIs and they could be expected to unwind their well-fed bodies from their taxis carrying cartons of chocolate, sweetened condensed milk, silk stockings most of all. She was not alone in expecting this.

Her daughter Doris (she who would be Celine's mother) was at secretarial school in the city every workday, but both women were at home on Saturday afternoon when the Americans arrived.

Celine's grandmother was, at that time, only forty. She had good legs. She was ready in her best frock which was from St Vincent de Paul's although 'you wouldn't guess'. When the door knocker echoed through the dark hot house she collected Doris and brought her to the door.

What was there revealed were four officers of the United States Army, or if not officers you would never know, for the fabric was so fine, the cut so flattering it made you feel sorry for Our Boys who had no chance at all, poor buggers.

The four soldiers stood there, together, their smiles extra-white, gifts held in their dark hands, that is, the Americans were as black as night, and Celine's grandmother, a Woolloongabber all her life, held her right hand against her breast while the left searched unsuccessfully for the daughter.

The men introduced themselves. Their voices were deep and melodious.

'Oh dear,' Celine's grandmother said when they were finished. 'There has been a mix-up.'

The soldier at the front was small, if only in comparison, but he stood proudly with his shoulders back holding his carton of Lucky Strikes. Peering from behind her mother's stringy shoulders, Doris smiled at him.

'I'm so sorry,' the future grandmother said. 'There's been a mistake.'

Doris had detected the scent of aftershave which she had never smelled before. Behind her was what you would expect: cabbage and mutton fat. Ahead was America: cleanliness and beauty and a young man, at the rear, so tall and slender with modest lowered eyes. He had a cherubic face, if cherubs could be black, and it was clear they could. The girl smiled; the young man smiled right back.

The mother was now pushing the door closed and the daughter was pulling it open.

'No,' Doris cried, and held it open.

'Shut up,' her mother hissed. 'I didn't ask for them.'

At this the smiling ceased.

'I'm sorry,' Celine's grandmother probably said. 'It's not your fault. It's just a mistake, that's all.'

And for a moment there was no pressure on the door.

'Well ma'am,' said the short wide-shouldered man with the proud expression, 'we are very sorry to have inconvenienced you. We will be on our way now, but it was not a mistake. Our Captain Cohen, he don't make no mistakes.'

Later Doris would possibly think her mother had been the victim of a prank, but at the time all she knew was that darkness had descended on the hall. The slap jolted her head sideways. She felt a sharp cruel pain, heard the loud heavy steps ascending the uncarpeted stairs. This injustice, this fear, was as normal as the smell of mutton stew and when Celine's grandmother's bedroom door had slammed, life remained as normal as could be.

At Doris's secretarial school a girl from Rockhampton was discovered wearing a scarf to hide the lovebites on her neck. She was sent away.

Time passed. Sundays were slow. Doris crossed back and forth on the tram between Stanley Street and the city, back and forth, without particular hope. The houses in Woolloongabba were perched high on sticks. She could hear the bands at the Trocadero – Eastern Swing, Lindy Hop, Jive – all happening just a mile away.

She turned seventeen. There was a song on the wireless late at night. It said that her lips were so close to his that she could not help but kiss him, and he didn't mind at all.

With her eyes deep in the pillow, Doris saw him very well. He was American of course. His uniform was tailored and his teeth were lovely and it had suddenly become a sin to prefer him to the Aussie boys as so many girls now did. They had wanted you to show hospitality to the Yanks. But very soon they started to hate you for doing what you had been told. You were an Aussie girl. Then you should only go dancing with the Aussie boys, your brothers who were dying for you, who had to wear the awful uniforms that the mingy government provided, not tailored, not slick, not even the right size. They were your flesh and blood, dear Aussie boys who had sunken cheeks, their teeth all pulled out to save the money on the dentist. The Americans were a knife twisted in their guts, overpaid, oversexed, over here.

Each evening at sunset Celine's grandmother locked the door. Outside, the trams from the city delivered more and more black men 'with one thing on their minds'.

The white Americans were kept in the city, but Stanley Street was near Brissy's 'black zone', that is, an area where black Americans were allowed to look for entertainment. The blacks were bees to honey pots at the Trocadero dancing to 'Chattanooga Choo Choo'.

Why us? Celine's grandmother wished to know. The authorities think we aren't no better. Can you see your father's face? He'd murder them.

You can forget that Victory Belle rubbish, her mother said. To emphasise this point she unplugged the hot water jug and doubled the power cord to make a whip.

Don't you even dream of going out that door at night, her mother said. She knew how to use that flex like the father used his leather belt. The flex hurt more than the belt. It left bright red stripes around the girl's very shapely calves.

Would her mother please let Doris go if she promised never ever to dance with a black man?

No.

How about the Red Cross Service Club? Aussies go there too.

No.

Doris was a good girl. She was very quiet and docile but she was wilful to a genetic degree. She folded her arms across her bosom. She returned to her room where she made nice French scanties from parachute silk.

Her mother knew all about French scanties. She

84

searched the room and found them and thrust them in the kitchen stove then sat down quietly with her darning. She knew what girls did in return for American stockings. She heard 'the authorities' would soon require blood tests for women seeking government assistance for their American babies.

Doris purchased more parachute silk and wrapped it in brown paper and hid it underneath the house. She sat out the warm winter days between July and October, but in November she managed to buy a pattern for the dress.

Her skin was not from Brissy but the moon – translucent, glowing. Her eyes were sapphire-blue. In her room she stood up straight and pushed her chest out – she might have been American herself. She listened to songs on the wireless and danced in front of the mirror. She had wicked dreams. She sat by the front door, her head meekly bowed as she picked old socks apart for knitting wool. She was ready, or nearly ready, but when the opportunity presented itself – when her mother finally left the house to attend the Temperance – she had nothing but gravy mix to give her legs a stocking colour. She tried to draw the seam but could not get it right. It was already seven o'clock and she had to scrub everything clean with cold water. That made her skin red and raw but she had no choice. She gave her legs a second coat of Gravox and when that had dried she knocked on the door of the old poofter who worked as a window-dresser in Barry and Roberts. The joke amongst the boarders was that he wore a wig, but when he answered the door his hair was perfectly in place.

His room smelled of peppermint and dirty socks. She was embarrassed to ask him to draw her seams, but when he finally understood what she wanted he was very sweet and kind, and also fast and accurate. He told her 'Mum's the word' and she kissed him on his soapy cheek.

'Don't get caught ducky.'

Of course she would be caught. There was no choice. She could already feel the sting of the flex whipping around her legs.

It was Thanksgiving on that balmy evening she got onto the tram, but that – if she had known – would have been of no significance at all. She had never heard of Thanksgiving. Australians did not give thanks. If you said thanks, your father would say, don't thank me, thank Christ you got anything at all.

November was a lovely time of year in Brissy. The tram had open sides and swayed and snaked towards the city and the girl sat up straight with her hands in her lap, seemingly unaware that she was beautiful. No-one dared to speak to her.

The tram rattled across the dirty old girders of the bridge, and her silk gown glowed pearlescent above the oil-slicked water of the Brisbane River. The dress had a scooped neckline and just three buttons down the back.

The American Red Cross Service Club was on the corner of Creek Street and Adelaide Street, just opposite the American PX. She walked from the tram stop with her little handbag, a clutch, beneath her arm, afraid of the attention she was drawing, surprised by the size of the crowd, Aussies and Yanks, milling in the evening air.

She had gravy-mix legs and a parachute-silk dress. She was going to be examined like livestock in an auction and be judged by men she wouldn't even fancy. The thick knot of uniforms pressed hard against her and she turned to go back home.

That was exactly when the most beautiful man emerged from the khaki tangle of sweat and beer. There was a brownout and the voltages were dropped but there was light enough to see him very clearly – golden hair, broad shoulders, a narrow waist and strong arms that pushed against the confines of his shirt.

'You are a songbird,' he said to her and she was astonished by the lilt of his voice as it slid upwards, tentatively, thus contradicting the assertiveness of his movement. You are a *songbird* question mark.

She should have been frightened but she felt relief that the auction was now over.

'Beg yours?' she said.

'You sing in the choir,' he said and she guessed his eyes would turn out to be pale and gentle like her own, as indeed they would.

'Yes.'

He beamed at her. 'I can always pick a songbird.'

'You must be a clever bloke,' she said.

'Oh no, Miss,' he said. 'It's very easy to see a songbird in this crowd. You do stand out.'

She was laughing, perhaps with relief, or just the simple wonder that someone would know she had a good voice, and when the man asked her would she like to go to The Society for a meal she was very grateful that she did not have to enter the churning scrum. He held out his arm and Doris took it, and as they cut through the mob towards Queen Street the crowd parted to let them through and she smiled more, thinking it a tribute to her beauty. She did not expect to be abused, but when the spit hit her cheek she thought, of course. I'm a tart, a traitor with a Yank.

16

Searchlights cut the empty sky and the tropical night was rank with beer and sandalwood, the latter the property of Hank, the American whose arm was now clamping Doris snug against his side, hurrying her to safety while the Australian soldiers called her tart and slut and cunt. She had a glob of slag on her cheek. She would not touch it with her hand, but in the doorway of a restaurant her rescuer produced a large white handkerchief and with it wiped her clean. In the midst of all the fear and fright there was space to know he was a lovely man.

The door swung open and she stumbled into the restaurant with a cry. It was too bright. She was exposed, embarrassed, in awe, of the flowers, the carpet, the American officers and beautiful women. She was set on by a very old head waiter in a long black coat.

'Pardon me,' she said. She knew her scanty line was showing through the silk.

'Two,' Hank said to the head waiter.

But it was at Doris the waiter looked. She was south Brissy rubbish. How dare she even breathe his air?

She smiled right in his sour old face. You are a coward, she thought, you will not turn a Yank away.

He didn't either. He told the waitress number 23. Then Doris and her handsome fellow were lead through The Society's crowded downstairs room.

They made a strong impression. Why wouldn't they? Doris had gravy mix on her legs, and spit-smeared makeup. She followed the waitress along the hall and up the stairs and of course it was a second-best room, with one table of Australian NCOs and, in a far corner, two plain American servicewomen in mufti, poor things, she pitied them.

Hank was not intimidated by anything. He announced they would sit by the curtained window i.e. not where they were put. He held out Doris's chair and waited for her to be comfortable before he took his place.

'It's lovely,' she said.

He was incredibly handsome, with full lips and straight white teeth. He sat so square and broad, a lifeguard she thought.

'I must look awful,' she said.

'You are perfect,' he said, and he touched her cheek where the horrid spit had been.

'Well,' she said, 'you're not so bad yourself.'

'I'm no angel, baby.' But his voice was so light and its inflection so tentative she laughed. He smiled too, and narrowed his eyes so that her tummy went quite strange. His eyes were pale and clear as water with no stones or pebbles or specks or flecks or injuries of war.

'You have lovely teeth,' she said, which was much too fast of her.

'All the better to eat you with.' As a joke, he bit his own hand and then showed her the bright red teeth marks embedded in his skin.

'You're a strange one.'

'Well thank you, ma'am,' he beamed at her, and took her fingers and kissed the inside of her wrist so gently that she had to snatch it back.

'Whoa, Dobbin.'

'Sing for me,' he said. And she might have (why not? who would ever ask her such a thing again?) but there came a great roar of men from the street below, as if a wicket had just fallen at the Gabba.

Immediately he drew the curtain back. She whispered you were not allowed to do that after dark but he said it was a brownout not a blackout. Someone shouted to close the curtain. He said, not quietly, that the Australians were always in a panic. She was more frightened of what was about to happen in the dining room than in the street and was slow to understand the scene below on Queen Street which was turbulent with pushing men.

She watched two American officers enter the street from the front door of the restaurant.

The first was knocked to the ground. She saw. The second was lifted into the air, his napkin or handkerchief still in his hand as he was passed like a side of butchered beef, over the heads of the crowd and thrown on the footpath on the other side. The Aussies made a circle around him then kicked his face.

There were now three, four, five circles in the crowd. An American would come walking down the street, the Aussies would grab his arms and legs and throw him up in the air to get him to a clear space to bash him more. Throughout there was a loud hammering, like blows on bone. Doris finally understood it was a mob hammering on the restaurant door.

'We can't stay here,' she said.

Hank sat down. He did not seem to realise that the

91

Aussies were coming in to get the Yanks and kill their whores, to break them limb by limb.

'They'll murder us.' She took his hand and pulled him up. He looked furious but he did allow her to lead him past the coat rack where she had the nous to grab an Aussie slouch hat. She pulled him down the stairs and through the stinking kitchen and out into a slippery laneway where the air was rank with fat and blood.

Beyond the alley was Queen Street and a howling mob.

'Come on,' she said, but now he had his arms around her and was pushing her stomach with his thing.

'Songbird,' he said. 'Sing to me.'

'Jeez,' she said, 'lay off, will you?'

She got the slouch hat onto his head and his situation seemed to dawn on him. He set the hat, tipping it back in the style favoured by the Aussies.

They were saved by the brownout and the happy coincidence that the northbound tram was tipped over just as they left the lane. There was such confusion. The American military police brought out their shotguns. All she could think was they had to get home, south Brissy, somewhere safe. She heard the first blast, then the second. She would have settled for a pillbox but it seemed every pillbox was occupied by men and women doing what she had never done, and would not do, no matter what she drank. She knew girls who had a 'bit of a pash' in a pillbox but she had never anticipated the stink.

'They'll kill you,' she said, but he wanted to pash into her there and then. He was strong and persistent, persuading her down into a lane, still very gentle with his mouth – soft little puffy kisses all around her neck. 'Sing to me,' he said, his hard arms around her, those mad kisses on her throat. She sang 'Danny Boy' for fear. 'Don't stop,' he said, 'don't stop.'

He was doing what she did not know.

'Don't stop. Keep singing.'

He had to let her go to fiddle with her bra and she slipped free and ran, unhooked, with her shoes in her hand, down Queen Street, thinking God Jesus let there not be broken glass. The tram for south Brissy was already rolling when she leapt aboard, and he was right behind her, she heard him, laughing like a drain.

The man and girl plonked down together on the bench, she in disarray, he laughing hopelessly, and the whole tram went silent on her and judged her for a tart. She folded her hands in her lap, covering her ring finger, pretending to herself they were engaged, going to live in Dee-troit, no longer Doris Crook, something better, safer, clearer, richer, thank the Lord he behaved himself. He put his arm around her shoulder and that is how it happened, when they arrived in Stanley Street and she saw, a cricket-pitch length from the tram's running board, the thirteen front steps of her home, that she was still holding Hank Willenski's hand.

17

Our sole responsibility to our ancestors, I had written, is to give birth to them as they gave birth to us. The houses in south Brissy were wrapped with skirts of lattice, as secret as a veil. Doris's mother had her bedroom up there overlooking Stanley Street. Yes, it was the noisy side, but she could be out of bed in a jiffy when the front gate clicked. You could rely on her being up there, waiting, the electric flex already wrapped round her hand.

The house was twelve feet off the ground and all the underneath was latticed too. If it had not been for the brownout the street would have looked so lovely – sky deep, black blue, and the latticed houses glowing like golden lanterns in the honeysuckle air, and if you shut your eyes and hid the trams and the pub and the shunting train and the drunk peeing by the lamppost you could almost think Woolloongabba was beautiful.

She brought Hank Willenski home, not knowing what else to do. When she jumped off the moving tram, she knew she would get caught. She did not doubt she'd get roared up. She wished for nothing better than the flex across the legs. The American was right behind her as the tram rolled on, its wheels screaming worse than nails on a blackboard.

She was for it now. Thank God.

'Home,' she said, quite loudly. She could make out his teeth. 'My dad will have waited up,' she said.

She put her finger to his lip to show he must not kiss her. He bit her finger, hard.

'That wasn't funny.' Why was she whispering? She wanted to get caught.

'Sing me a song.'

He got her around the waist and lifted her up in the air and she grabbed at the fence and felt the splinter drive into her injured finger. Why did she not scream? He had her over his shoulder. He was passing through the gate. Her mother would hear the latch.

But then she was out of sight, dragged underneath the house. There was stuff lying everywhere, snakes in bottles, axes, preserved quince, dead marines. She thought, he'll trip and fall.

'Let me down,' she said, 'I'll help you do it, honest.'

He set her down very slowly but then he was at it again, kissing her on the neck, holding her hands together tight, pushing his thing against her.

'I'll show you,' she said. Show what? Show where? She was embarrassed by the smell of her home. Nightsoil and honeysuckle, dirt and gas. He kicked the preserves and she heard a bottle crack and the smell of sugary peach juice making witch's pudding with the dirt.

'No, I'll show you,' he said.

And then he pushed her down so hard she fell. No glass. No cuts. Thank God, she thought. He had shoved her head onto the chopping block without knowing what it was. She felt the cold air between her legs. He was pushing and breaking and her tummy was filled with hurt but she dared not scream. His hands around her neck. He said, 'You better sing.' He was kneeling behind her, evil thing.

She could no longer breathe but she did 'Danny Boy'. The air came through the words and the air was ripped-up rags. His hands were large and very strong and she finally understood, without a doubt, he would kill her when he'd finished.

He clamped her windpipe. He shivered like a horse. The thing inside her was in spasms, like a cat dying from a hammer blow. And then *he* screamed, right in her ear.

Later she would know he had driven a broken preserve bottle into his knee and leg. But she was free. He was off her. She fled.

For once in all its history, Stanley Street was quiet.

'Mum,' she cried from the front gate. She heard a slamming door upstairs, thank God.

'Ma'am?'

In the street, against the lamppost she saw them, a black man with a hire-girl. Even at this voltage it was clear. The soldier left the girl. He crossed the tracks, his hand held out towards Doris. He looked drunk.

'Mum,' she wailed.

It was the very same GI who had arrived so sweetly at her door. He stood before her, swaying.

'Miss, what happened?'

'Are you going to do her or me?' said the hire-girl. It was Glennys Craig who had been the fastest runner in the grade.

'He's in there,' Doris said. 'Under the house.' The black soldier looked at Glennys Craig and then at Doris. Then, as the front door of the house yawned open, the soldier opened his wallet and gave the prostitute some bills.

'You're a mug,' said Glennys Craig, and teetered off

into the dark. The lights behind the lattice came on, one by one, and suddenly, in the midst of the brownout, the whole of 825 Stanley Street was a wooden lantern and the pansy window-dresser was sprinting – him at his age – turning on the lights as he passed each switch and Doris's mother was behind turning them all off.

'Now all the world can see,' the mother said when she arrived out in the street. She flashed her Eveready torch over the stunned black face and then across the parachute-silk dress which was marked with blood and spunk and woodchips from the past.

As the girl began to vomit on her shoes, Doris's mother confronted the American soldier who, drunk or not, was clearly the same fellow she had already turned away. He stood the same, shoulders back, squared off, his cap in one hand, explaining.

'Just go,' said Celine's grandmother. 'Before you get your balls cut off.'

18

Celine rose from the battered leather club chair. She returned my pages to the floor without saying what she'd read. She was not finished, that was clear. I watched as she chose a poker and, like a blacksmith, brought down a rain of blows upon a log already sheathed in glowing red and orange scales. How far had she got? Sparks glinted in her eyes.

I had done an extraordinarily professional job, but clearly she was not considering that. She blew the ash from her fingertips and pulled the kimono tight around herself and retreated to the hallway. Then I heard her retching in the bathroom, vomiting.

So she had reached that part. I was so sorry. But I would seem to be a hypocrite to say so. I returned to my seat and waited to be abused but I certainly did not expect her to return with a rifle at her hip.

'My father gave me this,' she said, 'my real father.'

Fire was dancing along the gun metal.

'He was the most decent man you could ever know. Strictly speaking, he was a criminal, but he changed my nappies when my mother couldn't. He left enough money for me to go to university. He cut my hair. He taught me how to shoot. How many rabbits do you think I've killed?'

'I am not wrong about Willenski. It doesn't make me happy, but it's true.'

'I brought you out here to get you out of Woody's clutches, you shit. But I had no idea of what you'd done.' She jerked the rifle violently, like a pitchfork. 'Can't you learn your lesson in a courtroom? Lying is not socially acceptable. Do I have to punish you as well?'

'It's not made up.'

'You're a convicted slanderer.'

'No.'

'My father is a rapist? You can't possibly know that.'

'Why do you think I didn't tell you at Monash?'

'You kept it from me, all my life?'

'Don't you remember the state you were in? You stayed with what's-his-name, the poet. Then Sando took you in. His landlady threw you both out and you slept in his car. You were too busy burning down the house.'

Sandy had taken her pain and held her and never let her go until he married her. I did not tell her how I had mourned her.

'How could you know shit about any of this?'

'There was only one American soldier who'd been photographed in Brisbane. The rest were Melbourne. The dates work too. Willenski was front page of the *Courier-Mail*.'

'And that's it? On the basis of this you write this? Anyone who knows you can see what you're doing. America rapes Australia. It's pathetic. Do you know how many Americans were here during the war? You want this psycho to represent them all.'

'I confirmed it again. Last week.'

'How could you?'

'I let my fingers do the walking for me, as the ad says.'

'You phoned my mother?'

'She's in the White Pages.'

'Why would she want to talk about this to a stranger?'

'People with secrets. It's what they do.'

'But why you?'

'It's a talent.'

'She would never talk to me.'

'As I understand it, Celine, really darling, you have been particularly unforgiving of your mother. She says you never took Gaby to meet her?'

'No. She met her.'

I raised an eyebrow.

'Don't get prissy with me, Titch. Who does all this muckraking serve? Not Gaby, that's for sure.'

'You came to me.'

Celine returned to her armchair and laid the rifle on the side away from me. 'No, you were Woody's contribution,' she said. 'He could not have expected to be so lucky.'

19

Doris's mother locked the verandah door in silence, I had written. Only when both women reached the kitchen did the elder woman unwrap her naked wrath. 'Filth,' she cried.

Crouching, wet rag in hand, she attacked her daughter's hem and thighs.

'Mum, please. You're making it worse.'

'Worse,' she cried, and tugged at the silk dress, ripping to reveal a raw abrasion.

'Jeez. Leave off. No-one saw.'

'No-one saw. God save me.' Her eyes were frightening but frightened too, clearly searching for an instrument to thrash the legs, the arms, the neck. 'I'll learn you, girlie. No-one saw.'

The girl made a break, upstairs, towards the safety of the bathroom but her mother was a scrapper, knees and elbows, in the bathroom first.

'Save the hot water for the boarders.'

'Please, Mum.'

And they were collapsed, crying, wringing their hands, grabbing for understanding, pushing violently away, and then the mother turned on the cold tap and threw a fist of salt into the claw-legged tub.

'Clothes off.' The girl might as well be six years old the way she was forcibly undressed. It was pull out your hair, rip off your nose.

'You smell of him,' the mother said. She wiped her eyes with the back of her arm. If you thought that meant sympathy, you were mistaken. 'Come on. Give me. Scanties.'

'Don't leave me naked.'

'You've got your bra. Use a towel.'

What occupied the mother was not disease or pregnancy. The issue was – who knew? Who saw?

'You could have picked a white boy but.'

Who was going to write her husband poison letters? She would burn the parachute silk and she wished she had the strength to destroy the house entirely. He was going to kill her. He would kill them both and who would blame him? Where there's smoke there's more smoke. His wife was not Miss Pearly Pureheart either.

The daughter locked the bathroom door and cried. She felt the sting of salt kill her germs and babies. It destroyed the lather so her body got coated with a grey scum which she would still smell in the morning, on the tram. The damaged part was not where you expected.

At secretarial school she was lucky or unlucky – her classmates could see nothing but the size of the stones in Maisie's engagement ring. Maisie's fiancé was an American called Captain Baillieux. Doris had her write it down. No-one cared or noticed that she kept the scrap of paper.

Of course Doris had not yet decided to become Baillieux, but she would not have told them if she had. She could not trust her girlfriends with anything important. She waited for her period alone and was relieved to see the blood. Next day she got blisters 'down there'. She used the salt twice a day and the blisters went away, thank heavens, but it wasn't over yet. The bank teller in the western room paid his rent on time but he was a pigpen. He liked his *Courier-Mail* and left it everywhere, including on the kitchen table where she saw the news, December 2nd, 1942. THE BROWNOUT STRANGLER. And there he was, the American, his perfect smile, his awful handsome face, his cowlick hair. He had raped six girls and strangled them and mutilated them in ways particular. After that she could hardly eat at all. Her period stopped. Her hair went dull and lifeless. If she had managed to eat a little custard, say, she would puke in the middle of her sleep.

Yet even as her appearance changed she found herself the beneficiary of unexpected acts of kindness. Late at night, after ten o'clock, she and the window-dresser listened to the wireless and the little chap was nice enough to brush her hair. Once he tucked her in. Her mother made a rabbit pie. You could taste the butter – although she had no ration coupons left. The girl resisted the awful need to read her stolen *Courier-Mail*. Finally, they had a lovely Christmas with the boarders and the window-dresser played piano. He was a strange kind creature with a white soft hairless neck below his wig, and the mother was happy and did not think what Black and White Rag might really be, thank God for that.

Then it was a different year. The rains arrived. The Allies took Buna in New Guinea. Then it was Sanananda. In Guadalcanal, the Japs had their tails between their yellow legs. In March they were blown to screaming pieces in the Battle of the Bismarck Sea. It was still mango season then. The bank teller loved mangoes so much he ate them in the bath. The girl ate them too. Her appetite returned. Then a letter came from Dad – he was back in Perth and coming home. Then Tom was in Aden waiting for a ship. And it was only then, when she knew they could all recover from everything, that her mother barged into the bathroom.

She was in the nuddy when the door slammed hard against the wall.

'You idiot. Why didn't you tell me?'

'I put the pounds back on.'

'Pounds. Dear Jesus help me, look at yourself.'

'It's been since Christmas.'

'It's four bloody months. No wonder you've been throwing up. You'll have to leave before your dad gets home. Don't cry. You should have thought about this. You can't be giving him a little piccaninny.'

Without another word, the mother went downstairs, soft as a ghost, an angel of the annunciation.

The girl found her kneeling at the front door polishing the knob.

'Mum.'

The mother's head was tiny as a coconut, the hair lank, eyes leached. 'You're an idiot,' she said, 'I could have helped you.'

'Mum, it wasn't the black chap. It was a white chap, Mum. You'll see. You'll be sorry for what you said.'

The mother's mouth was just a little line, a scar, a screwed-up sewed-up wound. 'Dear Mouse,' she said, and the girl shivered to receive the tenderness. 'We've got no choice, my titchy mouse. You'll have to be gone when he arrives.'

'I have to go to the hostel?'

'I'll say you got a job in Sydney.'

'Wouldn't he like a nice white baby?' she asked, but she

was already bilious at the thought of the mouse-sized Hank Willenski growing in her womb.

The mother's eyes were brimming, and she stroked her daughter's tiny ears.

'Do you even know his name?'

'Baillieux,' she said, and spelled it.

'Is he French?'

'I don't know, Mum. He didn't say.'

'Is he in New Guinea, love?'

'Yes Mum, he is.'

'God save him then,' her mother said.

'God save him, Mum.' She did not say the brownout strangler was dead already, murdered by the Aussies in his cell on Boggo Road.

20

'Did you ever imagine how it might feel for me to read this?'

I smelled Celine's acrid breath. I observed her blackened eye, the hard contusion on the cheekbone, the awful puce in the soft cave of the orbit. I reached towards her tenderly. She thrust my hand away.

I said I was not her enemy. I would never wish to hurt her. I was startled she couldn't see that I had been a time traveller on her behalf, that I had given her what she could have never known. Her life was a miracle to me. From Stanley Street to all those nights of mad applause on stage.

'Everything you've written is reprehensible,' she declared, and of course, the truth is ugly and often frightening. We have placed truth in our stained-glass windows but when it arrives in person, unwashed and smelly, loud and violent, our first act is to pull a gun on it.

'What you have written hurts everyone.'

I never wanted to hurt a soul, but a laboratory rat would have learned by now that I was doomed to repeat my action like some automaton in a Disney underworld. I felt ineffably sad. I stared at the monster log until it had burned through and collapsed onto a sparky bed of fine white ash. Celine gathered my pages to her breast. Her fingernails were delicate and uncorrupted, swimmer's nails, I thought, the colour of cuttlefish shells. I watched her turn my pages.

A single A4 sheet slipped free and glided towards the hearth. I snatched at it.

'Liar,' she cried. She launched a flock of paper. Two hundred and twenty-one pages struck my head, beat my ear, landed in the fire, white wings curling into black.

I had sworn this was the last copy on the earth and as I was being a good man I could not be a liar. I had no choice but to plunge my hands into the flames.

Then Celine was at my side, raking pages to the floor, stamping on their carmine skirts. The paper was like stinging nettles. I had expected it would have hurt much more than this.

'Stop it,' she said. 'What is the matter with you?'

In the kitchen I permitted her to plunge my sacrificial hands beneath the tap. She emptied trays of ice into a bowl and I watched my injuries: red and black palms, bloating like dead fish.

'This is bullshit,' she said softly and I could once more smell her acrid breath. 'This cannot be the only copy.'

'I know that.'

'Then why did you do this?'

I shrugged.

'Did no-one ever love you Felix?'

'I'm an awful person.'

'You wanted to hurt me, you should be happy. You've shown that my father is American.'

'So?'

'It gives them a claim on Gaby.'

'No it doesn't.'

'You're sloppy and careless. You don't know where you are. You told Woody I could not deliver Gaby. He believed you. He thought I had tricked him into paying bail. You just wandered off to bed and locked your door. I heard you.'

'I'm sorry.'

It was not Celine's character to have a first-aid kit, but there it was, a black backpack with a white cross in house paint. From this she produced a roll of white surgical bandage which she wound delicately around my injuries.

'Woody is your admirer, God help you. He'll kill us both.'

I should not have let her say this.

'Felix, did you ever ask yourself, why is Woody paying me so much money?'

'He's always been like that.'

'Yeah, right.' Even as she was sarcastic, she was also kind, tidying up both hands and securing them with small elastic clips. 'Gaby was not even arraigned,' she said, 'and I had Woody on the phone offering to pay her bail and legal support. Whatever he wants you to do, it's not for me. And now he will use this dirt you've dug up for him.'

'He offered bail. You said you asked him.'

The firelight caught the colours of her bruised and shiny cheekbone. Her fingers felt like feathers as she snipped away the loose threads of my bandage. 'I knew Woody when he was a Maoist with a red cashmere sweater.'

'Everyone trusts Woody.'

'I certainly trusted he would help me now.'

'Jim Cairns trusted him. Woody loved Jim Cairns, early, before he was the Treasurer, before he was Deputy Prime Minister.'

Celine poured me a glass of wine and held it to my lips. I sipped.

'Exactly.'

'You're being sarcastic?'

'Think about it, Felix. The Americans thought Jim was the enemy. Dr Cairns, the Deputy Prime Minister of their ally, was a communist. Gough talked about it – the "American Terror" that Jim would be briefed on Pine Gap. Imagine: a communist had got access to all that shared security.'

'And?'

'Don't you imagine they would have recruited someone close to Cairns?'

'So Wodonga is an American spy? Jesus, Celine. You never mentioned this before.'

'Calm down. I never thought of it before. Remember the photos on Woody's office walls. How does a Melbourne property developer get to play golf with the US Secretary of State?'

'I don't know, but he loved Jim. He'd do anything for him.'

'I worked in Jim's office when he was Treasurer. I do believe I remember you there too. Don't you recall how embarrassing Woody was? Cleaning Jim's shoes at the party conference at Terrigal? In public. And in the office, what a dogsbody. Woody is a sort of thug but there he was standing by his desk turning pages for Jim to sign.'

I picked up the glass and held it with both wrists and drank. She watched, as if waiting for me to fail. 'Jim had that effect,' I said and in the sad silence that followed me setting down the wine, I thought about those great men in that government which was overthrown in 1975. Gough Whitlam, the Prime Minister, was a patrician. But Jim

Cairns was from the basalt plain, from Sunbury. He had been a policeman, a champion runner, a working-class intellectual. It was Jim who had the moral authority to lead a hundred thousand of us up Bourke Street in 1970. My most intoxicating night as a young writer was spent staying up with Jim, composing captions for the pictures in his book on Vietnam. I admired him just as much as Woody did.

When Jim was brutally beaten by the Painters and Dockers, it was because he always had an open house. He was Treasurer of the nation and you could walk in off the street and meet Junie Morosi (Jim's lover and office coordinator), me, Woody Townes his millionaire intern, Celine with a kaftan and no bra. There were Nimbin hippies, confusion, awful instant coffee. Those were heady days to be so young and close to government. Australia had withdrawn from Vietnam, and recognised China. If Woody was a spy he was in a perfect place, except that he loved Jim Cairns.

'He is very loyal,' I said, and Celine picked up her rifle and ejected a single shell.

'Catch.'

I grabbed and missed. I heard the bullet bounce and roll. Then she was in the bathroom with her face creams and I was in the dark, alone with the smell of ashes.

21

So: clearly: the armchair was to be my bed. No-one brought a blanket and I slept like a reporter on the red-eye and woke to find a pale thing standing over me.

'What?' I asked of the pale thing standing over me.

'I keep hearing things,' she said.

Was this like me, to retreat from a woman's touch when it was offered?

'I'm scared,' she said. 'Would you come in with me, just for company?'

If I hesitated it was not because I was still a married man, but because I was nervous to go with her, and nervous to refuse. She was unusually fragile, even needy and I also remembered how she had been Medea, Antigone, Hedda Gabler, all these dangerous women.

I was an old man, but I was still a man. I had never been to bed with a woman without at least the possibility of sex and as the eucalypts of Smiths Gully tossed restlessly in the night, I lay very very still, too aware of that musky scent inside the tent. Celine went straight to sleep, snoring intermittently. Her frame was slight and birdlike. Her chest rose and fell. Broken sticks fell on the corrugated roof. Honey myrtles scrubbed themselves against the naked window glass.

Who doth murder sleep?

My father could not sleep, not ever. I would find him in

the middle of the night, in striped pyjamas, looking down at the car yard and all the unsold Fords gleaming on their gravel bed of quartz, like fish on ice. He hoarded pills. I forget so much about my childhood, but I can still recite his pharmacopoeia which included legal codeine and Valium which last he eked out because it was hard to get. He was awake and worried he paid too much to trade in Henry Wilmot's Holden ute. I was now worried that my present sleeping partner was unstable and that my supporter was a deeper and darker character than I could bear to think about.

I turned and discovered her staring patchy eye, a small and touching night creature.

'What might happen to us now?' she whispered, and lifted an arm, a motion as smudgy as a flying-fox wing in the dark.

'What?' I asked.

'Come here.'

I laid my head upon her shoulder and she stroked my hair with such sad consoling familiarity we might have been lovers after all.

'I can't believe you,' she said. In the cloud-scudding light, her lips appeared to be deep blue. I inhaled her toothpaste together with her pheromones. I did not doubt she was afraid. Somewhere far off, a car door slammed. Her body stiffened, but then a soft rain began, and there were no more noises and the corrugated iron played that song of safe childhoods, and Celine lay still and I thought of the house in Rozelle with our daughters beneath a sudden Sydney storm. It was unthinkable that I had abandoned them. It had been the only thing I knew I would never do.

The rain was louder and through the din there was a heavy thumping.

'Kangaroo,' she said. 'Don't worry.'

'What did you say to him? Woody.'

She propped herself on her elbow. 'Their own citizens don't count anymore.'

'Is that what you told him?'

'They murder their own people on the basis of suspicion. There are no boundaries of any sort. They break their own laws all the time. Half of them are locked in jail. And my daughter thought she could fuck them over. Say something.'

'What?'

'They say she infected their base at Pine Gap. Do you think that's credible? Is it possible? Is that her crime?'

'Did you accuse Woody of being a spy? Is that why he hit you?'

'That would make it all OK?'

It was not at all OK but it made a sort of sense. Woody was an emotional man. Loyalty was a big deal with him.

The rain had stopped and there was no sound but the occasional flurry of drips from the big gum tree overhead. Clouds had covered the moon and it was unclear as to whether I could see the shed roof or if I only thought I could.

'I was sitting in the sunshine yesterday,' Celine said, her inflection upwards in that mild hippie fashion she sometimes adopted.

'Yes.'

'I saw a tiny bird, like those spotted things, they live in New South Wales.'

'You mean a spotted pardalote?'

'They don't live here, Felix.'

'I think they might.'

'No, they don't. If you're in Pakistan, what are you to think if you see a little pretty bird that shouldn't be where it is?'

'This is not Pakistan.'

'Would I be mad to think it was a drone that could destroy me?'

'Sweet Celine.'

'Don't maul me, Felix. Turn on the light.'

'You don't mind people looking in?'

'Whoever comes to get me will walk straight in. Turn on the light. Open the cupboard door. Pick up that box.'

'This?'

'Open it.'

She was sitting on the bed with haystack hair and her legs crossed and a clay-coloured blanket pulled around her like a shawl.

'Do it, please.'

I opened the box and discovered, lying on a bed of discoloured cottonwool, the bloody remains of what I took, from the evidence of the colourful feathers, to be what she possibly thought it was. It had been mostly blown apart.

How extraordinary this was: the accuracy, the physical stability in the midst of turmoil.

'You shot this?' I asked. It was too late to argue about the habitat of the spotted pardalote.

'You know I did. I killed this lovely thing.' She began laughing, her big bruised lips crumpling and her eyes screwed up like paper in a bin, this miracle that began its journey underneath a Queensland house.

Who can foretell us? Who can limit what we'll be? Her marksmanship, I soon realised, was a natural gift, one recognised and encouraged by the rifle's previous owner, the man she sometimes called 'my father'. That is, Mr Neville.

Mr Neville was a most unlikely chap, a dear friend of that same window-dresser who had drawn the seams on her mother's gravy-coloured legs and, later, when Doris was thrown out of home, carried her cardboard suitcase to the tram. He had bestowed on her two envelopes. One was addressed to 'My Good Friend, Mr Neville Peterson'. The other contained thirty-three pounds and ten shillings.

'Be a brave girl,' he said, and kissed her on both cheeks. Did Celine not want this information? She herself had travelled the thousand miles in utero, unable to know anything except, presumably, that the waters of the world were full of fright and shame as her mother braved the Melbourne streets knowing that her cotton dress could not hide the curve of her belly to her bush, her thighs, bare legs. There was no-one to forgive her. She lugged her cardboard 'port' which is what they called a suitcase in Brissy, from the French *portmanteau*. In Melbourne 'port' meant cheap fortified wine which was sold, together with other necessaries, from Mr Neville's back gate and on occasions from his Bedford van. It was hard to credit the number of cigarettes and chocolate bars and nylon stockings stored inside that tiny space.

His house was in Dorcas Street, South Melbourne, which was working-class and industrial in 1943. It is still there, a single-story late Victorian twenty-two feet wide with a curbed corrugated-iron verandah and an ornate pediment on which the word 'Balmoral' stands in bold relief. It is on a deep block, almost two hundred feet, with access from the wide rear lane.

In 1943 the backyard held a trove of lumber, lead, copper, and various other valuables best traded after dark. The daylight merchandise lay on racks or stacked against the shed like sticks around a bonfire. Nearer to the gate stood the aforementioned van in which the terrifying driver, the left lens of his specs pasted with brown paper, made his expeditions to collect *windfall coal* or *bunny jumpkins* or *mushies* or *cackleberries* and there were many farms from the Dandenongs to Ballarat where the tall dry man with the cinched-in belt and no bum in his trousers was known and welcomed for no better reason than his nod, his tight-rolled cigarettes, his reassuring companionable way of saying 'yairs' (a spelling which misrepresents him in this age where such a thing looks comic). It is said authoritatively that there was no black market in the war.

Doris found her future half hidden by a bamboo thicket, behind Mr Neville's cast-iron gate.

As it was now noon the master of the house had just risen. He appeared at the front door with his first hand-rolled cigarette in the corner of his mouth, his slitted eyes peering through the smoke. He had a high nose, a long chin. His hollow cheeks were shining from the razor.

He accepted the crumpled envelope without a word. Having no sight in one eye, he read the two pages lopsidedly. Then he considered the subject of the letter.

'You don't drive I suppose?'

'Does it say I do?'

'No.' He folded the envelope once and then twice, making it much smaller than was needed to accommodate it in the pocket of his khaki shirt. 'Not exactly, no.'

'Why do you ask?'

He paused. 'Is he happy then, your Mr Clive?'

'Does he say?'

'Is he lonely?'

'I wouldn't know about that.'

'But he must have friends. Doris?'

'Yes, I'm Doris. What does he say about me?'

'He's a silly bugger our Clive. He has nothing to audition for except a role he is too nervous to accept.'

'He said you were a nice man.'

'Did he, darls?'

'Yes, he did.'

'Are you in trouble, love?'

'I must be the consolation prize,' she said.

Mr Neville pursed his lips and she saw that she had somehow hurt him.

'My, look at you,' he said. 'Is that a baby boy?'

'I don't know yet.'

'Can I eat him when he's cooked?'

He said that to pay her back. Why not? She was a cast-out tart with her stomach and her bosoms growing tight inside her dress. 'I'm so sorry.'

'Come in, come in by all means,' said Mr Neville, backing down into the darkness.

'I'm so sorry,' she said, inside the hall of Balmoral, with tears washing down her cheeks. 'I'm sorry.'

'Here you are, love, first door on the left, here.'

Doris felt all the cold of Melbourne autumn in the walls.

'Here we go, here we go. Just as his nibs left it.'

And he rushed ahead into a room such as she would never have expected. It was the window-dresser's bedroom, with pink silk bed and pink pillows and bows tied in the padded bedhead. Mr Neville laid her poor old port directly on the lovely quilt.

'He must have expected you,' he said, and squinted over his fragrant rollie and shoved his big dry hands in his back pockets so his shoulders bent towards her.

Which was, she understood immediately, his way of making peace.

She said: 'I haven't got a job or nothing.'

'That's all right.'

'You don't want a little baby crying all the night.'

'Can I be frank, darls?'

'It's your house, isn't it?'

'I'm a deaf old poofter.'

There was nothing in his appearance to show her how to take this – he was like a stick insect, 100 percent camouflage, all dry and wiry, with one brown-papered eye and smoke closing down the other.

'All right,' she said.

'You understand?'

'I suppose so,' she said. Then the old bugger winked at her.

'Don't let me worry you, Doris.'

'All right.' She guessed he wouldn't either. He winked again.

'It'll be nice to have such pretty company. Do you drive?' he asked.

'No,' she said.

He left her then and if he came back she did not hear him. It was hours before she discovered the pot of tea outside her door.

If Doris had been a bag of spuds it would have been the same to Mr Neville, and her relief at his lack of interest in her body temporarily obscured the quality she would soon learn to treasure – Mr Neville was a highly effective person.

He ran sixteen hot-dog stands. He did business with those American soldiers who had arrived in Australia months before only to be refused admittance to Port Melbourne because, although they had arrived to save our country, their black skin was not permitted by the White Australia Policy. Once this snafu was sorted out, the negroes turned out to be a big plus. Mr Neville was soon in partnership with a tailor reproducing their box-backed drape jackets, pants tight at the cuffs but loose along the legs. His 'threads' were made to a price and the fabric was what we used to call bodgie, that is, no good. That is how the bodgie gangs got their name.

Mr Neville resold V-Discs which included sets by Art Tatum, Louis Armstrong, Earl Hines, Coleman Hawkins, Lionel Hampton, Louis Jordan, Benny Carter and Fats Waller dreaming about a reefer five feet long. He had a secret source of butter at Bacchus Marsh which he maintained until 1945 when bodgie rivals burned the dairy to the ground. He had a 'working relationship' with the American 4th General Hospital, particularly but not exclusively its quartermasters. And by the second night, after Doris had met an obstetrician (an American captain) and gynaecologist (an American major), she understood that he could save her life.

Inside the Royal Melbourne Hospital, which the Yanks had stolen from the locals, her unborn child was pronounced healthy.

'Would you like to learn to drive?'

She would like it just as much as flying, maybe more.

Mr Neville shouted her the first Coca-Cola of her life. Then ('quick as a wink', Doris told me) her name became Baillieux, legally, spelled exactly like she wanted it. A week later she had her driving licence and it read: Mrs Doris Baillieux. He bought her one black suit and one black dress and she became his driver straight away.

It was not difficult for a man like this to lay hands on almost anything, say a Remington rifle manufactured in 1939. The weapon would later play a part in the bodgie wars but until then it travelled in the back of the van, sufficiently accessible for shooting rabbits or jam tins lined up along a fence.

After Celine was born, and named to match Baillieux, the boss observed how Doris wore gloves to touch her baby. He asked no questions but he made himself the master of the bottle feed and the sixty-second nappy change. He nursed Celine while the mother drove.

Celine grew up with driving, with campfires along the Lerderderg River, rabbit shooting above the warrens at Coimadai, jam-tin targets by the Darley road. She knew the high potato country up by Bungaree and the goldmines of Anakie. All these scenes are free on postcards but you must add the tall stringy man with the baby in his arms and his attendant driver: a woman in a black frock with violent red lips.

Would Celine ever understand how her mother brought

distinction to Mr Neville? She not only drove 'without jerkiness', she could wait for hours on end and never need to sleep or hum or read the *Sporting Globe*. She was always there, waiting, bright as a button. She was always calm, whether he was in a great hurry or a slightly drunken stumble or, on the occasion that the wars with the bodgie gangs reached their final stage, a little bit of both.

It was a very particular childhood for Celine, providing intense nurture but of a most distinctive kind. As for nature, Celine's body would turn out to possess an astounding stillness very like her mother's, and this would one day prove to be one of her most interesting qualities as an actress. This was what made her, Doris told me, a 'deadeye Dick. You know what that is?'

'An expert marksman.'

'Don't print that,' she said. 'She's a real dingbat. She's got a shocking temper.'

22

I slept with her, Celine Baillieux, good grief, of course it wasn't what it sounds like. I couldn't sleep at all.

Fifteen mg of Temazepam did nothing except dry my mouth so I set off, bare feet on ashy brick, seeking the solace of the vine. She had hidden the Jacob's Creek but the refrigerator motor drew itself to my attention, and Jesus Christ, there it lay, sweet sleep, Veuve Clicquot, glowing golden from beneath a plastic drawer. I'm sorry, I'm sorry, I'm really sorry. Never steal champagne. I found a tumbler. Seeking privacy, I slipped outside and the damp cold Victorian air washed over me. An owl cried, a mopoke. There was a possum thrashing carelessly around the branches of a blackwood.

As gentle as a safe-cracker, I closed the door. My hands were injured, the pain intense as I levered out the cork, a sweet and sneaky fart.

My feet were ice. I didn't care. I filled the glass and felt the bubbles bathe the desert of my throat. If I could do this I could do anything. A huge hand clamped itself upon my shoulder.

Celine was later nice enough to say she did not hear me scream. Supposedly she woke to white lights as thin as needles raking the trees and dirty bedroom windows. She thought to herself, I am on their kill list, this moment has been waiting for me all my life. She drew a blanket across her head and slid across the freezing floor and lay hidden, heart pounding. There was a distant motor running, then it died. She crawled into the dark hallway. The air was cold and ashen and she could see through the living-room windows and out to the bush where men with flashlights slashed the dark. Two human figures stood at her open door. One of these was Wodonga Townes.

'Don't do that again,' he said, and he put his arm around me and pressed me like a lover to his chest. 'Jesus, mate. There are people who care about you. Don't ever disappear like that again.'

'Sorry.'

Woody borrowed my Veuve Clicquot and took a swig. 'Christ, Felix. I thought you were a goner.'

Behind him were men with the word POLICE in reflective letters thirty centimetres high. They were thumping around the bush as loud as wombats.

'What in the fuck are you doing here, Felix?' A possibly affectionate mass of flesh collapsed around my shoulder.

'Looking for my source.'

'But that's my job. I bailed her. You're the bloody writer. This wastes everybody's time.'

'You could have just phoned me,' I said. 'I would have answered.'

'Yes, yes,' he said, suddenly, typically, distracted by another thought. 'You've got red wine?'

'Sorry.'

He released me from his lock.

'Dobbo,' he called. 'Go back and see our mate, the licensee.'

As he gave orders to the policeman his voice was clear as

ice. I observed the flash of paper money as he peeled it off a roll. I was confused, but not at all ungrateful.

'Buy a case of Château Nasty,' said Woody Townes. 'That should wake the bugger up. See if he'll sell you some steak. I'm hungry.'

I attempted to get back into the house but found my way blocked.

'Get those people off my land,' Celine said, not to me, to Woody who was hard behind me. 'Do they have a warrant?'

'My pretty Celine.' His tone was wheedling, creepy in conjunction with her injured eye. 'They're police, my love.'

Celine tugged her blanket hard around her. 'Put my champagne back where you found it.'

'I was worried something bad had happened to you.' The Big Fella handed me the bottle and took her hand. 'God knows who might have grabbed you.'

Celine folded her arms across her chest.

'Sweetheart,' Woody said, 'you are in a vulnerable position.'

'So you explained last night.'

There was a silence. What was going on between them? Celine stared right at him, fierce in her injury.

'Good,' he said at last. 'Then we're clear on that.'

Another silence, then she blinked and looked away. 'I'm sorry, Woody.' Only then did it occur to me: her daughter was very close nearby. 'Come in,' she said.

In the generous kitchen Woody peeled himself a banana, drank water from the tap, wiped his red mouth with paper towelling which he left crumpled on the draining board. From inside a cocoon of blanket, Celine watched.

'Darling, you've got a public road grown over. You must know that.'

She dropped his garbage in a tidy. 'I'm at the end of the road,' she said carefully. 'No-one comes here but me.'

'This is fire country. There is no direct access to the house.'

'They shouldn't be here,' she said.

'Why would you be pissy about them? They're here because I was worried about your personal safety.'

Celine snatched her champagne back from me. 'You're pathetic,' she told me, en passant. I watched with interest as she attempted, and failed, to stand the bottle inside the fridge door. Woody winked at me. 'You inherited this mansion from Lionel Patrick?' he asked.

'It's not a mansion,' she said and I understood that she had got involved with the long forgotten Lionel Patrick, a conservative attorney-general. She had been one of Lionel's girls.

Woody began shining his flashlight on her artworks, edging his way along the walls, around the corner. 'Lionel was a bit of a collector,' he said and I heard a door open and then close behind him.

Celine glared at me: 'Don't say a bloody word.'

Woody returned, holding a small canvas.

'Cliff Pugh,' he said. 'Cliff Pugh painted this.'

'For Christ's sake.' Celine poured her champagne down the drain. 'Will the pair of you stop touching my things.'

'Great artist, Cliff, bit far left for Lionel though. Didn't Cliff live up the road at Cottles Bridge?'

'Yes, he did. In a moment you'll reveal that you own his work yourself. It's a portrait of Jim Cairns isn't it?'

'Cliff was a big fan of the Deputy Prime Minister. Mate,' Woody said to me, 'will you rehang this painting for me. Sorry.'

By the time I returned, Celine was nowhere to be seen and Woody was affecting to read a book. I took my shoes to the dining table where I could sit and lace them.

'You know she isn't stable,' he said.

Was he explaining why he punched her? I stared at him. 'I don't blame you getting all shitty and sarcastic,' he said, not looking up.

'I wasn't.'

'Yes, that's what you're like. But you've never known her like I have.'

'How exactly would that be, mate?'

His book made a good loud thwack as it hit the slate.

'Don't fuck with me, Felix. You wouldn't be that stupid would you?'

'I'm a coward, you know that Woody.'

He brought his crocodile eyes to bear on me. Then he sighed and picked up a copy of the Melbourne *Age*. 'I wish to Christ you were that simple.'

I waited as he rolled up the pages, tying them in what I know as 'granny knots'. I watched as he heaped these on the ashes and assembled the remnants of the old fire and threw in some kindling. I was standing in front of it, warming the back of my legs, when the cops returned with a case of wine and a small soft parcel which would turn out to contain butcher's sausages.

Woody was now immediately active and you would have thought he was Rupert Murdoch who always liked to cook breakfast for his 'boys' down at his farm at Yass.

He was jovial, generous, benign. He set the snags to cook and cracked a lot of eggs into a bowl and addressed the gas cooker with one hand on his fleshy hip. When Celine did appear, in jeans and plaid shirt, she was not pleased to see this alien food invade her table. She stood before it, arms folded across her chest.

'Jeez, cut me some slack,' said Woody.

'You can't say the words?'

'You want me to apologise?'

'Take your fucking plates outside,' she said.

'These men have been up all night on your account,' said Woody.

'On your account, I think.'

I felt him stiffen, the whole weight of his body inclining towards her. Then he snorted, and picked up his sausages and scrambled eggs and led his men out of the house.

The magpies were carolling and the sky was cold and yellow. The intruders gathered on the terrace juggling plates and drinks like footballers at a barbecue.

I finally got some red wine only to have Celine grab it back. 'Later,' she said. 'You're meant to be a good guy. Please be a good guy. Please don't fuck up.'

'What can I do? I don't know anything.' I thought, what had she done with Woody? How had she inherited a house from Lionel bloody Patrick? 'You shouldn't piss off the cops. You know that.'

'OK, OK, go and eat with them. Tell them what a bitch I am. If they start poking around, just keep them away from the east.'

'Where's that?'

She closed her eyes, and squeezed them shut. It is a

credit to her character that she was smiling as she opened them.

'Where the sun comes up,' she said. 'Boofhead.'

23

Det. Sgt Dobbo clutched a handful of plastic bags, for what reason no-one said, ditto the matt-black equipment the others strung around their necks. Woody Townes carried a flashlight and a fresh-peeled stick, still slippery with sap, which he swung enthusiastically as he headed towards a slab-sided corrugated shed. His heels glowed fluorescent orange in the rising sun.

'I'm worried about her, Felix.' He whacked at a prickly Moses, slicing it in half. 'If you want to think about it, she was never good with stress.' He came upon a pale blue Cootamundra wattle, twenty-five centimetres high, planted just last spring. He whacked that too.

'Jesus. Don't do that.'

'You think she should grow *more* bloody trees? People get burned to death out here,' he said. 'I thought I knew Celine, very intimately, mate. But she has always had the great capacity to surprise. Did you know she had been bonking Lionel Patrick?'

'No.'

'But how does she seem to you? What's her state of mind?'

'Anxious, obviously.'

'She hasn't pulled any carving knives on you?'

'She did you? When?'

He paused, considering. 'When we were all young she was fucking amazing, the stunts she'd pull. But now . . .

Is she OK, really? She looks shaky.'

'Anxious, I'd say.'

'But isn't this a very fucking strange place for an anxious woman to have a house? She's got professional car thieves as neighbours up the road. Did you see that? The used cars scattered through the scrub. That's what we used to call a hide-out. Her road's all grown over. I had to leave the Merc at the bottom of the hill.'

'I'm sure it will be fine.'

'A Mercedes-Benz S500. Do you have any idea what that is?'

The Mercedes-Benz S500 is the four-door sedan preferred by Chinese businessmen, wealthy Americans and Third World dictators. 'No,' I said. 'What is it?'

'You don't drive? This one will drive for you. It's got three computers. This is the Merc for you, mate. It's got "Lane Keeping Assist". You could use that, for sure.'

He rested his hand on my shoulder and we walked a way together and it was difficult to resist the old habits of mockery and affection. 'It's got bluetooth,' he said, 'and Sirius and HD radio, USB and SD ports, you're not listening. All right, I understand. We'll save her idiot daughter if we can. I'm more concerned about mumsy. Has she compromised herself, Felix? Has she placed herself in any danger that you know of?'

'She does have a black eye, mate.'

Of course that gave him pause and his mouth entered one of those unstable states, never predictable in their conclusion, which resolved, on this occasion, when he took my hand companionably. 'We need her cooperation, you get it don't you? Habouring is a crime.'

'I'm confused.'

He blinked as if considering my 'confusion' from different angles. Then, suddenly, he was off walking earnestly towards the east, head down, thrashing passionately at the dogwood bushes. I had no way to turn him. 'How does she get her food?' he demanded. 'You never noticed that mailbox up on the road?' He blew his nose. 'Why is it so big? And when a great mad bushfire comes exploding across the tree tops, what does she do then? Why would she live somewhere so extreme?'

Then, certainly without me planning it – I did not even know it existed – we arrived at a forestry dugout. You cannot get a better fire defence than a dugout. This one had been driven directly into a hill like a mineshaft, with heavy wood framing around the entrance, tons of earth supported by a rough-adzed tree trunk. A dirty canvas curtain was set back a few feet from the doorway.

We stood together gazing at it and it was then I felt his massive stillness.

'So you're the country boy,' he said. 'Then tell me: why wouldn't a big fire burn all the oxygen inside?'

'That's a curtain. They wet it down. The tunnel will be L-shaped.'

'Ah, you've been in there?' I recognised a peculiar poker face from those long-lost days when I was agonising over my plans for *Drivetime Radio* and we played cards and drank all through the night.

'Why would I do that?'

He grinned as he took me by my upper arm and locked me tight. I thought, the Angel is in there. I'll get my interview.

'I should feel sorry for you,' he said, dragging me bodily towards the entrance. Suddenly I was afraid. I kicked at his knee and almost put my back out, and it was at that moment – just as the faint light of his flashlight reached the rusty canvas – that the magpie swooped. It hit as the white-backed males always do, with a rush of wings, a loud thwack, landing with sufficient momentum to jolt Woody's head a good eight centimetres forward. A moment later the assassin was back up his tree, indistinguishable from his brothers and sisters, safe from the passions he had unleashed below.

I have suffered the brutality of magpies all my life. In England, I am told, their magpie is a gentle creature. In Bacchus Marsh, in magpie season, kids would return from their run to the outside lavatory, heads streaming with blood, most of them in tears, while the more timid remained in the classroom, shitting in their pants rather than suffer the terrors of assault.

But lord, I never witnessed anything like this: Woody Townes, a hundred and thirty kilograms of meat, fell to his knees. Blood washed his forehead and filled his eyes he bawled like a heifer in a barbwire fence.

It is amazing, I thought, how such a large strong man, a beast electrified by his own barely suppressed violence, has so little tolerance for pain. He was left like the blinded Cyclops, his fluorescent feet all dusty, swinging his fat fist at what must have been my shadow.

Celine, of course, came running, 100 percent in character, black-eyed, barefoot, swinging her first-aid kit.

'Be still,' she told the fallen man.

There was a war between kookaburras and magpies

above our heads. I could hear the clacking of their beaks. Celine drew on a pair of rubber dishwashing gloves and separated the strands of Woody's hair.

He bellowed. Celine raised her hands.

I glimpsed a deep meaty gouge from crown to brow.

Celine said: 'All I've got is methylated spirits.' And she was pouring it, straight from the bottle, drenching his scalp before he had a chance to stop her.

'Shit. Lay off will you?'

'You need stitches.'

'Piss off.' He wiped his eyes and left his wrist a bloody mess. 'It's just a magpie.'

'Listen my love,' Celine said, way too tenderly. 'You are losing too much blood.'

'Bullshit.'

'Yes, but let's get you to the car.'

The argument was interrupted by Dobbo and his gang and their impatient boots, their long investigative noses, their professional judgements: 'That's not a magpie wound.'

'All due respect, Sergeant, but allow me to know what hit me. It was a bloody magpie. I got swooped.'

'Was it carrying a hammer and chisel?' said Dobbo. 'It must have been.'

'Come on Sergeant,' Celine said urgently. 'Help me please.' She had her hands under Woody's armpits and was attempting to help him to his feet.

'I can do it myself,' cried the patient. 'My legs still work.' At which his eyes rolled back in his head and he collapsed on the dirt.

'Sergeant,' cried Celine, which was the first moment I began to think about the mother plover, the habit of dragging her wing as if wounded.

Dobbo stood with his hands on his hips looking at Celine with unsympathetic amusement. 'You know why we can't even get the car up here, Mrs Baillieux. Because you've broken the law.'

It was at this point, I marked later, that Celine became completely manic. 'You have to help,' she said.

I thought, why is she antagonising him like this? She dug her hands under Woody's armpits again and showed herself ineffectual to an alarming degree.

'All right, darling,' Dobbo said, 'get out of the way.'

'No,' said Celine.

'Go on,' said Dobbo. 'Off.'

I did not think, not for a moment, that I was dealing with an actress, so I was alarmed to see her panic, to follow the fraught procession through the paperbarks, down into the blackberries, across the creek to Woody's computerised Mercedes-Benz. He regained consciousness for long enough to refuse to let anyone else drive, but when he was safely in the back seat Celine took a paper towel and wiped his indignant eyes and held a wad of red tissue against his wound. It was not pleasant, to see this tenderness invested in a man who had hurt her. The engine fired, and the black monster lumbered slowly down the corrugated road. Celine waved, although I doubt anyone was looking.

'Holy Christ,' she said.

24

Woody's hundred-dollar flashlight lay abandoned in the sunlight. Behind it was a lower part of his assassin's iridescent beak, clean ripped away. Behind this, was a small hexagonal nut and I spat on my finger to make it stick. It was only then that I saw, in the black mouth of the tunnel, my source. She was luminous with cloudy-climate skin and tangled wheaten hair. She wore a grubby singlet. Her collarbone was pooled with darkness. Her bare arms were folded across her breasts.

No-one introduced her. She stepped out to the light, and I saw she was not quite as symmetrically pretty as I had expected, also shorter, thicker waisted, sturdier than she had seemed on CNN. She looked me directly in the eyes.

I nodded but all the niceties, the civilities, everything superfluous had been rubbed off her and she was left with that isolated, glass-cased quality, that sheen and distance that so often accompany power.

'Sweetie, did you have to use that thing just now?' Celine said.

'Who is this?' she demanded.

'If they were suspicious, now they're certain.'

'Yes. Who is this?'

'This is Felix Moore.' I turned towards Celine only to understand she was a junior officer, dismissed, already walking back towards her house. There was no time to feel anything except: I had the interview. I would be worthy of it. My subject led the way and I was mentally recording: dancer's walk, shoulders back. The pocket of her jeans was torn. I followed into the earthen gloom, to a back wall supported by rough-cut planks – incontestably solid, clay showing between the timber. It swung smoothly open and I was admitted to what was arguably, at least from the viewpoint in Langley, Virginia, the most dangerous place on this earth. I remember my entry like a car accident, awash with adrenalin, very slow and very fast. The covert world smelled like a pottery, but also a teenager's bedroom. It was illuminated by computer screens, small video monitors beneath the ceiling which I would not really see until I was out in the air again: spooky black and white images, gum trees swaying, a car travelling along a dirt road, that same white feather of clay dust left by the police. I stumbled then tripped on an orange power cord. There was an indoor toilet, definitely, many small green lights, and a young man with the build of a bodyguard. His eyebrows were mad and heavy, his curling black hair explosive, and he stooped a little, as if he would not quite fit in the box he came in. He stood stiffly, his arms pressed against his sides like a schoolboy in short pants.

'This is Paypal,' she said.

I reached to shake his hand, an offer not accepted.

'Paypal. This is him. He's famous.'

If this was a story about hackers I was laughably ill-equipped. I had never heard of Paypal. I had never heard of the Crypto Anarchist Manifesto, or even the lowly practice of 'carding', the criminal process of using or verifying phished credit numbers.

When Paypal seated himself at a cluttered card table and fitted a jeweller's loupe beneath his hairy eye, I did not think this particularly strange.

'Your mother had this place waiting for you?' I asked Gabrielle Baillieux.

She hooded her eyes. 'Here is what you've got to know about my mother. OK? She's got to own the story. Whatever danger I am in she has to be in worse herself.'

There were two plastic milk crates on the floor between us. She kicked one towards me. 'You can't upstage my mother, that's the point.' As she sat, her jeans rode up and there was no evidence of the controversial anklet which had been a condition of bail.

She set a small black tape recorder on a milk crate. Of course. She was famous. She was accustomed to control.

'Don't you take notes?' she asked.

'No.'

She switched on her recorder. I thought I would have to instruct her, later, about the dangers of this game whose rules she did not know. There was no tape recorder ever manufactured that could protect her from a journalist, but she clearly thought there was, and her broad expanse of forehead had a tense uneven surface like wet tidal sand.

'You just asked your mother who I was. But you clearly knew already.'

'Yes. You're someone working for someone who wants to sell something.'

'That's unfair.'

'It's normal.'

'But not for you.'

'No, I'm a soldier.'

'You're also a person with a life.'

'Duh.'

Of course I had interviewed far ruder people, but not one of them had been in such extreme danger. Earlier she had decided to trust me but now I was here she baulked. She loudly worried that a book would jeopardise her further.

'I wish you'd read my work. You'd know I'm not just some slimebag who will pretend he's on your side then knife you. I won't be cheap or reductive. I won't ask you about politics and then leave out everything you want to say.'

The frown remained the same, but the eyes narrowed.

'Here's what I think,' I said. 'You want the world to actually understand you. You have put your life at risk, but for a rational reason. You are a sort of equation,' I said, not dishonestly, but not knowing exactly what I meant. I paused.

'No, go on.'

'Every life has a logic. Following the logic can be persuasive. Wouldn't you prefer to be understood in your own terms?'

Her face, in considering me, was totally expressionless but I trusted that feeling in my gut.

'You're trying to see if I'm wearing my anklet?'

Actually I had been touched by her little oblong feet, the chipped polish, all the toes of equal length.

'The Department of Justice is cost-cutting,' she said. 'So they buy the anklets from K5C who source them in China.' She affected weariness, as if no single thing would be understood by anybody else. 'They're crap, of course. They break down all the time. Then K5C hires a mob of amateur

138

hackers and recidivists to watch the monitors. The pay is shit and the kids are high and the monitors fuck up almost every day. When a monitor goes on the fritz they assume it's just a false alarm. How you fix a false alarm is wait for it to fix itself. Do you want the technical details? Would you understand them? Do you know what a Faraday cage is?'

'Not yet.'

'Maybe this is not a good idea.'

'I'm here to help you.'

'It's Paypal you should talk to. He transferred my anklet to a dog. They monitor the dog's progress. They think the dog is me.'

I thought, Woody Townes did not come out here following a dog. 'Someone stands to lose a lot of bail money,' I said.

'That big slob didn't buy me, if that's what you mean.'

'Do you know who he is?'

'He's a pervert. I've known him all my life.'

In the corner of the dugout Paypal seemed to be soldering a circuit. He was so big and stiff it was hard to imagine him doing anything precise.

'Give me back the beak,' he said, not looking at me.

Gaby took the beak and passed it to him in a gesture somehow so familial I had no doubt that they were lovers. He lifted an inert magpie from the bench, then ejected something, a black metal battery or perhaps a motor, from the bird's underside.

'You actually made this?' I asked him.

'We own it.' Gaby said. 'They made it.'

By 'own' I thought they had hacked it. Was 'they' a corporation or our favourite nation state? I looked to

Paypal but he turned his back on me. She also seemed to be in retreat.

'What exactly have you been hired to write?'

'Gabrielle, you agreed to this already. That's why I'm here.'

She shrugged.

'My job is to make you likeable,' I said. 'They want me to make the case for your good character.'

She almost smiled.

'Your mother is trying to save you from extradition. I can help with that.'

'Fear is not helpful to anyone.'

'You think I'm afraid?'

'Celine is shitting herself.'

'What if I simply wrote the truth?'

'People wouldn't like my equation. You won't either.'

I thought, she's a nightmare. No-one can control her. I have a contract, but not with her.

'You think you'll like me, but you won't.' She smiled and for a moment I didn't understand that this sweetness was for the idiot who had the unmanned aerial magpie hovering above his desk. The machine rose vertically like no magpie ever born. I thought, you're a waste of hope and time.

'My mother is a bad introduction to our situation,' she said. 'She's defeated by them before she even starts. It does not occur to her that we might possibly defeat them.' I thought she sounded paranoid and grandiose but she clearly did not give a rat's arse about what I thought. She was smiling at the curly-haired man-child as he elevated the drone almost to the ceiling. I heard the high pitched whine of an engine but when I felt my hair lift in the breeze I would not look.

'Them?' I asked her. 'Who is them?'

The machine dropped, like a catastrophic phone book, on my head. Maybe I cried out. Who wouldn't? Whatever I did, they fell around laughing like a pair of clowns. It was not my own fright that pissed me off, but their carelessness of who they were. I had a higher opinion of them than they did themselves.

'It was just a joke.'

There are many journalists, most journalists, who could be auditioned and mocked and still do a more than decent job. This juvenile behaviour would be a gift to them, not me. My head hurt. My hands throbbed. Fuck it. I stood. 'This won't work if you want to fight against me.'

'Oh, take a joke,' she said, but I was truly pissed off. This was what our great historian would call the flaw in my human clay.

'You've got plenty of enemies,' I told her. 'Go fight with them. Or find out who I am and get in touch with me.' And that was my character, how I normally fucked my life.

She smiled at me then, and touched my arm. I had heard she was casual with her hygiene. No-one had mentioned she was charming.

'Mr Moore, I am not nice, but I do know exactly who you are. Really I do. I first read you when I was still in high school.'

I tried very hard to disguise my pleasure, but knew that my smirky little mouth would be a traitor to my cause. 'Sleep on it,' I said.

'OK but I don't need to.' She put her small warm hand

in mine and I shook it and thought, dear Jesus Christ, she reads books. I'm saved. I said goodbye. I had done a good day's work. I emerged from the dugout as king parrots sliced the bush with their low trajectory, flashing their pretty sunlit colours above the darkness of the ridge tops. I filled my lungs with clean fresh air. I stretched my spine. I finally noticed, above the dugout entrance, in the tossing umbrellas of the gum trees, dozens of tiny whirling fans, each one camouflaged with mottled paint and strapped in place. Were there power cables? Yes, there, travelling towards the earth like careful lizards, down the dark side of the trunks into the exclusive story by Felix Moore.

25

I had not, previously, been thought of as the kind of writer who might make a difficult character loveable. My most notable work of fiction, *Barbie and the Deadheads*, had been a satire. As a journalist it was my talent to be a shit-stirrer, a truffle hound for cheats and liars and crooks amongst the ruling classes. These pugnacious habits had served me well for a whole career but the story of this young woman demanded I become a larger person, a man who had it in his heart to love our stinking human clay.

If I had been Tolstoy himself, I could not have been granted more than this, my almost vascular connection to the drama and its actors, a privileged role where I might be both a witness and participant in a new type of warfare where the weapons of individuals could equal those of nation states. I was a failed novelist but I saw I had the novelistic smells I needed (from shit to solder), the pixelated light, the women with related cheekbones, the great Australian bush rolling on out past Kinglake, ranges like ancient animals asleep, slender upper branches turned pretty pink by afternoon.

I had a lifetime of hard-won technical ability, but was my heart sufficient? Could I transcend my own beginnings as that stinging little creature who had been the object of Sando Quinn's pity? Did I have the courage for something more than a five-column smash and grab? Did I, along the way, truly wish to make myself a conduit for the corrosive hurts and betrayals of a guilty mother and an angry child? My own daughters would judge I had a better chance of chopping down a tree.

As I came to the top of Celine's steps I saw, high on the ridge tops, a magpie glide exactly like a hawk, *New hatched to the woeful time*, or words to that effect.

Then I sat at Celine's long table, drinking Jacob's Creek through a straw while she very kindly re-dressed my throbbing hands.

There was a large blister on one palm and a vicious lesion on the other. My fingers were scarlet and my nurse observed that I would not be typing for a while. I did not comment. She cooked, early. At an hour when Melbourne's office workers crossed the Swanston Street bridge on their way home, we ate. And then we sat before a mellow bed of coals, toasting bread and slathering it with jam and butter.

Celine still did not mention her daughter, except tangentially, to say it was a shitty time to be young.

It was always a shitty time. I said so.

But Celine seemed to have become romantic about our past. I was gently 'reminded' that we had one hundred thousand people on the streets of Melbourne for the Vietnam Moratorium. In her view we had 'won'. Then we voted in a Labor government. One moment Jim Cairns was the evil man who lead the moratorium. Then he was Deputy Prime Minister. Soon he would be Treasurer. We had learned that we could change the world.

She was completely correct, if only in the short term.

Change was what we wanted. Our new Prime Minister

didn't keep us waiting. In the first two weeks, without a cabinet, Gough Whitlam brought home Australian soldiers from the US war in Vietnam. Was it then that Washington decided we were all communists? This was a big joke if you knew Gough Whitlam.

The party was elected on Gough's platform and, by Jesus, he was going to honour it. He abolished conscription. He let the draft resisters out of jail, made university free, gave land rights to Aboriginal peoples wherever the federal government had the power. He, the Prime Minister of what had previously been a reliable American client state, denounced the Nixon bombing of North Vietnam. This outraged our ally, but that's what we had elected him to do. After almost two centuries of grovelling, we grew some balls. At the UN we spoke up for Palestinian rights. We welcomed Chileans fleeing the CIA coup. We condemned nuclear weapons in the South Pacific.

To Celine this list was proof that we had won.

I said our victory was built on the mad idea we would not be punished. For it was exactly these 'proofs' that caused Nixon to order the CIA review of US policy towards Australia. In our beginning was our end. Our victory triggered an ever-escalating covert operation which would finally remove the elected government from power.

Later it would be said that it was the world recession that had undone the Whitlam government. Of course that didn't help. But Nixon had made Marshall Green his ambassador before the recession hit. Marshall Green was the same guy who had overseen coups in Indonesia in 1965 and Cambodia in 1970.

Why didn't we see what the appointment of the coup-master would mean for us? Because the pilot fish thinks it is safe to swim beside its shark? Because we were not Chile? Because we thought it was our own country and we could do what we liked in it? Our newly elected representatives could actually raid our own security service and read all the misinformation in their secret files. Whose security service was it? The Americans thought it was theirs. We knew it was ours. We were thrilled to see the vaults of ASIO open to the air.

We were naive, of course. We continued to think of the Americans as our friends and allies. We criticised them, of course. Why not? We loved them, didn't we? We sang their songs. They had saved us from the Japanese. We sacrificed the lives of our beloved sons in Korea, then Vietnam. It never occurred to us that they would murder our democracy. So when it happened, in plain sight, we forgot it right away.

When the time came, no aircraft bombed the Australian Treasury, but our elected government was attacked continually and relentlessly in so many different ways from so many different quarters. Scandals were seeded in the clouds by hacks and circulated by Packer, Fairfax, Murdoch most of all. Misinformation rose into the sky above Canberra, like rockets that flared and died and left their lies on our retinas so we continued to see what was not true.

Gough's ministers set out to raise a loan to 'buy back the farm'. It's a shame they did not go about it in a more worldly manner, that they were forced to act without the hostile Treasury, that they permitted the minister for mines to get himself involved with a broker named Khemlani. Khemlani was a CIA stooge. His job was not to buy back the farm but bring down the government. Of course he never raised a penny of the $4 billion loan the government approved.

Finally Khemlani would arrive in Australia with a fat briefcase full of 'evidence' showing that the Labor ministers were all taking kickbacks from these loans. He was escorted before the cameras with bodyguards. He made a statutory declaration in which he swore his evidence. On the strength of his word, the free press was happy to report the people's government were crooks.

It was a death of a thousand cuts. Scandal, scandal, scandal. It was next reported that a Bahamas bank had issued a letter seeking $4,267,365,000 for the Australian government, an outrageous $267 million being 'proposed profit'. It didn't matter that the government had not sought the loan. The headlines were the size of bricks.

Then Cairns was also offered money by a Melbourne dentist and property developer named Harris. Harris came to Jim's office and offered to raise $300 million for a 'one time commission': of 2.5 percent. He had a letter he wanted Jim to sign. Jim, who had resisted the Khemlani loan, now refused this.

In parliament the opposition claimed he had approved this loan.

Jim denied it, naturally.

The opposition then tabled a letter which made our man a liar. There it was: his signature, giving his approval to pursue the loan on these terms. Thus was Jim ruined by a letter he had never knowingly signed. Today the question is, who slipped the letter in the pile? Who was the dogsbody? After the 'evidence' had been obtained, who fed it to the press and the opposition? Who destroyed the Treasurer? Who killed Jim Cairns?

There was more to come.

Gough Whitlam had told the American ambassador that Australia would probably, but not *necessarily*, extend the lease on the so-called 'US signals facility at Alice Springs'. This was and is Pine Gap, the same base that lets the US guide its drones today, but we did not have a clue what happened there, none of us, not even the Prime Minister knew what happened at Pine Gap. But the US would react so drastically to the threat of its closure, it was (and is) clearly so much more than a 'signals facility'.

The American trauma can be seen and measured in a cable, dated days before the Whitlam government was deposed. It is from the CIA to its close collaborators at ASIO. As a kindness to the reader, the following is both edited and summarised. SHACKLEY CHIEF EAST ASIA DIVISION CIA REQUESTED ME TO PASS THE FOLLOWING MESSAGE TO DIRECTOR GENERAL OF ASIO.

The CIA, the cable stressed, had cause for serious complaint. The Prime Minister of Australia had stated that the CIA had been funding the conservative opposition in Australia. This was true, of course, although the cable admitted no such thing. The American embassy in Australia had approached the Australian government 'at the highest level'. At this meeting the Americans 'categorically denied' that CIA had given or passed funds to an organisation or candidate for political office in Australia.

Next day the US State Department relayed the same

message to the Australian embassy in Washington. The CIA had not funded an Australian political party.

The effect of this, as the cable reveals, was unexpected.

PRIME MINISTER GOUGH WHITLAM PUBLICLY REPEATED THE ALLEGATION THAT HE KNEW OF TWO INSTANCES IN WHICH CIA MONEY HAD BEEN USED TO INFLUENCE DOMESTIC AUSTRALIAN POLITICS.

The Australians then publicly identified CIA agents working in their country under US State Department and Defense Department cover. This was outrageous enough. Then their Prime Minister revealed that Richard Stallings, the head of the Pine Gap facility, was a CIA agent.

CIA IS PERPLEXED AS TO WHAT ALL THIS MEANS. DOES THIS SIGNIFY SOME CHANGE IN OUR BILATERAL INTELLIGENCE SECURITY RELATED FIELDS?

The CIA were then forced to confer with their cover agencies and these agencies (State and Defense) stuck to their stories. This involved them claiming that Pine Gap's Richard Stallings was a 'retired Defense Department employee'.

Oh, really?

CIA CANNOT SEE HOW THIS [public dialogue] CAN DO OTHER THAN BLOW THE LID OFF THOSE INSTALLATIONS WHERE THE PERSONS CONCERNED HAVE BEEN WORKING AND WHICH ARE VITAL TO BOTH OF OUR SERVICES AND COUNTRIES, PARTICULARLY THE INSTALLATIONS AT ALICE SPRINGS . . . CIA FEELS IT NECESSARY TO SPEAK DIRECTLY TO ASIO BECAUSE OF THE COMPLEXITY OF THE PROBLEM.

That is, the American secret service could not talk to the elected leader of Australia. They had not forgotten Gough's threat to permanently terminate the lease on

Pine Gap which, as events transpired, was only days from expiring. Whitlam told the US ambassador: 'If there were any attempts, to use familiar jargon, "to screw or bounce us" inevitably these arrangements would be a matter of contention.'

IS THERE A CHANGE IN PRIME MINISTER WHITLAM'S ATTITUDE IN AUSTRALIAN POLICY IN THIS FIELD? . . . CIA FEELS THAT EVERYTHING POSSIBLE HAS BEEN DONE ON A DIPLOMATIC BASIS.

If ASIO could not fix this troublesome government, the CIA did not see how OUR MUTUALLY BENEFICIAL RELATIONSHIPS COULD CONTINUE . . . THE CIA FEELS GRAVE CONCERNS AS TO WHERE THIS TYPE OF PUBLIC DISCUSSION MAY LEAD . . . THIS MESSAGE SHOULD BE REGARDED AS AN OFFICIAL DEMARCHE ON A SERVICE TO SERVICE LINK . . . THE ASIO DIRECTOR-GENERAL SHOULD BE ASSURED THAT CIA DOES NOT LIGHTLY ADOPT THIS ATTITUDE.

Two days following the transmission of this cable the government was illegally dismissed.

Of course there was a conspiracy. We are old enough to know this now. There are institutions whose task it is to conspire all day long. They spy in every corner of our lives. They employ hundreds of thousands of workers and build acres of employee parking lots. If they are inefficient they are not always ineffective.

Of course the CIA could not do it all alone. It was like a brute-force attack on a corporate website. It required muscle, persistence, even luck. It required the conservative senate to block the supply of money to the government, which was unconstitutional. It needed Mr Murdoch and his collaborators to make this seem OK, to create a bullshit crisis which could only be resolved by the governor-general, the representative of the Queen of England, who would then dismiss the people's government. It also required the press to keep up the hysteria, to slander and criminalise an elected government, to name the process of its illegitimate removal 'The Coup' while insisting it was no such thing.

These events have mostly passed from mind, yet not completely. Mr Murdoch's *Australian* newspaper recently commemorated THE DISMISSAL – 30 YEARS ON:

> There was never blood in the streets. Hawke refused to call a general strike. The Queen slept in her Buckingham Palace bed while her prime minister was executed. The media repaired to a restaurant for the biggest binge in Canberra's history . . . We don't kill each other over politics. The army was not called out. Gough Whitlam, a constitutionalist to his core, accepted his fate and went to the hustings. In Jakarta, Gough's admirer, a confused President Suharto, summoned Australia's ambassador, Dick Woolcott, to ask, 'Why didn't the prime minister arrest the governor-general?' Good question. The conspiracists were unleashed and their phony claims about a CIA plot ran for years.

The events of 1975 have been the obsession of my erratic and mostly unsuccessful life, so now I cannot fail to note that Gabrielle Baillieux was born into a Labor

Party household in the midst of this traumatic Coup. It is therefore not insane to write about her life and activism in relation to this long-forgotten history.

26

Next morning at Smiths Gully, I prepared for my mission. I washed and scrubbed my human envelope and shaved three times. As the morning sun illuminated the opposite hillside, I was mentally composing my opening sentences. I wished to incorporate the colours of my native land, the warm pink and ivory and the bright underside of parrot wings. I placed the battered kettle on the gas, dropped two thick slices in the toaster, when bang, bang, bang, a big-beaked, square-headed kookaburra, just outside the windows, beat the shit out of a baby snake on the pergola.

I buttered my toast. The kettle boiled. I poured.

Bang, bang, bang. Nature was so violent. Looking up, I was startled to discover the kookaburra had become Wodonga Townes, slamming on the glass door with his open palm and second wedding ring. With a string of sausages he could have played the part of Punch. The kookaburra dropped the snake and swooped to retrieve it.

Celine hurried from the hallway towards the visitor and then, a metre from the glass, she paused and wrapped a towel around her hair. Did she sense what was about to happen? All I could think was, my first interview with Gaby must be aborted.

'Hoy. Let me in.' The Big Fella spread his arms and grasped the door. As I turned the locks the kookaburra ascended to its perch and resumed its murder.

Our visitor wore perfect Persil whites, a tracksuit with gold piping. He had a one-inch strip of shaven scalp, and six red stitches. 'What in the fuck are you doing?' he demanded.

'We're doing nothing, Woody,' Celine said. 'What are you doing?'

For answer he drank all my coffee and ate half my toast. 'Don't fuck with me,' he said directly to Celine. 'You can go to jail for harbouring a fugitive. That includes you, mate.'

'I'm working for you, remember?'

He looked astonished.

'That contract?'

'Relax Feels. I'm your biggest fan. Just tell me where you've got our subject hidden.'

Celine's eyes narrowed as she turned to me, but Woody grabbed her by the wrist and jerked her violently towards him. 'You must think I'm very stupid, Mum.' He was so clearly resolved to remove her by brute force that she stopped resisting. She was tiny but her cheekbones glazed with anger.

I told Woody to quit it.

'Mate,' he smiled, and reached out his hand to me and I smiled duplicitously and that was when the treacherous bastard shackled my wrist with his big red hand. Then he dragged us both behind him, out the door, up the steps, towards the dugout where he planned (it was obvious to me) to confront us with our own deceit. The kookaburra flew overhead and landed in the tree above the dugout amongst the whirling battery chargers. In the midst of all my other upsets I was certain it would drop the snake.

Our captor produced another hundred-dollar flashlight

and Celine took her chance to slap him rapidly, on both cheeks. Did he really spit at her? I never saw it. Certainly his face was contorted and later I wondered if he was more frightened of her than she was of him.

Once he had us inside the dugout it was over. I flicked a switch to no effect. Inside was total silence, not a milliwatt of illumination. There was a hateful smell. The beam of Woody's flashlight tracked across split truck batteries, wires ripped like prawn veins straight from the earthen walls. There were no computers anywhere. Blankets and sleeping bags were wet with what I first thought was gore but turned out to be the contents of the composting toilet. When Woody released my wrist I escaped into the light, trembling.

In the shadow of the entrance Celine was striking Woody's chest. That he accepted this confirmed my fears. They had murdered her.

'What have you done to my daughter?'

'Done to her? I've paid half a million dollars bail for her. She's got no choice. She has to go to trial. So where is she?'

'Woody,' I said. 'She doesn't know.'

'You're a sucker, Feels. This one,' he nodded to Celine, 'you cannot trust.'

'Me?' Celine cried. 'Oh, please.'

'No, I learned it a long time ago, but I keep forgetting it. You're a dickhead, Celine. The safest thing for you to do is go to trial.' With that he turned and strode into the bush.

As Woody crashed through the undergrowth, I put my arm around Celine and felt her strangely calm. I thought, if I had been privileged to have Gaby as a daughter I would have been going nuts, throwing myself into the metaphoric grave, pounding my head and rubbing ashes in my hair. Celine walked unsteadily to the house and turned on her computer. I thought, she's reading bloody email.

'Come here,' she said, and pointed: the cursor was moving, seemingly of its own accord, opening files and putting them away. We were hacked and owned by who we could not know. Celine held a finger to her lips, picked up the laptop between thumb and forefinger, and I followed her to the bathroom where she placed it in the tub.

Minutes later, with our iPhones and computer drowned in bathwater, we were stomping through the bush, Celine with a rucksack and a cardboard box, me with two bottles, a corkscrew, following the story, perhaps, or running for my life. We arrived at my former kidnapper's disgusting Holden parked in the midst of the chaotic refuse from demolition sites.

Celine opened the driver-side door and beeped the horn and here he came, her servant, my tormentor, on his way to work.

I waited while she spoke to him, but of course I understood what was about to happen. I went to the rear of the car and waited like a well-trained dog.

It was a tight fit for two, head to tail like a dirty joke and as the engine started Celine kicked and jabbed me and surprised me by farting as we set off down the rutted track. When she pushed the cardboard box at me I did not act well.

'Calm down.'

I do not like being told to calm down. We all know what that means.

'Check out the box.'

It was not wine, which was what I had hoped, but a mess of papers and a huge number of objects, the smaller ones like mahjong tiles, relics from the old unhackable technology: microcassettes. Plus, also, larger cassettes, C120s as it later turned out.

'I need access,' I said.

We crossed a culvert and I banged my head. Between my disappointment and my claustrophobia, I could have wept.

'This is access,' she said. 'You've got hours and hours of access in this box. Forget Woody,' she said. 'Woody will never hear these tapes. You can write this book to please yourself.'

PART TWO

I

He was an unlovely old scoundrel with his wide hunched shoulders and his long arms, carrying a cardboard box down onto the dock that morning. His hair was thick, wiry, not quite grey, in the style of forty years before, and if this contributed, to a small degree, to his furtive air the latter was not, it must be stressed, the consequence of his present situation. He had already, before this recent turn of events, been known as 'Wink' Moore and Felix 'Moore-or-less-correct'.

The celebrated journalist peered without enthusiasm at the place where fate had brought him: that is the banks of the great Hawkesbury River. He had been delivered there by a burly young woman whose dusty white Corolla smelled of her children's throw-up. She had not apologised for this, even when he wound down the window, and neither of them had spoken any word in the twelve hours they had travelled north from Melbourne. Only as they arrived at the little hamlet of Brooklyn, having suffered a lifetime's worth of seatbelts slapping in the wind, did she speak to him.

Good on you, mate, she said.

He had time to register the high emotion, but he was already anxiously searching for what awaited him in the concrete shadow of the bridge: a pencil-thin pontoon leading to a human figure, and an aluminium dinghy, known locally as a tinny. The Corolla drove away and the traveller understood that the next stage of his trip, across deep waters, would be navigated by a youth who was now securing his fragile craft with nothing more substantial than his hairy suntanned leg.

Up Shit Creek, he thought, without a paddle.

The hamlet of Brooklyn had seen this before, sedentary fathers who have been bullied into taking teenage sons fishing for the day. These sons could be sulky, or bored, or Game Boy addicts, or just generally embarrassed by the ancient party's lack of sea legs, nous, bait, tackle; they could also be, as in this particular case, solicitous.

Come on Dad, the boy called.

An observer watching from an unmarked car would have seen the son was a different sort entirely from the father. He was a river rat, from Broken Bay or Dangar Island possibly. You could see the story straight away. The mother had left the father years ago. She had gone to live with some careless barefooted potter or painter or dole bludger who had, to his credit, managed to raise the son to be at home on the water. That is how our doubtful hero would have liked his present situation to be understood because he was, as he shuffled towards this unknown youth, a criminal. He had never stood in this spot before and he was unaware of his destination, unaware also, of the exact nature of these tapes he had been dumped with. They had clearly been thrown together in a panic, loose pages and some batteries and two types of tape recorder to accommodate both the micro and compact cassettes. He felt no enthusiasm for this bloodless 'access', nor those notebooks, the spiral-bound kind you buy at newsagents, evidence that these so-called 'informants' imagined, in their innocence, might be useful to you, mate.

He reached the aluminium dinghy and passed his belongings into the care of the boy who would have been embarrassed to be told that he had the grace and balance of a dancer. He was perhaps sixteen, in any case legally a minor, tall and tanned with his fair curling hair lifting in the south-easterly wind which was, just now, raising the white tops of the cold bright water. The north-easterly had already travelled across the Pacific Ocean, past the old crouching beast of Lion Island and was now barrelling and bluffing up across what is called Pittwater, up to Brooklyn, under and over the bridge, seeking all those wooded bays along the way, swallowing the long wide stretch and then rushing into Berowra Waters and Pumpkin Point. Who knows where the wind doth blow? There would be very few waterways or mangrove swamps where an observer (if there was such a malevolent entity) would not see the water lift as it rushed across a shallow inlet of rippled sand.

The boy had a harder face than the curls might suggest, a little slit of a mouth that twisted in a sort of grin. Dad, he said.

The man hesitated. He was a most unlikely outlaw. Indeed, one might pity him his ineptitude, his nervousness around the water.

The boy had the box of tapes and papers in the boat and now, with his dinghy still untethered, took hold of his passenger by the arm and shoulder and the man then knew himself with the boy's hand, and was aware of his own age, frailty, softness. He sat heavily and the boy passed him an old hat and he immediately pulled it over his head and hunched down as the motor came to life and they headed out under the low bridge, Highway 1 in fact, which carried car loads of free citizens up the North Coast or south to Sydney where, presumably, people still sat in the Wentworth Hotel and drank champagne and ate nibbles and talked about all the crap and krill caught in the Murdoch filters. It was unlikely his photograph would be in *The Australian* just yet but they had some beauties in their files, Felix the rat, Felix the mole, Felix the pervert with his dirty raincoat.

'Feels, Feels,' the Murdoch guy had shouted. 'Look this way. Felix.'

Fuck you, he thought.

The wind at this hour was cold and the passenger wrapped his op-shop wardrobe tight around him, the old grey trousers, red checked work shirt, green tweed jacket, not nearly thick enough to keep him warm. There was a light chop and the boat rose and slammed and he was frightened that it would become rougher. Truth be told, he would have preferred the smell of throw-up to this fresh clean river air which promised nothing but discomfort and loneliness. It was of course beautiful, with stern khaki bush slashed with verticals in pink and white and grey and now and then the impasto yellow sandstone glowing ecstatically in the morning sun. It was like a picture postcard but it was not a picture postcard. The boat rose and slammed and the water was as hard as concrete and it was a great inhuman river and it opened its wide throat to him, and somewhere down to the left was Berowra Waters where he had once lunched at a famous restaurant of the same name. He had been ferried there by his sybaritic old mate who had been returning a certain favour. He had worked his way from the oysters to the quenelles to the soft chocolate pudding with the golden Château Climens which he had raised to the darkening afternoon and said what he had always said on such occasions: I wouldn't be dead for quids which, translated roughly, meant there was no money he could be offered that would persuade him to be deceased. It had taken a single envelope of cash from Woody Townes to prove him wrong.

He observed, with something of a start, that there was no wine in the dinghy, nothing but him, the boy, and the box which was now getting wet. Fuck you, he thought. Would he really be expected to continue writing, not only without a human source, but without resources of the liquid kind? Also, it was unlikely he would get any more money. Why would he continue with a book which was legally owned by Woody Townes?

Yet he did as Gaby's anonymous 'supporters' arranged for him to do. Because he had a fragile ego and they seemed to hold him in esteem. Because he had harboured a fugitive and was now a criminal and frightened of arrest. It seemed they would prevent that. More particularly, and knowledgeably, he understood that his own Australian government would never protect him from extradition and whatever variety of torture the Americans might decide was now due to him. Was he hysterical? Most likely. He was certainly not a brave or even good man. Indeed, he thought, he was a rat, a pathetic cringing thing being ferried across a wide expanse of water that would as soon rush down his panicking throat and flood his lungs. He sat too far forward and was drenched, and the journey seemed to continue a great time, and he entered a nightmare zone in which there was, for all the engine noise, no movement through space, the type of sensation that might, in other circumstances, have had him reaching for a Xanax, but there was no Xanax here, nor would there be.

By the time it occurred to him that he should pay attention to the formation of these little bays and islands, they had already entered a tributary and he realised he had no clue how to return to Brooklyn or Highway 1. A city of five million lay just an hour away. Who would ever guess it? They were now chugging along what might be the southern bank of a creek, or perhaps it was the eastern bank. Everything was in deep shadow and the water was very still and translucent green, and the boy throttled back the engine and drifted very slowly into a mangrove swamp.

High tide, observed the boy. He would understand that later, but at the moment it seemed like a mistake.

The boy, most likely, could already imagine mud crabs and flatheads to be caught and eaten but the writer saw mosquitoes and wondered how he could bribe the boy to bring him wine. The water was now shallow and coppery and they slid beneath the mangroves, ducking very low, until Felix could see, ahead, a bare shelf of yellow clay. The boy gunned the engine and the boat rose, stopped fast in the sand.

The boy removed the outboard and carried it up the path together with what was presumably its fuel tank. Then he returned and gripped the boat by its bow and, with his passenger still seated like a grand poobah, managed to drag it up onto the shore.

There glowering Felix alighted and clutched at his

cardboard box. With the load thus lightened the boy was able to pull the tinny so it slithered rapidly across the swampy grasses where, finally, he turned it upside down. Then the pair of them set off up a narrow path, the boy carrying the outboard and the fuel and Felix's heart lifting as he thought, perhaps he will take pity and stay with me a day or two.

2

The path led the pair of them up along the contour of a ridge to the foot of a weathered wooden staircase with open treads. Even as his companion stood to one side and encouraged the fugitive to go ahead, the latter had no sense that he had in fact 'arrived'. The steps were for the most part overgrown with wild lantana, and if he noticed, in the deep shadow, a set of sturdy posts such as you might use to support a rainwater tank, he was too alarmed by the jungly tangle to pay attention. He believed the pretty red flowers with yellow hearts to be the habitat of shellback ticks.

Beside the banister grew a large rough-barked tree, close enough for him to touch and to note, without enthusiasm, the line of ants streaming upwards in the twisted valleys. This was an ironbark tree he decided. If it had not been an ironbark it would have had to be a ghost gum or manna gum. He acknowledged no other species.

He was tired and hot and his heavy lids and fleshy nose shone with perspiration, yet when he arrived on the threshold he was not particularly giddy. This one-room hut, which would later shake and shudder in the westerly winds (rippling in the gusts like a sailing boat), was on that sunny morning open to the benign south-easterly, and when the dishevelled fugitive arrived at the top of the steps he was surprised to find his quarters hospitable. Of the many things his eyes might alight upon, he did see a garden spade, hanging from a hook inside the door but he overlooked the words 'Shit, Horse' burned into its wooden shaft. There was so much else to look at. The glass-less 'window' above the old porcelain sink was occupied by a huge elephant-skinned angophora (ghost gum, he thought). The smooth pink and grey bark was luminous in the sun and the characteristic rusty blemish on the trunk harmonised so well with the stained sink that the latter seemed artfully intentional.

He kept his box clutched against his soft stomach, staring at the tree which he would later know in quite another way.

I'll take that, the boy said. Meaning the visitor's possessions.

But the man's belligerent attention had now shifted to some half-dozen shelves that had been fixed in place beside the window. On one of the lower shelves, abutting an assortment of canned beans and Campbell's soups, stood a number of four-litre casks labelled 'Hunter Valley Red', a description that gave no assurance that the wine inside had not been oaked with a shovel full of chips, stirred with a garden rake, and strained to reach its present 'market niche'. The visitor made a dove sound. His cheeks hollowed (briefly) and his mouth puckered (privately.) He placed his box on the rough counter top beside the sink and, being unconscious of his own sigh, plunged his hand deep in his pocket.

Don't wash the eggs, the boy said, not until you want to use them.

What?

Eggs.

Felix then saw, beside his box of evidence, a dark blue plastic ice-cream tub containing a motley collection of eggs – small, large, brown, white, not one of which was untouched by shit. He stared at his guide solemnly. He nodded, to register his understanding, as he would soon nod in response to fresh apples, pumpkins.

Typewriter, the boy said, scratching at his calf and leaving contrails of white across the brown skin.

How had he not seen it? Whoever had prepared the accommodation had positioned the machine thoughtfully in the middle of a folding table of the type once available for $10 at any army disposals. Had they known it was for him? Had the 'supporters' read his books? What did any of them really think about what they were doing?

An Olivetti fucking Valentine identical to the one he had destroyed in 1975.

It was of course a bright red little portable. Now he removed it from its sturdy plastic case and gently touched the spools of ribbon there revealed.

He turned to the boy who grinned.

Of course, thought the fugitive, there is no electricity. He sat in the awful canvas chair and selected a single type bar, the letter L, raising it from its nest, examining it so closely that the boy might have been reminded of a naturalist tenderly banding the thin legs and long, agile toes of a white-faced heron.

Having, in the course of his hard-typing years, broken the fonts from the type bars of so many Olivetti portables, the fugitive was at once astonished that such a thing might still exist and touched by its frailty and appalled by its clear inability to withstand what he must now do to it.

While turning his wide bookish back to the curious boy, he plunged his right hand in his pocket and removed a sheaf of that distinctively slippery Australian currency, clearly designed for sneaky business.

The boy, meanwhile, had placed reams of paper on the table, found the mosquito coils, had picked up an orange pumpkin from a pile in the corner of the room. Clearly it had been feasted on by possums so he did what anyone else would have done i.e. he threw it out the window. As there was no glass or screen to impede its progress the pumpkin crashed like a tumbling wombat through the bush.

Of course the fugitive was alarmed, but only very briefly. His greatest concern was that he would be compelled to drink inferior wine. So as the pumpkin exploded on the rocks he revealed his hand.

The boy saw the slippery money and was suddenly in a frantic hurry to get away. She'll be right, mate, he said. Fridge, cooker, matches, gas, he continued. The old man came at him with his legal tender, red and orange like a bird-of-paradise flower.

Water, the boy cried, and turned the tap on and off.

You could do me a favour, the fugitive said, perhaps too desperately.

The boy held up his hands and pushed at the air between them. I'm fine, mate.

Could you get me a case of McLaren Vale shiraz, and drop it back.

I'm sorry.

I'll make it worth your while.

I'm only sixteen.

Get your brother, anyone.

Mate, no, I can't come back.

I'm not going to see you again?

That's the idea, mate.

But someone else is going to come?

I couldn't say.

Why not for Chrissake?

Couldn't say.

Couldn't bloody say?

Kero for the lamps, he said. My ride is here. I got to go.

Take a twenty anyway.

Good on you. Mate. Good luck and that.

And with that he was out and gone, tripping lightly down the stairs, leaping like a goat down the path, bounding so fast that the new resident, following him, bravely if not elegantly, arrived in time to see a tinny was in the process of nosing out of the mangroves.

Help, he called.

The sun glinted on the aluminium and broke into the shade. He removed his shoes and dropped his trousers and with his long jacket flapping in such a way as to make his sturdy white legs, his point of greatest physical insecurity, appear even shorter than normal, he set off beneath the mangroves, mud squelching obscenely around his urban toes.

And so it was that the 'most controversial journalist of his generation' was abandoned, untrousered, like some creature in a Sidney Nolan painting (*The old man who was up bathing himself in the dam*) and he soon saw, through the light-netted mangrove leaves, another aluminium dinghy and a woman with long blonde hair, like Julie Christie, he imagined, or at least Celine as she set off to lead the revolution from the front ranks of the 1972 Melbourne Moratorium. Squatting he could see her, the tanned skin, the hair flying behind.

Fuck fuck fuck. He proceeded up the narrow track carrying his trousers, socks, his shoes, suddenly aware of how soft he had become, a frail old fellow pricked by sticks, stones, and those little stabbing bindi-eyes which he had thought existed only in suburban lawns.

Finally, standing at the open window, with his trousers still flung across his shoulder, he stretched his legs sufficiently to wash his feet in the sink. He managed to find a tumbler, open a wine cask, and pull out its wrinkled concertinaed genitalia. Shuddering, he poured a purple glassful and then found, in the small gas refrigerator, a lump of cheddar the size of a house brick. He cut himself a slice, and was about to taste it when, with a great rush of winds, a fucking kookaburra arrived from nowhere, took his cheese in its bucket beak, and flew out the door.

He remained then at the sink, for a long time, looking balefully out through the foliage to the blue glint of the water. He accustomed himself to the wine. He was a highly specialised creature, he thought, sometimes, on a good day, capable of a single function, not much more.

He dried his feet with his trousers and laid them carefully in a parallelogram of sunshine beside the desk. He then wound a single sheet of paper into the Valentine and found it far from blank.

To Mr Felix Moore, posing as a radical, it read, and continued thus: We know exactly what you did and did not do in 1975. Wouldn't your fans and readers be shocked

173

to discover their great radical didn't have the balls. You were just like our parents: down on the ground crying how unfair it was.

The roller of the Olivetti turned, thus revealing:

It won't help us to reveal your sad moral failure, but it would help you to honour the gift you have here been given. This woman is a human being and it will be your honour to celebrate her real life without hysteria.

Celebrate her real life without hysteria. Celine Baillieux had used these words in Moroni's.

All you need is to be humble, the note continued. If you can manage this we, her friends, have the ability to publish you digitally around the world. We are legion. Ten million readers are now within your reach.

Yes, right. He twisted the corner of his wine-stained lips and began to bash the keys. His fingers hurt like hell but he would not dishonour her by being her hagiographer. He would write or overwrite until he bled. Go celebrate your arse, he thought. Ten million readers. Bullshit.

3

Many Hawkesbury mornings had now passed. As this
new one began, a grey lizard, aka a skink, a member of
the family Scincidae, a nervous neckless creature with
tiny legs, made its cautious way up the pitted trunk of
the angophora and stopped, still half in the night. A
butcherbird sang like Ornette Coleman, fluffed out its
untidy chest, and shat. The windows were filled with
smudgy dawn but the voices of two women could be
heard, sometimes in unison, sometimes in discord, then
in lone confession, and this variation was emphasised or
diminished by the man in puffy overalls, who sat on the
edge of his desk or kitchen table, using a large discoloured
toe to raise and lower the volumes of two quite different
tape recorders.

The river was opaque, a greenish grey. The crack of a
whipbird cut through the human voices. The magpies and
lorikeets and king parrots added their calls and the pink
early sun, finally, revealed the awful hairy glory of the
fugitive.

The 'most controversial journalist of his age' would
have thought it pathetic to grow a beard deliberately, but
the razor had been left on the top of the beam above his
bed and now he had discovered it . . . well, too late. He had
a 'sort of' beard and it had shocked him to see its reflection
in a spoon, his sensual mouth all hidden, leaving just the

fleshy nose and his creased and pitted bark. He looked a hundred.

The women were still speaking, as they had done for days, and he let them go together, waiting for . . . he did not know. Of 1975, not one single word, no rage, no pity, no word about revenge. He no longer cared. He had received so many different instructions on how to tell the story, the only sane thing was to let it show itself, to wait until it crept out of its hole. Sometimes he was very patient. Sometimes he hated the women, sometimes he was amused by how often they agreed with the person they complained of. If they had been butcherbirds they might have almost qualified, in spite of all their acknowledged opposition, as a 'bonded pair'.

Sometimes he reported their comments. Almost always he 'fixed them up' and oftentimes he distilled Gaby's slang into something more worthy of the ideas she was expressing. Would you trust a woman who spoke of 'lossitude'?

In the Supreme Court of New South Wales the judge had asked him did he make up quotes.

He admitted freely that he not only made up quotes but had also been accused of making up quotes, 'but never of the quotes I actually made up'.

When they did not laugh, he attempted a quick lesson in the nature of dialogue, explaining how the actual words themselves were far less important than was generally thought by laymen. It was more accurate, he said, to understand the spoken word as the product of the tectonic forces working below the surface of the human drama. It was these forces (none other than the insistence of a character's greed, love, ambition, etc.) which were important. It was these forces which the writer had to know. It was as a result of them banging against each other that the dialogue emerged.

The prosecutor asked him if he could report an entire conversation which he had not witnessed. He said he never claimed that ability.

Then what ability do you have?

He compared himself to a forensic palaeontologist which caused unfriendly laughter. But he insisted on it. His job was to dig up the bones, piece them together, and from all the known information about diet and habitat, be able to construct the creature itself.

You mean, said the prosecutor, a whippy figure with an enormous high-ridged beak, you made up words and put them in my client's mouth.

He said he would have been happy to quote his client exactly if the client had not, in spite of his Christian Brothers education, the unfortunate tendency to switch tenses, inject 'ummm' or 'ah' into sentences and use 'gonna' instead of 'going to'.

If your client's subjects agreed with his verbs, said Felix Moore, then there wouldn't be the temptation – or necessity – to ever clean up his quotes.

This is what he did above the Hawkesbury River: cleaned up quotes and lined them up in readiness like fresh-caught flathead in a killbox.

As he worked, a dinghy thumped and whined its way towards Wisemans Ferry while, just below the hut, he could hear the first slap of water from its wake. God, it was lonely. If there had been a safe place to go he would have found a way there.

The tapes aside, he had not unpacked the cardboard carton until the fifth long day when, in spite of his depression and his fear of being controlled or imprisoned, he had laid out his forensic evidence across the floor and began, as follows:

4

She was Gabrielle Angela Quinn Baillieux on her birth
certificate. She was born in the Royal Melbourne Hospital
on November 11th, 1975. We can pin down the exact
minute of birth from the parliamentary broadcast which
was, on Celine's evidence, playing in the delivery room. As
the baby slithered into the midwife's brown hands, both
parents heard the governor-general's secretary: 'God save
the Queen,' he said, the creep.

It was 4.40 pm.

The baby wailed. The pulsing squiddy cord was cut.
The insistent force of life was now brought to the mother's
attention and her naked child was laid against her chest.
It is a moment when new parents often weep, but when
this pair wept it was not at the miracle of life, but because
the legally elected government of Australia had been
overthrown.

Fuck them, Celine cried. God fuck the governor-general.

Shush, said the obstetrician. There's no politics today.
You have a child.

Celine cupped her daughter's universe inside her hand
and inhaled the musty rutty sex-smell of her hair. There
are politics every day, she said. Only a fool would forget it.

It would be the child's likeness to the beautiful mother
which everyone would emphasise. The daughter would
later insist that this was artificially emphasised, the result

of her mother's vanity, but who can rely on these agitated witnesses? The nature of the resemblance – the cheekbones and distinctive lips, the thick, almost wiry, yellow hair – was real enough. Likewise the electric pale grey eyes, identical to those of the reckless parent, and that mischievous muscle you can see today, joining the pert nose to the mobile upper lip. These uncanny similarities made strangers smile. Even those who had become disenchanted with Celine were smitten. It took the theatre director Betty Burstall to be 'puzzled' by the way the mother's hair just happened to match the four-year-old's urchin curls.

Gabrielle Baillieux was born into bohemian comfort in the inner Melbourne suburb of Carlton and thereafter grew up around actors and writers and radicals and became precocious in the way you might expect. Betty Burstall was her godmother at a time there was no God. 'I had a very happy childhood,' Gaby said on tape, which made Felix Moore wish he had been trapped with her in her stinky dugout, quietly noting how, say, she used her lip chapstick obsessively. Stuff like that.

The alleged terrorist was born golden. She grew up knowing prime ministers and junkies and barristers and alcoholics and had regularly fallen asleep in a fug of marijuana, but for twelve long years she was reliably loved, safely handed from one pair of hands to another, at home, and in the Footlights Collective, and at the Women's Action Theatre in Nicholson Street, and there were, through her childhood, perhaps twenty houses which she could walk into without knocking and find adults who would feed her or admire the artwork in her schoolbag. She attended Carlton Primary and had Greek and Italian and Lebanese friends who petted her blonde hair and never called her skip.

These were the years when the conservatives once more ran Australia, when Woody Townes, who always had his nose or dick in everything, was buying up the old Carlton terrace houses and painting the exterior walls ultramarine, the window frames maroon, like Persian rugs, and no-one ever dreamed they would look as shitty as they do today. It would later turn out that Woody Townes owned the company that owned Gaby's childhood house in Macarthur Place. It was the narrowest house in Carlton, as wide as a suburban driveway, dove-grey, salmon-pink, with a high cast-iron verandah where you could have seen, at any moment, the tight press of Australian art and politics. Gough Whitlam stood there. Clifton Pugh. Felix Moore Esquire. This was the house where Australia's tallest playwright famously walked from the front door to the kitchen fridge in just two strides. It was a small house much envied, much derided, for how could two bohemians afford this, the cutest house in Carlton with its windows opening onto the park?

This was what Celine called 'my Carlton' which is less nauseating than it might seem. She really managed to own Carlton for a year or two – not only by being a beautiful young woman with great legs and a Nepalese kaftan with tiny mirrors sewn into the embroidery. In those days, before she made the soup commercial, Celine Baillieux was an activist actress of note. If she was sometimes mocked she also had a following and she used it, not always to her husband's advantage. God knows what Sando felt when he opened up the newspaper each day, and if his wife was never photographed with Yasser Arafat it was only because she never had the chance. Celine was liked because she was both beautiful and not 'up herself'. She put herself at risk. She was beaten, more than once. She stood in the rain outside King & Godfree selling *Direct Action* with the actor Matty Matovic, who was not yet a prisoner of the state. She was fearless, always in the front row of everything.

She bicycled from household to household, from play-reading to rehearsal, past the Italian greengrocers, the group houses with windows open to the street playing Van Morrison throwing pennies on the bridges down below, up to the Brunswick baths, down to the Victoria markets for fresh puntarelle with her string bag suspended between the handles and Gaby dripping gelato on the seat.

And of course she did love Carlton (as she understood it) for its unlocked doors and open windows, for Macarthur Place, for Lygon Street, for its Lebanese hashish in Johnny's Green Room, its sly-grog shop in Chummie Place, the welcoming Italian families, the intense and clannish Greeks, the intellectual pubs and radical politics and fabulous cappuccinos and Readings books and Professor Longhair's record store of loving memory.

The hard men from the party's King Street headquarters filed into her doll's house and sat in the small front room with cold beers held daintily between thumb and forefinger. Sandy was their up and coming man. They had watched him since he left his storeman's job at Dunlop to get a degree at Monash University. They observed him in the Monash Labor Club. In 1970 they shoehorned him into the Vietnam Moratorium Committee where he began his association with Sam Goldbloom and Jim Cairns. They were very happy when he became a family man, and if

Celine was not exactly what they would have wished, she managed, when she was in their presence, to make them forget it. Did she flirt with them? Lay her hand upon their arms? Did they permit this? There is no evidence, none at all, none on a tape, none in a notebook or scribbled on the typing paper, but of course she flirted. What else should she have done?

Sandy had strong support from the socialist left and, unusually for Melbourne, the right as well. For the men in King Street he was a natural for the state seat of Coburg, and it did not hurt that he was promoted by Woody Townes. The Coburg branch, however, was a local branch i.e. parochial and bloody-minded. They agreed that Sandy Quinn was working-class, dinky-di, ridgy-didge, from Williamstown. They said nothing about Mrs Quinn (not her name) but she was probably what they were thinking about when they said Sando was not local, that they did not want an outsider 'parachuted in'.

Celine never would understand that she was only bullied into living in Coburg so, in the branch's opinion, she would get to know 'real working people'. Real? The party did not really know shit about Celine. And if Sando thought she could be forced to live in Coburg, he did not know her either. She would rather die than have a backyard, or a Hills Hoist or a barbecue or a privet hedge all of which arrived in her life when Mr Neville died and Doris 'liqui-dated' the home her daughter loved. Within a day of the auction Doris had bought a taxi business on the other side of Melbourne, in Springvale. She began to drag out photos of 'Dad' and no longer mentioned Mr Neville.

Celine understood the madness later. At the time she

smelled it like a gas leak, the loneliness, the nothing of Springvale. There had been nowhere to escape the fear. There was not a bookshop in Springvale, certainly no Bach or Botticelli, only the culture-hating xenophobic mediocrity.

To live in Springvale, Celine said, was to endure long hot afternoons and airless nights alone and a five-kilometre walk to a chlorinated swimming pool and burning concrete and stupid boys peering through the walls of the changing shed.

I would die in Coburg, she told her husband. He told her Coburg was not Springvale.

He did not understand. The streets of Springvale had been empty but for some poor lonely 'housewife' trudging up to the shops, past blind and empty houses in one of which Celine was reading 'Howl'. Doris did not have to live in Springvale. She could have afforded Carlton. This very house, this lovely slice of terrace house on Macarthur Square. To Doris it would have been a slum.

Celine was not leaving this for Coburg. Coburg was a hot basalt plain. Coburg was the road to Sydney. Coburg was where they manufactured hats and shirts, Kodak film, Agent Orange. Coburg was the poor fucked-up Merri Creek seeping through the council tip past Pentridge Prison to the quarry.

It would be no bad thing, just the same, said a certain George Papadopoulos of the Coburg branch, to get your missus to understand: in Coburg there is space to have a proper clothes line.

Sando laughed when he passed this on to his wife. He kissed her. He made her laugh about the clothes line. He told her that he could not have loved a wife with a clothes line. He would not ask her to modify her views, to dress more carefully, wear a bra, or consider the party platform before she made pronouncements about the Middle East. He said he was the one who would be elected, not his wife. She was an actress. She should act, he said.

Sando was the only 'good' person Celine had ever met. He set up an office in a cupboard just off Sydney Road in Coburg, and she was proud of him. There, each night, after his day teaching school, and on weekends, and on holidays, he filled out forms and wrote letters for all factions of the immigrant community, mostly Greek and Italian at first, but then the Lebanese from Denbo, who needed more assistance than the Turks.

Each night he returned to her in Carlton, to the black trunks of the elms and the birds quarrelling in the branches of Macarthur Square. There, on the top floor of his skinny house, Celine watched him breathe their daughter's shampooed hair and listened while he read her *The Midnight Cat*. She was jealous sometimes, not for long. Every child should be loved like that.

5

'All happy families are alike; each unhappy family is unhappy in its own way.'

Is there a more famous line in all of literature? Is there a greater writer than Tolstoy? Only in some lost corner of the earth, in a shack above the Hawkesbury for instance, might you find a wine-caked fool thinking to himself – hang on, Tolstoy, not so slick: it may not be a case of either/or.

This family of Quinn's and Baillieux' had definitely been happy. For ages they had story-reading, beaches, opening nights, election-night parties. They cuddled up in bed on Sunday mornings. All happy families are alike in that no-one gives a shit about them. This sort of language, Felix Moore had been warned by powerful friends, did nothing for his credibility.

Being now employed to explain a life using nothing more than over-oaked wine and tape recordings, he did not argue with Tolstoy. Instead he thought, this is a family that will be unhappy. Even during the happy years there must be 'storm clouds gathering'. These clouds would make the happy years more interesting. As luck would have it, there was a real actual storm cloud: i.e. a dreadful lie: that the grandma was allegedly dead and unavailable. When in fact she had been alive in Springvale all this time, this trauma victim abandoned by her daughter.

Then she turned up, alive, at Macarthur Place.

Gaby remembered it exactly: she had been in the front room, standing, reading at a music stand. The book was *Wolf Children* by Lucien Malson. (There's another first line for you: 'The idea that man has no nature is now beyond dispute.')

Looking up to reflect on this happy Marxist fantasy, Gaby saw her grandmother in the window.

She took the old lady to be a wino, from the Salvation Army hostel. She was sixty years of age, more or less. She wore a fox fur. Her hairdo made Gaby think of Edo Japan, although the effect was not artistic or refined. A huge tortoiseshell comb kept the structure in its place and the woman's face was very white and her lips very red. If her face was fabulously wrinkly, she had lovely bones beneath.

When the old lady tapped on the glass, the hair on the girl's neck stood on end.

She had nothing to give but her jelly beans. She had them lined up on the music stand. She held up the black one and the crone nodded enthusiastically and pointed towards the door which the girl reached at the same moment as the visitor.

Black one, she said, very chirpy. Thank you.

She was not a wino obviously. She was dressed in a long worn black coat with sleeves rolled back and silver bangles.

I'm sorry, the girl said, confused by the jewellery. It is all I have. And was then taken by the sight of the stranger unwrapping an oblong object, cosseted in white tissue paper. She feared it would be an heirloom offered for sale. I haven't any money, she said. Truly.

Yes, yes, lovey. She smelt of fish, like a cat. Just look.

187

She saw a tiny snapshot framed in silver. The glass was splintered and the old dame's finger had been cut and was smearing blood across the tissue.

You're bleeding.

Look.

The photo showed a woman and a little girl, taken long ago. There was a black van in the background although to call it a van was to make it sound far larger than it was. Although the subject in the photograph was much younger than the woman at the door, she shared the strong lipstick and penchant for black. She was eccentric, Gaby understood, but quite artistic and very beautiful. Somehow she assumed the little girl had died.

Macarthur Place was a very 'come in' sort of house and she led the injured visitor to the kitchen where she found the bandaids and sat her at the table and took some pleasure in cleaning the wound with Dettol and securing the bandaid.

Would you like a cup of tea? she asked.

Her guest set the memorial on the table. Gaby thought, oh dear she really wants to sell it to me. Tea?

That would be nice dear.

A bickie?

You don't happen to have sardines I suppose? She had removed her fur and coat and revealed another layer of black, a smartly tailored suit cut quite snugly. So much better for your memory.

On toast?

A fork would be lovely.

Gaby found the sardines and put the kettle on.

I'm Doris, her guest said.

I'm Gaby. Gabrielle.

It's a very pretty name. Were you practising your music?

I'm reading.

Do you like to read?

Yes, but this book is a little hard.

The old lady had deep-set eyes, and a very straight mouth that occasionally revealed the smallest most beguiling movement in the direction of a smile. Your mother was a terrific reader.

Well, everybody knew her mother, or claimed to, even if it wasn't true.

The visitor ate her sardines from a cereal bowl. She slid the photograph across the table. You know who it is?

You look very pretty.

No, the girl.

That's your daughter?

That's right. And who is she?

What do you mean?

I am your nanna, the old lady said, using a tiny handkerchief to remove sardine oil so delicately that the lipstick almost survived intact.

How do you mean?

I'm your nanna. I'm your lovely old granny, dear.

Gaby sat down suddenly. She looked through the cracked glass, at the image of her mother. It was not like her at all. Her clothes were awful, like a refugee, like things from a lost and found. She had long socks up to her knees and a tummy showing through her poor tight sweater.

I am Doris, the woman said.

She reached an oily hand to touch her granddaughter's hair. Gaby drew away.

And you are the most beautiful, she said, of all of us.

Then she permitted the fishy hand to stroke her hair. She entered a disturbing variation of that hypnotic state she sometimes experienced when her hair was cut. Who can say how long the trance might have continued if the front door had not opened.

Here, the old woman said hurriedly. (It was a business card, a little oil-stained, SPRINGVALE TAXIS.) This is me, darling. I am at your service for anything you wish. The zoo, the Dande-nongs, I'll take you where you like. She was gathering her coat when Celine entered.

Hello, said Doris.

Did Celine know who it was?

Visiting my family, the old woman said. I brought you a present.

Gaby watched as her mother examined the framed photograph with its crazed glass.

Keep it, Doris said.

Thank you, Celine said, quickly placing it behind her.

Goodbye, Doris said to Gaby who was startled to see her poke her tongue out at Celine. And then she left, without explanation, soft as a cat, out the front door and out of sight.

I thought she died, Gaby said.

No, Celine said. Of course not. How could she be dead?

It was not her mother's lie that shocked Gaby but her grandmother's fur, the sardine smell, the poked tongue. She ran upstairs to wash her hair, knowing that she had been saved to live a happy life.

The unhappy part arrived soon enough.

She came home from soccer practice to see her father arranging polaroids along the mantelpiece. She closed the front door and the draft blew the photographs across the floor. He yelled at her.

She was a beloved child and this was unacceptable. She rushed to her room and locked her door. She waited for the apology. It did not come.

She heard the front gate squeak and knew it could only be her mother returning from her run. She unlocked her door and spied from her tent of darkness at the top of the stair: she saw that the photos had been restored to the mantelpiece. What did her father expect would happen now? Once more the door opened. Once more the photographs swooshed across the room. This time he did not yell. He watched as his wife knelt to pick them up and all was quiet a moment.

Then she throws them in his face and the child is electrified with fright. This never happened before. Sandy falls to his knees. He stacks the fallen pictures as tenderly as a boy with swap cards. When he speaks, his voice is very slow and very reasonable and it is clearly understood, by everyone, that he is in a towering rage. His face is unshaved and savage like something washed up on the beach.

The mother demands, We are not going through this again.

In a cardboard box, years later, there will be a faded polaroid of a weatherboard cottage, a dying lawn, a high lifeless brick fence like a blindfold on its eyes. Who would keep such a photograph and why?

He says, We won't ever have a chance to own a house again.

Did this all really happen? Of course. She, the beautiful young woman, steps forward with her hands backwards on her hips. What did you say to me, Jack? (Saying *Jack* to make a stranger of him.)

He says they now have a chance to own a house.

She removes her headband and flicks her fair hair back over her shoulders. She says, You said it was obscene. 'It' was the Saturday real estate circus, the yuppie home buyers who travelled from auction to auction in Carlton, double-parking along Canning Street, coveting the old working-class cottages.

Anyway, she says, we can't be 'home owners' even if we want to, not even in Coburg.

The man moves to a kitchen chair. The woman resists the implication that she should join him, but clearly he has something new to say. Go on, she says, from the doorway. What is it?

We have been offered the deposit, he announces.

Christ, the woman shouts. (Christ, the girl hears.) Can't they just leave us alone? Can you win the election or not? Are you the best thing Coburg ever had? Does the idiot branch understand they've got themselves a cabinet minister in the making? Tell them to fuck off. We don't want to borrow their dirty money.

Then he smiles. It is such a relief for the girl to see her daddy smile.

Not borrow, he says. Some blokes.

Blokes what?

They will make us a gift of the deposit.

Some Greek bloke?

No, not him.

She would have been outraged to know the money would come from Woody Townes. That particular revelation will be delayed until the divorce, at which time their so-called 'marital property' will not be theirs at all, but an asset of one of Woody's secret shell companies.

You be bloody careful Jack, she says. Honest people don't have that sort of money.

There are great places with big backyards.

I can pay next month's rent. All of it. I'll get a second job.

He shrugs and stares into the fridge.

They want me to go to Coburg? Why? You got elected living here. Don't turn your back. You think you can force me? Do you not understand anything about me?

There is nothing the girl can do to affect this conflict, which she will relate years later. Anyone listening to her adult recollection will hear how little distance she has from the event. She may be a 'habitual law-breaker' but she still knows what it is like to flee to her cold bedroom and switch on the blower heater. She can tell you how she locks the door and waits. All her room is vile and empty. She wishes she had a kitten. If she was dead they wouldn't know.

It is an eternity before her parents understand what they've done to her, and then they come creeping up the creaking stairs. Then they love her. Then she curls up in her mother's lap. Publicly, she is her mother's replicant. Privately, she feels herself to be a plain square little thing. She traces her mother's beautiful face with her finger and calls on all her will, the great engine of her terror, to make them laugh and love each other. She can do that. She does it constantly. She performs a handstand and reads a poem. She clears the table without being asked and, when she finds the stack of photographs, she hides them in the drawer reserved for string and rubber bands. She knows she has the power to make her parents love each other. She is the force swinging between them. She is the heat and electricity and she will turn it off, forever, if they frighten her by shouting.

Sando and Celine apologise for their 'dreadful character'. They show their consideration by only fighting late at night (as if the girl can possibly sleep when she knows her whole life is at stake). She notices how her mother now refers to the 'Labor Party machine' and 'machine politics'. Likewise her father refers to her mother's 'radical friends'. 'Your Carlton tribe,' he says, sarcastically. He says the Labor Party will die when it becomes the party of 'your tribe' rather than the party of Coburg.

She begins to 'sleep over' at friends' and stay late at soccer practice and lock herself in her room and listen to Midnight Oil. There was no sleep. The beds were burning. She would recall the lyrics all her life. She turned up the music so loud the bass shook her windows and they did not even try to stop her. Ditto: there was nothing she could do to stop them, not even bite their legs.

She gets caught shoplifting from HMV but they do not even blame her. She smokes cigarettes that they do not seem to smell. They forget her thirteenth birthday until it is a day too late. So she gets into her mother's closet and tears two sleeves off two different dresses. Nothing happens as a consequence.

There is a warm windy night when Celine and Sando fight until the early morning, stamping up and down the stairs, to the bathroom, to the fridge, out the door and in again. By dawn, they are all worn out and drunk and snoring. Then the child takes her backpack and her homework folder and her soccer ball and leaves the house by the kitchen door which opens onto a narrow bluestone alley.

Later she will hear that you could fix this feeling by cutting yourself. But she has no-one to advise her, so on this particular morning she does not know what to do about the pain. She dribbles the ball up the centre of Macarthur Square, and sprints across empty Rathdowne Street, the way to soccer practice. She has the power to make them seriously sorry, more than they can ever know. She catches the green light up at Swanston Street and dribbles across the silent tram tracks. The sun is behind her as she enters the empty streets of the University of Melbourne, into Queen's College. She keeps the ball between the double lines without a mess-up, *pushing* with her laces, not slowing but *anticipating* College Crescent where she is stopped by two-way traffic. She waits, all lit up by yellow sodium, doing switch keep-ups on the curb, seeing the white startled faces in the cars. Where is that girl's mother? Why is she abandoned? Then she is off, through the traffic, a clean calm line through a hysteria of brakes.

For the first time, by herself, she enters that long spooky path through the middle of the Melbourne General Cemetery. She sees herself from way on high: straw hair glowing, a dead girl risen from her grave, dribbling, cutting left onto the green field, completely, totally alone. She lies on the hard thirsty ground pretending to be dead. What else is there to do?

She can hear the lions and hyenas roaring in the nearby zoo. Now and then she opens her eyes to see if anyone is creeping up. There is dust in the wind. The yellow streetlights look like murder. She stays and stays until sun bathes the faces of the terraces on Royal Parade. No mention of 1975 at all.

6

It matters that she did not mean to slap the fox terrier or hurt its head but she got woken by its tongue dragging on her skin. She hit its face in fright. In return it bit her leg. There were four other dogs, maybe five. Maybe they just wished to play, she thought, years later on a microcassette. She had freaked. A spotted bitzer jumped and scratched her and she screamed and got her soccer ball and ran with her book sack thumping like panic on her back.

The dogs blocked the way to Carlton so she ran west towards Royal Parade. It was the little patch-eyed fox terrier who was the scariest, maliciously nipping at her heels as she ran straight across Royal Parade, behind the tram, before the truck. She heard the squeal, the awful howling, but she was already fleeing into The Avenue which runs around the back of the big old terrace houses on Royal Parade. There she recognised Frederic Matovic's rusty corrugated back fence.

She did not know him well enough.

Blood was streaming down her leg as she let herself into the yard. Her sock had turned pink. She had never been invited into Frederic's, but she knew that was it, ahead, a shocking tacked-on sort of shed with rusty corrugated walls like the back fence. His dodgy mother lived inside the house at the front, upstairs in a large single room which was apparently lined with the second-hand dresses which were her business. She sold stuff from her van and little shop.

This was Parkville and therefore fancy but the social structure here, from Royal Parade across to Nicholson Street, was always smudgy, layer to layer, Italians, Jews, skippy working-class, lawyers, academics, Housing Commission kids, playwrights, junkies, boarding house proprietors and fences of stolen goods. It wasn't often that you saw a family slide from one group to another, but in Frederic's case there had been a lurch. His father had once been famous, on the cover of *TV Week*.

Frederic, Gaby called his name. When she heard him breathing on the other side of the door, the hair rose on her neck.

Who's that?

Gaby. From school.

What do you want?

Let me in, she demanded, waiting.

She knocked again. I'm sorry.

Just bloody wait.

I'm hurt.

Wait.

The chain shook and rattled and was withdrawn through its jagged hole. The door opened a little and there he was, blinking, the beautiful boy with long black hair and black fingernails, his face quite red as if from violent scuffing. He looked down his nose at her.

What?

I need someplace to crash, the child said.

The door opened and she saw that he had covered himself in a strange blue raincoat. You should come to the

198

front door of the house, he said.

But I'm all messy.

He stepped back and she followed him. To her surprise he took a box of Kleenex from a desk. Obviously his mother had been removing makeup here. Gaby saw her stuff was everywhere in the sleepout, not just crumpled tissues but her trash and treasure, racks of clothes she could wheel into her van, from there to Footscray or her musty little shop on Faraday Street where everyone went to find fur coats, loopy wedding dresses, cups with triangular handles.

The sleepout smelled of old lives, dead people, the cats that had once lived with them. Take your shoes off, he said. Sit here.

Gaby rested the box of tissues on her lap and Frederic took them one by one and dipped them in his glass and washed her bleeding ankles.

I'll get rabies.

No you won't, he said, and she did not ask him how he knew.

I'm sorry I woke you.

What happened to you?

Dogs I said.

You want to sleep?

What if I foam at the mouth and bite you?

He pulled back the bed cover and she climbed in and he tucked her in so nicely her neck felt strange. Don't tell anyone you've been here, he said.

There was a computer on his desk. She had seen one previously on television, and also in a comic strip, but she had never seen one in real life, not this tiny screen joined to a keyboard the colour of old bones.

What do you do on that?

You wouldn't understand.

It's your mum's?

He shook his head irritably.

I'm a girl so I must be stupid? It's in Hamburg, she said, reading off the screen.

It's not.

Welcome to the Altos Hamburg Chat System.

Mind your own business.

The bed smells nice.

It's lavender.

Your mum will go nuts when she gets the phone bill.

Go to sleep. You're so completely wrong.

Won't she though?

Go to sleep.

You're very clever, aren't you?

If you can't stop annoying me you'll have to leave.

She lay on her back and closed her eyes. He was in Germany somehow. She was leaking blood. Everything smelled funny, borrowed, stolen, used, former weirdnesses and misery, old men drinking port from flagons, country girls, nurses, matrons, cats comforting their chilblain toes. On the wall it was handwritten: IT IS AGAINST THE LAW IN MELBOURNE #1 To wear pink pants after lunch on Sundays.

It was too hot for him to wear that coat. He had scrubbed his face so hard there were scratch marks on his burning cheeks. There was a big chart pinned onto the wall above the desk, a web of tunnels and caves with tiny spider writing dense as lace. She did not guess that this was where she was going to live. She read: 'East Temple Room.' Later, he stood and added to the writing then returned to the keyboard, his fluttery butterfly fingers dancing, his cuticles like the wing cases of black Christmas beetles that lived inside the walls.

The sun got higher and the hot corrugated iron made loud explosions as it pulled on its nails like Jesus Christ and it was too hot to lie in bed fully dressed and she could not leave and could not sleep. She would never have thought of Frederic like this before. He never spoke in class except when the homework meant he had no choice but read aloud. He stood apart, always, alone, tall, straight, too big to be teased or threatened. He would have been bored to be a goth but his skin stayed very white and his hair fell on his shoulders like a raven's wing, and he walked rather carefully with his head tilted to one side, so the hair, she guessed, did not obscure his view. He was already over six foot and he had to shave once a week, but he had a very soft sibilant way of speaking which, now she knew his place, exactly matched the room.

Gaby had first met Frederic at socialist youth camp in Healesville when he had given a report on child labour in Third World countries. Gaby found him afterwards, totally alone, throwing stones into the bush. Not long after that, his father got kicked out of the party. Then his parents split up and you would sometimes see him standing with the handsome rock-jawed dad selling the Trot paper. The dad was not charming: 'Do you or do you not agree there is a crisis in capitalism?' He was one of Celine's 'tribe'. Sandy said he was a crim.

When Frederic's mother got her shop together she could afford to also rent this jerry-built addition for her son. At first she worried he would be murdered or mestered and she was mad as a watchdog, running down the stairs in the middle of the night, barefoot on the concrete path. With this one disadvantage the bedroom/shed was the best thing that ever happened in Frederic's life. That, and the Mac IIx his father had delivered late one night together with some 'white goods'. The computer came bundled with its disadvantage too: his mother might go to jail for 'receiving'.

It was too hot in the sleepout. The sun brought out the hidden smells which had lain like mosquitoes sleeping amongst the hanging dresses, deep in the carpet with the dust. Gaby put on her gluey socks.

Thank you, she said.

For the first time he smiled, a nice smile.

Anytime, he said. It's been a considerable pleasure (he talked like that).

And he gave her something, a coin, not a real coin, a heavy medal. On its face was a hurricane lamp, bronze relief against the silver. She asked what it was.

Look, he said.

It is pitch dark. And you cannot see a thing.

Where is it from? She meant from what country.

He closed her fist around the medal. It is from the past, he said.

And with that he raised her hand and gently kissed it, not like a boy at all, and in her fright and joy she would have rushed straight out the door again except he had to unlock the padlock before she could be released.

7

Royal Park is a significant site in Australian history. It is from there that Burke and Wills set off to lose themselves and die. It is where General MacArthur's forces camped. The trees had grown since 1942, but Royal Park was still as flat as a parade ground. It was across the road from Frederic's daggy back fence. Here Gaby removed her blood-pink socks and discovered she smelled of dead rabbit or day-old butcher's paper. She kneeled on the dying grass and twisted uncomfortably to examine her injuries, two U-shapes overlapping, brown and pink and now raising red around the edges. Did rabies look like this?

The yellow children's hospital was visible through the trees, waiting to tattoo her with the name of her disease. Car loads of super-normal families headed north along The Avenue. She imagined their intimate fug, lost Minties, old travel sickness, the boring safe comfort of a Saturday. She touched the tooth stabs with her forefinger, pressing to see how much they hurt. Looking up she was startled to discover Frederic – now dressed in retro drainpipe trousers, brothel creepers, Hawaiian shirt – as he closed his corrugated gate behind him. Then he was sloping off along The Avenue towards the city moving in his famous Frederic way, his tall body very straight, his head on one side, hair flopping, an entirely distinctive, very cool style of tiptoe walking that she would finally understand (not for

203

years and years) as the expression of his gorgeous shyness.

She had left her soccer ball behind. She had not meant to. She certainly wanted to be let into that magic room again but she was too proud to have played a cheap trick to get there. Like, I left my comb behind. Pathetic.

She made her way back across Royal Parade and then around the cemetery. As she emerged on the Carlton side she felt herself being looked at. She had wished them to think that she was dead and all their fault, but by the time she was walking along the grassy strip in the middle of Keppel Street, she felt stupid and ashamed. When Katie Humis and Eve and Robo and the others erupted from the front door of a bright white terrace house, five screaming girls dressed in black like crows, it took everything in her not to run away.

Oh my God.

Ring your mother.

Use our phone.

Katie and Eve had wide leather belts at their hips. They would have been surprised to know they were severely judged for it. Gaby would have been incredulous to know she would ever want to be their friends again.

Your mum was freaking out.

It was the first time that she properly understood she was not one of them.

Who were you with?

No-one.

You did it?

What?

She did it.

What did I do?

You shagged him. Eve said that and was clearly shocked by the ugly thing she'd said.

Who would I do it with?

Their faces were red and overheated. Martin Boosey, they said, together, idiots, clones in black.

They did not know how to look at anything. They had not even noticed her bites and when she left them she made a fuss about walking backwards, waving, making it sort of funny, although she was disgusted they would think she was shagging.

She had wrecked her life much worse than that.

She turned down Cardigan Street, jogging, pretending she was coming back from soccer. Looking down the wide straight flat road towards the city she saw him, Frederic, now crossing at Elgin Street. He was dodging traffic, carrying a very large cardboard box.

At the Rathdowne Street traffic lights she stopped to examine the medal he had given her, the bronze hurricane lamp on its silver ground. *It is pitch dark.*

Her life had just changed in some serious way but there was, as yet, no external sign of it. Entering Macarthur Place she walked close to the buildings on the north side, then slipped into the lane beside her kitchen. What had happened? What had changed? All the empty beer bottles had been taken away leaving a single line of sickly yellow grass between the asphalt and the wall.

Her radical mother was in the kitchen wearing makeup.

Are you all right? the mother asked, staring at her. Celine looked so weird, like the enemy, someone from South Yarra. She was wearing pressed embroidered jeans and when, on tape, Gaby tried to evoke the cocktail of emotion that had caused her to cry, she mentioned the jeans more than once. Celine had dressed in a bourgie black linen jacket with padded shoulders. Her daughter had been missing a few hours and now she was dressed up for the police and social workers. She had pressed her jeans to make it not her fault.

Gaby had not known that she wanted comfort until she saw her mother's frightened stare and knew there wasn't any comfort to be had.

Are you all right?

Yes, the girl cried, I'm fabulous. She pushed past and ran up to the shower. Not for a moment did she consider what a shower might mean to her mother. Gaby wished only to wash the rabies germs away, and she locked the bathroom door, which you were not allowed to do. She washed her legs and rubbed her skin too hard. The bite began to bleed and she thought that must be good. When she was dry she used her father's aftershave which stung just as much as she had wished. She placed a bandaid on every tooth mark. Then she dressed as if for soccer, with new clean shorts and long white socks still smelling of the laundry. She slipped her shin guards into place.

And then she presented herself again in the kitchen where she apologised. By way of acceptance her mother made a chocolate egg flip, one of those indulgence foods supposed to give you strength and comfort.

Are you OK, sweetie?

Don't let me disturb your hangover.

Oh baby, Celine said, please let me brush your hair. And she had the hairbrush waiting, her instrument of love, and Gaby sat on the kitchen stool and stretched her neck, bending forward beneath the weight of the brush, not showing how much she enjoyed the tug, the pain, the battle with the knots and curls.

You shouldn't yell at each other, she said. I can't deal with it.

I know.

But it was not until Sandy returned that they actually hugged and she knew how thirsty she was for the tender sorry way he touched the skin on the back of her hand.

We've been awful, he said. I am ashamed.

Celine should have been ashamed but instead she had pressed her jeans with a crease right down the centre of the legs.

I got bitten by a dog, Gaby told her father not her mother. What if I've got rabies?

She would never forgive Celine for the relief that then illuminated her puffy eyes i.e. she was reassured by the possibility of rabies. Even though everyone knew what happened if you had rabies – they pushed a huge needle, a centimetre thick, straight into your stomach, thirty-three times.

Better than shagging, was what Celine had clearly thought. She was just so thankful, obviously.

8

Felix Moore's present residence had been built on a sandstone outcrop which, in the shadow of lantana, and in secret places beneath the floor, looked like a fine-ground concave lens. It showed silky sedimentary lines in mustard and ochre, but when he wanted some pretty rocks to secure his papers against the wind, there was no sandstone of a useful size.

The rocks that finally held his fluttering papers were dark reddish-brown, volcanic and blobby, or quartzy, sometimes white, streaked with black veins. They did the job, holding his information fast through two lashing storms, although nothing could be done about the rain which had, during the second 'weather event', blown straight through the hut, causing him to flee up the ladder to the bed where he sought the comfort of the previous tenant's padded overalls.

Now he was confronting the resistant nature of the information in the carton. This was not, in any sense, a 'source'. It was the sort of shit schoolgirls left in their abandoned bedrooms, old projects, medals, ribbons, school reports, VHS tapes, CDs, lipsticks, thirty types of cassette tapes of bands they were ashamed to say they ever liked. These tapes were not music. He knew that from the start. The microcassettes were Gaby's, the motley lot Celine's. On and on they talked, on and fucking on, invisible to the reporter, without an editor to rein them in. Other presumably vital evidence was provided by spiral-bound books with pasted photographs and scraps of art, larger books with brown paper pages not unlike those 'guard books' they used to keep in the advertising departments of newspapers, awful old ads for dreary suits held in place by so-called 'milliner's solution'. A flat airless soccer ball might have lifted his spirits, but instead there were enigmas beyond all understanding e.g. a book with a hand-lettered title in Flintstone block capitals. WANK, it said. This caused the pathologist to play unhappily with the scraggly edges of his moustache. What would it serve to open this unsavoury door?

In 'The World of Wank' (as it was subtitled) each of the pages had another glued on top of it. Their distinctive fold marks suggested they had been through the mail.

```
<ROOM ANTECHAMBER
   (LOC ROOMS)
   (DESC 'Small Room')
   (EAST TO LIVING-ROOM)
   (DOWN PER TRAP-DOOR-EXIT)
   (ACTION ANTECHAMBER-F)
   (FLAGS RLANDBIT LOCKEDBIT)
   (GLOBAL STAIRS)>
```

RLANDBIT, he thought, LOCKEDBIT, he thought. AGENBITE OF INWIT. U.P.:UP. FUCK YOU.

Time passed. There remained just two casks of Hunter Valley red to deal with. He had found a single stick of pale blue chalk inside his overalls and with this he drew a circle on the floor and placed the book inside it.

The water slapped against the shore. *Ah hate this place. All ah hear all day is them damn waves, floppin' down.* What garbage he carried in his head. There seemed no order or meaning in the contents of the box, but this was all he had been given, like his too long arms and too short legs. He turned off the mother and increased the volume on the daughter, and took the 'Shit, Horse' shovel off the wall and picked up the dunny paper and set off up the back stairs which led to the high ground above the roof. He managed to dig a hole in shallow soil. He could hear the pedagogical daughter briefing him on tape, so much he had to learn, she lectured. His knees hurt. He watched a pelican as it changed its landing plans and plunged, untidy feet down, head first, into the river. He shat, in spite of all the cheese, and afterwards he filled the hole as best he could and ignored the white ribbons waving from their grave.

He had a tinny, an outboard, a tank of fuel. What to do with them was something else. If his wife had been here she might have had a sensible plan to save his neck again, but he was dead to her and he must cauterise his memory of her and so he returned to the hut and sat on his desk. He restarted the tapes and was amused to hear that – here, once again – the two voices were disagreeing, but dwelling obsessively on the same concerns. They both circled the purchase of the house in Coburg. Fucking real estate, he thought. This is how you change the world?

Next he listened irritably to Gaby's detailed explication of 'Frederic's mental processes'. She thought this should be the basis of his book. The style should be 'experimental'. He fast-forwarded, paused, rewound. It was 'important' that he understood. 'Truly remarkable

Frederic' had a continual silent conversation in his head, in words and symbols, not only when seated at his Mac IIx – which was both his true and his secret life – but even walking along the streets of Carlton where his compass-point orientation and the actions of his limbs were expressed, by him to him, in Zork Implementation Language, aka ZIL, a computer language related to LISP, now obsolete. Felix Moore MUST take notes, he was instructed. Frederic was not autistic. His skin smelled of coriander. This was said, unprompted, three times. But whether going to school or delivering 'seriously discounted' electronics for his father, he was secretly a machine, conversing privately like this:

```
>go north.
>go east.
```

When Frederic picked up Gaby's soccer ball he allegedly thought >pick up soccer ball. Then he held it in front of him, his burnt-sienna nail polish hidden in the dark. He carried the soccer ball as an act of love, under sodium streetlights and into the seaweed shadow of the park, coming down the central axis of Macarthur Square he would make the world he entered 'SUBTITLE GABY'S HOUSE'. Stuff like that: <DEFINE EAST-HOUSE.

And also:

```
In there is a small window which is <WINDOW
['WINDOW'] ;object's name
  ['SMALL' 'TRANSPARENT'] ;adjectives for window
  < + OVISON, OPENBIT, BREAKBIT> ;things you
can do with object
  [ODESC1 'There is a small window with 4
panes']
```

```
[ODESC0 'A window is here']
BILLS-OBJECT ()>


<DEFINE WINDOW-OBJECT ()
<COND (      <VERB? 'BREAK'>
      <TELL 'Watch out for flying glass!'>
      <>) ;'Prints sarcasm but doesn't handle
the command
   (   <VERB? 'EAT'>
   <TELL 'Nah, the glass gets stuck in my
teeth'> ; does not allow eating window
   >>
```

Who talks like this?

Machine. Plus, also, Frederic Matovic stood outside the railings of what would soon be the lost house in Macarthur Place. He looked in through the dark front room into the kitchen where he could see the three of them at table. He remembered, he would tell Gaby often, a scene of mythic beauty, golden, the father wide-shouldered and narrow-hipped like a surfer, you could almost see the sand, his short tousled hair, the mother sexy like an actress which of course she was and Gaby, ethereal with dirty nails he would bring home to touch his keyboard.

He thought in many languages but ZIL was from the world of Zork. >put soccer ball on doormat. He placed the soccer ball on the mat, knocked on the door and ran away, into the park, 'raindrops glued onto his shiny back', wrote Felix Moore-or-less-correct, slamming the keyboard of the Olivetti.

King parrots feasted, dropping seed-casings on the noisy roof.

Felix Moore rewound, played, rocked the tape back and forth across magnetic heads. He finished one A4 sheet and placed it beneath a rock. He wound in a new sheet, already swollen by the damp.

Coo-ee.

It was a human voice, and it caused the great journalist to tug shoes onto his bunioned feet. With laces still untied, he fled up the dangerous back stairs pushing through the wild lantana where a lorikeet, as pretty as a Persian miniature, was moulding itself into the flowers, and then he was above the roof of his hut looking out across the empty river and down at a rainwater tank half covered in dry leaves. He could see nothing near the shore but mangrove leaves.

Coo-ee.

His eyes were dark and hollowed.

Coo-ee.

What would happen to him now? He climbed back down the stairs, walked through the hut then down towards the water.

Hello? he inquired. An outboard sprang to dirty life.

Coo-ee, he bawled. His knees hurt and he was an arthritic dog jumping through swordgrass, arriving at the shore, out of breath, one shoe in his hand. The visitor had departed, was beyond the mangroves now, and the throttle of the outboard opened wide. He was slow to see what had been left behind, there, on the edge of the mudflat, two gleaming gutted fish and three bottles of clear rum.

His creased eyes filled and he smiled and stamped his foot and if he was laughing with relief, or disappointment, he did not know himself. Must go on, can't go on, he uncorked the rum, drank, and coughed. To be continued.

9

Frederic Matovic had left Gaby's ball outside her door, thus removing any excuse for her to ever visit him at home. When he passed her in the hallway at school he would not even look at her. It was rainy and windy all that week, and on Tuesday his vintage brothel creepers got soaked which meant she could always hear him, even when she didn't see him, squelching, please shut up. She wished she had rabies. She would go mad and bite them all. On Wednesday he charged out of Miss Hanson's special maths class and shoved his pointy books into her chest. She chose this moment to insist: her ball had been left at his place by total accident.

All right, he said, not listening.

I don't play those games, she said.

OK, he said, and ducked away, leaving her breasts bruised and angry.

Gaby was unhappy, irritated with everybody, even Bree, whose birthday it was this coming Sunday and for whom she had decided to make a pair of happy pants. Celine had a treadle Singer and Frederic's mum had some '50s fabric, the planets Saturn and Jupiter on a black background, ten metres of it displayed in her Faraday Street shop. Gaby had walked to this window every day after school, always in the rain, her ankles sprayed by passing cars. 'Back Later' the sign said. Gaby huddled against the door and the sign

215

was still in place two hours later, and again on Thursday when she returned. It was early, before school, but there was a light inside. She knocked, without hope, but without relent, and finally there was Meg Matovic and a bald man in a dirty singlet.

Yes.

I'm sorry. I've got the money. I know what I want. She could hear Meg's visitor peeing out the back, it was awful, on and on, he sounded like a horse.

Mrs Matovic had not priced her fabric yet and did not want to sell a short length but finally she gave her two metres, and pushed the girl out into the rain.

At home that night her father was forced to light a fire although it was so warm they had to keep the windows open. The problem was the rising damp so the rain snuck up the walls like sap from the foundations. It bloomed in white and furry mounds on the painted hallway and, more seriously, in Celine's built-in wardrobe. Sando was a 'bush carpenter'. He had strung cords beneath the high ceiling of the little living room and all Celine's clothes hung safe and dry, like sails above their heads.

Gaby's bedroom wall was damp as well, but she had happy pants to make. By the time she was threading elastic she was called to set the table and found Celine removing the skin from chicken thighs which meant, twenty minutes later, short-cut coq au vin. She lit the candles.

Celine was in a good mood, translate as maybe stoned. She had actually AGREED to inspect a house in Coburg on the following weekend. All this was on her tape. She and Sando drank wine from long-stemmed glasses. They were 'loose as gooses'. Sando got himself all folded in his chair. He had news but he held onto it, that was his way, to have treasures hoarded for a rainy day: he had got the funding for the day care centre for the migrant workers. You could see he was in love with them. His eyes caught the reflection of the candles. His mouth stretched along the coastline of his wobbly smile.

Celine was not competitive but she had good news as well. The Footlights Collective had been given a 'development grant'.

They finished the bottle, Gaby said, and then they got stuck into the cask wine so it was time to leave them be. She returned to the elastic waistband of the happy pants. Downstairs everything continued chill. They were playing *Astral Weeks*. For God's sake, find something new. Gaby read about Etruscan Mania and drifted into sleep.

On Friday morning a fresh mass of rainclouds were rolling across the Great Australian Bight but the serious rain did not arrive in Carlton until early evening. Then the fat drops hit the iron roof so heavily that they all had to shout. The rain made her happy, and safe, and the house filled with delicious smells as Celine reheated the leftover chicken. And everything felt like it was soothed and better until Gaby caught Celine cheating on the mashed potato. She was using water instead of milk. It's healthier, Celine said. Translation: I am beautiful and you are fat.

Gaby returned to her room and locked her door and sat cross-legged making Bree's wrapping paper, lettering with a thick gold Sharpie.

i'm skinny, so i must be anorexic.
i'm a girl who eats lunch, so i must be fat.

217

i wear black, so i must be a goth.
i'm into death punk, so i must cut my wrists.
i'm irish, so i must have a drinking problem.
i like brancusi, so i must be a poser.
i hang out with gays, so i must be gay too.
i'm a virgin, so i must be a prude.
i'm single, so i must be ugly.
i'm christian, so i must hate homosexuals.
i'm young, so i must be naive.
i don't like the sun, so i must be an albino.
i'm intelligent, so i must be weak
i'm a westie, so i must be obese.
i like blood, so i must be a vampire.
i love kafka, so i must be a loner.
i don't like to talk about my personal life,
so i must be having problems.
i have been to therapy, so i must be crazy.
i'm not like everyone else, so i must be a loser.
i'm a teenage girl, so i must not have a clue.

She returned to the kitchen. Celine criticised her for
having gold paint on her hands, then announced that she had
to cancel her visit to the Coburg house. She said the grant
money had to be spent on a workshop over the weekend.

What a liar.

If we don't spend it by Monday we have to give it back.

You said you got the money yesterday.

I just *found out* yesterday, sweetie. Apparently we've had
it for a year.

Yes, this was a lie, Celine said on tape, but the point was:
she knew Sando had gone and bought the house without

her. She had found the account from the solicitor. She would not mention this for years.

Well, her husband said quietly, perhaps you could pop up to Coburg at lunchtime. And look at the house then.

You sneaky wilful bastard, Celine thought. The drag is, darling, she told him, I just can't. The workshop is out of town. Of course there was no workshop but she already knew what she would do.

Sando laid down his knife and fork.

At Moggs Creek actually, Celine said, coming around the table to kiss his neck.

Sando stood, took one step around his wife, and scraped all his mashed potato into the tidy. Never mind, he said, staring deep into the bin.

No-one knew it but this was really the last day in the family's history. It was then, exactly, that Frederic called through the window from the street. Gaby watched her mother with amazement. How pleased she was to see him all at once. Come in. He must come in. Celine was so completely false, but WTF: Gaby's eyes were blurry as Frederic passed beneath all the hanging clothes. Her father finally lifted his foot from the kitchen tidy and gently helped the visitor escape his sodden coat.

Frederic's black hair was like seaweed on a martyr's skin. He was offered food. He accepted. He sat next to Gaby and did not look at her.

Thank you for bringing the ball back, Sando said. Gaby was relieved. Weren't you baby?

We go to school together, Frederic said. His eyes hid behind his gluey lashes. You could see the candles deep inside his head.

Celine served him more mashed potato than she would ever give a girl.

You arrived at a historic moment, Sandy said.

Dear Jesus, Gaby thought, please do not embarrass me.

We have found a house to buy in Coburg, he said. (What the fuck was he doing?) Do you know Coburg?

My dad lived there for a while.

Sandy was thinking, oh shit, oh what have I said? His dad is Matty Matovic. He lived in jail in Coburg, oh shit.

And how was that? Celine smiled brightly.

Shut up, Gaby thought.

Frederic actually smiled at both of them Where is the property you are interested in? he asked.

Patterson Street.

Patterson Street is cool.

Celine was acting 'excessively delighted'. He knew Patterson Street? She could not stop looking at his lacquered nails.

They shot Jimmy Gifford there.

Shot? said Celine.

The film, said Sando quickly. He means they shot the film there.

I never heard of *Jimmy Gifford*, said Celine. Who was in it?

Gary Waddell, said Frederic, and it was, most likely, on account of this single brilliant lie that Frederic, in spite of what he did, would remain golden in Sando's eyes.

Frederic grinned like Vengeance.

We were going to look at the house tomorrow morning, said Sando.

Frederic was smiling blatantly.

We're sad because we've just found out that Gaby's mum can't come.

I'll come instead, said Frederic. Obviously.

Obviously? No-one really knew what to say.

I made a present for Bree, Gaby told Frederic. She was smiling too, could not stop.

You're so social, he said.

Happy pants.

Show me, show me. He splayed his hands across his cheeks and made Celine smile, not because she liked or didn't like him but because, clearly, she thought he must be gay i.e. no trouble here.

Can I show Frederic the present?

Frederic was a genius. He fairly danced up to her bedroom and no-one thought to stop him. They closed the door. They read the wrapping paper, kneeling side by side.

They hate each other, right?

It's awful.

Is she having an affair?

No. I don't think so.

She is, said Frederic. Take my word.

Gaby snuggled into Frederic's chest and he kissed her cheek, and then, most particularly and delicately, her earlobe.

I want to teach you cool stuff, he said.

She did not understand him, but who cared? She took his hand and, seeking some unknowable transgression, slipped two fingers in her mouth.

10

All night the wind blew and her parents snuck out into the park to have their argument which was lifted and broken and thrown like cans and newspapers rattling in the laneway and Gaby played Tracy Chapman with the volume at the max.

She woke in daylight with the Walkman cord around her neck. Her parents' bedroom door was shut. The stairs were sour and spilled and smoky. In the shivery kitchen, the remainder of the chicken shared its stale confusion with the sharp fresh slap of Celine's perfume. Could she not have applied her perfume in the car? Which of course she took. Thanks Mum. Don't worry about us. We'll get the tram to Coburg.

Back in the front room at the top of the cold stairs she found Sando sleeping like a death scene, diagonally across the bed. When she spoke he turned to reveal a face cut with the red lines of crumpled sheet. He was bloodshot and sad. His handsome mouth was desiccated. I'm so sorry, Gaby. You don't deserve all this. Et cetera.

I'm just going to get Frederic, OK. Then we'll go?

We don't have to go anywhere, baby.

Yes, to Coburg.

Do you really want to go without your mum?

Yes, I do.

He swung his big legs off the bed. He dragged her to

222

him and he smelled like someone else, like dirty laundry and uncleaned teeth. She was squished and smashed and scared and she understood that she had, finally, done what she would never do i.e. she was on his side.

Is it really come to that? he asked and she could not be certain he meant what she thought he meant.

And Frederic, she said.

Of course.

I can cook you breakfast.

I'll go to Johnny's Green Room.

I'll get Frederic.

The girl in the bathroom mirror had swollen eyes and a broken smile. She set out to brush her hair then flung the hairbrush from her. She showered and washed her hair and piled on the conditioner. She scrunched up her towel-dried hair with Protein+ and gel, and she used a T-shirt so it scrunched up really good, and then she let the gel dry and then she put on even more gel and then scrunched it again and listened to Tracy Chapman when her fair hair was like a dandelion in seed and it did not matter that her smile was hurt and bruised. She outlined her eyes with kohl.

Sando had already left for Johnny's Green Room. She visited her mother's wardrobe which was hanging from the ceiling. She chose an old blue Marimekko shirt dress with a Mao collar. Celine never wore it and anyway, so what? There were spotted bleach marks on the sleeve.

It was too big, but cool that way, and she put it together with daggy white socks and dirty sneakers. She tied on a red hair band but it was dumb and then she tried the old man's hat she had bought at the Footscray market, and it was dumb too, because it would ruin the hair, but it would not be dumb if she never took the hat off.

The wind blew all the way to Parkville so she kept the hat in her hand until she was at the back gate at Frederic's. She had never dressed like this in all her life, but she would not arrive at Frederic's door looking like a high-school clone.

She had closed the corrugated-iron gate and was heading past a pile of huge sodden cardboard cartons and blocks of styrofoam, across the broken concrete to Frederic's locked door when she was intercepted by a slender black-haired woman in a pink kimono.

Mrs Matovic wrapped her arms beneath her breasts and the pale circles printed on her sleeves were very beautiful and strange like suckers on an octopus. She wore no shoes or slippers and her feet were remarkable with no veins, perfect straight white toes.

She was staring at the Marimekko dress, as if it were someone she knew or might like to meet.

Can I help you? she said, not friendly in the least.

I was looking for Frederic.

Why would that be?

I'm Celine's daughter. You know me. I go to school with Frederic.

Mrs Matovic lit a Marlboro, tapping her finger against the white cylinder, not to loosen any ash. At last she said, We're a private family.

I thought other people lived here.

Yes, we don't like people sneaking in behind our backs. Celine's daughter should come to the front door and knock.

Can I talk to him now I'm here?

224

Just knock on the front door.

You mean now?

Sorry, darling, yes I do.

Walk out to The Avenue and come round the front on Royal Parade?

That's it, she said.

Gaby had imagined she liked Meg Matovic and her interesting artful choices and her brave distinctive son but in fact she was a creepy thing that would squirt ink into your eye.

Thank you, Gaby said and walked to the back gate, holding her hat on her head like a girl at Sunday school. She closed the gate very carefully and checked the latch. She walked slowly along The Avenue, for as far as Frederic's mother could see her, and then with all the dread of a bad girl being sent to see the principal, turned into Royal Parade. She did not know Frederic's street number but only one of the houses had not been yuppied up. That one had peeling paint on its front door and this was where she knocked.

Frederic answered in white Indian garments, pyjama pants and a sort of shirt. He was like a waxwork dummy.

You better not come here, he said.

She smelled cigarette smoke and knew the squid mother was lurking back there in the dark. Sorry?

He could at least have made a funny face, but no. You have to call first, he said. Telephone ahead.

I didn't have the number.

My mum will give it to you if she wants you to call. We're pretty private.

Gaby mimed her outrage but he would make no sign to her, and he remained there like a great big pudding.

It's all right, she said, I don't want it anyway.

She returned to Royal Parade with her face already wet and her nose running. She got snot marks on her perfect hat. The stupid magpies went on carolling and the stupid sky was a cloudless blue and the stupid Sydney Road continued to carry its trucks and cars north across the dreary bluestone plains made in the days when volcanoes vomited across the future suburbs, and streams of lava ran like toffee, pooling in the hollows up to sixty metres deep. Liquid basalt spewed from her chest and rolled down the Merri Creek, boiling eels, and sending blazing wallabies to spread fire through bush.

At Macarthur Place she threw herself so hard upon the bed it broke. When the doorbell rang her eyes were bleeding black across her cheeks and she did not care to hide the damage.

There was Frederic: cruel, in stovepipes. She threw her fists to break his chest.

I had to say that, he said, finally grabbing for her wrist.

Let go. Your mother is just rude.

He released her and she hit him in the stomach.

Jeez, lay off.

She will decide to grant me her phone number? Jeez.

Quit it. Don't hit me.

What if I knocked on the front door? How would you even hear me out the back?

Frederic could have said my father is a thief, mother is a fence. But he said nothing and she began to cry.

He lifted her wet hand and brushed his lips across her knuckles.

What did I do wrong? she asked. Just tell me what I did.

His dark eyes were unnaturally still, more like a nurse's than a teenage boy's.

I'll get you your own key, he said and, with his index finger drew a line through the wet kohl on her cheek. That frightened her, the key. It was Saturday morning, not yet ten o'clock.

11

On a red Olivetti Valentine, the man known as Moore-or-less-correct reported that Gaby Sando and Frederic were on a Melbourne tram, travelling north along Lygon Street to Brunswick, past clothing factories, cyclone fences, faded signs for English lessons. They entered familiar Holmes Street. They felt the tram shake itself and do a dogleg dance and Gaby tumbled into Frederic who smelled of leatherwood honey.

Everything was fine and sunny: clouds the size of little farts. The tram rattled north, passed all the cast-iron verandahs that, at that date, had survived the council's planned destruction of all memory. They got off at what was meant to be a posh street but the footpath was in Coburg and therefore narrow. Sando was bristly and bloodshot as if he had been playing pool all night.

The street had a snotty name but the trees were weedy, starved of love, survivors with hessian bandages. Gaby was shocked by the cracks in the concrete, the lonely quiet, the little houses shrunk inside their borders, alone, disconnected. They saw a malevolent cluster of boys like rats with mullets, operating on a Datsun 240Z, roaring, revving, sending oily smoke across the intersection. One lay on the mudguard, deep into the engine, his plumber's crack shining at the sky.

Frederic smiled excessively and annoyed the boys with mullets who thought he was a poofter cunt. He was blatantly some unknown quantity who would get her father bashed. They escaped into the dead end of a suburban street, unscathed, and she understood that the liver-brick shitheap right in front of them would be, forever, That Coburg Place.

Broken pickets. Weird old flowers. Red-hot pokers. Cactus with shark's teeth growing along the edges of its flesh. The house was one hundred years old, at least, dying in deep shadow, with a wide low slate roof and verandah tiles like a mansion you pay to visit on a boring Sunday, blues and terracotta which turned out, in this case, to be smeared with illegal skid marks. The garden smelled of gas and cat's piss and there was a tall palm tree with a dead frond. Complete and utter lossitude. She could have cried.

Wow, said Frederic. Oh wow. Mr Quinn, do you have a key?

Sando kicked the front door and it swung into the gloom. The previous inhabitants had lit a fire in the middle of the living room and burned a hole to the centre of the earth. The injured floorboards were wide and waxy and marked with motorcycle skid marks.

This was their clubhouse, right? Frederic asked. The White Knights? This can be so good.

Sando took Gaby's hand in both of his and led her, in this ungainly way, from one room to the next, through violent debris of a type you might not expect to see unless you were, for some unexpected reason, on the run, frightened for your life.

There's a lot of room, she said.

So cool, said Frederic and she did not know what to think of him.

Plaster hung in shards held by ancient horsehair, moving gently in the breeze.

Sando held his hands out: Will it be OK? he asked his daughter.

She saw it in his eyes: someone had been murdered here but he had bought it because it was so cheap. Celine would have a shit fit. It would be Gaby's job to make it all OK. And it would be Frederic's talent to know all this without being told. He understood the role. He was Matty Matovic's son and therefore knew the cost of lead and copper. He had attended auctions all over Melbourne. He knew the value of these internal stone walls. He knew the squiddy underbelly inner-city pubs and midnight runs, and he would, for his reward, have her beside him in the tunnels of the world of Zork.

He perched fearlessly on the corner post of the front fence and saw what no-one else could see, that the leak in the bedroom corresponded with one broken slate, that 'this must be Gaby's room'.

'Gaby's room' had a narrow window with a view of an empty laneway. It's quiet, he said and his voice made her tailbone hum and he was being the power, the generator.

We can get kids from school to help, he said.

No, she said sharply.

Why not?

It's not your house.

But I'm helping you.

Gaby, honey, said her father.

He's not helping me, she said. He's creeping me out. I don't even know him.

And she saw Frederic's hurt face through the hot blur

230

of tears. Her father was restraining her, holding her, squeezing all her breath out. She wished to be back in her own home which was being taken from her, mother gone, father crumpling like paper in a bin.

12

Frederic refused to be offended, no matter what she said to him. He already knew what she was like. He said that. He may have even been correct. But then he told her he would teach her to code, and assumed that was just so attractive. How totally up himself. She was a girl so she must want him.

On Monday, after everything she had said to him in Coburg, he tried to catch her eye. Even while she ignored him she wrote 'Frederic' in her notebook and scribbled over it, obliterating him forever. She went into the loo and ripped him out and tore him up so small no-one would ever know what she had done.

She got back home and a telegram arrived – the first telegram she had seen that was not in a movie. She signed for it and left it on the table for her father who threw it in the trash when he was finished with it. Soon it was covered with spaghetti bolognaise, so obviously it was from Celine.

Is it Frederic? her father asked. Is that why you're so sad?

That was *him*? Saying *she* was sad? What had been in the telegram?

I'm studying Cicero if you want to know.

Gaby, I'm not sure Frederic likes girls.

Oh aren't you? she shouted, without warning, even to herself. Really? she yelled at him. She threw her book on the floor. Who was he to talk? What a mope. Letting Celine get away with all that shit.

He patted his big hands before his chest. He said, it was just my feeling.

And what are you, a homophobe?

It was as if she had slapped his face. Oh God, she thought, please Daddy, don't be drunk.

Why don't you just go and get her back? she said. Just get her and bring her home.

Then he was *offended* and shook his head at her, like some awful TV actor trying to convey disappointment. Then he stormed out of the house. Up to the Albion, of course.

And this was just one of many incidents that occurred in the two weeks when Celine was sending telegrams from Moggs Creek. On another night: Gaby had been looking through the cardboard box of Dylan Neil Young Jefferson Airplane Beatles. There was Rickie Lee Jones doing 'Chuck E's in Love'. She had danced to this track with her mother when she was a little girl, Celine crooning. *He learn all of the lines, and every time he/don't stutter when he talk.*

On this night, Gaby thought, Frederic! *(And it's true! It's true!)* And then, the needle scraped across the vinyl and her father was home and the vinyl was flying through the open doorway out onto the dirty street, and all her insides were cold spaghetti. Her father was insane. Why would anyone do a thing like that?

Because – duh – it was a song about an actor. Celine was with an actor. Shagging. It made her sick. He was not even a Christian so was he putting up with Celine's bullshit to make a happy family? Was he turning the other cheek? If so, don't do it on her account. She stood on a kitchen chair and pulled the hems of Celine's dresses, tugging, dragging until clothes pegs popped and clattered against the wall. She twisted clothes hangers beyond their useful shapes and the room got lighter and brighter until finally the ceiling was all bare and she didn't know who she was cross with but she fetched the black rubbish bags from the kitchen and stuffed them full of Celine, five full bags of them and tied them up with yellow ties. She was a cat running screeching over lily pads, nothing to support her, each pad sinking as it took her weight. She waited and waited but her father stayed upstairs. Finally she locked the front and back doors and the window to the lane.

At her father's door she called to him. Are you OK?

The streetlight illuminated his blue shoes protruding from the murky blankets. She found a place beside him in the musty tangle.

Will Mummy come back?

Yes my love. He tucked a quilt around her and she did not wake until the middle of the night when he carried her back to her bed. In the morning she found him in the kitchen drinking instant coffee. The black rubbish bags were now lined neatly against the wall and Gaby saw that the attack on Celine's clothes would not be undone now. Those body bags would still be there, lined up in evidence against her, when her mother finally came home.

After school the four girls, the Keppel Street Quartet, as they called themselves, were walking north along Rathdowne Street. They were not really a quartet at all. They were Gaby and Katie and Nina, but they always had to include Katie's little sister. Her name was Jenna and she needed a good whacking.

Crossing Elgin Street they all saw Frederic carrying another cardboard box entirely on his lovely head. It was a shock, Gaby said, to see his beauty displayed in public and to recall how she had bled onto his sheets and listened to his feathering clicking nails, black as beetles.

Jenna said, Hello Frederic. In a cheeky tone of voice.

Frederic lowered his burden to the footpath. As anyone could see, the box contained a brand new Knoll office chair, but Jenna asked: What's in the box, Frederic? The lurker loser, it was not her place to speak at all.

Frederic said it was a chair. He was being funny. They did not get it. He was a hundred times brighter than the lot of them.

That's nice, Jenna said. Did it fall off the back of a truck?

Gaby said, Shut up Jenna. She gave Frederic a quick nod.

Hubba-dubba, said Jenna and the other girls stayed silent. Katie lifted her finger at Jenna who stuck her tongue out. Frederic picked up his heavy box and continued up Elgin Street without any sign of strain, walking with that beautiful bounce, presumably towards his home.

He's strong, said Nina, as he walked away. He has endurance.

At which Katie and Jenna both burst into laughter.

You're really rude. Gaby spoke to Jenna but she included Katie, obviously.

I'm what?

Your little sister told him his father was a thief.

Get real, Gaby, said Katie. His father is a thief. Everyone knows that.

His father is an anarchist, said Gaby. Did you know that?

Gaby, darling, Katie said, selling left-wing newspapers doesn't stop him being a thief.

Have you ever heard of Proudhon, Katie? No, you haven't. Don't smirk at me, Jenna. You couldn't even spell it. Just look it up, Katie. See what Proudhon said. And leave Frederic alone.

Hubba-dubba.

Babe, you'll only get your heart broken, Nina said. I had a friend who fell for one of those. It destroyed her life.

Well, I don't have that sort of problem, said Gaby who was amazed with herself for making up the story about Proudhon.

Well, you have some sort of problem.

No, you do.

What sort of problem do I have?

This, cried Gaby, swinging her bag by its straps so it whizzed past Katie's freckled button nose. And that was how they temporarily resolved their problem shrieking all the way to Keppel Street. Ob-la-di, ob-la-da in vinyl talk.

13

Celine drove home through a hurricane, along the Great Ocean Road with her eardrum broken, buzzing, throbbing. The driver-side windscreen wiper stopped working as she passed the little church at Mount Duneed. She was one-eyed through Geelong in a hailstorm, and up the endless, awful Melbourne road.

It was and would remain, she told the tape recorder, the stupidest thing she had done in all her life – no, not running away to Moggs Creek with Fergus, no, she meant letting Sandy put her in the wrong.

So she committed adultery. OK. But Sandy bought the house without her, and left her name off the deed. So who was the biggest liar and cheat? She did not even like Fergus, but he was there, waiting, ready, able, unemployed. Also he was intellectual and working-class and would beat the shit out of Sandy soon as look at him.

Sandy was like some Labor Party saint. He would turn the other cheek. He would not cry out when tortured. Fergus was the un-Sandy, with unapologetic calculating eyes, a million miles from all those smooth-faced creatures who made up the Footlights Collective, actors who were still having to relearn the Australian accents they had lost while auditioning in London, artists who could only impersonate what Fergus really was. He argued as he acted as he fought, dance like a butterfly, sting like a bee, from Nietzsche to Solon and back to the dangerous edges of Douglas Credit. By the time you had assembled your rebuttal he had moved on elsewhere. Žižek before we even heard of Žižek, Celine said on the tape playing on the floor a thousand kilometres away, twenty-five years later. It was perfect casting: the fucked-up energy, the rawness of his speech. He was mad in bed, wide and barrel-chested and covered with fine curling hair like a beast and his penis had a distinct upward curve to it as you might imagine on a satyr or a pig.

Celine had always been inflammable, easily intoxicated by her burning bridges. She wasn't nice, she knew, but how do you compare that to leaving your wife's name off the title deed?

Based on all available evidence, Sandy had cheated her. Fergus had wanted her, had flattered her, had listened to every single word she said. She knew what he was doing, as she always knew when men did that nodding thing. She was not at all surprised that when he finally had her in Moggs Creek he never agreed with her again. She had not come for conversation anyway. Once he had fucked her she could not get away with anything, and she was in the mood for that as well. It was dangerous. You could not bluff him. There was no dare he would refuse. Celine would have to go out further, beyond the Moggs Creek surf, if she was to be with Fergus, which was what she had done for all those weeks.

Then they drank whisky and he told her she was a yuppie bitch.

She was high as a kite, reckless, off the map. She told him he was feral. She said some other things, quite personal.

And the bastard nearly killed her for it.

The rain stopped at Werribee and she drove back into Melbourne along Dynon Road where her mother had learned to dodge the Yankee trucks, up past the hospital where she was born, and into Carlton. She blew her nose and heard the air whistling out her broken ear. She came home incorrectly labelled with disgrace. She parked, badly, at Macarthur Place. She was no more in the wrong than he was.

It's her, Gaby cried, but stayed where she was, halfway down the stairs.

Celine heard the stairs creak and then saw her husband's legs and then his face peering down from the upper floor. He did not speak.

She noticed all her clothes were gone. She did not connect this absence with the bright black bags.

She closed the door quietly and sat on the sofa as if it were the middle of a set. The audience knew exactly who she was.

OK, she said, and put her hands up in surrender.

How stupid.

Gaby retreated up the stairs as Sando descended and Celine knew, as they passed each other, that an upsetting intimacy had developed in her absence. As he emerged from the shadow Sando was older, with two stark new creases from his nose to the corners of his beautiful mouth. So he had suffered too. She thought it was fifty-fifty and he would join her on the sofa, but he stood over her, towered above her, with an expression she took to be a sneer. Then, as he shook his head, the light caught an actual teardrop. She was appalled then pleased. She moved to one side and he surrendered. She gave him a tissue and held his hand. It was not yet clear to her what she had done.

14

Cockatoos were ripping the bark off the angophora while the oily-haired fugitive inserted four new Duracell batteries and played a cassette he had labelled 'Celine 4'. His eyes were dark and hollowed and he stared at the machine with his head cocked.

Is this what got you boys so hot? she said.

Pause. Rewind. Sip. Play.

Is this what got you boys so hot? That I would blow myself up? That I would do anything? You knew I had fired my mother. That must have looked like something but when Doris did not come chasing after me, when I ended up sleeping in Sando's car, I cried myself to sleep each night.

Fast forward.

You saw me in my mother's house, back in Springvale, ripping photographs from frames.

The fugitive had never personally witnessed such a thing.

Fast forward.

It was the same in the stupid business with Fergus, she told the tape recorder. Sando must have heard my ruptured ear whistling but no-one saw my hurt. No-one knew how I wanted to be forgiven.

A spy would never see the beauty speaking to the journalist, but he might hear grief, a certain flatness of affect, or even wonder why so many of us talk like that.

So I came back from Moggs Creek, she said, and guess what? I did not exist. Gaby vanished me. Sando wrote his bloody letters or read about saintly Samoans exiled in vile materialistic Australia. He was steely. It is not how people talk about him but he could be totally unbending. And of course, she said, he would not make love to me. He could be very cruel.

Pause.

Play.

I had thought we shared the blame fifty-fifty but now I just wanted him to love me like before. He had lied and cheated with real estate and I was the only one who said sorry. I was weak. I traipsed after him to Coburg and waited to be forgiven. I did penance. I ripped up the lino and killed the slaters and the cockroaches and kalsomined everything as was required. Of course the whitewash only served to emphasise the jagged shadow where the floorboards failed to meet the walls. As everyone said, the house had good bones: large square rooms and massive sash windows and once the filth was scrubbed off or covered up, it should have felt wonderful. Yet even when the morning sun washed across the hallway floor, it was clear that something awful had happened there. This was not 'the electorate'. It was a site of trauma, a place with unsafe floors, where the fabric of society had been ripped and torn. This was where the saintly Sando brought his wife and child, to get away from 'your Carlton tribe'. And although he and Gaby had got their way, I know they felt what I did. My dialectical materialist was made angry by talk of ghosts, and he turned sarcastic when I suggested that rooms might contain echoes of their past. Just the same: the hair rose on his arms. He had me buy him curtains and kept them drawn at dark. The junkies parked their car in the lane, so close to the kitchen window that you could see the flare of the match against the silver foil.

I should have abandoned them. I stayed.

Sando was shitty with me because I made so little money, but I was exactly the creature he had wished me to be. I had been going to teach school just like he did, but he *wanted* me to be an actress. It made him amorous to sit in the theatre and see me on the stage. Naturally I made no money – what did he expect? But after Moggs Creek I agreed to do those soup commercials and that got me kicked out of the Collective.

Gaby was so triumphant I had lost Macarthur Place. She became an instant Coburg girl with made-up vowels. She set off each day up the narrow footpath, lumping her backpack to Bell Street High School, up past the stripped car, the broken syringe, the clinker-brick St Bernard's with its depressing '50s bronze statue of the saint. Whatever happened to her each day I was not allowed to know. She refused to see anything was less than perfect. She insisted Bell Street High was 'really, actually, academically the best school I could be in' i.e. she was siding with her father.

Bell Street High School was rotting, neglected, faction-ridden, falling apart. In heavy rain the power points exploded, sending extraordinary blue sheets of Pentecostal fire dancing above the pupils' heads. The Anglo kids were called skips or bogans, as a matter of course. Gaby's Turkish classmates boasted as if they had personally killed the Australians at Gallipoli. There were, naturally, second-

and third-generation Greeks and Italians who were not suffering the cultural shocks of the Turks and Lebanese, but by the time my daughter arrived the suburb was filled with disorientated Muslim families who had begun life in the poor and isolated mountainside of Denbo. There was a boy who had been kept in prison alongside decomposing bodies. There was a girl who drew decapitated heads in pools of magic marker.

Gaby was in the foyer on the day it collapsed and hurt the gym teacher. Where had the state funding gone? Ask her father. She had a fifteen-year-old classmate who had been left in charge of the family while his father returned to Denbo to marry another wife and thereby protect the family's property. The school hired an Arabic teacher, but it turned out he was a Coptic Christian and the Muslim families did not trust him. The teachers doubtless gave their all, but everywhere there was cultural resentment and misunderstanding. Gaby watched her maths teacher insisting that a Muslim boy look him in the eye, a request the kid could not obey because it was disrespectful. Even she knew that.

She was in the Roman room when a mild, polite Turkish boy urinated into the plastic bin containing Lego blocks.

The urine could be seen, quite clearly, pooling in the bottom of the bin.

What's this, Feyyas? the teacher asked. The liquid was pale yellow.

It's water, Miss.

The teacher was also a mild and decent person, up to that point anyway. She was buxom and pretty with long dark hair. Get a cup, she said.

The boy fetched the cup and the previously mild teacher tried to make him drink his urine and the previously mild boy punched her in the chest.

So I wasn't surprised to find Gaby sneaking back to Carlton to visit her old friends. Was I a bad mother for letting her? Sometimes I was left in Patterson Street alone and I hated it, but I was always happy to think she was somewhere better than I was. I was not complacent. I was vigilant in fact. If she was sleeping over I would always call her at ten o'clock and – when I had got past the recorded message – we always had our whispered conversation.

Patterson Street was neighbourly enough. The Greeks were polite but stand-offish. The Italians were chatty, united by their hatred, of the plane trees, and of the council which neglected to collect their fallen leaves.

Gaby was soon friendly with them all. With me she was different, displaying a sort of moral vanity. The complications of the game were beyond belief, descending to her hiding or destroying her hairbrush and therefore preventing me brushing her hair. Of course I had a hairbrush of my own, but that went missing too.

None of this could be acknowledged or addressed directly.

I had been hysterical and deceitful but I had loved my daughter, indulged her, cooked her the food she liked, helped her with her homework, set aside those long erratic Melbourne summers so she would know that she was loved.

I would not abandon her. When the Sydney Theatre Company cast me as Yelena Andreevna in *Uncle Vanya* I stayed in Melbourne rather than abandon my daughter.

Apart from all the branch members who annoyed me

shitless, the only visitor I got was Frederic's mother. She scraped her dirty van against my fence and produced, from the passenger door, my red-faced daughter. Meg Matovic had come to demand that she, Gaby, stay away.

Your daughter has a key to my house, she cried but I was more concerned that our neighbour could hear her. Mrs Messite was sweeping her plane leaves down my way. I wanted to get Meg out of earshot, but I didn't want her inside my house. She was waving something silver at me, a key.

Read it.

There were words engraved on it. *Pick up key. Go west.*

This key fitted her front door, Meg said. If she ever found my daughter inside her house she would have her done for Break and Enter, don't say I wasn't warned.

I thought, was she really saying that my heterosexual daughter had designs on her clearly homosexual son? I asked her what we had to be so frightened of.

She snatched off her ridiculous cloche hat and I saw her dirty pinned-down hair. We are very private people, she shouted at Mrs Messite who retreated down the lane.

It's just a game, Gaby said. Please, Mrs Matovic. It's really just a game.

Where do you think she sleeps? Where? You're her mother. Do you know?

I had no choice but get her inside, seated at my table. I told her Gaby stayed with her girlfriends on Keppel Street.

Do you know the parents?

Don't insult me, Meg.

Her eyes were roaming the dining room. I thought she was coveting my Clarice Cliff vase.

Call them, said Meg Matovic, handing me my own telephone. Ask them if your little angel has been sleeping in their house.

Gaby sat with arms folded, refusing to engage with either of us.

I dialled the number. It was answered.

Gaby's lost her homework, I said. I wonder if she left it at your place.

Meg Matovic smiled sarcastically as I heard the answer she expected.

So, she instructed, ask this woman when she last saw your daughter.

Had I not called that very number three or four times a week? Had I not always found my daughter on the phone? Confidently I asked the question.

Gaby returned my gaze. She knew what I was hearing and she showed no fear.

He phreaked you, Meg Matovic said as I hung up.

Gaby rolled her eyes. It was, apparently a huge offence to use 'phreak' as a verb. As for me, I heard 'freaked', I did not understand that her disturbing son had been able to divert my call from Keppel Street to Parkville. Gaby always picked up, and I always saw her, in my mind, in a nicely furnished renovated terrace house in Keppel Street. Why would I possibly think she was in bed with a boy in Royal Parade?

You understand?

I understood like you understand you have fainted in the street.

So, said Meg in a nasty singsong voice, I had to take away his phone line. They won't be pulling this one again.

Yes.

Good, said Meg Matovic, and your little grass will stop snooping in my house.

I did not see her out. I stayed at the table looking at my girl. Her lips were swollen and her eyes puffy which I recognised from occasional symptoms of my own. So my daughter was sleeping with a boy. I was not stupid enough to think that I could stop her now.

Frederic must be very clever, I said.

He's a genius.

I did not see that would be the problem. All I recognised was the urgent need to get her on the pill. I did not say this right away. I made tea and put some biscuits on a plate. I tried to use the notion of Frederic's alleged 'cleverness' to get around to contraception but when she understood what I was doing she was outraged.

You're pitiful, she said. All you can think about is sex.

You sleep with him, don't you?

You are such hippies.

Gaby, do you sleep with him or not?

We're not dogs if that's what you think.

I was thinking, he is bisexual, of course. They all are now.

That's so stupid, and disgusting. Frederic has a computer. You couldn't imagine what we do.

No-one I knew had a computer so I imagined some huge mainframe thing. Men in white coats. *2001: A Space Odyssey*.

What is it you do, darling?

Don't even ask. It's called Zork, Mum. She pushed away the biscuits and took my hand. Really truly, you wouldn't understand.

247

It's called what?

That's only part of it.

Of course I did not understand, nor did I try to. I thought, at least she touched my hand.

Rewind. Pause. Play.

15

Frederic lost his phone line and he did not once blame Gaby. What that tells you is: he loved her. Meg had also hidden his coupler modem. Gaby explained exactly what a coupler modem was i.e. the thingo that connected your computer to the phone line. Without a phone line and a modem Freddo was completely cut off from the secret online world that had previously filled his whole existence.

All Gaby knew was you did not need a modem to explore Zork which was contained within the computer. Zork was enough for her and, almost unbelievably, it was for Frederic, for a while at least.

It was as if they were the only people in their world, the first explorers to map its tunnels. At this stage the maps were everything. Without a map you could easily waste an entire weekend searching for locations you had found already. Just one glitch: Frederic's writing was awful, like the trail of an ink-dipped spider.

This was Gaby's opening. She became the cartographer. Zork maps were what she dreamed about. When she read 'sacred pleasure dome' she immediately saw the world of Zork. She did not care that the game was so pre-Nintendo, almost prehistoric. She liked it better than anywhere else she had ever been.

At the high point of THE ERA OF MAP DEMENTIA there were over twenty poster boards in Frederic's room.

Most were pinned on the Caneite walls, but there was a huge one on the ceiling. These were not simple maps, but lists of clues and cheats, for instance: how to short-circuit the restriction on how many objects you could carry. (You inflated the raft and put all your stuff inside it and then deflated the raft.)

There was an epic RIP card behind the door. Meg Matovic had to look at this every time she finished her inspection. It memorialised the time Gaby had landed in an oubliette which she could only escape by dying. She would bash herself unconscious, then wake up and have to start again. It took five hours to die, but she would not be kept away from Zork.

Then Frederic cracked the code of Zork. Now they could invade and rule it, write new tunnels and new caves. They could introduce new characters and rename existing ones. This was the first time they experienced total ownership. You have just entered Twisted Zork.

Gaby stole a drill and keyhole saw from Patterson Street and removed four floorboards under Frederic's bed and whenever Meg rattled on the chain she crawled beneath the floor and lay on the stinky gas and cat-piss dirt until she left.

Of course she lived part-time at Bell Street High School where she became mates with the black giantess Solosolo and through her, the brothers. Aleki and Peli introduced her to a better 'recreational facility' than she could ever have in Carlton i.e. the wasteland of rocks and thistles past the old Kodak factory, between Newlands Road and Elizabeth Street where a gang of stringy bogans ran a scrap yard and would sell you a 'shit-bucket', e.g. an unroadworthy

Datsun, for twenty bucks. Peli was Solosolo's eldest brother, nineteen years old. Her younger brother – Aleki – drove the clapped-out Datsun around the paddocks across the creek from the Agrikem factory. Peli lay on the bonnet pouring petrol straight into the carburettor, flame erupting, burning hair and eyebrows while massive Aleki made 3D figure eights, sneezing and bouncing amongst the pitted brown rocks and boxthorns and purple flowering thistles.

This was fucked-up Samoa, not Fa'a Samoa, the 'Samoan way of life'. They left the Datsun's bonnet lying in the paddocks so the girls took possession and floated and dragged it down Merri Creek, between wattles ripe with crops of plastic bags, until they reached the rusty FJ Holden stripped and abandoned in the water. Solosolo was the six-foot centre-back of Bell Street girls' soccer team, but she was afraid of spiders. She sat with the little white girl on the slimy bench seat of the Holden, shrieking at the cold water on her backside.

Frederic waited for Gaby in solitude, rewriting Zork. He was the tapeworm. He crawled into its belly and became its god.

Fast forward.

Sometimes Gaby was lonely. Sometimes she hung with a kid named Troy who had been expelled from Clifton Hill. Troy claimed to have a girl in Northcote but she was blatantly imaginary. He had cute lips, curling wild black hair, and mild brown eyes which secret softness he kept hidden in the shadows of his hoodie. His one true love was *Cannabis indica* and Gaby helped him search for it amongst the tree violet and fennel of Merri Creek. This wild weed was as imaginary as the girlfriend. When they finally did find a homegrown crop in the lane behind Service Street, a bald-headed bogan came at them with a shotgun. Get out of here youse little cunts before I blow your brains out. Gaby thought, I have seen an actual gun.

After school she and Solosolo raced and chased each other screaming amongst the wild mad fennel, two metres high, rolling down the bulldozed spill from Whelan's tip, not stopping until they were wounded by a brick or buried spring.

The white girl thought, my life is starting. She was alive all day all night. The best part was when Meg left home to sell at the markets and Gaby and Frederic were free to do weird shit in Zork. In her ignorance, she did not miss being online at all.

One Sunday Gaby went to *lotu*, which was Samoan for church and prayers. Church, her mother cried. You can't. This might have become a family story if there was a proper family anymore.

Frederic had a plan to steal a new modem and to access his neighbour's phone line. He would not tell her how he might do that, but she never doubted he would do it and it would be against the law. They did their homework side by side and criticised their fucked-up parents. They ate pizza and searched for gold and jewels in the tunnels of the world of Zork. At this stage, she was the bossy backseat driver. Go there. Do that. Pick up. He smelled of lavender and his cheek was smooth.

Blind cars and feral trucks roared up and down Royal Parade. The trams rang their bells. No-one had any clue that behind that peeling pale-blue door there lived grues, zorkmids, and dwarves. Frederic introduced new actors and renamed the old cast. Thief was the first renamed identity.

'Thief' in Zork became 'Dad' in Frederic's version. The differences were not so great.

Like Thief, Dad carries a large bag. He is never seen by light of day. He likes to wander around the dungeon. He likes to take things from you. He steals for pleasure rather than profit, so he only takes things you have already seen. Of course he prefers valuables but he is often drunk (see *shickered*) and takes worthless stuff by mistake. From time to time he examines his take and discards booty he doesn't like. He may occasionally stay with you in a room but more likely he wanders through and rips you off. For a long time Gaby thought that this was fiction.

'Pick up sword' and 'kill dwarf' both give a good feel for Zork-talk. However, the machine will understand you if you type 'put the lamp and sword in the case'.

I would tell you more but it would be wasted on you, Mr Moore, Gaby said to the unwashed fugitive she could not see. Who could have foretold the straggling hair on his upper lip? Zork, she said, begins in total darkness. You have to 'get lamp' and then you can 'take', and 'drop' and 'examine' and 'attack' and 'climb'.

She emerged from her secret summer pale as a vampire just off the boat.

Stop, eject, play.

Celine said she had become a thick-waisted 'hoyden'. She blamed McDonald's.

Stop, eject, play. She returned to Bell Street High a wonder to the big-hair girls and the white-shoe boys. So many kids had NES consoles. They played Super Mario which Gaby had never seen. She hung with the Samoans who hadn't seen it either.

By winter when the Samoans were mad for football, Frederic had still not got his phone line back. They were enclosed in their own world.

Fast forward.

They could hear the animals in the zoo, the crowds at Carlton Football Club. They did not prefer one to the other.

Meg promised an NES console so they could play Ninja Gaiden.

Zork was under new management. Its name was changed to Wank.

All the terrace houses have been restored by the Troll except one with a grungy blue door.

>*west*

The house has two windows.

>*open window*

The window is locked.

>*break glass*

The window is barred.

>*turn doorknob*

The lock is broken. The door swings back and you are in the hallway which is tangled with old bicycles and flyers from Safeway. There is a parcel on the floor.

>*get parcel*

The parcel is addressed to Frederic Matovic. You are Frederic Matovic.

>*open parcel*

In your hands you hold a Phoenician blue garment with gold embroidery on its hem.

>*take off clothes*

They have no value in this game.

>*put on gown*

You are wearing the gown. It is so light and DIAPHANOUS against your bare skin. You have become a girl.

>*you are a pervert. go west*

You are in the kitchen. On the table is a baggie of Sumatran grass.

>*get weed*

A passage leads to the west and a dark staircase can be seen leading upward. To the south is a small window which is open.

>*go south*

You are likely to be eaten by Meg.

>*go south*

This is the last time you will be warned about the fierce and random Meg. You find yourself in a narrow east–west alley.

>*go east*

You face a brick wall.

>*go west*

In the distance is an overgrown garden containing the wet mushy packaging of stolen goods. To the right is a red corrugated-iron wall. There is a hole in the door and the wall. A chain is threaded through the door and is padlocked.

>*pick up doormat*

There is a key under the doormat.

>*get key*

The key is blue and glowing faintly.

>*unlock*

>*unthread chain*

You are inside a musty room where long-dead cats have passed their lives. Their ghosts swim in disinfectant. There is also an odour of mothballs. To the east are racks of clothing, fur coats and brides' dresses from long ago. To the west is an unmade bed. To the north is a desk. On the desk is a computer.

>*turn on computer*

The screen reads: You are standing in an open parkland east of a row of old white terrace houses.

>*take off gown*

How can you be a girl when you have a penis? Before you is a cherub boy with strong legs and breasts. Her nipples turn out, L and R.

>*go down*

There is no down.

>*go up*

There is no up. This is one of the locations you are transported to randomly when you least expect it. The boy has breasts, the girl has a canna lily, a poisonous flower that will make you vomit if you swallow. Anything is possible in your life.

Fast forward. Play. Gaby was totally in love with his black lacquered fingernails, long hair, sibilant voice. I would do that for you, she said to him. I wouldn't mind.

The voice on the microcassette was peeled of all protection. Was she alone? She said she had made the boy quiver and had smelled the Selsun in his hair. The fugitive lived on cheese and apples. He pictured Frederic, disconnected once again, pining for a modem, selling second-hand clothes at Flemington markets. He smelled the stink of tanneries, abattoirs and the heavy-metal mud, saw Footscray Park, the awful palm trees, unnatural in the poison yellow light.

Fast forward. Play. I didn't mind anything stinky, Gaby said. I did his nails for him. And shaved his legs.

16

What was spooky about the house in Patterson Street had nothing to do with murders or the bad vibe left by the White Knights Motorcycle Club. Everything could be traced to sad parents coming and going with no explanation, one sleeping in his office in his socks and underwear, the other attempting to plant flowers, shouting shit, hurling her trowel against the garden fence. Fast forward. Gaby tried to stay away. Saturdays Frederic had to work with his mum at the Trash 'n' Treasure. Fast forward. Gaby hung out with Troy. Troy always travelled via the lanes. He taught her how. In some parts the lanes had been colonised by the adjacent houses and they climbed the corrugated-iron fences, jumped across the beds of puntarelle, chased lizards within a hundred metres of Sydney Road.

Troy and Gaby smoked in the lanes but the true lanes existed only in Frederic's Mac IIx.

On two Saturdays Gaby rode her bike to Solosolo's house in Thomastown but then Solosolo said her mother was forcing her to tidy up for her *palagi* visitor, so forget it Gabes. But Peli was now a cable tech with Telecom and he had the perk of a Toyota HiAce van for use on public streets and highways all weekend.

Peli was six foot tall and over a hundred kilograms with his back tattooed 'Fa'a Samoa' to show he had no fear of pain. Peli was strong. He liked strong weed, thank you Troy, who brought him over to Frederic's place one rainy afternoon when the NES console had just arrived. Who else but stoned Troy would put those two together: Peli was like a refrigerator in board shorts; Frederic had satanic nail polish and eyeliner and careful floppy hair and a considered whispery voice. Peli was a big dog examining a whippet, sniffing, and pushing him with his paw.

But then they smoked and leapt to the Mac IIx, to Wizard's Crown, with magic weapons named Frost, Flaming, Lightning, Storm. Frederic was polite. He used Plus-category weapons so the visitor would pass out ('The opponent lies unmoving') but not die outright. The Samoans had no video games, but Peli was a duck to water. Dark, Doom, Soul, Demon and Death were his weapons of choice. If you are taken out by these weapons you are dead except with a resurrection spell.

Then Peli spied the Nintendo. It was his. He must play it now. Then he morphed into Small Mario, trotting left to right across the Mushroom Kingdom, collecting gold coins, dodging Bowser's armies. Peli was addicted. Could he come back? Frederic thought that would be so, so cool.

Here, by accident, was an unlikely gang glued together, Gaby said, by not much more than dope and games, or so it seemed. Frederic, Gaby, rabbity Troy, Solosolo and red-eyed Peli took the HiAce cruising in the early morning, hooning through the S's on The Boulevard, three passengers unsupported, rolling, bruising and cutting themselves amongst the racks and cables. The HiAce had the aerodynamics of a garden shed which was frustrating to its driver who was a 'man of spirit'. It was Peli's continually expressed desire to swap the Toyota engine for a Chevy

V8. He lay on a beanbag in the sleepout and performed the television news report in a deep blissed-out voice: 'A Toyota HiAce van marked with Telecom insignia drew away from a police car already travelling at a hundred and sixty kilometres an hour.'

Frederic loved Peli straight off. Peli was slow to get the hang of Frederic but he was there to be with Gaby. This was obvious to everyone but her. She was so dumb.

When they set off cruising in the HiAce, Gaby must sit beside the driver in the front.

Someone else should get a turn, she said.

Nah, you don't get it.

What don't I get?

Cappuccino, he said, meaning expensive white froth, black coffee. Drive the racists mad, he said.

Let Frederic sit here, Gaby said.

I don't drink that brand, Peli said.

The boys played Wizard's Crown and Mario Bros.

Frederic said no word about Peli's job, but surely this was the first thing he thought about Peli, that God had sent him a Telecom van. Peli could deliver him all the free phone lines that he wanted. Within days of their first meeting Frederic had 'located' a USRobotics Courier, way better than the modem he had lost. Gaby didn't see that at the time.

Frederic did absolutely not social-engineer Peli. Gaby said this. Peli's family would later say he had been conned by the *palagi* kids. This was so untrue. It was Peli who loaded the gear into the HiAce. It was Peli who drove so carefully along the shadowy streets. Fast forward. Play. Gaby was beside him, natch. It was her job to keep her eyes skinned for pods, those pieces of municipal furniture you never notice until you do, foot-high metal Mario mushrooms everywhere, parked in clear suburban sight, melancholy purple in the yellow streetlights so common in those Melbourne nights. The pods were packed with phone lines like spaghetti squash, waiting to connect with that new modem and catapult you into teenage worlds of wonder unimaginable in Patterson Street Coburg or almost anywhere on earth that year.

Later Gaby would be persuaded that perhaps Peli had a conflicting sense of loyalty. He did not hate Telecom like everybody else did. Telecom gave him a good job and a vehicle. It did not occur to anyone that the way they slagged off Telecom might have been offensive to him. In any case. For whatever reason. Peli wouldn't touch the pods. Troy, on the other hand, got his beaky nose inside the pod. Troy hooked a line, stripped its wire, attached alligator clips and ran the hundred metres of cable, an umbilical cord, a garden hose, like a shadow along the front of those suburban fences, then around the corner to the van. Meanwhile the driver played Tetris, super-cool.

Then Gaby saw the delicious dark side of Frederic, the kid who had already spent two years flying online solo, messing with two different computers, learning to write programs, connecting with local BBSs and doing mischief on his own account. He was the sort of alienated boy who might have set fires down by the Merri Creek but it was way more fun to invade and incinerate a certain local BBS (Pacific Fire) which had banned him. Rewriting Zork was cool and retro, but by the time he got a replacement modem and Gaby caught her glimpse of the online universe,

Zork seemed like *Play School*. Frederic had traded a set of passwords for the local dial-up number for Minerva, a system of three Prime mainframes in Sydney.

It was certainly less *convenient* to go online via one hundred metres of cable, but it was a rush as well, to be faster and smarter than anyone, to be a trickster amongst governments and corporations run by complacent admins, with carelessly protected networks. These were anywhere you looked. From Peli's HiAce Frederic could stroll unhindered into a massive computer known as Altos. Watch, watch, he said, and if Gaby did not know what she was seeing, Frederic told her. He was sweet and patient and excited too. He gave Altos the digital version of a masonic handshake. And Altos thought he was a fucking corporation.

Crammed inside that van with fuggy boys, Gaby was no longer the tangle-haired cherub dribbling a football across the green in Parkville. She was five kilograms heavier. Her breasts pushed in against Frederic's back. Her cheek was against his cheek and she liked that he had stolen the modem. As his pretty fingers fluttered like moth wings across the keys, she wandered from world to world in a universe she had not known existed.

Now she understood how it had felt to him to lose his phone line. Being REALLY online was like Zork to the millionth power. From a dark street in sleepy Moonee Ponds, she was teleported into NASA. Frederic passed her the keyboard and she could write nothing better than FOO WAS HERE. How embarrassing, she said on tape, please don't report that. No-one would believe it anyway.

17

Gaby said, We had to deal with Dad aka the Thief aka Matty Matovic. He was snake-eyed, slim with a pool-hall hunch, always stalking around some imaginary table. He was drop-dead handsome until you saw his missing teeth. Also: he was bitter. He favoured white T-shirts and lamb's-wool sweaters, even on a rainy night. Like when we were summoned, Gaby said, to his back corner of Toto's with his unsold copies of *Direct Action*, grey and sodden, on the table. He looked more like a betting man, but he really was a fence, Gaby said: I thought, I have seen a gun. I have seen a fence. My life was turning out quite well.

Frederic's father wouldn't look at me, but I could not help looking at him, so creepy but also graceful, rolling a cigarette with his long yellow fingers. He felt me watching and he twisted his body sarcastically – which he could really do – and tossed the menu at his son.

Saw your mate Peli, he said to Frederic. We waited. His eyes were in that state we then called OWTH (offended-waiting-to-happen). Frederic hid behind his fringe, studying the menu.

Hey. Dad rapped the table.

I could have slapped his face.

Frederic said he would like lasagna and a can of Coke.

Hey.

Frederic flicked his hair back. What?

You, he said, having no clue he was addressing a genius.

Your mate, the Thief said. Peli. You never told me he worked for Telecom. He helped me shift some stuff to Melton Self Storage in his van.

I'm hungry, Frederic said.

I knew the Thief would never pay for me so I said I was on a diet.

He put his stained hand across his mouth, just like a girl whispering in class. You know what trashing is? he hissed. Of course we knew. Like trashing a hotel room? I suggested just to watch him curl his lip. No, sweetheart, like picking up the trash from Telecom.

I told him I didn't think that would be his sort of thing. He looked at me. Up and down, as if he were astonished I could speak. He said, Girlie, you wouldn't know 'my thing' if it bit you on the bum.

I knew what Break and Enter was. I said that sounded like what he had in mind, but he wasn't interested in me.

You'd only be taking waste paper from the bloody government, he told Frederic. If they wanted it they wouldn't throw it out.

Frederic said he wasn't sure.

What if I talked Mum into reinstating your phone line?

She won't, Frederic said, but he looked my way, signalling: we wanted this.

Not interested, son?

Frederic licked his lips. I thought, oh shit, is this going where I think it is?

You and Peli. He's got the wheels. And you'll know what's worth snaffling.

He tried and failed to tousle his son's hair. Then he

called the waitress and considered her body and ordered one lasagna and a glass of water.

He told us that his mate had told him that they had some interesting devices in those Telecom exchanges. He knew they were devices that should be studied. His mate could use the hardware, but he reckoned the waste paper was where the money was, thousands of Saudi credit card numbers, people who think nothing of putting a BMW on their Amex.

Dad, your mate's a wanker.

But all Dad wanted, he said, was for Frederic and Peli to pick up the recycling. He didn't need them to hang around reading it. They could pick it up and piss off home. Study it at their leisure there. If they found anything interesting, they could copy it down. They could have it. It was theirs. They could even share it with Miss Uptight here. Then Peli could bring the bag to him in Brunny.

You'll get ripped off, Dad. You won't know what you're selling.

So you don't want your own telephone line?

Apparently Gaby and Frederic wanted a telephone line more than anything that I, Felix Moore, could ever imagine. So when Frederic stood up, when it was clear he intended to walk away, when Gaby should have been relieved, she was, she admitted to me, disappointed.

Frederic said he didn't want the lasagna. He would think about the offer.

Bullshit, said Matty Matovic. Is that fucking mascara running down your face?

Gaby had to rush to catch him at the door and then, in the spotlights of the cars turning right from Queensberry

265

Street, he kissed her and she held him and he told her how he loved her and that was all that mattered in his life. He said he wanted to marry me, she said. I think I cried. We walked back to Park-o-tight together, and I was in love, and I do believe it was then, on that night, I learned that deep in the maze of Telecom the techs scrawled user names and passwords, restricted 800 numbers, 'secure' information that they then threw in the bin, scraps of paper, cigarette packs, the backs of envelopes, on yellow dockets. There the honey massed, in thick black plastic bags, in dumpsters, a harvest worthy of a dungeon and a poison moat. Pick up key.

In the 'twisty little passages' of the computer underground, Gaby said, there was a species dedicated to the collection of discarded information, furtive scholars, jesters, fools, hackers, phreakers, practitioners of the black art of recycling who picked the locks of Telecom exchanges and, like dung beetles busy with their ancient occupation, rolled their holy shit into the night. The passwords and user names would be useful in so many ways e.g. when you got an actual phone line you could go online free of charge, and clicky clacky there you would be: lying in bed with your BFF, jumping off the Hamburg springboard, shooting the shit, hanging out on the bridge where no-one knew the girl was a girl.

Dad was a thief, but for Fallen Angel and Undertoad (as they would be known) the highest value of this information was best appreciated in terms of the culture of the gift.

If you were us, Gaby said on tape, above the noise of running water, you gave the info to other hackers in a BBS. One hard-to-get 800 number got us invited into a private

BBS, then past the rope of a restricted BBS we never guessed existed. Fallen Angel and Undertoad were quickly cool. They talked to Justum. They met Quark. They got higher up the pecking order.

Peli was never a thief. No-one ever asked him to be one either. Even Frederic had never picked a lock before but when the first one popped, Gaby said, he was so completely hacktified. We were IN. Running, white bright neon light. Flinders Lane exchange, 3 am Sunday morning, oh man, you cannot know, IN IN IN, black trash bags, bat wings, unimaginable, to ourselves I mean. We were so swift, so cool, and back outside before Peli got to the second level on Tetris. Who knew he had Tetris syndrome? Go, go, I screamed. Go, go, go. And he was stuck to the screen like a fly to flypaper, illuminated, and the bloody cops cruised past. But nothing happened, because nothing ever happened, and the only consequence was: Meg finally placed an order to reinstall a phone line. Then we would have everything we needed to fly around the world, like they say Satan does, all night. We would enter through the weak front doors of systems, build our own backdoors to guarantee return even when the admin dopes got off their arses and fixed the hole. You've got no idea how easy it was back then, she told me. People would use their own names for passwords. We would wipe away our meece tracks, return through that back door to read pissed-off messages from admins who we roasted, toasted, flamed to fucking death. We abandoned Zork forever.

Undertoad and Fallen Angel both had school of course. There was Ritalin involved in consequence, and this was the giddy, high, overstimulated time, the night-before-

Christmas sort of thing, when they were innocent but not at all, when they lay naked together and did things they thought they had invented and knew the possibilities of life were about to become wilder and weirder than anything their hippie parents dreamed. They were bound together, grown together, wrapped like strangler figs around each other's trunk, inseparable, waiting for a dial tone.

18

Frederic's mother had her temperament upgraded with a huge TV, a VCR, a refrigerator, two air conditioners. Then everyone was perfectly sedated, playing Mario Bros. Suddenly Meg liked me, Gaby said. It was an unexpected side effect.

Stringy Meg Matovic folded her black balletic legs beneath her and snuggled up beside the Blondie child. She flicked ash onto the floor and begged the child to teach her Mario Bros. Technically, she was unteachable, the most awful player you ever saw, yelling, screaming, falling into blackness, hitting the invisible block, being killed by the Firebar, missing all the Bloobers, a giggling fool, happy to die at the hands of Goombas and Koopas and Buzzy Beetles, shouting like a soccer mum. Meg was possibly bipolar. She was certainly the first parent Gaby met who was a blatant stoner. She crashed her van on the Eastern Freeway. She stayed at home on school days, getting high, waiting for Telecom to show up.

Teleprofit, Telescum, Frederic called it, hissing and narrowing his kohl-lined mystery eyes. Hackers hated Telecom, he said. Telecom were morons who could not even use their own technology. The line noise was so bad you got logged off continually and the faster your modem the worse the problem was. Soon they'd have a modem with error correction, but not that year, not yet. Telecom were jackboots. They could raid your house, tap your phone line and seize your equipment any time they wished. Service? They could not even give you a phone line when you asked for one. Oh no, you must wait three fucking weeks.

Mrs Matovic resigned from Mario Bros. She took up Wizard's Crown and hogged it so much Peli, direct from work at six o'clock, had to play it with her. Meg was way too flirty for her age. Groan. She never knew a black person in her life. Scream. She absolutely loved them. She got poetic about the Samoans' size and colour and their frizzy hair. She wanted to live in the tropics, and always had. She and Frederic were going to run away to Nimbin and live off papaya and 'be really healthy like Samoans'.

Peli had been back to Samoa only once. He had been pissed off beyond endurance by houses with no windows.

Gaby noted Meg laid her hand on Peli's knee so when Solosolo stormed outside and slammed the door, well, of course she knew the problem i.e. Meg was a hundred. Peli was nineteen. She followed her best friend across The Avenue to the place where she had once had rabies.

She's awful, she said. I'm sorry.

Solosolo spun around and her face was bunched up like a fist.

Don't you shit on my brother, she said.

I didn't shit on anyone.

Telescum. Teleprofit. You never bloody stop.

So?

Didn't you notice but? My brother bloody works for Telecom.

He's Peli. He's not Telecom.

Don't make me hit you, bitch.

270

Soley, I'm your friend. Please don't call me that.

Well, you get Frederic to show him some respect.

We do.

You're going to put 240 volts down the phone line? That's your plan. You're going to kill Telecom workers.

That was a joke.

Why do you think our father brought us to this awful *palagi* country?

Gaby saw the point of view. But she also knew how much her Samoan friends didn't like Samoa. Didn't like it here. Couldn't stand it there. Women had to spend their whole life making food, all day, every damn day, hot rocks, fire, how many Samoans does it take to get a pizza?

OK, I'll be the bunny: why did your father bring you here?

Shut up. Peli did what was asked of him. He got the education. He got the job. So when you call it Telescum you piss on my whole family.

No.

And then you make him go and rob Telecom.

I make him?

You think he likes Frederic? You're joking. Frederic's just your pimp. You sit beside Peli in the van. And then you piss on him. You're lucky I'm a Christian. Soley's eyes were black, unknowable. You're lucky I'm a Christian or I would bite your pretty face.

Gaby thought, she has a temper. It will pass. But when she came back into the sleepout she saw all the bullshit in Peli's eyes. Before she went outside she had been sitting on the floor beside him, but now she moved away. He looked at her all mulish with his heavy chin and fluttery eyes.

What had she ever said or done to make him act like that?

So now she stopped sitting in the front seat and then, without a word being spoken, they were at war. Why? What right? He drove stop and start, went too fast, scraping along a tram on Swanston Street.

They had all – everyone agreed – retired from trashing so what then happened should never have happened. Dad went direct to Peli. If Peli did it, he did it for himself, but then Frederic could not let him run it on his own. Then Gaby had to go. Then Solosolo came too, acting as if it was all Gaby's fault. Well, hello. Who was paying Peli?

Frederic rode in the front. Solo and Gaby were not talking but they had to ride together, alone, between the racks of cabling equipment, wrapping themselves in mover's quilts and straps. Peli made the ride as nasty as he could, taking them through seasick curves. At the end of the journey they hit a speed bump and they were in the lane behind the East Kew exchange. Gaby had big black yard bags. When Frederic popped the lock Peli's face was imprisoned by the Tetris glow.

The trashing at East Kew was fast and easy except, as was made clear later, something happened to Peli while the others were inside. The police had cruised past the lane, seen the van, seen the illuminated black face, and come to have a 'chat'. They were polite, allegedly they 'made inquiries'. They were informed that Peli was 'waiting to drive his boss home'. It was three in the morning but Peli was a Telecom employee in a Telecom uniform and a Telecom van. The police did not regard this as 'suspicious activity'. If they parked their car in the street, it was only so they could buy some Cokes and Chiko Rolls. They were eating them when they heard the van engine and saw the 'vehicle' emerge from the back lane faster than they would have expected, given the size of the speed bump. The 'black gentleman', spotting the police car, waved his hand in greeting.

He had no-one in the passenger seat. To the police this meant the boss was bullshit. They observed the van 'proceed in a southerly direction', at an estimated sixty kilometres per hour, and they were wondering, they later said, what to make of the absence of the boss, when the van made a right-hand turn and, as it vanished from sight, the driver accelerated so hard the squealing tyres could be heard from blocks away.

They turned on all the bells and whistles and set off in pursuit which had the comic effect of making the Telecom van accelerate even more. Clearly it was not rational for the driver to expect that his Japanese bread box might outrun a Holden Commodore VN SS, but that is what he seemed intent on, heading along Studley Park Road then left onto Walmer Street where it became clear he was unstable, for he chose, he actually *selected*, the Yarra Boulevard, a serpentine progression of loops that had already, two weeks ago, brought a Porsche unstuck.

The magistrate asked if they had considered slowing.

No, they had wished to apprehend the suspects.

Suspect, the magistrate corrected.

Yes, Your Honour.

Inside the dark van, Gaby could feel the fury, see the flashing lights, as they began to tip. She accepted a blanket and wrapped herself head to toe. Then they lay together, the three of them, clinging onto the wire-mesh door of the equipment cage.

Frederic said, Here it is.

Then they felt, very briefly, their stomachs float, and then their bodies became hostile to each other, on and on, then stillness and a loud hissing.

And it was Solosolo who was on her feet first, who kicked the back door open to confront a bright-lit stage.

Solosolo twisted her ankle. Gaby knew she would be blamed. Frederic saw Peli, his eyes closed against the quartz-white glare, by the riverbank. He was holding his hands in the air, slowly turning around as if to show that he had no weapon. He did 360 degrees then kept on going. Then, with his broad beautiful back to the police, he jogged twenty paces to the Yarra River and dived in.

Frederic, whose high forehead revealed a single trickle of bright red blood, grasped his glittery fingers behind his vampire back and slowly followed to the bank where, not having yet become 'the prisoner', he was free to stare at the water, black as anthracite, the lethal current no more visible than electricity beneath its gleaming skin.

19

The Hawkesbury River writer-in-residence had made himself at home, which is not to say that he appeared physically comfortable, but that he had a folding chair, and had become familiar with a domestic situation that required him, while clad in unflattering boxer shorts and a matted sweater with unravelling sleeves, to lay his trousers on a rock to dry. His beard had filled in somewhat, and his hair had reached a stage where an undergarment was required to keep it out of his watery eyes. Also, he had a dog, which was in itself sufficient to make him appear (if he was ever unfortunate enough to be observed) a local. The dog was the right sort, a short-legged blue-heeler bitch. Of course she was not his dog at all. She was an opportunist who had the manners to remain and doze a while after she had eaten. He called her Lizzie.

It had long been the fugitive's 'character' to eschew all vanity, and yet he would have admitted, had he been caught in the act, that he was indeed keen to tan his city legs. This was not vanity, but part of blending in, and with time his knees acquired a certain smooth brown texture such as might be expected of a river rat.

On the other hand, of course, he had the larger of his two cassette players in his lap and he was zipping back and forth through what had once been eighty-five metres of screeching tape searching for a few centimetres where Celine was not talking about her marriage. The tape had been accidentally exposed on a sunny windowsill, so the length to which it had been stretched was anybody's guess. But somewhere (fast forward, pause, rewind, play) he expected to find an account of the death by drowning of a young Samoan. In his mind's eye he could already see the police car with its blue disco lights flashing in the dark black skin of the Yarra River. He listened with his head cocked, at the same time keeping a windblown eye on the Hawkesbury River, the ultramarine sky, the hard blue water, the tiny chop, numerous anonymous craft, any one of which might contain his enemies. Also, the water police were out today and there was a single Tupperware cruiser put-putting out beyond the mangroves.

None of this was as he would have imagined, for the terrifying truth (it seemed) was that he was so unsuited to solitude that he would have almost welcomed a visitor. Now, at the sight of a heavy-set dark-haired man crossing the deck of the Tupperware cruiser, seeing the bright orange heels of his sneakers, he felt such a wild surge of dangerous hope that this might be Woody Townes.

Celine was talking about her marriage and Gaby's difficulties at school and he could choose to look at that as narcissistic, or consider that she was being a better human being than he was. What had he done, once, to acknowledge his missing wife and children? Was this because he was an arsehole? Or was it beyond the habits of reportage? Or was it that when his family threw him out he just closed the door and sealed it? He had no tolerance for pain.

A light aircraft passed over, too high to interest him. Meanwhile Celine was talking about acting in commercials, and what a relief that was for her.

The man on the cruiser was a dead ringer for Woody Townes.

Was he waiting for Woody to rescue him, even when he knew Woody was his enemy? Felix Moore assumed he was now known to the government of the United States and although it seemed hysterical, it might not be fantastical to discover that he could be rendered and imprisoned until he betrayed Gaby, even if he had been unable to find any sign of her expected animus against that nation, which had suffered, so to speak, collateral damage. It was not fanciful to think that paid mercenaries might strip him naked, put him on suicide watch so he could not even kill himself. Not so many days previously he had tried to catch a fish with a handline. He was, as always, inexpert, and the sight of the worm's response to the hook filled him with fear of pain. He tortured the worm and drowned it and didn't catch a thing.

Now he hoped the Duracells would run out so he would have an excuse to wave for help, or Woody would save him, as he saved him before, rescued him from his own reckless pursuit of principle, helped him avoid his own destruction, pulled him back from a situation his conscience had demanded he embrace.

Fast forward. Play. Where else (the voice groaned basso)? Where else but Carlton would it be a big *scandale* to be cast in a commercial? Fast forward. Her tribe had sat in a circle on the dusty floor and excommunicated her from the collective. Only the junkie would not raise his hand in condemnation. Stop. Fast forward. Play. In the straight world, meanwhile, the commercial was a big success. Forward (squawking). Play. She had secretly (seeeeee-creeet-ly) deposited half the money from the commercial in her own savings account. How else would she ever be able to afford to run away? Fast forward. Play. Sandy had caught her. Henceforth he was good. She was bad. She was marooned in Coburg. Fuck. Fast forward. Play. She had to act the wifey with the branch members who could never seem to meet at the electoral office but must come back to the house. Woody was on the finance committee. Arsehole, she knew he had engineered the move to Coburg.

Without pausing the machine, the fugitive rose from his seat. When he turned to pay attention to his drying laundry, he revealed the back of his brown legs to be pale as the belly of a flounder. He turned the damp side of his trousers to the afternoon sun.

Peli was about to drown. He had found that spot before then lost it.

Matrimonial difficulty had caused Celine to double her sleeping pills which made her groggy all day but wide awake at 2 am when the police called. How come Sando didn't stir? she would have liked to know. The voice on the phone asked her was she Celine Baillieux. Yes she was. This was Sergeant someone of the Victoria Police. Did she know where her daughter was right now?

She thought rape. She could not say the word. Her throat closed over. She was drugged, and confused, also angry that Sando could lie naked like that, chaste and naked with a pillow across his head. She said she would come to the station straight away. Later he would blame her for leaving him to sleep. It was an aggressive act, he would say.

She rushed from the front gate, thinking she had failed to make her daughter sufficiently afraid of life. She drove along Moreland Road and headed south on High Street then into wide empty Hoddle Street where the railway line ran parallel beneath its lethal web of wire. The grass in the median strip was mangy as a worn-out dog. She remembered passing Ramsden Street where she recognised the site of the Hoddle Street Massacre: that banal suburban railway crossing, that dreary low billboard from which hiding place the assassin had shot thirty people, one by one. She was spooked by the low dark roofs beneath the poison sky, the plain unlovely park, all these somehow melded with her daughter's fate.

In the twenty minutes it took to arrive at Gaby's side, her head swam with images of evil things. She relived the night Dominick Swayne was murdered, stabbed to death in the backseat of a parked car. She had not known him, but she knew the poor pregnant girl who did it, and when the girl was arrested Celine was taken to Russell Street police headquarters, and that hospital in Commercial Road where they injected 10 ml of Valium in her bottom. That had happened just up the road, two kilometres from this police station, slick and modern as a bank, with blue and white checks like the band on a police hat.

Her commercials had cursed her, made her famous. Now she fretted someone at the station would identify her. MP's wife. MP's daughter. She was both relieved and disappointed to be a nobody and be made to wait on those long rows of vinyl chairs backed against the untidy noticeboard with its twenty missing persons, three of whom were Aboriginal, she had counted, and remembered, a chaos of bright-coloured violence, alcohol, police recruiting, all in contradiction of the bleak corporate order of the waiting room. There was a front desk and five tall dark wooden doors, all locked. In another situation they might have suggested farce. From these portals there now surged bright-eyed graffiti rats, accompanied by their pissed-off parents. Celine's name was called as 'Baily'. She was escorted through a locked door by a female officer or constable with a flustered red appearance. The actress observed that she had a particular way of doing 'cop face', speaking very slowly, very deep. Here, in the ashy air of the inner corridors, the policewoman was not prepared to answer her questions. The sergeant would inform her of the facts directly. Celine passed the statuesque Samoan girl standing behind a glass pane, looking out as at a distant ocean view. Her handsome face betrayed not even a flicker of recognition.

The interview room, so called, smelled of tomato sauce like the Caulfield races. Mrs Baily was to wait for the sergeant there. She had noted that there was no desk and that the chairs were chaotically arranged. She managed to observe the Big Mac box lying on the floor before she saw, like a discarded blanket thrown into a chair, the child she had brought into the world. Gaby's face was burnished, closed. There was a scratch below her eye.

What happened, darling?

Where is Frederic?

Has someone hurt you, darling?

What have they told you?

Gabrielle, has anybody harmed you?

Harmed *me*? she said indignantly. You haven't got a clue. They've taken Frederic.

Very well, darling, I'll get someone.

Gaby wound herself in her blanket and let her mother discover the door was locked.

We had an accident. OK? We rolled the van.

What van?

Solosolo's brother ran away.

Who has a van?

I think he might be dead, she said.

Pause. Rewind. Play. I think he might be dead.

No-one told Celine that the dead boy loved her daughter.

She must not try to hold her child. She offered a small pack of tissues and was pleased it was accepted. She told her that she loved her, which was like throwing wet potato into boiling oil.

It's not about you. Leave me alone.

The sergeant would later be tabloid-famous, but on the night of Peli's death he did not look like a candidate for jail. He was a handsome sort of man, whose greying close-barbered looks would have suited the pilot of an Ansett flight, or of those ship's captains they had once used to promote Ardath cigarettes. He did not like Celine Baillieux.

It's dangerous out here, Mum.

I know.

You know do you? Is that a fact?

He did not require an answer. He lectured Celine about all the kids he knew who never had much of a chance, Mum. Their parents were poor and ignorant and alcoholic. But what about this little girl of hers? She has been an accessory to Break and Enter. Or hasn't she had a chance to tell you that part? He bet Celine would know a terrific lawyer. Frank Galbally was probably a mate of hers? Was Frank her mate?

Celine had not been thinking of a lawyer. She had imagined she was there to witness him interview her daughter. This was apparently not the right thing to say.

Anything else I should do for you, Mum? Interview? Park your car perhaps?

She said she hadn't meant it like that.

What would 'that' be?

So she grovelled.

That's all right, Mum, he said, it's been a pretty rough night for everyone.

That 'rough night', said Celine, had presumably included recovering Peli's body from below the Hoddle Bridge, and a session with Matty Matovic who, having been called in as Frederic's father, had signed an autograph for an aging fan, and then got himself tangled in the investigation to the extent that his son had accidentally 'assisted the police' with more inquiries than they could have made without his help. None of this information was provided by the sergeant at the time. Nor, for that matter, did he do what he was obliged to do, that is, interview Gaby with a parent as a witness.

Perhaps he wanted a drink or his wife had just left him or he simply would not have an actress order him around. Perhaps he already had what he needed to put Dad in Pentridge for two years. So why would he waste his time typing up a needless interview?

Did he think, I'll 'caution' her then fuck the rest of it?

In any case, he cautioned Gaby until she cried and then he gave her a Kleenex and opened the door. He did not quite tell them to piss off.

Mum, he said, you are free to take her home.

But you haven't interviewed her.

The sergeant seemed too tired to laugh. Do you want to leave, or do you want to stay? It's not a comfy way to spend the night.

Gaby said she could not leave till she saw her friend.

She's with her family, love.

I mean Frederic Matovic.

Everyone was with their families now, the policeman told her. Fred was with his dad. Her mum would look after her. Nice cup of cocoa, something like that. And by then he was shepherding (shoving) them up the hall, through the waiting room which was crowded with German back-packers.

Why did this sergeant hate Celine? Did he know she had thrown marbles beneath police horses? Was it just because of this that he walked them all the way to the car and folded up Gaby's police blanket so neatly?

Take care of her, Mum.

Gaby refused the front seat and climbed in the back.

The sergeant tapped sharply on the glass and waited until Gaby buckled her seatbelt.

As she pulled out into the road Celine still had no idea what had happened. She looked in her mirror and saw her daughter slip sideways out of her belt and lie on a hard bed of books and paper. Celine had no religion, no faith in anything much more than the fact that the lichen on a gravestone lived forever. She thought, God give me another chance to love my child.

20

It was just on dawn when they got home, Celine said. Gaby went to her room and locked the door. Sandy emerged from his office, dressed for work. His eyes were always pale in love or fury but this morning they were glass.

So he was at me from the get-go, she told the stretchy tape, demanding I tell him who was driving the van. How old were they? Who was charged? With what offence? How could she possibly leave the police station without learning the circumstances of her daughter's detention?

The sergeant had told her to go home.

So she did what the police told her to do? Since when?

On and on.

Years later, she said, this same sergeant was called before the court where the judge asked him why he took prisoners out of jail to eat at restaurants and visit 'known criminals'.

I do what I want to do with my prisoners, he said.

Celine washed her husband's cold, egg-encrusted breakfast dishes. There was no news on the radio. Sandy went into his office to take a call – in private. He returned to say that Matty Matovic (whom he had once called comrade) had been arrested for receiving. He was now on remand awaiting trial, but no-one could locate his wife with the result that Frederic, if Celine was even interested, was being held at Turana, aka, Parkville juvenile detention facility.

She shrugged.

He judged her for that, but why would the criminal Matovics be her concern?

Then Sando turned his attention to their daughter's bedroom, kneeling at the locked door, whispering like a monk.

Why this was so intolerable Celine still could not explain, years later. Nor could she excuse her own behaviour, for she had gone to her bedroom and locked that door. Thus she had been a child and was doubly in the wrong.

They did not know how she needed them both. She could never tell them even now. She had sat on the bed, listening to every sound. She heard her daughter open the door and admit the supplicant. Then they had locked themselves against her.

Her failure was unbearable. To her shame she took three sleeping tablets which provided a wet narcotic habitat. The earth moved around the sun. Satellites maintained their orbits. She heard the telephone, once, twice, a hundred times, who knows. When she dragged herself to the surface, she was astonished to find her husband was still in the house. He told her Peli Tuputala had drowned in the Yarra River. Did she know him?

No.

Neither of them knew the dead boy's rank and status, but Sandy was the one to sigh, as if it was Celine's job, only her job, to know their daughter's friends.

Why do I make myself appear so ugly? Celine wished to know on tape.

The writer thought, she had never seemed ugly, only spirited, emotional. She had always been so beautiful, so brutally self-critical, he would have forgiven her for murder.

Sandy left for a meeting with constituents. Celine sat at the dining-room table and tried to not need anything from her daughter. When she finally knocked on Gaby's door she was astonished to find herself wanted, even more surprised to see Gaby at her little student desk, already in a black dress and blouse, strapping on a high-heeled sandal. Her knees were bruised, her eyes were swollen and her mouth lopsided. Celine was permitted to make her sliced tomatoes on toast and Earl Grey tea.

Celine had not liked Frederic from the start, but she assumed Gaby had dressed like this to visit him in Turana. She asked would the girl like to be driven somewhere. Yes, she would, to Peli's family in Thomastown.

They set off around four o'clock, that is, peak hour for the building trades, travelling north along roads lined with warehouses: auto parts, steel sheds, garden equipment, Melbourne transport, interstate transport. Behind these light-industrial ramparts she discovered clusters of false-bright optimistic houses with dying lawns. Celine had never been to Thomastown before. She did not wonder at the large number of cars parked along Peli's street, signs that the grieving family was playing host to relatives, some of whom were approaching in that Boeing 727 presently leaving white scratch marks in the sky.

She was instructed to wait. She double-parked and watched the poor creature wobble on her unaccustomed heels. Celine had no idea of what was at stake. There were three steps to the front door and the girl tottered to the uppermost where, unprotected by a rail, she rang the bell.

The street was quiet and empty, each house a mausoleum. In the Tuputala home a curtain moved. Gaby made her way across the front lawn, to the high side gate. She let herself in.

Then the front door opened and a solid grey-haired man walked down the steps and out along the concrete path. If he had been a Sikh from Kuala Lumpur she would not have known. He had a slow, wide strut, big thighs, pigeon toes. He walked diagonally across the street and entered another house and of course she had no clue of where she was or what was happening, not even that every human being inside those houses knew the dead boy had been the victim of his love for Gaby Baillieux.

When Gaby emerged from the side gate her mother recognised Solosolo, hobbling on crutches, behind her. Gaby pointed to her mother's car and then Solosolo threw down her crutches. Sitting, crying, she flung a fist of dirt. Celine started the engine and unlocked the door. By the time Gaby was in the car the street was once more empty.

Celine asked her what was that.

Can we just go?

Celine stalled the car, started again and turned into a driveway, then reversed. At the same time she provided a handkerchief.

Shall we find Frederic? she asked brightly.

She had been so bloody weak, she thought. She had made herself a doormat when she should have taken charge.

You can just drop me where he is.

Do you know where that is?

You know, Gaby said.

Once Celine had delivered her to the parking lot of

Turana youth detention centre – like a suburban bank, she thought – she found herself dismissed.

How will you get home?

I'm not a baby, Gaby said, and followed the Volvo out onto Park Street and waited until Celine turned the corner.

Celine stopped at a newsagent in Brunswick and found Peli and Matty Matovic in *The Herald*. She learned the Tuputalas were sort of royalty. At home Woody's assistant was calling on the phone. Then Woody made her wait and wait. When he finally came on the line he was beyond his normal smarmy 'Mrs Quinn' sort of bullshit. He 'let her know' that he had been forced to squander a great deal of his 'social capital' to keep Sando's name out of the news.

This was a lie. Gaby was a minor. No-one could publish her name and her father must remain anonymous.

Next Monday morning Gaby went to school as normal. I most definitely, Celine told the tape, I most definitely encouraged her to 'see someone'. Please don't think I didn't. I knew she had to be in therapy, but I could not force her. I could not make her change a shoe if she didn't want to.

Meanwhile Sandy seemed protected by a carapace of blame. Fair enough, she thought. He was giving himself hives working for Bob Hawke's re-election. She was an awful wife, but she made him a healthy breakfast and watched him leave for the electoral office in the rain.

How could I have left him then, even if I had the money?

It was only three or four days later she had a telephone call from a woman who introduced herself as 'your daughter's bookkeeping teacher'. Her name was 'Miss Aisen' and she said she had just received some visitors and she hoped Mrs Quinn would receive them too.

Who are they?

They are on their way to see you now.

They turned out to be two young men with 'depressing zip-front track jackets' in 'dead' colours, sad maroon, gloomy green. One or both of them were from the Parkville youth detention centre.

The young men placed a worn tennis ball upon her scrubbed hardwood table and showed her how it had been slit. They invited her to squeeze the ball and look inside where she discovered a note, written in her daughter's hand.

Her daughter had been throwing balls into the Parkville centre in the middle of the night. Balls like this, the young men told Celine, normally contained marijuana but in this case they held letters addressed to a boy who had only stayed in Turana on a single night. He had been discharged from the facility before the balls arrived but the staff had been disturbed, they said, to recognise the 'ink'.

Actually Miss Baillieux, it's blood.

Whose blood?

They looked at her with pity.

Celine read: *Hullo BFF.*

She pointed out: Frederic's initials were FM, not BFF.

She was informed that BFF meant Best Friend Forever and was normally reserved by teenage girls for members of their own sex. *Hullo BFF, I will die without you, please let me in, please let me be with you. I am all alone in Aisen's class at Bullshit High. I cannot stand myself. I cannot bear life without you. We can get married. Ask me again I will get high just breathing the air coming out your nose.*
XXXXXXXXXX

Celine paid no attention to the blood business. Her first thought was, he isn't gay at all. She told the social workers it was romantic. Had they never done the same themselves?

Oh no, this was not romantic. This was self-damage. Her daughter was under severe mental stress.

Meaning what exactly?

She has been cutting herself.

Celine said, I thought they were ridiculous, but they left their business cards and a pamphlet about girls who cut themselves. I was such an idiot I let them take away her love letter.

Then Miss Aisen called again, basically ordering her to present herself at the school.

So, once more, she said, I was reminded Bell Street High was a dump. Also: I would never have sent my daughter here if I had known how huge the boys were, how they occupied all space, how smug and certain in their expensive sneakers and M. C. Hammer pants. No wonder her grades were so depressing.

I arrived in a sort of lumber room to discover Miss Aisen and a single Apple computer which turned out to be her own. She was less than middle-aged, wiry, a swimmer surely, with short grey hair, intense brown eyes, no makeup and a cotton frock she may have made herself. She had an unnerving gaze, a sort of uninhibited curiosity.

She said, I know you must get this all the time.

I thought, how have I fucked up now?

But she and her father used to see me at the collective. She could list the productions. She had been really upset to read I had been kicked out. Oh God, she was a fan. She asked me did I know who Solosolo was.

Yes.

Did I know they had had a fight, then she corrected me before I answered. It had been a physical fight. In the park, she said.

I see.

No, she meant the car park, the public park, the lane leading to the old man pub, where the big tree was, with the basalt boulders underneath. This was where the boys fought, and she said how much it disturbed her. What they fought about you could not tell, perhaps a wrong look yesterday, or a massacre centuries before. You would know there was to be a fight when you heard the audience gathering. Then, if you looked, you would most likely see the weaker boy, the one who knew he would be beaten.

Celine thought, too much information.

A boy would turn up first and stand beneath the tree. His pride did not allow him to be saved. Then his assailant would arrive and he would cuff and punch the first boy until he was on the ground where he was punched and kicked in the head and the girls would call out, You guys are animals, you guys are sick. Then the boy would go away. Then the girls would go inside.

And the point was?

The point was that Celine's daughter was the first girl to stand and wait in the shade beneath that tree, beside those jagged rocks. It was no secret: Gaby wished to fight with Solosolo, and each afternoon the staff had been pleased to see Solosolo walk straight past Gaby.

When Solosolo put aside her crutches Gaby spat at her, she whose family were now obliged to bury her brother Fa'a Samoa, and pay for airfares for their grand family, and feed them when they could barely afford to feed themselves. Solosolo slapped Gaby so violently you could hear it in the staffroom like a sound effect. Gaby was smaller, but always dense and solid. She ducked inside the tall girl's reach. She hit her at the balance point and brought her down, bare limbs on the gravel, and the boys were ugly as hyenas, dancing, loose-mouthed, and it took the shop teacher Mr Junor and Miss Aisen between them to pull the scratching girls apart.

I was gutted, Celine said. I pretended I had seen the wounds. I explained Gaby would not see a shrink, not anyone.

No, listen, Miss Aisen told me. She was kind to me. Listen, she told me. She laid her hand on my wrist and said my daughter was way brighter than her grades. She was attracted to the most difficult and interesting computer issues. She had a burning sense of right and wrong, of course I must know all that.

Of course, I thought, you are a socialist. Shut up, I thought. Don't tell me who my daughter is.

If I was lucky enough to have a daughter like this, Miss Aisen said, I would want to know she spent most of her day hiding in a drain beneath Pentridge Prison. A teacher at the primary had seen her come and go. Stop. Swap. Play.

After Peli died, said Gaby.

Rewind play.

After Peli died I was spied on. Everything I did was significant. If a boy fights a boy no-one cares, but if a girl fights a girl she must be psychologically disturbed. My teachers were so clever. They knew without a doubt that I was imprisoning myself as punishment for Peli's death. I was torturing myself by burying my body below Frederic's father's cell. I imagined Frederic was in prison so I had to be locked up too. If no-one would punish me, I would do it to myself.

I'm skinny, so I must be anorexic.

I'm a girl who eats lunch, so I must be fat.

I wear black, so I must be a goth or death punk.

I'm a death punk, so I must cut myself for thrills.

If they had taken the trouble to ask me I might have even told them I started sneaking down into the drain because of little Troy, my sole surviving friend. When the Samoans turned on us, Troy lost his protection. Now he was exposed e.g. to Jasim, a vast Lebanese kid who said he would execute him as a drug dealer.

No-one had ever stood beside Troy in his life. Obviously. Now we stood beside each other, at the midpoint of the drain or tunnel at a place where we could see the light at both ends. Troy said his father was a doctor. He said he was going to get a gang and bash Jasim. I told Jasim that Troy had renounced drugs. From that point Troy only sold after school from the lane beside my house. He stopped coming to the drain completely.

As for me, I was a person of interest to the authorities, so I went where no-one could counsel me or 'get you through your grieving' (please drop dead). None of them could imagine what I lost, but if I had known it was Miss Aisen who had her sights on me, I would have asked her please come in. She had the only thing I wanted: a 1988 Mac IIx she lugged up and down the stairs once a week. She had cruel-looking magpie eyes and a squishy secret sparrow heart. I did not know she was full of love and yearning and plans to change the world, so I did not let her guess how much I wanted what I wanted.

That Mac IIx was my only plan for life. Plus how to get a phone line and a modem. Then find Frederic. He would be on Altos in Hamburg. Even if he changed his handle I would know my BFF.

Hi, that u?

Yup.

That would be enough.

It was raining on that day Miss Aisen sooled my mum on me. I was in the drain alone, talking to Frederic in my mind, on my screen. Five centimetres of slimy water pushed in around my wrinkly toes.

I thought something like the following, more or less:

A dark staircase can be seen leading upward out of the drain. To the west is a small window which is open.

>go west

Inside is a white clean chamber. Frederic no longer wears his gown. His skin is like ivory. He is in a trance.

Celine came towards me and the light burned the edges of her silhouette and I didn't know if it was a man or woman, big or small, young or old. I thought she was a man i.e. INTRUDER. The flashlight made a second halo of her harm.

I pressed myself against the wall, in the shadow of a pier, listening to splashing feet.

You are in the cavern of cockroaches.

When the light rushed at my face I screamed and tore it free. I was mad, not nice, screaming keep out, stay away from me. Then I woke up, sort of, and there was my mother, bleeding where I hurt her arm. She was shivering, quivering. I put my arm around her and we limped towards the light like sewer rats. Outside on Elm Grove, beside the primary school, we were both embarrassed by ourselves. At home I ran a bath for her and made her bread and butter and sugar and drenched it in warm milk. What did I want? I watched her eat her baby food and I told her I was not cutting and then she told me Frederic's mother had taken him up to northern New South Wales. At least I knew he had not dumped me.

Celine asked would I be happier back at school in Carlton. I said I had to learn programming. This was maybe not a total lie, but what I really wanted was to hook up online. I imagined Frederic's fingers flying like moth wings all night long. Even now, when I cried myself to sleep, I knew he must be messing with root, account passwords, building back doors. My parents had to get me a computer and a modem. Then I would find Frederic on Altos. We would build a s3kr4t back room i.e. with just two members where we could invent, imagine, talk soft and dirty to each other.

I told my mother I must learn to program I didn't care how hard it was. I would be the biggest swot she ever met. I stared at her with such bright mad attention I knew I could draw her from the water like a yabby, put her in the pot and eat her up for dinner. I was a selfish little cow.

Celine made me take off all my clothes and checked I wasn't cutting. If this was creepy, WTF. I stood on my bed and she shone a flashlight on my not quite virgin thighs. To compensate me for this humiliation she would pay for private computer lessons with Miss Aisen. I was guilty about the money, so I gave her something in return, not much – I showed her the bottle of brown ink the idiots had thought was blood. She swore she had not read the letters, which was a lie. She apologised for believing stupid social workers. I could have asked for my own computer then, but I had no clue of how easy it would be. Miss Aisen had already told my astonished parents that it would be a 'crime' if I was hindered in my desire to learn.

21

Gaby delivered the first ten dollars to Miss Aisen. Thirty minutes later she was back home, sweaty, out of breath, holding a tiger snake in a jar against her little breasts. It would have freaked you, Celine said, to see the poisonous creature with its head squashed like a garlic clove. My daughter was glowing like she had just been kissed.

What about the lesson?

I have to get something.

You have to get something? What do you have to get?

The girl grinned and placed the viper on the shelf between the kidney beans and lentils.

What do you need for your lesson?

Don't worry about it, Gaby said. She'll make up the time tomorrow.

Pause.

Start.

A worker's cottage in Darlington Grove, Gaby told me, a block over from Patterson Street, with a super-loamy vegie garden. Aisen had been born there, in her mum's bed. It had been her mum who had improved the soil with chicken manure and lake weed. Her father had also been born in Coburg. He was Mervyn. He had grown up when it was all 'rock and rabbit farms', paddocks wild with boxthorn bushes and Cape broom. Some moron would always 'drop a match' and burn everything from McMahons Road right through to the lake, millions of sparrows and starlings rising in the air, blocking out the sun.

Miss Aisen had been taught at St Bernard's and Bell Street High then studied to be a secretary, then to be a bookkeeper and worked with IBM accounting machines which were already dinosaurs. Then she taught bookkeeping at Bell Street. She never married. She was careful with her money. When the Mac IIx arrived she could afford to buy one and thus became 'the oldest hacker in Melbourne'. Fast forward. Play. She was not a criminal. Stop. Fast forward. Play. She had seen Celine and Gaby emerge into the steamy drizzle from beneath the Pentridge Prison walls. That lovely actress, she had thought, all her talent, and there is her angry ugly daughter living in a drain. But that was what Miss Aisen was put on earth to fix. From each, to each etc. Fast forward. When Gaby arrived that first Saturday morning, she found her living in an island of white people. One neighbour was Mr Howard who trained the apprentices at the Government Aircraft Factory. Alice and Bob McNaughton were on the other side. He was 'with' a timber yard on Gaffney Street. He raced pigeons, you get used to them, according to Miss Aisen's dad. Melbourne's oldest hacker had once had a front garden but now it had a wheelbarrow, a rusty Subaru and a motor scooter with a fruit crate strapped onto the back.

Gaby arrived in shorts and bare feet. She edged sideways through a nest of bicycles and reached the front verandah where the boards were nice and cool. It was Miss Aisen's dad who answered her knock. Mervyn was short and wiry, in a working man's navy singlet, shorts and plastic thongs. He was what we might call 'a bit of a character', a pensioner yes, but also a frisky dog who wants to play. He carried a white tea towel across his brown shoulder and a dead tiger snake in his right hand.

Gaby had grown up with Labor Party 'characters'. She was also on familiar terms with the snakes of Merri Creek: browns, tigers, red-bellied black snakes too. They swam with their heads held high around the car wreck where Gaby had smoked with Solosolo.

You got a Tigger, she said.

That's correct, a Tigger. He had a walnut face and all sorts of knocks and blemishes on his pate. He grinned and showed a bright gold tooth.

I'm here to see Miss Aisen, she said. (The snake's head had been bashed.)

Did you meet him down the creek?

He was looking for a tête-à-tête. He asked, You know what that means?

Yes.

Of course you do.

He had comic eyebrows and bandy legs, sun-brown on both sides.

I got bitten by a taipan once, he said, opening the door for her.

I bet you did. (She had learned to talk like this by listening to her dad.)

Mervyn's thongs slapped against the morning light. The girl could smell burned toast, fresh-cut grass, water sprinkling on hot soil.

I thought that would be a bit fatal, a taipan.

Old wives' tail.

Did you use a tourniquet?

299

Beer and a Valium.

By the time she arrived in the kitchen she was smiling. It was a small room, painted a wild bright yellow, filled with sunshine, hanging herbs and garlic, high stacks of newspapers along the walls, a blackboard with rosters of names and dates, a laminex kitchen table with three odd chairs.

Mervyn continued out the back, through the flywire.

Your visitor is here.

The familiar computer was in front of her, the IIx that she knew from school.

Take it down the creek, Miss Aisen called, before it starts to pong.

Next to the computer was a modem, a bright red cradle. This was probably the only surviving coupler modem in Melbourne, but I didn't have a clue. I understood that you took Miss Aisen's normal everyday phone off the hook and placed it here, and I could, if I ever dared, if I ever got a sneaky chance, get onto Altos.

Miss Aisen wore short shorts and a sleeveless T-shirt and gardening gloves. She had a shiny sweaty face.

So, she said, you want to learn to code.

All I wanted was to get online. But I insisted on the code. Not baby language, I said.

BASIC is a proper language. The fun bits get you to the hard bits.

So I could write a program in BASIC?

And what did you want your program to do?

Fool around, I said, yearning for that bright red cradle.

Do you know what that is there?

What?

What you're staring at.

Is it a modem? I asked.

Have you seen a modem before?

Can you teach me?

Listening to the tapes, it was comical how Gaby highlighted her deceitfulness. She was her mother's daughter after all.

I'll teach you to program, Miss Aisen said. We can do that as a project, but we are not going to give up on BASIC.

I don't think I want that, no.

If you want to be serious. BASIC is exactly that.

Maybe not.

Was Miss Aisen intrigued by this resistance? Surely, yes, she was a teacher, but then her father was demanding a jar to put his snake in. He had thirty-four bottled snakes which he planned to bequeath to the Melbourne museum. She dealt with this issue and then returned to her pupil.

Gaby, what is it you really want?

Yeah, right.

I beg your pardon?

You'll get crabby.

I think we should trust each other a bit more than that.

When can I come back?

We haven't even started.

Yes, when could I come back?

You don't want a lesson now?

No.

Tomorrow morning if you like. But why?

I need to get something.

What do you need?

Can I really come back tomorrow morning?

Then Mervyn was demanding attention.

And so, of course, Miss Aisen went, as per usual because, as she told him, she was his doormat. And she gave up her bean jar and he coiled the snake inside it and poured the illegal formaldehyde and he finessed the coils with a piece of dowling. When he was finished she returned to her pupil but now with her father right behind her, polishing his horrible jar with his clean white tea towel.

What do you think of this, young lady?

The child became beautiful.

I brung a gift for you, he said.

The girl reached for the bottle and rubbed her index finger at the place where the snake's crushed head lay against the glass.

It's a beauty, she said.

I'll get you a little Super Glue to keep it safe.

Miss Aisen watched her father glue the lid and saw how the girl was filled with light. She watched her leave, that summer car-park hop, as she carried the bottled snake, dancing across the gravel. Who would not want, with all their heart, to be a teacher?

22

Of course the fugitive was on the Hawkesbury and never once laid eyes on the astringent little Aisen or inhaled her hallway, her kitchen floor polish, Stove Black, or 1950s plastics heating in the sun. Regardless, it was clear to him, inarguably so, that it was not merely an antique modem his subject had found, but surrogate grandparents who would, in their own ways, be prepared to love her unconditionally and thereby provide her with a history she had not even known she lacked.

Her first recollections of Darlington Grove are of soil, loamy, clay, dry, wet and are only interesting because they are so clearly disconnected from anything she could have experienced until that time.

All her language describing Mervyn Aisen (an 'old shoe' for instance) indicates a comfort she could not have felt when first meeting him. Indeed, on entering their kitchen, her intention was to deceive them both, something she pointed out not once (fast forward) but many times. She fled from her first lesson in order to fetch her collection of passwords and access numbers. You can't understand, she said. You can't possibly understand what I felt. I did not have to die. I WAS GOING TO USE AISEN'S MODEM. It was as if Frederic had anticipated this very moment and had made a stash of everything I would need when he wasn't by my side.

He already saw the shit ahead of us, and if our files were to be wiped or arrested we would store them where no-one would ever look. On paper. You've seen the Federal Police leaving those suburban houses with their cardboard boxes, floppy disks, hard drives, cables, modems. Did you ever see them with *The Lord of the Rings*?

Frederic stole two copies from Mark Rubbo in Lygon Street and we turned them into paper brains. We assigned numeric values to the ten most common letters a-e-i-o-u-h-n-r-s-t. (a=1 and t=10). Do you think the Australian computer crime squad would even open *The Lord of the Rings*? Would they see the pinpricks? Do they even know now, years later? A single volume held as many 800 numbers as there are blackberries growing beside the road to Eildon. In any case, the Altos twelve-digit NUA was in there: Book Three, Chapter Two, 'The Riders of Rohan'.

Gaby returned to Darlington Grove on the Sunday but then lost her nerve. She begged another lesson, ten more guilty dollars, lost her nerve again. It was stinky hot, she said, summer holidays. My mother was cast in a movie and was filming at Mount Macedon. I waited three days in an empty house then came back to the Aisens' so early in the morning that I was given the job of collecting the woodchips for their bath heater. My face was still bruised and yellow from the accident but they decided I was a good girl when I was actually a thief and burglar. I made lethal black tea the way they liked it, and two grilled cheese sandwiches. The old fellow went to see a man about a dog and I sat and waited, watching Miss Aisen swallow her dark brown tea. It got thundery. Then she went out to draw the shadecloth across the lettuce, almost enough time, not enough. Those early Macs took a long time to boot up.

I had to endure one more lesson in writing BASIC about which I had only second-hand opinions i.e. BASIC had a fat arse and took up too much space. Aisen could not grasp how I could be at once so desperate and so bored.

She taught via games, she said. She compelled me to choose what my game would be.

Doctor Who on Mars, I said, because I was a show-off. She forced me to start dividing things up in classes. I came up with 'World classes' and 'Actor classes'. I was so impatient. Mars was a 'world', Doctor Who was an 'actor'. I had to make Doctor Who move but not all actors would need to move so she got me to invent the subclass 'Movers'. So on, forever. I was so so bored.

I tried to trick her into leaving me alone. I said I would work on this by myself and show her what I'd done.

She was, OK, continue. And would not leave my side.

Finally, it was 'nature calls': she was going to the 'library' i.e. the dunny out the back. By the time the screen door slammed shut the thunder was overhead. Her phone was on the desk beside me. All I had to do was drop it on the modem which clasped it tight like sex. 800. Remember that old-time dial-up signal? Then I was like IN. Minerva. And I had the Altos NUA out of my pocket. Then IN again: that intro page at ALTOS I had first seen in my honey's bedroom, now so sweet and familiar. I hoped he was waiting on the bridge.

```
WELCOME TO THE ALTOS HAMBURG CHAT SYSTEM!
What's your nickname?
Fallen Angel
Where are you from?
```

`Undertoad, where are you? Need 2 dialog`

You're a tricky little thing, Miss Aisen said.

And I was going, Ah, I don't know. What is it?

But she saw exactly what I had done. She asked me how I got there, and I began to cry. I'll pay. It's a local call.

Local call to what?

Finally I told her it was called Minerva.

She had clamped my shoulders with her strong little hands, but when I said Minerva she released me. OK, log off. She watched, her arms folded across her chest, her head cocked.

Now, log on.

I thought she had no right. I thought Frederic would kill me. She watched me while I went through Minerva and introduced myself on Altos. I was almost at the limit of my skills.

`Speedball: Welcome back Fallen Angel. Wassup? WTF with Undertoad?`

Aisen asked: Who is Undertoad?

I would not say.

This is the boy who was in trouble?

I glared at her and she touched my head like someone who never had a pet before. She said, Show me what else you can do?

Will you let me use the modem still?

If it's a local call, yes.

She had a way of looking at you I can't describe, as if there was an error in your genetic code and she was searching for it, line by line.

You'll find him, she said. Her eyes were pale and brown, too clear to hide a thing.

How do you know?

You will.

She could not have known. Actually, he was with hippies in Nimbin and could not get online. But I believed her.

The lightning was raging but the line noise was OK and I tried to take my five-foot teacher travelling. I wanted to show her I could do it, but I didn't want to give anything away.

Good heavens, she said. Look at you.

God knows what she was thinking. Then, jeez Louise, the bitch logged me off. I sort of shouted at her, not thinking where I was. She goes, Do you really want to go to jail?

It's not illegal, what I did. I dialled a phone number. That's not wrong.

And the password, did you steal it?

A baby could have guessed it.

But those same eyes were on me. She could be a scary old dame. You better go home to your mother now, she said. I will not help you to break the law.

You promised I could find my friend.

Yes, but now you should go home.

I understand now that she liked me, and that she was afraid of the police like everybody but at the time I was outraged, deceived, betrayed. Also, completely inept.

You'll still teach me BASIC? I said. I have to know BASIC, which was a lie of course. But she was in love with teaching, so I faked it, never thinking my lie might one day become my life.

She said I won't help you to break the law.

Well what am I going to do? I said, and I was really crying because I could not find Frederic without her. I have to learn BASIC I cried. I bawled and bawled to make her sorry for me, so she would let me back and I could have another chance.

OK, she said, I'll think. You better go home for now.

Back home the rooms were dark and empty and loud with rain. I did not know what I would do. I was angry, and I was frightened I had shown her Frederic's secrets. There was cask wine on the fridge and I filled a tumbler. It was red and bitter and I didn't like it but afterwards I slept and dreamed. I was writing in some amazing language which was also, somehow, music and a kind of graph. The object was to make the graph go high. I was actually programming and playing the game as well and suddenly I understood it was all so easy and the graph started to go high, then it went higher and higher and I felt something so maximum, elegance, perfection, perhaps I gasmed, it was like that. The graph went off of the top of the screen and a voice said, You have broken through!! And I thought, I have got him back again, I have found my hedgehog boy. And I woke up, so sad and disappointed to learn I had killed Peli and it was all crock, crap, disgustitude inside the empty house.

23

My lips in the bathroom mirror were dry and scuzzy with red wine. I splashed my puffy eyes then air-conditioned them with the open fridge. It was eight o'clock at night but I left the blinds as they had been all day, drawn against the heat. The phone had been ringing through my sleep and now it began again. As before, there was no message, not from my mother who was shooting at Mount Macedon, not from the Great Sando who was at a conference called Socialism in Shorts. I suppose that was meant to be lighthearted, in any case he would not be home tonight. I collected the coins from his office floor, enough for pizza.

Then bam bam bam on the front door and Miss Aisen called my mother's name and I was Gregor Samsa in the dark, peering through the chink below the blinds. There she was: sodium-yellow in the electric light, sun dress, wiry legs, homemade hair. She left the porch, and passed through the squeaky side gate. Then bang bang on the back door.

Gaby, she called. I know you're there, she said. The door rattled in its frame.

When she finally gave up and walked away I knew I was in more trouble than before. She would tell my parents I was a criminal.

So I stole Dad's parliamentary envelopes. I locked myself in the bathroom and used the toilet lid to write snail mail to Frederic Matovic c/- post offices in Nimbin,

Uki, Murwillumbah, Byron Bay, Bangalow, needles in haystacks, all the hippie towns I knew in northern New South Wales. I begged him to come back. I had one more glass of wine and imagined I was doing stuff with him.

So I slept.

Next morning, my mouth an old carpet, my stomach acid, fuck my life, I kept the blinds down and windows closed against Miss Aisen. I cooked eggs they made me retch. I went back to my room and smoothed out the envelopes which had got all crinkled in the night. Then came three sharp knocks on the bedroom window. Thank God, Troy. He would go to the post office for me.

I lifted the blind and it was Aisen. Perhaps I should have cried or charmed her but I fled to the bathroom and locked the door and finally she went away.

Later I looked in Sandy's drawer for stamps. I had a glass of wine and cleaned the crud off my teeth. All I thought was, Undertoad, where are you? I tore out the best pictures from my *Macworld*s. I collected wine cartons in the kitchen and a Stanley knife and a Sharpie and a roll of silver gaffer tape. By lunchtime – this will sound insane – I had made a life-size model of the Mac IIx. This was desperate, but it was how my dad and I spoke when we loved each other, sitting on the floor, eating pizza, drinking Coke, making stuff all Saturday afternoon. It was what they call a cry for help. Ha-ha.

I was starving and vomitous but I constructed a card-board monitor, a keyboard, twin drives with Apple logos. I made three realistic floppy disks. I had it completed, on his desk by midafternoon when he walked through the door in his socialist shorts and thongs. I was hiding in the corner behind the sofa so I saw him smile. I jumped him and he laughed and hugged me and I thought, yes! He will definitely buy me a computer now. He ordered pizza and Coke and then I unplugged the phone so Aisen could not tell him I had broken the laws of the Commonwealth of Australia.

But then he washed my dirty eggy plates and pans which I understood to mean he would not buy me what I required.

You need to get out in the sunshine more, he said, and that was the same thing said another way. Why bother being surprised? We were always broke, but I was also a wilful little cow, so I persisted. When the Turkish pizza arrived I transferred my votive object to the kitchen table. When Sando laughed, I hoped. And I kept on hoping, even while he was saying no in various different ways e.g. wibbling at me about how pale I was. You need to get out in the sunshine, etc. as if getting skin cancer was good for my future. I should go to the Coburg pool, he said. I did not tell him the Samoan girls were waiting there to bash me up.

I asked could I have a glass of wine. He said just one. He had two or three himself. He called me darls. He was upset my mother could not get a day off the shoot to appear with him at an event. The greenies were being unreasonable. He had to demonstrate to them, again, that he was publicly opposing MetWat's plan to concrete the Merri Creek. If it had been Greeks or Turks inviting him, he would have been there like a shot, but these were 'environmentalists' which was code for white people. Of course they were his constituents, and if they wanted him and his wife to come and plant some trees, then he better bloody go.

I was a treacherous jealous little thing, so I laughed at

the idea of my mother planting trees. He told me not to, but he couldn't stop smiling. So I was into it. I laughed so violently I blew Coca-Cola out my nose. He said that was enough but I invited him to picture my mother planting trees, in a fury with everything which would not submit to her, not just the spade, the earth, the soil itself would play an evil force.

He thought I was hilarious. His upper lip lengthened. His nostrils contracted. Celine loved the country, I told him, but her love involved a lot of glass, one to hold the wine, the other to make a window that would keep all the nasty bugs outside.

No, he said. You must not speak about your mother in this way.

How could I not love him? He was like this with everything in life. You should have seen how he was with his electorate, shy smile, nasal Arabic, lumpy Greek. He was tall and strong. He looked great in shorts and when he listened he crossed his arms and hunched himself down and folded himself into the other person's life.

So I said I would go tree planting instead of Celine. Looking back now I see this was the beginning of my life, at the stage when he was still my hero, where I would do anything for him, even let him kill me in a car accident. Early next morning we were in the Volvo dodging the murderous trucks and semitrailers on Carr Street, speeding to meet the volunteers. He was an awful driver. He should have watched the road. Instead he pointed out the highlights of the mullocky landscape, backhoes and cranes intent on turning the unloved stream into a proper drain. It was just after dawn. Scavenging seagulls rode high in the thermals above the rotten-smelling dumps.

We found the white people were all gathered, in all their daggy glory, beside the degraded stinky creek which was to lead me on my path. I only pretended to be excited to carry a tray of poa tussocks. A boy with unfortunate hippie hair was trying to balance three mattocks and a crowbar.

I was not even paying real attention. The embankment was not a real riverbank, but a mess made by bulldozed mud and ancient garbage. From here you could look down to see the poor fucked Merri Creek threading through the body of Coburg like the vein in the dead body of a prawn. The descent was steep, shoulder-high with fennel. There was a spewy smell. Factories occupied the high ground above the creek, below the power pylons. The actual watercourse was marked by abandoned cars and broken industrial equipment including a sabotaged dragline crane with its long steel boom twisted like a swan's neck.

The heat was already murderous and although the sky was dirty grey I could feel it burning through my long-sleeved shirt.

As I came down to the level of the watercourse, to the natural bank, I saw sheets of burlap, all neatly pegged to the ground. Here, amongst the smell and the squalling seagulls, a man and woman were working neatly and swiftly, with the confident rhythm of gardeners deadheading perennials. They were cutting holes where my poa grass would go. Today I was a good girl, eager to help my daddy help them.

Gaby, Miss Aisen cried.

I was so ashamed I could not even look at them. But they were rushing me, laying down their tools, relieving me of my grasses, leading me off the mulch sheet to a tiny tartan rug. Here Miss Aisen laid her hand against my cheek and sort of patted me like she had earlier patted my head.

Have a choccy bickie, she said.

I said I just had breakfast. My saintly father stood dangerously close, along from us, on the bank. He had no idea what I was like.

Mervyn had a flask of tea. I accepted a mug and sat on the rug. The Aisens were so very nice, which completely creeped me out. I took that chocolate biscuit after all. Why were they keen to talk with me? I didn't understand this at all. Of course the dear people liked me, loved me even. I didn't see that yet.

Mervyn told me that every injury to Coburg went back to Pentridge Prison. The bosses build the prisons, he said, and I thought, he is telling me I am going to end up in jail myself.

To build the prisons they needed stone, he told me, and that leaves a lot of quarries and then the council makes a dump and throws in everything that no-one wants.

Miss Aisen stared at me in such a way that I knew to pretend to listen to her father.

Mervyn had grown up across the road from a Coburg council tip, he said, you learned not to smell it. The creek was running through it.

The seagulls loved it didn't they? Miss Aisen encouraged him. At night they would go down to the sea to roost.

As for me, said Gaby, I was still waiting for them to get to the point. I didn't know this was the point, the talking. The *Coburg Times* photographer had arrived and my father was digging with a crowbar in the rusty graveyard soil.

Once this happens to a piece of land, Mervyn said,

everyone wants to hurt it more. Once you've done this devastation you've got a perfect place to put the sewage works, and then you straighten the creek and make a drain, and you can run ring roads through it and degrade it any way you want.

Miss Aisen was patting the rug and I sat a little closer to her. I was realising her computer might not be out of bounds.

MetWat has decided to make the creek a bloody drain, Mervyn said, and I looked at him like I was really interested.

They already straightened up one stretch, he said. What they pulled out of the creek, he said, they didn't cart away, they just left it in big smelly muddy heaps. They brought in that dragline crane. They dredged out the bottom and dumped the toxic mud and then it got washed back in. The holes I swam in when I was a kid are only twenty-five centimetres deep. That's the thing that done it, that mongrel of a thing. He meant the dragline with the broken neck.

My dad and the photographer were waving at me.

That's Mr Quinn, said Mervyn. He's our local member.

He's my dad, I said.

Quinn? Mervyn said. He looked completely gobsmacked. You're not Quinn.

Pause micro. Play compact C120.

The Aisens always knew who I was married to, Celine said. Always. From the first time I met Aisen she knew my name was Baillieux and Gaby's father was Sandy Quinn. Then they pretended they didn't have any idea of the connection. They were cunning as a pair of cockatoos.

315

24

Gaby was a Labor Party child. Even as her family fell apart she continued to hand out campaign literature, answer the phone in the electoral office, and act as Sando's human handbag when Celine stopped communicating with the local branch. But Merri Creek marked a turning point.

She came to parliament to hear her father speak, not for the first time but the first time of her own volition. She saw him announce the Green Front Coalition, an alliance between MetWat, three local councils and all the local interest groups. She was smart. She paid attention. Sando's pride in seeing her politically engaged was only dampened by his fears about Mervyn Aisen's influence.

He would do nothing to discourage her activism but as time went on, and as she went off regularly to work beside the Aisens, first at the creek, then later at the VINC tree nursery, he was not quite jealous, but certainly disturbed. He revealed none of this to her. What he showed her was his happiness. He was always awake to kiss her as she left the house just after dawn. He welcomed her at dusk when she was red-faced, sweaty, scratched and dusty. She lost weight and he was smart enough to never mention it. Her brown skin suited her.

Celine was away again, filming. That was fine. They were similar, father and daughter. Together they were both voluble and silent, generous and withholding. For instance

Gaby did not tell her father that she was spending ten minutes a day at Darlington Grove where she was permitted to log on to Altos. She did not say she had found Frederic. Sando did not reveal any of the horse-trading and treachery of political life, or divulge that classic line he shared with everyone else: 'I don't know why he shafted me, I never done him no favours.' He did not learn that his dinner was cooked by 'Fallen Angel'. They both argued frankly about the Merri Creek and its ancient enemies, town planning, ring roads, MetWat and the State Electricity Commission. Sando did not risk telling her that the Aisens were the loopy left, a tiny ratbag faction in the Coburg branch, enemies of any Labor prime minister who could actually win elections. It would be safer to ask her to shave her armpits and he was not brave enough for that.

Clearly it was the Aisens who lent her that battered copy of Felix bloody Moore's *While We Were Sleeping*. He did not ask, he did not have to, but his pride in his daughter was clouded by a sort of dread as, in this, and other ways, he prepared to lose her.

She told him: Capitalism is a bull charging a chook house shouting it's every man for himself.

He knew exactly who that came from.

He saw Mervyn's other mad opinions introduced into his house. For instance: Jim Cairns was only interested in the capitalists making profits. And: Bob Hawke had used his moral authority to prevent the general strike in 1975. 'Hawkie was always at the US embassy. Don't tell me the Americans did not tell him call your dogs off, mate.' Sando thought this was insane, but Mervyn thought it was 'outrageous' that Gaby could grow up not knowing a thing

317

about the Coup of 1975. She brought this back home as well, in the same bag as her sudden environmentalism. You could have called a general strike, she said.

Me?

The Labor Party.

Who told you that?

Can't I have my own ideas? she asked. What else would you do if your government was stolen? It was illegal. It was unconstitutional. Don't sigh, Dad. I'm not an idiot.

I actually was there, you know.

Yes. So don't you agree there should have been a general strike? Do you agree or not?

He told you it was the CIA?

You mean Mervyn? Say his name. It doesn't matter who it was, Dad. Once it was done it was done: the people's government was taken from them. So what about the unions?

What do you know about the unions?

Don't patronise me. I know a lot about the unions.

A general strike would have been a step towards armed conflict.

So?

Did your friend Mervyn tell you that the governor-general had the armed forces on stand-by? Did he tell you that? The Queen's toady was actually Commander-in-Chief of the Australian Defence Force.

Kerr, I know who you mean. He was the governor-general.

Kerr called in the defence chiefs. He conferred with the American embassy. He briefed intelligence agencies. He had the armed forces on a 'red alert'. You want to send the unions out to face that?

318

You were afraid?

Of course.

What about Mum?

She was on red alert too.

Ha-ha, what did she want to do?

No, she was not in favour of a strike.

Why have you never talked about this with me?

She looked hostile, spoiled, superior and he couldn't bear she would regurgitate this stuff.

Is it shame? she asked.

Shame?

That you were cowards.

That was when he told her what he really thought about the Aisens. That their so-called ecological activism was an attempt to return to some fantasy of white Australia populated by good blokes and mates and everything was dinky-di and the blackfellows fed themselves unhindered on the creeks of Coburg. It was territorial, Sando said. Did you see any Turks or Lebanese amongst their planting party? No, of course not. The Aisens were using the language of socialism to reassert white privilege.

Listen to you, she shouted. Listen to yourself. You sound insane. They're fighting these polluting bastards and so are you.

But Sando was sick of talkback-radio racists ranting and arguing about who they would permit to be called a 'real Australian'. Doesn't even smell like Australia anymore, you know what I mean, mate? No you listen, he said.

His daughter then told him that her new friends were 'real radicals'.

Real? he asked. In what way?

Well, she said, do you know who sabotaged the dragline?

He cringed on her behalf, that she should so carelessly give away this information.

Mervyn did that?

She returned his stare and he thought she looked smug. Someone did it, she said.

No-one wants to support vandals, he said.

But who is the vandal? cried his musky daughter. Are you blaming the people? Shouldn't you be calling out MetWat about this shit? Are they under your 'purview'? she said, twisting the word like a weapon.

What sort of word is purview?

She would not answer him but she knew he knew where purview came from.

No, he said, they are under the purview of the minister, and this was surely the moment Sando decided he would rip his daughter out of Bell Street High. Certainly he had made up his mind before Celine returned. He consulted no-one. Gabrielle Baillieux went to bed that night not knowing she was about to be removed from Miss Aisen's classroom and established five kilometres further south, as a student at the R. F. Mackenzie Community School.

25

Celine had just finished shooting *Mrs Fischer* which would later cause such controversy at Cannes. She returned to Patterson Street refreshed, invigorated by a brief uncomplicated affair. She was carrying thousands of dollars in cash. She was finally ready to leave and start again.

They had both ganged up on me again, she told the author Felix Moore. I had deserved it all, OK, but they were so hurtful and I would have loved to hurt them just as much. But when I realised how wounded and angry they were with *each other*, I knew I had to fix it. I was the one who had got us entangled with the Aisens.

I had thought I was using her with her computer lessons which cost less than buying my daughter the computer she wanted. I was so cheap. Sando was cheap too. But the first day I was back from shooting I drove into the city and bought the Mac IIx. It put a big hole in my runaway money. Don't get psychological on me, Celine said. It was as straightforward as I say: no need to visit Aisen anymore.

I came back from down the creek, Gaby said, and there was a big white box on the dining table. I saw the Apple logo and felt sick with what I'd done. I had gotten everything I wanted and I knew exactly what it cost and I knew my parents could not afford it. Money was what they fought about, the house, the repairs, the advertising gigs, even the computer lessons and now, of course, Celine had done the thing she had been so against, and she had not bothered to discuss it with my dad so then he went bananas about how selfish she was with her money.

I lugged the box to my room and locked the door behind me. I tried to be happy, because I should have been happy. I smelled the brand-new Mac IIx, all clean and Appley. I heard that startup tone, that single note descending. I saw the happy Mac icon, the real thing. I acted out my happiness, with no-one to see me do it. I was a psycho and a fake. I wrote some stuff in BASIC because what else was I to do? I had no phone line and no modem and I could not ask them to spend more money now and so, of course, I was deceitful and made up stories so I could sneak out to Darlington Grove and go online to hook up with Undertoad. Undertoad and I made a private back room on Altos. He told me his mum was returning to Melbourne 'for treatment' but she had moved him to a different school.

I thought Frederic extremely dangerous, Celine told me, but I hid all that from Gaby. I acted very sympathetic. I suggested that the poor boy must hate his life without electricity. (Gaby answered that he did.) I then supposed the New South Wales education system did not even know he existed. (My daughter did not disabuse me.) I supposed Meg must have taken her business with her. (Gaby didn't know.) I said northern New South Wales was beautiful. (No, no, Frederic was continually the victim of the groundsel bush which left his eyes streaming and his sinuses blocked and swollen. He owed his life to eucalyptus oil. Even when people were so nice to them and let them crash and fed them free, night after night, on baked vegetables from hippie gardens, endless pumpkin, he always knew his noisy breathing made him an unwanted guest.) From all this, Celine said, I concluded that Frederic was eight hundred kilometres away from my child, whereas Meg's van was already heading south towards me.

My parents began spying, Gaby said, so naturally I lied. Somehow they found out I was still visiting Darlington Grove. Celine took Sando's side. Mervyn was 'your father's enemy'. He was a shit-stirrer and ratbag, she said. He used the word comrade constantly, but had I noticed he had no comrades? He could not work with other people. His real specialty was embarrassment, direct attacks. Also, she went on about how much she had spent on the computer.

But Mervyn had already taken me to visit what he called 'the jewel of Merri Creek', a dull yellow-brick building on McBryde Street in Fawkner. It was next to some dreary paddocks with starving horses and across the road from some small suburban houses like you might see in any of the poorer northern suburbs.

There was a wooden sign by the road that had been hand-carved in a folksy sort of way. It said 'Agrikem'. The factory had a gravel car park like a hardware store and nothing to suggest that it was dangerous in any way.

It was after five o'clock when we arrived and all the workers' cars had gone and there was no-one to see us climb through the fence into the paddock, a girl and an old man going to talk to lonely horses. Mervyn was carrying an iron bar but he often carried one tool or another and there was always a reason, in this case the bar was to lift a concrete inspection cap with two U-shaped loops. Really it was an inspection plate for a sewer, but as I walked towards it I thought it must be a well for water.

323

I watched him fit the bar into the loops, and saw the tendons in his neck go tight as he lifted.

He asked, You hear that?

Is it water?

Have a look.

It smells bad.

In the beam of his flashlight I saw a small pipe draining murky liquid into the sewer.

What's that? he asked.

Drain water.

Where does it end up?

I don't know.

Did you ever hear of dioxin?

No.

How about Agent Orange?

At school.

OK, he said.

And that was it.

He took my hand as we walked home. This was the first and possibly the last time he ever did that. If we talked I don't recall it. Nor did it seem strange that we did not. What struck me was not the sewer or the smell but the confusing emotions generated by that big dry hand, the comfort that I took from it, my queasy guilty feeling of betrayal.

26

That night the fugitive writer would find himself carried like a baby through the dark bush, as if he were, in his own words, a sacred slug or silkworm protected by the empress's guard. But now, as day broke on the Hawkesbury, those noble guards were presumably still resting in their Manly barracks. At this hour, upriver, the fugitive was attending to his toilette, carrying his spade up the rocky hill where he made a bad-tempered search for a place to do his business. He scraped a small depression in the resistant earth, removed his lower garments and laid them on a tuft of grass. Then he squatted, glaring bleakly at the river. No-one saw him. No-one knew his aching knees. He was Felix Moore and he was aware of his position in his country's history and thus saw himself from a slightly elevated perspective, deriving some dour satisfaction from his similarity to Dürer's portrait of the hermit Saint Jerome.

For breakfast he had a bruised apple, after which there was nothing to do but return to punishing the Olivetti. For lunch he took cheese and a single glass of wine. As the hours passed, the pages accumulated and he secured them with a knobbly stone. When this day was ended, he would add these to the treasure already hidden in the black garbage bag at his feet. He was offline, strictly analog. There were various other black bags-in-waiting, all moist and ready to

325

be disposed of, but the bag beneath his feet was dry and clean as a prayer in the wilderness.

Thus had his days passed, like writers' days have always passed, in solitary labour, and just as housemaids, nuns, priests and religious devotees of all kinds are known to form their bodies to the shape of their trade, producing lasting physical distortions once recognised as distinct surgical conditions, Felix Moore hunched his wide shoulders around his machine. As he typed he waved his hands and sometimes muttered but his ear was always pitched beyond his own inner tumult, alert for the voices of the river, not only the shouted conversations of fishermen, but the fucking jet- skis, the regular beat of the mail boat, the lonely thud of distant tinnies hammering against the hard unbending river. There were also 'gin palaces' and 'Tupperware boats' and 'hot water tubs' of different varieties and he would abandon his chair from time to time, simply to confirm that he had identified them correctly. What he feared was confused and ever-changing, but on this occasion it was silence, the sudden absence, the cessation of an outboard motor, which caused him to jump upright, then to climb, like Ben Gunn himself, up onto the top of the hut, where he peered down, uncertain as to whether the aluminium craft now gliding silently beneath the mangroves was bringing him supplies or was, finally, the expected assassin.

Ow, he heard. It was a boy's voice, sharp with indignation. Then a man's voice.

Quit it, the boy cried.

The hermit scampered down the ladder from the roof. He re-entered his dwelling and rushed to and fro, his long arms sweeping floor and desk. He discarded a malodorous black plastic bag and picked up the treasure from beneath his chair. Into this he thrust all his morning's work and then, sitting, grunting, he collected the tapes, batteries, notebooks, pens, posters and other archival matter, hurling them into the bag as if they were no more important than potato peelings.

Don't, he heard.

And then a man's voice, singing tunelessly.

He tied the bag and encased it within a second bag, tied that too, did the same a third time, then ascended, in bare bunioned feet up to the roof where, finally, he hurled the bag towards the river far below. If he expected a splash, there was none. He waited but could wait no longer. The visitors were already on the path, the man singing in a voice so flat, so blithe, so confident that it raised the hair on the listener's neck.

You better watch out
You better not cry

Felix Moore returned to the hut nursing a freshly injured elbow, crossed to the doorway, pausing to scoop up a stray Duracell and to select an apple from the bottom of a cardboard box.

Let me go, cried the boy.

The hermit leaned, 'nonchalantly', against the door-frame.

Making a list . . . checking it twice
Looking to see who's naughty and nice

And then his pink-cheeked red-lipped patron emerged, dragging a protesting boy by the ear.

Hello mate, said Woody Townes.

Mate, said Felix, and bit into his putrid apple.

327

As the visitors paused at the midway landing the man sought his prisoner's attention.

Ow.

You ever see this bloke before?

No. Ow.

As Woody tugged the boy onwards he reached to take the hermit's apple. In this moment of distraction the prisoner pulled free, and fell, then rolled, protesting loudly all the way to the bottom of the stairs.

Give me the fucking apple.

Fat bastard, cried the boy, and had already turned as the apple hit his shoulder and burst apart.

Stupid cunt, said Woody Townes, simultaneously embracing his writer, crushing his hairy face against his canvas shoulder, crooning tenderly into his single naked ear.

They see you when you're sleeping
They know when you're awake
They know if you've been bad or good
So be good for goodness sake

At the sound of an outboard motor roaring to life, the property developer, without releasing the hermit, produced a telephone from his clever canvas waistcoat. His thumbs were distressingly large, but he dialled precisely. Mate, he said to the slender phone, let the kid go.

The hermit tugged free. You see me when I'm sleeping? he cried. What the fuck is that meant to mean? He had already seen the cruiser with satellite dishes on its cabin. Who told you where I was?

Woody Townes did not bother answering. He took the single chair and shook his head in a style that might be 'rueful'. He had lost weight. The stomach staples had evidently worked, or he had been at the gym. When he returned his telephone to his waistcoat holster, new biceps stretched his shirt.

Pull up a pew, he said, and placed a liquor flask and a peculiar revolver on the desk.

The hermit showed no reaction to this ugly weapon. Instead he fetched two smudgy glasses from the sink and dragged a plastic crate to serve as a chair.

You always liked that bit, Feels.

What bit?

Come on, this is for you. Your all-time favourite interview. Murray Sayle snares Kim Philby in Moscow. Intrepid Aussie journalist tracks down Pommy traitor at the Moscow post office. The spy agrees to the interview. When the journo arrives the spy is waiting with a bottle of vodka and a revolver on the table. You didn't get the reference?

What are you doing, Woody?

The literal answer would have been, I am now raising the revolver and pointing it over your shoulder. Woody Townes, however, did not reply directly: I always thought Philby must have been a drama queen, he said.

The hermit's hand may have been less steady than his friend's but he displayed a modicum of courage. That is, he unscrewed the flask and poured. As he raised the glass (formerly a receptacle for peanut butter) the most colossal explosion occurred.

Shit, the hermit cried. His body jerked. He stood. He sat. He turned towards the sound of running water, a trickling garden hose which turned out to be red wine spurting from a punctured box. He stared at the wine morosely. It was the visitor who spoke:

So give me my fucking pages.

The hermit reflected that it had been awful wine in any case.

Give me my fucking pages.

How can I have pages? I haven't got a source.

So why are you here?

To get some fucking peace.

Woody Townes laid his weapon down, and dragged the Olivetti Valentine across the table. He unscrewed the pair of orange knobs which secured the spools of ribbon. Having removed these, he affected to read the ribbon like a strip of film.

Were there people somewhere like San Antonio, Texas at, say, a former Sony computer-chip factory, who could really decode a typewriter ribbon? Of course there were. Whatever weird shit you could imagine, they could do it. The spools flew like yoyos across the room and Woody Townes tilted back to ask: Tell me this, why am I the one who always has to get you out of the shit?

You're not.

Shut up. This is not the New South Wales branch of the Labor Party you're trying to fuck with.

I wrote two hundred pages. They sent a kid to pick them up. Not that kid, another one. He said he was from you.

Bullshit. You won't want to be here when I send some-one.

There's nothing here. You can look for yourself.

You've got the hots for her, fine. So now's your chance to be a hero. Give us a chance to defend her. We need info-fucking-mation, mate.

I'm not sure I should be trusting you Woody.

You're not?

Nothing personal.

Talking of personal. I was chatting to Donno at the *Telegraph* the other day. Donovan? Yeah I know. I was sort of hinting there might be an interesting Felix story. He was saying, We know everything there is to know about the grandstanding little cunt, you know how he talks. But of course that's not true, is it? We've got all sorts of shit on you.

The fugitive became still.

Do you remember, Feels, when you thought you could take on Hawkie? People don't know about that. Felix Moore vs. the future Prime Minister of the nation.

This is what you told Celine, isn't it?

Woody shrugged. There were a mob of you, as I recall. No-one had more moral authority with the unions than the head of their collective body. Hawke used all that clout to stop the general strike? Right. He was a mate of the US ambassador. Etc. etc.

He was. You know he was.

And then you, my nervy little mate, do you remember? You were auditioning for *Drivetime Radio*. Someone was on holiday. Matt Cocker? No, not him. They gave you three weeks to try out *Drivetime Radio with Felix Moore*. It went to your head, no? Just a teensy bit? Somehow you thought you could call a general strike from the fucking ABC. You were worried, as I recall, how you would fit eighteen left-wing union leaders into a little studio on William Street. Eighteen. That was optimistic.

331

You weren't against it, mate. As I recall, you sort of egged me on.

Let's just say, I was very interested in everything you had to say. You were born in a country that never had a war. You were blessed, but you thought we should suffer like the Bosnians, the Rwandans, the Palestinians, everyone. I never heard anything so fucking stupid. You really wanted civil war.

Whatever. You were on my side.

Oh, mate, he said and he cocked his head and the expression on his face was almost fond.

What?

What do you think?

You weren't playing on the other side?

Other side of what? Other side of bloodshed? You bet. Fortunately you didn't have the balls for it. You were shitting yourself, I remember that, looking for any chance not to follow through.

You told Celine this?

You were frightened of where your imagination was leading you. Remember we sat up half the night before? You got so pissed you couldn't walk. You slept at my place in Neutral Bay. Do you remember the morning?

We drank all your tequila.

No, not that, mate. Your car caught fire.

Of course I remember. You were with me. You're the one who dragged me out the passenger side. It was not my fault the car caught fire.

No, it was my fault.

Bullshit.

Yes, me. I fucking saved you from yourself. You should

be grateful I gave you your excuse. Although you could have still got to the studio if you'd really wanted to.

We had to wait for the police.

Ah, look at you, said Woody Townes, delighted. The boy who cried pig. You've spent a lifetime screaming at everyone for being so gutless in '75. To the barricades, and all that shit. If there was any credible opposition you had them, every available pinko and ratbag, waiting to go on *Drivetime Radio*. What will your little girls think of their daddy when they hear all this?

The wine was dripping, but only very slowly. The hermit turned his attention to the visitor's flask from which he slowly refilled two large glasses, one of which he drank.

Why? he asked his biggest fan.

Woody leaned back, as if to give the writer a sporting chance to grab the gun. Mate, you know me.

He slid the second glass across the table. Felix Moore did not reject the gift.

So you've got nothing to give me, Feels? Not a single page?

Sorry mate. Wish I did.

Woody stood. He kicked irritably at the tangled typewriter ribbon as he slid the gun back inside what was, clearly, a highly specialised garment.

You're not up to this game, he said. You'd like to play at this level, but you never could. Here, take my phone. When you realise what shit you're in, call me on my landline. It might not be too late.

It was an iPhone, the latest model, but Woody left it without regret.

The hermit remained in his doorway as the visitor

continued down the path. When he heard the gunfire he felt no particular alarm. Woody, he understood, wished to use his weapon, and firing the last fifteen rounds at an aluminium dinghy was the best he was going to do today.

27

The queen had locked the saint in a tower room filled with straw and ordered him to spin the straw into gold, on pain of death. And how he worked. He slammed at the spinning wheel, night and day until, one morning, it was necessary to shove the gold into a plastic bag and hurl it from the tower.

Cleverly done. Well saved. But when peace returned it was no simple matter to retrieve the treasure. The saint lay down on his stomach and stretched himself full-length on the edge of the outcrop, peering down through the undergrowth and scrub where he could see, in nets of light produced by slapping wavelets, the aerial roots of mangroves poking up like nails from yellow sand.

The so-called 'outcrop' was host to a jungle of wattles, wild lantana and various bits of prickly stuff. Here, just a hand's span below his fleshy nose, grew a knotted little eucalypt with a trunk no thicker than an axe handle.

Further down, a man's length he calculated, there was a convenient ridge in the rock where he might gain purchase with his toes. Below that, he could not really see.

As a schoolboy he had achieved serious status as a hundred-kph spin bowler, in spite of which he had been, sporadically, unpredictably followed by boys swinging their arms and making 'chee-chee' monkey cries. That is, duh, his arms were long. But, as his mother once said when answering a query re his testicles, God put everything there for a purpose and now the time had come when his arms would prove their Darwinian value. He grasped that twisted eucalypt and, completely forgetting his age, lowered himself in the direction of the ridge.

His arm was yanked like a bone from a rotisserie chicken. He kicked at the rock and gained no purchase. He swung with his feet twitching and shuddering like a hanged man. As always, part of his mind was administered by a cartoonist and he was encouraged to believe he might somehow slither down the remaining inches to the ridge.

Instead, he fell, scratching, scraping, slipping past whatever ridge or ledge he had imagined. Death awaited him. He awaited death. He landed in a twisted eagle's nest of wattle and lantana where the black plastic bag was pushed like a horse's arse against his face. All three bags had been partly inflated with accidental air, so it was this, not the sand, which cushioned the final fall.

His face stung. He loudly fucked and shat. A fierce pain assailed his shoulder as he splashed along the waterline. He wrapped his arms around his treasure, binding it to his chest, like a spider with a sac of eggs. Cautiously, he made his way under the gloomy mangroves, amidst the forest of aerial roots, until he arrived at the place where he had beached so long before.

He showed not the least interest in his bullet-riddled dinghy but hurried along the track, breathing through his open mouth, squelching up the protesting stairs. When he entered his former refuge the air was cold and sour with wine. Typewriter ribbon adhered to his sodden shoes and he did nothing to untangle it. He sat in the gloom, gingerly, embracing the bag, mindful that it might hold evidence that would prove Gaby Baillieux innocent. What would Woody do with that? What would he do himself? He did not wish her to be innocent. He wanted her fearless, guilty of courage, of principle. If his writing would get his name on the so-called 'Disposition Matrix', he wished her to be worthy of the pain.

Now he lifted the remaining vodka and touched it to his stinging lips. For once he did not drink. He examined the abandoned iPhone, turned it on, then failed in his attempt to throw it out the window. The screen glowed briefly then went dark. There was no illumination but that provided by the deep charcoal-blue of the Hawkesbury River.

Felix?

The voice was close, in the doorway, but there was insufficient light to distinguish the doorframe from the space it might have defined. He held the plastic bag like a child with a pillow.

Felix, right? Mr Moore?

The voice that of a young man. He was perhaps tall, with fair hair.

Who are you?

We're the pros from Dover.

He was slow to register the 'we' and slower still to understand that these friendly wraiths who had appeared at his door were a subset of a caste of Sydney surf lifesavers, once known locally for eating live canaries in bread rolls and sticking their naked backsides out car windows during late night shopping. These anarchic characters would now exhibit towards the hermit an intoxicating sort of reverence and he found himself wishing that his daughters could witness this moment of redemption or, at least, prestige.

What's your name? he asked.

Mate, the publicly available tools for making yourself free from surveillance are ineffective against a nation state.

I don't understand a word you're saying.

Time to go.

Now?

The visitor explained that there was no longer a safe way out by water. So they must walk back up the ridge. The moon was good.

The fugitive did not resist or argue although he insisted, from the start, that he carry his own bag. This he managed well enough, but his sodden deck shoes rubbed his delicate heels and they were not even at the fire trail before he was limping. The track was a pale yellow, and there could be no better conditions for walking in the night, except that his calves were soon cramping and his blisters were bleeding and then, when it was clear he could not keep up the pace, when it became obvious he must be unmanned and suffer the indignity and pleasure of being carried, he was moved by their tenderness towards him. A fireman's lift, of course, is not the most comfortable way to travel and Felix Moore passed through the Marramarra National Park from the Hawkesbury to Forest Glen with his head down, filled with blood, dropping pencils and paperclips and Duracell batteries along the way.

He was a stick-case moth enveloped in silk, finally redeemed, the treasure of his nation.

The night seemed endless. He saw no 'spectacular ridge-top colours of iconic Hawkesbury sandstone' or 'gullies of bright red waratahs and Gymea lily'. His escort would not permit him to walk, but merely shifted his load between them, until the lights of a four-wheel drive could be seen bumping below, snaking up the switchbacks.

Time for your pill, mate, said the first man who had spoken to him.

For what?

Travel sickness.

I'll be fine.

Take my word.

The hermit held out his hand and took the pill.

What is it?

Men in Black, they said.

Whatever chemical that was, he would never discover, but it was sufficient to ensure that it would be eight hours before he awoke in what was clearly, on the evidence of the shiny bedspreads and pastel-pink art, a motel. His wet shoes were on the floor, stuffed with newspaper. There were bandaids on his heels. He drew the curtains aside and saw a concrete paved courtyard, almost empty, and beyond this a two-lane road and mountainous bush.

On the desk there were two bottles of McLaren Vale shiraz, a large washed rind cheese, a Triumph-Adler Twen T180 electric typewriter. There also, God help him, were tapes, new tapes, and enough batteries to play them for a year.

As to where on earth he was, there was no newspaper or television to solve the problem. One door led to the bathroom. He tried the other, and although it was, unsurprisingly, locked, he could hear the murmur of voices on the other side. He wrenched out the wine cork in the grim knowledge that he had, for the first time in his professional life, been worthy of a suite.

339

28

The eighteen-wheeler semitrailers roared past the motel all night. You could hear them from miles away, descending through eight gears, then a screaming ninth, air brakes exploding so loud you might imagine the glass-walled reception area shorn away and frosted donuts liberated, rolling down the middle of the road.

Meanwhile the tapes continued at 7/8 of a centimetre/ second, more or less, as Gaby made her didactic 'confession', explaining, for instance, why it was thought there could be no female hackers. She would not even discuss rule 37 (devised by adolescent boys) which asserted there are no girls on the internet. Google it, she told her listener, as if that were something you could do on a Triumph-Adler electric typewriter. Search, she said. Look for 'teenage-male voyeur-thrill power-trip activity'. Look for this actual sentence or, same difference, 'don't find female computer intruders, any more than you find female voyeurs who are obsessed with catching glimpses of men's underwear'. This will take you to Cornelia Sollfrank in Rotterdam in 1999. Full credit please. 'Women are very, very rarely arrested for sneaking around in the dark of night, peering through bedroom windows. Teenage males are arrested for this all the time.'

This is so morally satisfying, but it is just total crap and cruditude, she said. Not even the sisterhood could imagine me, she said. I could not exist. I must be doomed to rage and skin rash. But what if? What if you wished to obliterate, eliminate the corporatists? What if your Bonnie found your Clyde, if your Sid found your Nancy, then you would be blessed from your clitoris to your earlobe to your small pink toes, no shit, to find a boy who would allow you to become wwb, a world-wide boy yourself, to become Fallen Angel or even Fnu (first name unknown) Lnu (Last name unknown), to be a boy, a girl, a silver shark. We can be anything we wish, Gaby said, unaware she was addressing a captive with bandaged heels.

My bourgie parents, she said, tried to remove me from every good influence I had discovered. My mother only bought me the Apple to get me free of the Aisens, and my father dragged me out of Bell Street High for the same reason. Frederic was safely exiled, or so they thought, but *The Superior Person waits for wisdom and clarity* (as the fat book says).

R. F. Mackenzie Community School, she said, was a ten-minute bike ride from B. S. High, but it was another universe. I scowled and would not say my name. I walked into the so-called 'home room' a very bad girl and there he was, a pop-up, my laughing boy, girl-boy, returned from Nimbin a man-boy now.

So guess what my mother said when she finally saw him? He was 'strapping'. He had such shoulders. Celine was a sex maniac but she would always hate what Frederic was, even if he had been a manly man fixing roofs with Claude Poulos, Meg's Northern Rivers lover. Claude finally did do time for carding, but he was not, primarily, a criminal. He was a grey-haired cyber-hippie with a motto: 'If you engage in behaviour that carries the risk of negative consequences from an adversary you must be invisible.' Claude existed on no database. He did not fit the pigeonhole. He appeared to be a plumber surfie with bleached hair and earrings. In real life he was a cryptographer, author of an elaborate banking system so private that not even the bank would know how much you had. So while Frederic's mum was getting on heroin and screaming and shrieking her way off it, Frederic not only learned to surf, he became an apprentice plumber and cryptographer whose aim was to live beyond the reach of any 'nation state'. When he came back to me at R. F. Mackenzie Community School he was a total wave of possibility, far beyond the world of Zork.

Celine could have used a little I Ching, her daughter thought i.e. *Because you are the foreigner in this setting, you have no history to acquit you. Watch, listen, study, contemplate, then step lightly but decisively on.*

In the motel, Celine's tapes never touched Gaby's tapes. They stood in different piles, each had its own machine. The trucks roared down the hill. A note came beneath the door to tell the occupant to stay away from the window. Return this page, it said. His meals would be delivered to the shared bathroom. *Slide this note back to its sender. The connecting door is always locked. We will unlock it when required.* On her stretchy tape Celine said, My daughter thinks I am a homophobe. How can she be so dumb? My one true father was a faggot. He nursed me. Like a wasp burying its eggs in a corpse, he left his baby's education waiting in his will. When he died Doris found tons of gelignite stored above the hallway ceiling. It was not a symbol, but a fact. Not a bad symbol just the same. She said, I wish I had been conceived like Tristram Shandy. How sweet and innocent to wind the clock. Now I can see the semen and the crime. I wish I never knew. I wish I had been nice to Doris in those years. I was such a cow. Can this ever be repaired? I should kiss the damage, bless the glove, forgive me.

I wanted to do better with Gaby, she said. The situation was not unredeemable. She liked the new school after all. She brought her projects home to me. Would you believe it? Cardboard boxes, an alternative education built on supermarket leftovers, projects on the history, geography, biology, chemistry, ecology of Coburg, Pentridge, Merri Creek. She was happy, even when she was drawing cancer maps. They were so pretty, pink and yellow empires, like pâté en croûte, with delicate black lines and annotations. Then Frederic came back to Melbourne.

When he turned up at Patterson Street, Sando greeted him, apparently not knowing who he was.

Hello mate, the young man had said.

Hello mate, said the local member of parliament.

Mind if I come in, mate?

When Celine got home from rehearsals the visitor was well ensconced, his long legs stretched out in front of him. She did not recognise him any more than her husband had. The buzz cut tricked her, the lack of makeup. Only the lashes finally alerted her: they almost, but not quite, obscured his bright insistent eyes. It was that single glimmer (that living being inside the burrow) which would always be, for her, the most disturbing feature of his face.

Celine dropped her heavy groceries on the counter top. She poured herself a glass of wine and observed her strangely tranquil daughter, sitting on one end of the long sofa facing the young man, her lovely strong brown legs folded beneath her skirt.

The visitor tilted his head and Celine saw him hiding there, the fey prancey child who had preferred old fur coats and eye shadow. He wore a checked flannel shirt from Kmart like a working man. Dear Jesus, she said. (Deeeer Jaysssus, said the tape.) He had come to destroy my girl.

Gaby sipped a beer. (Since when was she allowed to drink?)

Frederic? Celine asked.

He grinned. She offered her hand and found his rough and dry.

Hello, Celine.

He had never called me by my name before, she said. (Dear God he expected to be hugged.)

Sit, Celine cried. What have you been doing? she cried. My God, how old are you? she asked, shocked by the man's body she had felt against her own. The creature began to tell her what he had been doing and of course he knew she did not want him here, unravelling all her good results.

You've both been through *so* much, Celine said (waiting to see if he even knew what had happened to Gaby because of him, but nothing, not a thing).

She asked what school he was going to. How he answered she could not remember, except he didn't tell the truth. As a result, she could not understand the triumph on her daughter's face. She thought, don't you, don't you, don't you dare throw your life away, my girl.

If it's not one thing it's another. Soon they went off to her room and they must be having sex, but no: Celine heard that Apple noise and was not smart enough to be afraid.

The computer had been a waste of money. Gaby never used it. As far as Celine knew she had transferred all her cybermania to the reclamation of Merri Creek. The new school encouraged this from the first day. Her study group planted trees and hunted carp on Saturday afternoons. They used the school PC to make charts of invasive species and native birds. That was enough. Who would have alerted her to Agrikem? Frederic? How would he know?

No, Celine said, Mervyn Aisen introduced Gaby to Agrikem. This was pure malice. He 'proved' to her that MetWat had issued Agrikem a secret licence to release 'limited quantities' of dioxin. Gaby was Gaby. She was immediately outraged. Mervyn wound her up and she rushed off to attack her daddy.

Sando had to be the good guy, Celine said. It was what his life was for. He could not bear it that his daughter would think otherwise. Of course Gaby knew that, and she was totally relentless. She took him to visit dying gardens in the little houses on McBryde Street. She nagged at him until he actually raised the issue in parliament. This did nothing to calm his daughter and he was mocked by the minister who was the one, presumably, who arranged for a 'reliable source' to leak him a chemical analysis of Agrikem's effluent which showed no trace of dioxin at all.

He was a politician, Celine said, as the semitrailers shrieked, so therefore he must be corrupt. But the poor darling could be completely unworldly and when he was fed bad information from the left faction, he believed it utterly. He sat Gaby down at the kitchen table and went through the printout with her. He gave his solemn word that there was no dioxin in the Agrikem effluent.

I wasn't there, Celine said. I can imagine: how it must have hurt to confront his daughter's grey and hostile eyes.

Pause. Rewind. Play.

What if you wished to obliterate the corporatists? the Angel said.

29

When two headlights arrived directly outside his window Felix snapped awake and stumbled towards the white-quartz glare, naked arm held across his red-rimmed eyes, but nothing else to ensure his modesty.

There came a violent thumping on the connecting door behind him.

He drew one of the curtains and saw, through the mountain fog, a tall windowless van with a high old-fashioned radiator which he would later learn had the singular virtue of being unburdened by computer operating systems. For now, however, the thumping on the door took precedence.

At other times he had pressed his ear against this door, sometimes his back. Sometimes he had heard laughter, sometimes television. No-one had ever knocked on it before. Who's there, in the name of Beelzebub? He had, until that very moment, assumed that those on the other side like the woman who had driven him from Newcastle, the boy who delivered him upriver, that whole tribe of river rats and dry drunks who had kept him supplied with food and drink, the crew of surf lifesavers, all these people had a benevolent intention towards him. He knew them to be brave individuals who revered his occupation and would place themselves at risk to ensure the story was told in all its complexity, no matter what pistol-wielding thug might try to stop it.

What? he asked the door.

A white paper napkin slid in over the carpet, its message clearly visible.

KEEP AWAY FROM THE WINDOW.

He retreated to the vicinity of the bed and donned a pair of boxer shorts.

He imagined he could hear newcomers entering the next room of the suite. There were sounds of distress, although they possibly had been produced by a television soundtrack. Someone coughed. He thrust his papers, tapes and batteries under the mattress and remade the bed. Then, with his heart beating loudly in his ears, he slipped beneath the iridescent quilt. He waited. He faced the door with his knees drawn up. He embraced his pillow like the child of divorcing parents. He threw off the blanket and pulled his trousers on. He took three steps to the connecting door which, being of the hollow-core variety such as can be purchased at Mitre 10 for less than $50, was no serious barrier to anything. Perhaps he might have kicked it down.

He knocked.

The voices ceased. TV ditto. The door flew open. He saw several young men and women fleeing like cockroaches from light. He saw a woman with two gold earrings shaped like shells. On her slender wrist there was a bracelet, also gold. She reached to grasp a hand. He was shocked to realise that the hand belonged to Claire Moore, his wife. She wore a long man's coat and tennis shoes. Her perfect girlish legs were bare, as if straight off the court, and she was flushed.

You've lost weight, she said, and held out her ruined potter's hands.

Celine Baillieux, who did not know her, then placed her hands familiarly on Claire Moore's shoulders.

Felix Moore felt the force of emotions he had imagined safely locked away.

His wife was searching his face. She asked, How much are you drinking?

I fucked it up.

Idiot, I love you.

The fugitive held up a single finger, then two palms, then retreated to the bathroom where he confronted the embarrassment of his crumpling mask, the snot in his mad beard, the red wine stains on his dirty teeth.

Fubsy, Claire called, let me in.

But he was ugly with snivelling gratitude.

Let me clean my teeth, he said. But he had no toothbrush [sic] and when he finally emerged his eyebrows were mad and his wet hair stood on end.

His wife then informed him that Gaby was Celine's only daughter. So would Felix please write what Celine wanted him to write.

Claire patted the bed and he sat beside her. He was very pleased to have his hands taken.

You've got a lovely wife, Celine said now.

You shouldn't be here, he told his wife. There are people trying to kill me.

I went with them, Claire said. I'm here to drive some sense into you. They're on deadline. They're editing right now.

He registered that his writing was being fucked with. At the same time he beheld that dear familiar face and understood that she would take him back.

I was at Five Dock tennis club, she said. The game was nearly over.

You walked away from a third set?

She honoured him with a private smile.

That was who Claire was. She was being taken to see her estranged husband but she was a good citizen, she would not let down the others. That was who she was. She could not play singles because she had no killer streak, but she was an ace at doubles because she could never let her partner down.

Listen, Celine said, listen to what Claire wants to say.

Claire's hand was pressing on his knee. Felix, she said, please do what they want.

What do they want?

Are you really making Gaby seem as if she's guilty?

In the midst of this upset, the fugitive was pleased to feel his wife's restraining hand.

You will not fiddle with my words, he told Celine.

Listen to your wife.

What is all this 'editing'?

We are fixing your awful spelling. We are *preparing* the digital edition. But it reads like you want my daughter dead, so maybe you could think about that.

Then don't publish it. Burn it. I don't care.

Fubsy, Claire said.

The fugitive looked into his wife's brown eyes and when she had taken stock of him she shook her head and laughed. He can't be changed, she said and, with the back of her hand, brushed the tangled beard. Dear old fool, she said. Don't be brave.

He was frightened that he would make an ugly scene by

crying. See you soon, he said, and abruptly turned his back. She knew enough to let him be, and he was stupid enough to let her climb back in the truck without once saying that he loved her.

When it was quiet he returned to work as he had left it. That is, he knew his subject had no wish to be innocent. It was her job to be the guilty one. They will say there are no female programmers, she said on tape, and everything is there to make sure your gorgeous boy is on the fast track, making deep algorithms while you are likely to get yourself stuck in some fucking data centre mounting servers, changing tapes, and running cable under the floor. If you drop out of high school your workmates will be idiots trying to feel your tits, managers who want to fuck you and 'promote' you to marketing or customer support, on the phone all day explaining technology to morons. I almost did this to myself.

I thought I was being brave but I was being the girlfriend without knowing it. I had so much fun hacking that I spent almost no time programming. I was my own worst dream: a fucking 'hobbyist' or a 'power user' sitting in the dunny reading old issues of *Macworld*. But when I got it, she said, I got it: writing software is so intensely pleasurable it should be against the law. I was not employed to do this. You don't get paid to do it, it pays you. You go to sleep at four in the morning. You are awake at seven, with your brain already working: why is that program running slowly, what is causing this lurking bug. Girls don't program? Bullshit. When I was a daytime suit I was a good suit because I knew more than the programmers. Even in the years when Frederic was an overpaid public genius, when he grew his

351

hair, long like a Beatle, wore button-down shirts, narrow black ties, and slim tight single-breasted jackets, through those years I was a suit by day, we binged at night together.

Code is simple to understand. It is a language to talk to people and machines. Think of Montaigne writing an essay, shaping ideas, seeking beauty, clarity, simplicity and concision. A good code language lets you do this. When you are on fire then *beauty* arises. It's like, for instance, Euclid's proof that prime numbers are infinite. Or it's like Brancusi's *Bird in Space*, elegant solutions to complex problems. Some coding languages make this impossible and some computer programmers are the walking dead, but if you're working in an expressive language you spend your nights all over the heavens quote unquote.

From the beginning, Frederic and I were builders, she said. We reconstructed Zork when we were babies. Later, much later, we would make architecture, feature by feature, clamp interfaces together, squash bugs, supercharge the hotspots to make them faster still. We built in air and electricity, in 1's and o's and nothing more.

But when Frederic came back from northern New South Wales, we built a physical structure in the paddock outside Agrikem. This was the premier event. This is all you need to understand.

30

It was winter. There was frost on the grass and Frederic and I were cockatoos, keeping watch on McBryde Street while Mervyn crawled beneath the fence. He was dressed in rubber boots and waterproofs, so this was not an easy thing to do. Plus he had gaffer tape to close the gap between his sleeves and his rubber gloves and he wore a motorcycle helmet with a visor. Not bad for a man of seventy-five. He opened the sewer plate and lowered in a billy can and we watched as he retrieved it and poured its contents into three brown bottles. He took his time, wrapping each one in a plastic bag. Finally we met him at the fence and held up the barbed wire for him to get back out.

We were there because Mervyn was a relentless old codger with a long history in the labour movement. His mate Herby Waltzer was a former secretary of the Australian Manufacturing Workers Union. Herby had a nephew at the Batman Institute of Technology (BIT). The nephew was doing a PhD in environmental science and would be 'honoured' to analyse our effluent for free. Even better, he could do this under supervision by the acting head of his department. All we had to do was get a sample.

The BIT tests took a whole month. Herby Waltzer's nephew had found a furan ($2,3,7,8$-TCDF) and other toxic polychlorinated dioxins. His supervisor had written: there are no safe levels for dioxins and furans. They should not be entering the sewage system at all. They are dangerous in the sense that they can cause harm to the environment in even very small amounts.

This arrived by snail mail in Darlington Grove and I went to Sydney Road and paid for photocopies.

This was when I would bridge the gap between my father and Mervyn. Maybe Mervyn was a stirrer and a ratbag but corporate crime was right up Sando's alley. This was the best gift you could give him: a polluter, caught red-handed, and shamed with solid proof, printed out in rows of numbers from the Batman Institute of Technology. I said nothing about Mervyn yet. It was the numbers that were the point and when my father had finished reading he dragged me into his chair and there, with me all bruised and tangled, he kissed my head. We've got the bastards, he said. I was not going to screw this up. I said nothing about Mervyn. I cooked him tuna casserole instead. We washed up together and then he took me through the BIT report which he clearly understood.

He said that this student had found 1.4 parts per billion of the furan 2,3,7,8-TCDF. This level was equivalent to 143 parts per trillion of dioxin 2,3,7,8-TCDD. Don't worry what it means. Just understand that 0.038 parts per trillion in water is enough to start killing fish. Agrikem's effluent also contained chlorophenols, the precursors for the manufacture of 2,4-D. Several different types of these chemicals were found, including dichlorophenol and trichlorophenol. The samples contained one hundred times Agrikem's allowed limit of their Trade Waste Agreement.

My dad called the minister on his private line, at night. We were not nervous or intimidated. He said, Goodso, we got the bastards, and then he faxed the report straight to him. This was Sando at his best. It was worth living in a creepy house to see him shine like this.

So the minister would table the report, no wucking furries, but he could not possibly do it until it had been officially signed by BIT. He was not in the business of defaming a manufacturer. BIT said this would be routine, and then the analysis was misplaced, then found, and then there was a letter from their legal counsel stating that the institute would not support 'unsupervised work' performed outside the department.

But you can read it out in parliament yourself.

In my dreams.

But you do have that privilege?

Sweetie, no. I can't.

Yes you can. If you want to you can. (I suppose I was obnoxious.) You have to, I said.

For Christ's sake, Sando cried. Shut up.

That's where it turned, in a nanosecond, Gaby said. I told him he should apologise. We were standing in the kitchen. He had a jar of peanut butter in his hand and he threw it at the window. Glass sprayed around the room. There were shards in my hair. I was afraid and angry all at once. He tried to hug me and say that he was sorry. I told him he was a failure to his whole electorate. I asked him how many birth defects had been reported in Fawkner. I just made that up, based on nothing.

He laughed at me. Who ever made you think you could talk to me like that?

Don't you laugh. Stop it.

But he wouldn't or couldn't. He crunched across the glass.

I told him he was drunk, although he wasn't. I said he was abusive. I stuffed clothes in my schoolbag and bicycled around Brunswick and Royal Parade looking for Frederic's mother's van.

31

I hurt my father and so he changed. After that I was always innocent or stupid. If I learned or questioned something, it was because of someone else. If I criticised him, I had been *influenced*. This way he could keep on loving me no matter what I did.

He discovered the floppy disk 'Find Gaby's Pussy'.

He would have had no clue about how to access it. He just blamed the school for what he feared it was and he visited my home-room teacher. He didn't like that she was a 'girl' with torn jeans and spiked-up hair. Her boyfriend was in Cosmic Psychos or The Hairballs, one of those. Crystal was a punk revival feminist. She dealt with my father and calmed him down. When he left she played the game. Of course she got the joke, that Frederic was my pussycat. Then she went through the code afterwards, learning from us, line by line.

There were teachers who were always stressed by the lack of structure. They thought they were radicals because they walked off the job when an Education Department inspector arrived. But not all of them were suited to real life in a democracy. Crystal was born to be our teacher. She encouraged us to take votes. She smoked with us in the 'man hole'. She taught us by learning alongside us. I had become obsessed with the Merri Creek, so that was very cool with her. She had known nothing about the soil, the history, the politics, the birds and trees, so we all started to do the work together.

When my dad chickened out on presenting the dioxin numbers in parliament it was just natural that I took the BIT analysis to Crystal. This was what she was on earth to do. She added Agrikem to my Merri Creek map. She got us studying herbicides, which led us to dioxin, which led us to Agent Orange, to Australia's part in the Vietnam War which had finished before we were born.

She went to MetWat's head office in Flinders Lane, down near Spencer Street station, and returned with an annual report. We were righteous and outraged by what we found in it, pictures of the men to whom we had given custody of the most precious commodity on earth, our water. They were 'corporate advisors specialising in debt, performance improvement'. They were on the boards of Genteck, BankWest, National Australia Bank and Bank of New Zealand, CSIRO. They were Civil Engineering, M. Engineering, FAIM, FIE (Aust.), B. Science and Engineering. They had backgrounds in the manufacturing industry. They had worked for mining companies and multinational accountants. We were not persuaded they could be trusted with the common good.

Am I ranting? Alone in a room. Talking to the wall. Will anybody ever hear me?

In class Freddo and I wrote a very buggy 'Active Agent Puppet' game in BASIC. Dioxin was the active agent and the puppets were the shiny-faced men on the MetWat board. Crystal was a published writer. She helped us to imagine individual characters, pathetic, fretful, boastful, or falsely innocent like the amoral Harold Skimpole in

Bleak House (which we had to read). Skimpole said he was innocent as a child. So we put him on the board as well. Not even Frederic could resolve the code issues, but our fire spread throughout the school.

The mad beaky-nosed art teacher projected images of the board members on wet cartridge paper and we painted over them, making bleeding, fuzzy portraits of men with shadow eyes, and vast gold buttons on their creepy suits. The shop guy was Doug the Organic Mechanic. He taught mitre cuts in fifth-year shop. Then his class made real frames so we could have an art show and an opening. Our portraits hung round the edge of the upstairs gallery where mad Methodists had once studied scripture in compartments shaped like segments of a pie.

Are there schools like this today? Probably not. We all thought we were inventing the future which we imagined would be better than the past.

We had a class visitor I recognised from Lygon Street: a punkish older guy with thin red hair and rings and screws and safety pins like medals on his face. He used to set up a folding table some Saturdays. He displayed awful pictures of deformities and bubbling flesh. He had red sunglasses. I had always thought he must be nuts.

In our home room, Eddy Margolis asked him what band he was in. He said shut up, don't be a smart-arse. He had been a sergeant in the Australian army handling herbicides. They had made him ill.

I smiled at him in sympathy. He stared right through me.

After his gruesome talk he said he was not there to encourage us to break the law but he himself was going to pay a personal visit to the sewer on the map we had made. He had not known about it previously, but he would confirm or deny the analysis on the spot. Me and Undertoad went on our bikes. When we arrived we could see Crystal's beat-up van and some figures in the smudgy gloom beyond the barbed-wire fence. It was damp and cold on McBryde Street and the wind was blowing from the east and we squeezed under the bottom strand and found our teacher and our class all huddled at the stink hole. Our expert was still wearing his red-coloured dark glasses. He lifted the plate without any iron bar, just with thumb and forefingers. He did not even set it on the ground.

OK, he said. What do you smell?

Chemicals.

Like what?

Like manure, like cow shit.

Yes. Nitrogen-rich. What else?

Like plastic?

Like plastic yes. Does anyone know what silicone caulking smells like?

No-one did.

It smells like manure and plastic and silicone caulking. There is no smell like it. Whose eyes are running?

Everyone's.

So, said Crystal, what would you say if MetWat swore there was no dioxin?

Stay away from here.

What can we do?

Nothing. Stay away.

We crossed the sodden overgrazed grass and slipped through the chained front gate. It was all so ordinary. The streets, the little houses, the bad smell, a plumber's van reversing from a driveway. Crystal gave me a sort of hug and said, Promise you will stay away now. She did not know me very well. I hardly knew myself.

Freddo and I went up to the musty ceiling above the school and he took off my clothes and drew his finger down the middle of my chest and told me I was beautiful and I said I was going to take off all my clothes and roll in the dirt at Agrikem.

He didn't say anything, just looked at me with his secret glittery eyes and I felt a hot patch right above the bottom of my spine. He never tried to stop me. He knew I wouldn't like him if he did. He kissed me all over, in all the crazy places like the back of my knees. We had an electrical connection. We were doing 'pair programming' before we heard the term or learned it was uncool. Pair programming has a gripping immediacy: you live with your partner inches from your side. You feel his heat, his brain, and each half of you must understand the code, there, then, as it is being born. Pairing may be invasive, but so is sex.

No-one but us knew what we planned or what we thought. We annoyed people. We locked the others out. We got deeper and deeper into our own shit. The school had an old super 8 camera which no-one bothered with. A Canon 512XL. While our classmates were running round making arty videos, while Cosmic Cosmo was making a wine rack from plumbing parts, we took the Canon apart and put it back together like soldiers with a weapon.

We sneered at the new video cameras and called them 'products'. We introduced the word agitprop to common parlance. Our 'appropriate technology' could not record sound so our agitprop would be completely visual. We would destroy MetWat on the television news.

We would go further, play harder than anybody else. We would destroy my perfect skin. We paid for one roll of film which was exactly two minutes and fifty seconds of footage. We performed our action in rehearsal. We timed it to fit that single roll.

1. Three seconds of Agrikem sign.
2. Establishing shot of factory, zoom in to sewer.
3. Gaby walks into frame and strips to her undies.
4. Gaby rolls on the poisoned soil.

We planned this on paper and then we followed our own directions. This is how it has always been for me. Once it gets to the real-life action you are beyond fear. You are simply in the mechanism. First you do this, then you do that. It is no more scary than stripping down a gun. On the day of the action it happened to be cold. My naked skin was like a plucked chicken, smeared with mud and poison. I crouched and hugged my knees while Frederic ran across McBryde Street to find a house that had a telephone. He took ages. I hoped he might get a blanket to bring back but we hadn't thought of that and so he came back empty-handed, waiting to execute the next part of the plan.

5. The ambulance arrives.
6. Paramedics run across paddock.
7. Paramedics carry Gaby to ambulance.
8. Ambulance drives away with Gaby inside.
9. Agrikem sign.
10. Title: 30 days later.
11. Gaby's skin with chloracne bubbles and pustules.

Frederic took his shirt off so he would be as cold as me. That one was worthy of my dad. We waited for the ambulance together. He offered me his shirt which made me start to cry. He touched me and I pushed him away and thought things that surprised me. I thought, you carried a bloody tripod on your bike but not a blanket. I imagined I could feel the blisters starting on my back and tummy. I was less together than I would have expected. I cried because my father wouldn't listen to me. I cried because Frederic would admire me for being brave but now he would not marry me, or would marry me and have affairs with women with unblemished skin. I thought, fat chance our film will ever be on television.

The bone-thin starving horses stood against the fence of the next paddock, their sad faces towards me, their backs to the wind.

The ambulance came. I was hysterical and the neighbours came to watch and Frederic had to cry as well, just so he could travel with me.

32

When we refused to process our film, Crystal got unexpectedly shitty.

We said we weren't ready to hand it in. We were waiting for something.

For what?

A scene. We can't tell you.

Probably we displayed bad attitude. The class all thought we were wankers. Fair enough. But what could we reveal to them? That we were waiting for the vile sores to break out on my back and stomach. Then, only then, could we shoot the scene, finish the roll, process it, and get it on the Channel 9 news. The class could see it then. They had no idea of who we were.

We were waiting for the sores and lesions. Every time I came back from the loo he was looking at me, his eyebrows raised. He already had our press release, but jeez, back off, Freddo.

Don't get me wrong. We were in total agreement with each other. We had performed 'a necessary action' but, honestly, now we had cooled off, I was not exactly thrilled by the prospect of being marked for life.

I went to the State Library, sans Freddo. I saw gross pics which freakerated me. Later I would get labelled ignorant and hysterical, which was more or less correct, although that was trumped by my mother who called me a masochist.

If I had been a soldier I would have been a hero for putting my body at risk for the greater good. But I was just a girl and so I must be a masochist.

Crystal had been an ideal teacher but when we wouldn't hand our project in she became a snub-nosed hard-arse. Why? We had school-based assessment so I could not see why she should get so stressed. Finally she flipped and 'ordered' Frederic to bring his backpack to her desk. No-one ordered anyone at R. F. Mackenzie.

I called for a vote.

Crystal said shut up. Bring up the bag, like now.

I made a note. She saw me doing it.

The Canon was in Frederic's bag, and in the Canon was the film. That was the point. Frederic did not move. He also made a note, and then gazed up at Crystal.

The room was frozen-still. Crystal did not threaten or repeat herself. Frederic remained at his desk. Then he made another note and laid his pen back down. It was sort of thrilling to see his defiance. Next he uncoiled himself and his eyes were narrow and his movements informed by some undeclared intention which made him glorious.

He threaded his way through the desks to the coat rack and I thought, shit, I love you, I love you, you are going to carry our film right out the bloody door, or maybe, just expose the film in front of everyone. I knew he was thinking what I was thinking, that's the way we were.

As he delivered the bag to Crystal I was in the zone. He placed it on her desk. Right. He unzipped it. Right. He removed the camera and held it high, taunting.

Then he fucking gave it to her. I watched it in its full awfulness. Frederic held his head to one side, and if it was meant to be sarcastic, it was not. He stood in all his powerlessness and waited while she rewound the film.

Crystal removed the film and gave him back the camera.

The film is our property, he said.

Tough.

We paid for it with our money.

You'll be reimbursed. Now, please take your place.

Please take your place. Who said that? I made a note, of course, but this was no longer our school. R. F. Mackenzie was not like this at all, and the whole home room were like POWs, shocked, and hating Crystal except – to be honest – maybe those who thought Frederic and I were too up ourselves, and of course they must have been the majority.

But even then it did not occur to me that the chunky spike-haired little band moll would actually process our film.

Later, on the due day when everyone presented their projects, nonstop, 9 am–5 pm, I watched her set up the projector and lace our processed film, and she was still hard-arsed, but when she saw the Agrikem sign her face softened and she glanced at me and I was pleased because I wanted her to like me after all. I knew I must be the most radical, the coolest student she ever had.

Frederic had shot the scenes in sequence so what was projected on the pitted wall was a kind of rough assembly of what we actually shot. Not quite the script, but close enough. Each take was short, three or five seconds, and Crystal's face changed in sync with what she saw, as if she were entering the rhythm of the argument. 1. Agrikem sign. *Good*. 2. Wide shot of factory, *good*, zoom to sewer. *Good*.

3. Gaby takes her clothes off, *OK*. 4. Gaby rolls in the dirt. *No, no.* 5. Ambulance. 6. Gaby escorted to through fence. 7. Ambulance leaves McBryde Street. 8. Royal Melbourne Hospital. Ambulance arrives. *No, no, no.* Crystal in total panic.

When Crystal ran from the room everybody stared at me. Freddo drew on his pad as if he had just had some really cool and urgent idea. Crystal came back with the temporary coordinator, a person not well suited to that role. When the temporary coordinator had seen the film she said she had a legal responsibility to show it to our parents.

We read *Bleak House* all afternoon. I hated it, that sweetie goodie Esther Summerson.

I asked Crystal did she like her.

Crystal said we were looking to go beyond 'like'.

Doug the Organic Mechanic arrived to announce that he 'very much doubted' you would even get a zit from a single exposure to the dirt at Agrikem. Melissa and Nada tittered. Doug ordered me to pull up my T-shirt and I said he was a perve. I said it was 'inappropriate' and so he left the room. Then Crystal made me show my unmarked fat.

It was the worst day of my life.

My father made a big impact at the parents' screening. He said what a relief it was, and what a happy occasion that no-one had been hurt, that no harm had been done and the best thing, he said to everyone, was that we had learned about the importance of doing homework. They all pissed themselves with laughter and I felt a fool. My father wore an open-neck shirt and a daggy unravelling sweater – pitch perfect for R. F. Mackenzie – and he looked so bright, and handsome and in charge. The Premier had just increased funding to suburban libraries. One of which was just across the street, Sando said, and his daughter could have learned everything she needed to know about dioxin's side effects without getting herself muddy.

This was just so psychologically wrong.

He put his hand on Frederic's mother's shoulder and she stared at him like a cocker spaniel. Stoned. He tousled Frederic's hair (which Frederic *really* didn't like) and he hugged me and Celine to him in a monstrous family fake. I had never seen him so energised. He bullshitted and bulldozed the temporary coordinator and made a speech about Crystal's amazing dedication. He thought the government's negotiation with her union on pay scales would make her very happy.

Did Frederic understand what had happened? Of course. Exactly. But he led his dazed mum away without speaking to me. I had my bike so was excused the parental car. The Volvo was at home when I finally arrived, its radiator pinging as it cooled, and I wheeled my bike down the side and came in through the laundry. Once inside I discovered Act II was over and this was now Act III. All dark and comfortless.

Sando had clearly stewed on everything since leaving school and by the time I came into his presence he was triumphant. He could not wait to point it out: I had failed to prove my point. He had been right. I should have believed him, not Mervyn Aisen and his sloppy graduate student friend. He would be a minister by next year. Would I believe him then?

He became reflective, speculative. What, he asked me, what if I had succeeded in my film, what then?

Academically speaking, he said. What if my skin had erupted? Did it occur to me how I would have hurt all of us, not only myself, but him? What would it have done for his future in the government?

I did not recognise the person who I had sided with against my mother.

How could you do this to me? he demanded. Why do you believe everyone outside the house but not your father?

You abused your beauty, he said. I told him he was pathetic and went to bed and locked the door so he had to apologise from the other side.

Then Celine tried to be the peacemaker. She must have been seeing Lionel Patrick (who was old enough to be a pensioner) but she sided with my father. He loves you, more than life itself, she said.

He's a baby, I said.

All men are babies when they love you, she said, so vain.

33

At first, when Frederic surrendered our film to Crystal, I did not understand how much I had been betrayed. Frederic saw it, though. That was one of his amazing talents, to always see the contrail of my thoughts.

To the home room, we must have seemed unchanged: the up-themselves pair with matching eye shadow, and army boots. Freddo stroked my neck and blew in my ear in public. No-one had a clue, but he was asking me to forgive him when I wouldn't admit that there was anything to forgive. He told me with his eyes that he needed me and I really couldn't bear his need. It was so completely unappealing. No-one knew what was happening. I just went off him, in public. I wondered had I ever loved him anyway.

Then, quite soon, in days not weeks, without this ever being discussed, he was switching from Apple to PC. (What the fuck was this about?) He morphed into Freddo Version 3, all brisk and definite. PCs were just more serious, he decided. He was 'polite'. He noticeably did not stroke my neck.

He was not going to say sorry for making a compete fool of me on film, showing my fat to the class without any bigger social benefit. Instead he produced *Effective C + +* by Scott Meyers, and read it as if it were a newspaper.

Was it really that easy for him, or was it: you punish me, I punish you, that sort of thing?

From then on I lived in the middle of a thunderstorm. I dreaded school each day. I obsessed about the wrong things, like my weight, like how did he get money for expensive books. Finally, one warm evening, after school, I walked the wrong way up Sydney Road. That is, not the way we had always walked together. He let me go. I did it to myself. By the time I got to Cornwall's Hardware, I knew we had broken up.

Next day I returned to the home room. Let it be the same, I thought. I sat where I normally sat. I waited passively, already dead. When Frederic took his usual place, I thought, thank God, but when he turned to me his eyes were leaking, black and murderous.

I said, I don't know what's happening.

He said, I have to help Cosmo.

Cosmo, who later became the notorious Paypal, was the biggest dork in a home room totally full of misfits and dorks and refugees from all sorts of marital, pedagogic and political disasters. His father had Palermo Plumbing and Gas Fitting out the back of the Coburg mall. Cosmo was at R. F. Mackenzie because he was thought unteachable. His father had four other sons, and no room for the youngest in the business. But Cosmo was like a dog that won't leave your door. All he did was make models and machines from plumbing parts. He was already six foot tall but he had no sense of personal space and it was a nightmare to even walk down Sydney Road with him because he was always bumping into people plus he had a loud hysterical laugh. Plus he was a PC gamer which was, of course, the point.

Cosmo needs help, Frederic said, rubbing his eye, smearing black across his wrist.

OK.

So I'll just help him for a bit, OK?

I looked back at Cosmo. He winked at me, which was not his privilege.

OK, I said.

I was slow to appreciate that my gentle polite Frederic was about to permanently sit beside the nerd and they would now spend days whispering to each other about all the games available for PC.

When Cosmo lent Ultima VI to Frederic everybody knew I had been dumped. No-one in the home room was sorry for me. No-one came to save my pride which would have been so easy. Beyond R. F. Mackenzie was outer space, no life on any other planets. I had pissed off Troy. To the Samoans I was dead meat. I had been so fucking superior with the Keppel Street Quartet that they had long ago stopped trying to phone me. My father had become distant, and Celine arrived drunk at night expecting what she called 'girl's talk'. Yuck.

But Christmas was nearly here, ditto summer, so I could hide from myself at the creek where the council mowed down our saplings because, of course, there could be no life between the tractor wheels, and we should have known to plant our trees at one-metre intervals. Someone somewhere was having meetings with the three councils and MetWat, but I was just replanting. I hung out with wrinkly old people. I worked hard and tried not to feel too much. I volunteered at the plant nursery and did my best to get along with my father who could not get over himself. Night after night I stayed at home eating takeaway until I was brave enough to call Katie, who had been my alibi when I was sleeping with Frederic at his place.

I deserved nothing from her, but she was going to the Mechanics Club in Brunswick that night, where her boyfriend's band was playing. He was a drummer in a punk revival band called Snot, something like that. He had the early gig and they would meet me out in front, OK.

Really?

Are you joking? I miss you.

I had spent so much time being Gaby-and-Frederic I no longer knew what I should wear to listen to a bloody band. I knew those girls, they would arrive so cool and cute and I made myself totally vomitous attempting to 'get a look together'. Finally I smoked a joint and dressed in all the second-hand stuff I normally wore. When I arrived at the club my old friends were all waiting, hooing and cheering that they loved my look, they loved me. I was original to them. There was no-one like me, although of course they would have rather died than look like me. Their clothes were all clearly expensive (not to boys, but to girls it was completely obvious).

The Mechanics Club was a ratfuck, the band itself was crap. The boyfriend was handsome but too pleased with himself. WTF. I jumped around and had some drinks. Katie shared a bump of coke with me. There was what they called an 'after party' and the drummer boyfriend put my bike in the van and I was so pleased to be included in the normal world. Katie sat in the front seat next to her drummer. He drove with his arm around her shoulder, serpent scales in blue ink from his sleeveless top down to his fingernails. Katie kept on flopping her hand over the back of the seat. Then:

duh: she had a condom. My friends had become babies while I had been gone.

The after party was in East Kew. I had lived in Melbourne all my life and never saw a house with gates like these, four-metre-high spears tipped with gold fleurs-de-lis, like the owners were waiting for the revolution. A bright yellow Porsche was parked inside. The punk revival drummer lived here with his mum and dad and little brothers. His left ear was rolled and pierced like a weird piece of pasta, but he was very well mannered. He carried my bike from the van and showed me where to leave it. Damn, I thought, fuck it. Have to ride it home.

The parents were away. There were frantic kids in every direction, speed, molly, coke, hash oil. They were so private-school, and I was the freakiest thing they ever saw, those silly little girls with white powder still clinging to the philtrum of their Botticelli lips.

I thought, I will have a pee and try and find my way back home.

But the loos were locked and filled with idiots. I went downstairs and found, amidst the chaos, the moronic thumping base, shrieking, vomiting, not a loo but a brand-new Mac IIci. It turned out to be upgraded with a 50 MHz Daystar 68030 board, and it connected to a Hayes Smartmodem 96 and it was surrounded by silent kids some maybe as young as twelve. At the keyboard, like the most perverted seminarian or Sunday-school teacher, was Frederic Matovic.

The little boys hung on him, on his shoulder, pressing in on him as he did his fluttery feathering Frederic typing, and I knew it absolutely was not sexual, but just the same my stomach tightened. It was, to me at least, so completely intimate. Those rhythms were his rhythms, created by commands and responses, by pauses, by almost violent returns, when he shifted in his seat, the way he did, and nodded his head as he had first done when he had a fringe to flick away. I knew that he was breaking into something good. When one of the munchkins hooked him up to a brand-new snail's-pace StyleWriter it was clear he had a shitload of treasure to take home. I had meant to run away, but I barged in and tapped him on the shoulder and he was like, Hi.

He pushed a skanky skateboard child away and I, just, took my place.

What had he got into? A few years later it would have been email. That year it was a CSIRONET account. Holy Shit. He was inside MetWat's *Secretum secretorum* where correspondence was still headed Memo and RDM as in Restricted Distribution Memo. He made a Frederic noise, indeterminate, a sort of moo, and left me with his mullety crew while he relieved the StyleWriter of its burden, reading as he stacked the pages.

We should go, he said. He flicked the fringe that was not there.

I stood. (I should have reacted how else exactly?)

OK, guys, he said. The water is on me.

I was staggered he would do this. Leave these little anklebiters running like mice inside MetWat, but perhaps that was the fee he had negotiated with them, or perhaps he was safely pissing on the Federal Police, or engaging in class warfare by getting the Computer Crime Squad to hit East Kew. His normal procedure would be to not interfere

375

with any site he had entered, to build a nice back door perhaps, but to tidy up after himself and do no damage to the system.

Not tonight. IDIOTS. YOU NEED BETTER PASS-WORDS. WE ARE TWELVE YEARS OLD AND WE OWN YOU.

I found him a plastic bag in the kitchen and he filled it with his heavy printout and we left the house together, and walked out into the hot night air.

And there, in the front of the palace, behind the high iron gates, beside the Porsche and the BMW, we kissed and kissed and kissed, the softest widest lips. I kissed his secret feathery eyes. He smelled my neck. He said, Happy birthday baby, in my ear and I was so busy crying, I did not understand exactly what was in his zorky little mind.

34

The fugitive, it can now be reported in this edition (fifth digital, first paper), had been moved from place to place at night, for instance on the pillion of an ailing Honda 750, along a hundred and thirty kilometres of winding mountain road, from the Golden Wattle Motel to the Koala Lodge in Katoomba, a town famous for its touristic virtues including the steepest railway incline in the world, the steepest aerial cable car in the Southern Hemisphere, the vertiginous Scenic Walkway, with its sublime scenery so precipitous and perilous that a perfectly sane man might be tempted to cast himself screaming into the abyss.

The pillion passenger's character would not be tested by the great sublime. On the contrary: he was accommodated with a view of the Koala Lodge's inevitable concrete forecourt, and all the extra advantages of generous self-catered accommodation with editors 'en suite'. He had a cooktop in his room so he could have spaghetti and grill sausages and lamb chops and, at this particular moment, launder his underwear which ballooned from the boiling saucepan in shivering dome-like tents suggestive of soap bubbles and the Sydney Opera House.

In his new location, he sat, as he had sat while covering the war in Bougainville, the events of 1975, the first hunger strike at Villawood, day after day for almost fifty years, in front of a typewriter. Tapes were supplied. Pages were taken by arrangement. There was continual loud dripping from the bathroom which he ignored. He wore a grubby bath towel around his hips. On his wide bare shoulders he revealed a hard hairy saddle of flesh, a dense pad reminiscent of that rounded structure on the dolphin's forehead, the so-called melon which produces sounds for 'communication and echolocation'.

It was night, as usual, and the headlights from the nearby road washed across the ceiling and the voice of Celine Baillieux was without relent. Likewise the dripping, which finally caused the fugitive to leap from his seat as if he were a character in an early Pram Factory production, as if he were, say Archbishop Mannix half mad with paranoia, imagining himself the actor in a drama being observed by all the world. His trousers would not dry but he was the son of an ingenious mechanic. He fetched the wire hanger from the back of the bathroom door and made a hoop about twenty centimetres in diameter. This he sprung into one trouser leg to keep it fully open. He then threaded a belt and cinched closed the waist. He laid the wet garment on the floor and positioned the motel hair dryer in the tunnel entrance to the left leg. As he turned on the dryer, hot air rushed up the trousers and the apparatus filled its sails.

Cop that young Harry. He said. Out loud.

The newest tapes were seldom free of irritating comment. Really, really, said Celine Baillieux, most of what you have submitted is untrue.

But Felix Moore did not *submit*. To anybody. He turned the cassette off. He stood and approached the connecting door, only to be interrupted by a blue police light washing across the steamy ceiling. He thrust tapes and paper beneath his mattress. He moved typewriter and tape recorders into the cupboard and dragged his towel in after himself as he closed the sliding door behind.

The underpants continued bubbling. The blue light strobed through the steam. The cupboard remained closed. By the time he slid the door open the blue light had changed to red.

He arranged his towel, turned off the lights, and peered around the blinds where he was much relieved to see a young man strapped to a gurney being urgently propelled towards an ambulance.

Celine said, You quote my daughter to make it seem we were alienated. You know that isn't true. We were close then. We're close now. If you were honest you'd make it clear that everything I am doing is because there is no-one in the world I love more. Love does not make you perfect, as far as I recall. It does not wash your sins away, but when I drove back to Coburg, late at night, it was not to talk about my life with Lionel, as you suggest, but because her father would be out of the way. He was enraged by her Agrikem film. He was furious that she had tried to damage him. He was snoring in what had been our bedroom, and I came to give her comfort.

Yes I was 'going out' with Lionel Patrick, so what? He gave me a nice place to live. What was I meant to do? Of course Sando thought I had chosen a conservative to hurt him. He hadn't even met Lionel. Maybe once to shake his hand. But you want to discuss Gramsci? Lionel could do that. Or Terry bloody Eagleton. Lionel has been to performances I would have killed to see, even if I'd had to work as an usher for the privilege. Paul Scofield, Gielgud,

Olivier, and he had an astonishing memory of every one. I was quiet and contented at his place, a house in Caroline Street which he had filled with such lovely things, nothing that was not beautiful, but nothing preening either. I loved his soft leather slippers, the pyjamas he wore around the house with their thin white piping.

Sando never understood the theatre in the least, except he loved to watch me on the stage. It filled him with adulterous passion to know he would soon be schtupping Hedda Gabler.

Lionel was far more refined in every department. It was a pleasure to go with him into the bush, up to his house at Smiths Gully, filled with paintings by these people he had known, the Boyds particularly, and Percival, but also Clifton Pugh and Peter Glass. He tried to teach me the names of trees, but it was so far beyond my own upbringing. With Mr Neville the world was divided into gum trees, wattles and scrub, and that was it.

So two or three times a week I drove across the river and snuck into my own house to talk with my daughter. Perhaps I had had a glass or two. I wouldn't say that I was ever drunk. She was overweight and isolated and depressed and that boy had dumped her, the creep. He was the guilty party then. He always has been. Of course I spoke badly of him. Jesus. Then they were back together, so I had to be punished.

Does she remember how she slagged Lionel? I do. She thought it was 'gross' he was so old. It made her sick to think of it, whatever 'it' was. She repeated things she got from Sando, who seemed to think that Lionel had invented capitalism. Meanwhile the Labor Party were trying to out-capitalist the capitalists. Sando was already becoming bitter. He had been in parliament so short a time but he was being run by bureaucrats and technocrats. This would be his failure, not because he was weak or bad, but he was up against things he could not control and he had, unbelievably, not expected it.

He persuaded Gaby that my relationship with a former attorney-general would be scandal that would hurt not only him but the party. What a joke. Malcolm Fraser lost his pants in Memphis. He was the damn Prime Minister and even this did not hurt him politically. I could have walked behind Lionel carrying his trousers, and no-one would have reported it. I could live with him for weeks on end, be seen at the theatre and the opera and Moroni's and what the hell.

But I was destructive and narcissistic, I heard.

So why then, you may well ask, why did Gaby choose to consult with me about the 'Water Leaks' memoranda? Wouldn't a destructive narcissist be the worst person to confide in? Yet it was to her mother she revealed the contents of a David Jones shopping bag. Two hundred pages, easily.

I suggested she just give them to her father.

He'll burn it, she said.

When I properly understood what she had got hold of, I was frightened for her. MetWat were indeed issuing secret waste-disposal licences and worse. I was also appalled by that fucking R. F. Mackenzie school which hadn't bothered to teach its students that there would be consequences for their pure and lovely actions.

Of course I wouldn't dream of telling Lionel, but he had

been the attorney-general and he was a very experienced lawyer. So it was not at all weird to talk about the law, in general, hypothetically. Forget the conversations. I don't recall them anyway, but what I concluded was that this printed evidence would never see the light of day. The memoranda were stolen property, the product of a crime. In this case the criminal would be my daughter. This is what I told her. She would be punished and not get what she wished. She shouted at me, of course. I was a defeatist. I was bourgeois. She would get the story in the media. I told her that our news had become driven by press releases and managed events. PR flacks outnumbered journalists at the rate of four to one.

She almost spat at me. You think I don't know this? What do you think our film was there to do? She said, I am making history. You haven't got a clue.

If I was such crap, why was she bothering to tell me?

Because you are my mother, she said.

And her chin went rubbery, and I cried and so I completely failed to notice what she was clearly telling me: she would manage an event which would force the government to act.

I drove back to Lionel dewy-eyed. I was her mother, said Celine Baillieux, speaking with that strange flatness of affect that marks all varieties of Australian speech, whether it be Lebanese from Denbo or Samoan or the descendant of a man who expected to live in the Lake District all his life. The fugitive imagined he detected a deep historic grief in the voice of Celine Baillieux, as familiar to him as the sound of wind in lonely European pine windbreaks planted in L-shapes in the paddocks, the denuded land from Balliang East up to Morrisons and Bullengarook and Maryborough. That was our fate, he thought, to love that abused landscape, in spite of the evidence before our wind-wet eyes.

The writer turned off the burning gas below his underpants and rescued his scorched trousers from the bathroom floor. He inserted another cassette, a young woman's voice which would whisper in his sleep.

35

Now Frederic and I were back together I had thought that Cosmo would disappear. Next Monday morning we had 'Monday remarks' as per usual. Frederic had previously considered this a waste of time. Now he wanted to raise the issue of 'Cosmo's gun'.

I could not be embarrassed by Freddo but this was pretty close. Cosmo's gun was an infantile steampunk gun he had constructed from antiqued copper and brass tubing and several eccentrically shaped 'steam chambers'. He had made it with Doug in shop, which was OK. But when he brought it to home room and acted like it was 'significant' he got completely pissed on. No-one knew what steampunk was and didn't care. It was guns they voted against. This was why Crystal failed to recognise the R.F. Mackenzie teaching moment. Cosmo the loser had raided Palermo Plumbing and found totally new uses for flexible copper tubing, hose clamps, thermocouples, heating elements, copper and brass fittings, all sorts of crazy Jules Verne shit that his father would never let him work with in real life. I did not speak against him. Even when he said Macs were for girls. I was just sad, because he was so big and damaged.

Frederic had generally exhibited disdain for the class's good opinion. Now they were outraged by his nerve, amazed to find themselves the subject of his sexylove.

And Cosmo with his staring eyes and long chin and

great Sicilian schnozzle, huge Cosmo, pressed rigidly into his desk, mustn't he have thought, why is this happening to me? Did it occur to him there would be a price? Had he decided it would be worth anything, to get a social upgrade in this unexpected way?

I thought it was about Cosmo. I was so pissed off, I didn't see it was for me. Frederic was always a sort of bowerbird, building astonishing displays to court me, and he did this again and again over many years. Just when I thought he was bored with me, he would perform his mating dance. How would I guess this was one of those? He was so sly and devious and funny, and he forced the home room to admire Cosmo in a totally Freddo way. He gave them a talk about steampunk, in whole sentences, with punctuation: Jules Verne, H. G. Wells, Hayao Miyazaki's *Laputa: Castle in the Sky* blah blah blah. Steampunk was an alternative history of Victorian England, the Wild West too, separately, together. It was a variety of science fiction, set in a post-apocalyptic future. Steampunk featured anachronistic technologies like Cosmo's gun which as anyone could see (apparently) harnessed steam and gas for its propellant force.

Crystal had her mouth open. I thought, she is hypnotised. I thought, she loves Frederic in spite of everything. He was so perfectly 100 percent R.F. Mackenzie, showing the teacher what a syllabus she could have built from steampunk: literature, physics, the study of naval vessels. Steampunk brought you slam-bam against Charles Babbage who designed the world's first computer in 1822. And so on. Frederic was an actor's son. He walked between the desks. He was deft and sibilant while the apparent object of his speech sat locked inside his big stiff body, blushing, glowing, his black curly hair erupting from his red bandana.

The class had never seen Frederic in this way. (I'm not sure I had myself.) Certainly they did not understand where this creature came from, and they were indignant to be charmed, to be asked, by him, to tell him what steampunk music might be like. They had no fucking idea. They looked to Crystal who did not help at all.

Cosmo never spoke in class, but Fred asked him anyway: what might steampunk music sound like.

Cosmo beamed, as if he could hear a private orchestra: synth, brass bells and bagpipes and he wasn't going to share. He was so happy, me too, weirdly happy, proud and astonished and in love beyond salvation.

Frederic's mother was back in rehab so after school Frederic and I crawled into the back of her van and when I was all relaxed and dozy he listed every obstacle to exposing MetWat, and how he would personally overcome them one by one. I can do this, he said. He described it like a quest game, with different levels.

First problem: the toxic dishwater was flowing through the dark, buried in the ground. We will raise it up, he said, or something sort of biblical. This was like stoner talk. I was slow to realise he planned this for real life. Freddo could not draw for nuts, but he drew the sad overgrazed paddock beside the Agrikem car park, all the time talking about plumbing, PVC pipes, Bostik plumber's weld. He drew a sort of cobra which turned out to be a giant garden tap rising from the sewer.

You don't know how to do that, I said.

Don't worry. He could fix it. As we publicised the true

effluent analysis we would also raise up the actual poison, see it, smell it as it descended back into the public sewer. Then we would turn off the tap, on television.

We would need Hazchem suits for a start, he said.

I thought this would look cool and scary on TV, but where would we get a Hazchem suit? How much would it cost?

Don't worry. I'll fix it.

Of course he did not know how to fix anything but he was, instinctively, creating an event. He was seventeen. It was *Field of Dreams*, if you build it they will come. He had recruited Cosmo. Cosmo didn't know that yet.

I told him how I loved him.

He said, We could get into a lot of trouble.

I said I knew. I was totally high on danger, on justice, righteousness and rage. It was not my fault my father failed. It was not my fault that this was left to us to do.

The following night I brought Frederic to Darlington Grove and we sat around the kitchen table. It was scorching hot and the sprinkler was sighing in the garden. Miss Aisen wore a tennis dress and her father shorts and a navy singlet. Miss Aisen sat on her hands and would not look at me, and I thought, we have made a big mistake here. She will not break the law. Plus Mervyn had been having trouble looking at Frederic. I hadn't thought of that: Freddo was back on the eye shadow and nail polish. Mervyn directed everything to me.

Later I discovered Miss Aisen was waiting for me to say I was pregnant. She was working out her position, although she never told me what that was. Was she Catholic? Maybe. All I could feel was the very heavy vibe and I was incapable of asking for what we really wanted. I babbled. I regurgitated everything they had taught me: MetWat's brutal mistreatment of the creek, its totally misconceived attempts at flood control, its deceit over Agrikem's effluent. I did not reveal that we finally had the proof.

Miss Aisen asked me, Is this what you came to talk about? She put a hand on her father's arm, and I thought, he is too creeped by Freddo. He can't even look at him.

It's to do with that, Frederic said. In that area.

To do with MetWat? Miss Aisen asked while Mervyn studied a salt shaker.

Yes.

Oh, she said, and totally beamed at Frederic.

Mr Aisen, Frederic said, Gaby tells me you took the dragline in hand.

Sabotaging the MetWat dragline had been a serious crime. No-one had ever told me Mervyn had committed it. Now I must have seemed a gossip and a dangerous girl.

She did, did she? said Mervyn. After which he went back to his salt shaker.

I said I was very sorry if I had been wrong.

We all sat in awful silence until Mervyn finally allowed his smile to show. You tricky old codger, I thought. So I told him about Frederic's hack. Frederic offered to go online to show them how, but Miss Aisen did not want to break the law.

Her father said she was a nervous little mouse. He winked at Frederic.

So she let Frederic do it, in the kitchen. Then she was so excited and angry she donated a floppy so we could have a screenshot of our evidence.

You'll need a plumber, Mervyn said.

I've got one already, Frederic said.

Today we could have dealt with Agrikem differently. We could have hacked their system and instructed the plant to shake itself apart. But twenty years ago remote access to physical assets was a different matter – a business like Agrikem would not have had the level of instrumentation of the modern sort. Everything was operated in person. You opened a valve by hand. You set the speed of the centrifuge manually. Twenty years ago we needed four metres of 80mm PVC pipe, four metres of 80mm flexible agricultural drainpipe, a two-into-one 45-degree PVC junction, a joiner, a tub of Bostik PVC Weld, a plastic bucket, a roll of gaffer tape, a metre of 3/8 steel rod from Surdex Steel in Edward Street Brunswick, two 3/8 nuts and washers, a scrap of 8-ply, a hacksaw, a jig saw, tap and die set, an adjustable spanner, a drill, a 9mm drill bit, a jemmy, eight Undertoad suits and Cosmo natch.

36

So, Freddo gave Cosmo the chance to build a PVC drain system with a plunger that would induce a suction action to expose Agrikem's toxic dioxin effluent to the public eye. Cosmo became scarily excited. He began to make dumb jokes so often, he was a liability. I took him up to the Ferguson Plarre and bought him a neenish tart and said he must not even say our names. He could not even tell Doug what he was doing.

What should he say to Doug?

Say it's steampunk, I said and Cosmo looked so winded that I bought him a malted milk and then, quite clearly, the great wilful dork went back to Doug the Organic Mechanic and spilled the beans.

Doug was like one of those whiskery barkless dogs with a traumatic stare. Whatever dog that was, Gaby did not know, only that his most prosaic shop instruction was whispered. *Draw a line all round and cut it off square.* Doug had lived in Japan. He taught woodwork with Japanese handsaws. He was also a furtive sci-fi fan and *manga otaku* and Cosmo's sole supporter amongst the staff.

Now, suddenly, Doug began publicly distancing himself from Cosmo. He used his *loud voice* so everyone would hear he would no longer let Cosmo Palermo drag 'all your crap' into the classroom. Go find somewhere else, not here. We're not a plumbing business, mate.

But it was Doug who found us a safe place where we could assemble the pipes: an abandoned building site just near the school on David Street. Under the awning was a rough workbench. Below the bench were a few empty beer bottles and a lot of fag ends sort of composting themselves.

Doug was fulltime engaged with his own innocence. He said Cosmo better take more time with his English literature he would end up an unemployable moron.

Go to my office. I'm sick of you, Palermo.

Then they spent about an hour compiling the list of stuff that Cosmo would need to make his pump.

We were not worth a plumber's bootlace, but somehow we managed to assemble the basic structure of his pump with not much more than a hacksaw and a tub of Bostik PVC Weld. We had it done in one weekend and it stayed there unprotected for five more days until Mervyn brought his mate the Catholic Worker. The Catholic Worker had some very complimentary things to say about how Cosmo had attached the brass spigot to the PVC. Being an activist himself, he understood we must have a steel cage to protect us from the cops.

The cops never did arrive but that cage, chained to that sewer manhole, is what most people remember of the action: a steel-mesh cube imprisoning two operators in Hazchem suits. One of these operators was Mervyn and the other was his Catholic Worker mate.

It was later said I was the innocent tool of left-wing unions, but in fact the opposite was true: it was my will that drove our war machine. I was the one who 'borrowed' the Hazchem suits. I was the one who would reveal her face to the cameras when I removed my hood. I wanted to be responsible. Look at this young girl. If she can do it, why can't we?

There were many people who I represented. I would have given credit if they wanted it, not just to Mervyn, but about fifty people we never even spoke to, not least the now famous band who supplied a van and driver to take the unassembled pieces to McBryde Street. This is how it would be all my life. I would be the one who everyone could love or hate. But you cannot be a solo artist and release asylum seekers from their corporate jails. I was, always, in every single action of my life, spoon-fed by others. It is hard for my mother to accept this, but it is my job to take the heat and do the time.

It was frosty again on the day of the action. Even before I got off my bike, the two men inside the cage were waiting for the PVC weld to set. No-one in this part of Fawkner was awake. There was no traffic. Frederic and I dressed in our Hazchem suits in the middle of McBryde Street.

The so-called steampunk pump was already rising from the earth. Now Mervyn withdrew the steel rod with its plywood circle and there was a thrilling sound of liquid passing up the PVC tube, a lovely slowly elevating slurp. Driven by the forces of cohesion and adhesion, the toxins travelled vertically, then turned horizontal, then emerged from the brass spigot, like bathwater heading down towards the sewer. Suddenly the air was filled with the vaporous horseshit poison. We let it run, but it was in our public power to turn it off, poor Daddy, now I am sorry for the hurt I had to cause.

37

There are writers who will thank their editors, bow and brownnose and then enjoy the blue pencils driven through their wrists. The author Felix Moore was never one of them. Trapped in the Koala Lodge, with editors next door, he has been turned into a mill puppy, a poor bitch locked up for breeding purposes, who must forever have her children removed. The hammered sentences, the deeply imprinted pages, are delivered to others with no guarantees of what parts will be excised, what calumnies inserted. This was not what he had expected when he accepted that fat brown envelope from Woody Townes.

There is no direct exit from this room, one door to a shared bathroom and the other to what one might call 'the editorial suite'. It is from this grimy bathroom that he collects his gruel and frozen peas. Here also, on the closed toilet seat, he leaves his daily pages to be removed and edited without his approval or involvement. It has been said that this is for his own safety. He is a national treasure, too important to be a witness to a felony, to face the dangers of the front. Yet in spite of this cosseting it seems likely to him, now, as he writes, that he will soon be shot and killed. Stet. His wife will read his last words, he loves her. [*sic*] Leave tenses as is or are. He treasures her, regrets more than he can say. Nothing is lost to memory, the nest of sheets, smells, baby throw-up on his shoulder, in the middle of an interview, in the midst of history. He has not forgotten, even near the end of his wasted days, the nights spent worrying about the dyslexic daughter, her too-pretty sister who was just too confident to survive another day.

As he writes he is bilious, sick with memory and uncertainty, fear that the end will come before the end is told, that there will be no end. He had wanted Gaby Baillieux to do what he had failed to do on *Drivetime Radio*. He wanted more than that. How pathetic his ambition now seems, how small his own imagination. He had been a journalist with one story, one cause, one effect. He had been born in the previous geologic age while she was born into the Anthropocene age and easily saw that the enemy was not one nation state but a cloud of companies, corporations, contractors, statutory bodies whose survival meant the degradation of water, air, soil, life itself.

She, Gaby Baillieux, was once a schoolgirl. She stood on the crispy cold grass, in the middle of the Agrikem paddock just after dawn, in the company of blowflies, sad horses, amidst the perfume of dioxin. She wore a yellow Hazchem suit. The poison flowed from fresh white plumbing, as dull as ditchwater.

Disguised humans clustered around the sewer inspection hole, blue and yellow figures like cartoon gnomes in Hazchem suits. All Melbourne's TV channels were there, their OB vans parked in McBryde Street, their satellite dishes turned towards the rising sun. Inside the barbed-wire perimeter, shivering crews crowded around the cage.

Inside the yellow suit, sweaty, blinkered, the girl was afraid of someone sneaking up beside. There were sixteen blue and three yellow-suited figures. She no longer knew which one was Frederic.

A large car, a black Ford LTD, entered from the direction of the factory, driving very fast, steering directly at the cage of gnomes. The starving horses scattered. The girl's throat was dry and she wondered would she even be able to talk when her moment came. She turned to face the Ford as its front right wheel dropped in a ditch and the whole pitched sideways. The roaring engine seemed quite distant. She clearly saw the driver crawl up an incline to the passenger-side door. He was very wide-shouldered and although not tall, possessed by a powerful fat-necked big-chinned fury. As he came he shouted something. She saw he had fat thighs and a distinctive pigeon-toed walk. He was carrying a rod, or tyre lever.

She thought, he does not know I'm just a kid. He will bash my head.

He was using the word trespass. She had time to think, good handle. I am Trespass. I own you.

The crowd of men and women in blue Hazchem suits shuffled and crinkled and now enfolded the Agrikem executive in what the Chinese call a cabbage defence, that is they wrapped loosely around him like the leaves of a cabbage, at once passive and impenetrable, so he was locked in the place where his effluent streamed back into the sewer.

The ABC picture had a cool aesthetic quality. The viewers saw the blue plastic petals open to reveal the Agrikem man. At Patterson Street Coburg, the local member sat on the floor before the television, waiting to hear the angle on the nurse's strike.

395

The yellow figure removed her hood. The cameras became agitated. The girl was too shockingly young. She had blonde curls and thoughtful soft grey eyes. The manufacturer was broad-faced, thick-necked, his face unexpectedly sensual. His lips were bows, his cheeks buffed like apples. When he saw the girl he laughed in disbelief.

In Patterson Street, Sando watched his daughter read aloud the chemical analysis her boyfriend had stolen from MetWat. As she recited the contents, he thought, she has made a huge fool of herself. At the same time the ABC rolled the analysis like film credits. He thought, this has taken hours to set up. In all that time not one of the stations had sought a comment from the government.

And where did you get this information? the Agrikem executive asked. He was a hard-nosed bastard, Sando knew.

Gaby said, The state government has a zero tolerance for dioxin. Is that right?

This is all a nonsense. We have MetWat anaylsis. Talk to them.

This is the MetWat anaysis.

Where did you get these?

The girl had a small pimple on her tumescent upper lip. It only emphasised her beauty.

She said, Will you promise to stop this poisonous effluent?

I'm calling the police.

So you won't turn it off?

Of course not.

Very well, she said, then we will.

How could you do that you idiot? he asked. Clearly he had not really taken in the nature of the plumbing. Now he watched as Mervyn turned the brass valve and the flow was stopped completely.

The man later identified as Ken MacFarlane walked to his beached car, paused, and proceeded to his manufacturing facility. Simultaneously the Premier of the state was being called by all of Melbourne's media. Gaby Baillieux appeared on the television, again and again, on the huge screen in City Square, on Swanston Street. The Premier of the state cancelled all appointments and spent the morning in conference with MetWat and his environment minister.

This was how Gaby and Frederic and Cosmo and other unnamed individuals closed down the Agrikem plant. Her later exploits would be less visible and more far-reaching, but this was the first, the intoxicating spectacle that would lead her, eventually, to the Koala Lodge.

38

None of the following was available when the first edition was rushed so urgently to publication.

Woody Townes had burst into the Koala Lodge, dragging Celine Baillieux after him. The great bull danced and pranced, enraged that the journalist, in a state of fright, continued typing, transcribing lines of dialogue written as spoken. This was not intended as provocation.

Felix Moore was not noble. He feared for his own safety first of all. The connecting door had crashed open. He was finally unprotected, exposed, as vulnerable as a rat fleeing across a ballroom floor.

Woody Townes wore that premeditated jacket with all its useful zips and pockets. He snatched loose pages from the writer's desk and shoved them into a plastic shopping bag which already held the great bulk of this manuscript. Meanwhile Celine was signalling desperately. She nodded and grimaced. What did these signals mean? Was Felix Moore meant to give Woody what he wanted? Yes? No? He handed him twelve numbered pages in a manila folder. Then he rolled a fresh sheet of paper into his machine. He wrote because he could do nothing else. He wrote to tell his wife what was transpiring. Woody Townes read over his shoulder as if he owned him every word.

Woody said, Tell her you are sorry to have been a coward and a waste of space.

Felix Moore reported this, and made gnomic notations on all the abuse that followed. This was not his usual style.

Gaby Baillieux then entered the room and he was moved, again, by the small bare feet the chipped nail polish. He experienced a deep and complex familiarity with a woman he had met only once before. At her side was a wiry whippy man, perhaps thirty-five years of age with deep-set eyes and sunken cheeks. The barcode tattoo on his wrist identified him as Frederic Matovic, but could this man have ever been the girl-boy with the eye shadow? If so he had been distilled, reduced, burnished and he confronted Woody Townes like a hard man, with his right hand held down along the seams of his jeans. Felix Moore had never seen an actual 'shiv', but the whole of Frederic's body suggested he held one in close against his thigh.

OK, famous Frederic said to Woody Townes. What you got?

The property developer's eyes were small, pouchy, bloodshot, dangerous. They settled on Frederic and stayed on him throughout the following silence. When he reached into his jacket he produced two Australian passports and tossed these on the desk.

Using an aluminium jeweller's loupe Frederic inspected one and then the other. He took his time.

Judith, he said, delivering the first passport to Gabrielle Baillieux.

If this was a joke, no-one smiled. Woody offered a fat brown envelope. Gabrielle Baillieux counted the contents and Frederic's eyes did not leave Woody Townes.

OK, said Gaby.

Airline tickets, said Frederic.

399

Celine was already searching in her handbag in the manner of a woman who fears she has lost her keys. Shit, she said, I put them in the glove box in the car.

Woody groaned.

I thought they would be safer, the actress said.

OK, said Frederic, this is what we are going to do. Gaby and Celine will stay here. You will give me your keys, mate. I will go and get the tickets.

You're joking I hope.

All right, you tell me how to do it.

Woody narrowed his eyes and Frederic held out his left hand, leaving the right down by his side.

Flashlight too, he said.

I haven't got a flashlight.

Bullshit.

Woody paused and when his hand emerged from inside his jacket the writer was relieved to see only a flashlight.

Frederic departed with key and flashlight. The writer typed. Woody Townes instructed him to cease. He was unable to comply and was abused. Woody Townes then turned on Gabrielle Baillieux to whom he delivered a sarcastic lecture on the future of the earth: the planet had always been going to die; there was nothing she or anyone could do about it. In 5 billion years the sun would go cold and the story would be over. So save the fucking whales. Was she such a spoiled superior up-herself cunt to think this would not apply to her?

He was a dog on a leash barking. If Frederic tried to nick the Merc Woody would have him killed. It would be cheap, a thousand bucks. He promised that the manuscript would never be a book. It would be 'properly gone through by the authorities' then Felix Moore would go to jail. He sat heavily on the bed which spewed Duracells onto the floor. He produced the revolver and rested it on his massive thigh. No-one spoke. Still Frederic did not return.

Woody got up and stood by the connecting door. He pointed the weapon at the women, each in turn. All typing ceased.

Celine, he said.

Celine's mouth crumpled. No, Woody. Don't.

Shut up. You go and find him. Bring him back. If he is not here straight away I will have to get serious. You understand what I'm saying?

Celine turned to her daughter wringing her hands. The girl held out her arms to her and kissed her eyes and ears. I'm OK, Mummy. Go.

As always, the omniscient narrator had a very wobbly grasp of what was happening. He certainly did not know, for instance, that the OBD-II port of a Mercedes S500 is under the lower right side of the dashboard, that it is possible for a malevolent device to send instructions directly to the CAN bus through this connection and thereby to *own* the car's network which can, in turn, be controlled remotely via a smartphone. It did not occur to him, as the prosecutor would finally suggest, that Celine might have somehow left the tickets in the car by prior arrangement with 'the other conspirators'.

Felix Moore was flattered to be accused, even briefly, of aiding and abetting a hack of the type described. Yet he could never have dreamed that such a feat was possible. All he wished was thirty minutes, a chance to finish the book on a grand note. But when Frederic finally returned, the author was ordered to collect all his manuscript and source material, most specifically the tapes, and carry them out to the Mercedes. By then the revolver had been returned once more to its holster. There was no explicit threat made or any apparent danger. The worst he expected was to be shoved into the boot.

Woody Townes had left his car not in the car park, but beside the road. He walked around the Merc inspecting the tyres with his flashlight. Whatever he was looking for he did not find. When he popped the boot it was only so the manuscript and tapes could be locked inside the dark.

He shone the white-quartz light in the writer's raddled face.

You are a silly prick, Felix.

Yes, mate. I am.

Just a tip: I wouldn't hang around here now if I were you.

You couldn't give me a lift back, mate?

There was silence. The writer thought, I've surprised him.

If you could drop me somewhere I could get a cab.

Silently, Woody opened his door and sat behind the wheel. Felix presented himself at the passenger-side door. He waited optimistically. The engine started. He heard a click and reached for the door handle and narrowly avoided serious injury as the Mercedes accelerated.

Abandoned in the yellow sodium streetlights of Katoomba, Felix Moore made a forlorn figure. His shoulders were hunched and his shuffle clearly audible in the mountain air. There was no-one to observe this moment in his life, nor any indication that he was on the

402

very brink of becoming a publishing phenomenon. In the short time since he had carried the tapes out into the night, a previously prepared digital edition of his account of the so-called life and crimes of Gabrielle Baillieux had been unleashed on the World Wide Web. In the few minutes it took him to reach the motel suite the PDF file titled 'Amnesia' had been downloaded over five thousand times. Fast forward.

39

My old mate's connections were such that I was almost immediately arrested by the Federal Police and, as a result, it was my fate to not see my wife and children for many months and then only through the glass wall of the visitation facility of Barwon Prison, a high-tech Supermax prison not so many miles from my home town of Bacchus Marsh. Here I was held on many charges including conspiring in the murder of Woody Townes whose car had last been seen intact as it passed the Pennant Hills Golf Club at 240 kilometres per hour. Two kilometres later it left the road, briefly airborne before it flipped and exploded in a ball of flame.

I was also held liable for causing billions of dollars of damage to property by means of the malware (what the media dubbed the Amnesia Worm) which had been so neatly packaged inside the PDF file of my book.

How this file was tampered with, what was done to bring certain chapters to the attention of certain corporations and their legal advisors, I do not know, only that the book's 'editing' involved embedding codes designed to cause extreme disruption to many international corporations and individuals who might be typified as 'climate change murderers'. I did not personally attack these corporations for that would be an act of terrorism.

Although the Commonwealth alleged that Celine Baillieux and Frederic Matovic had hacked the computers of Woody Townes' Mercedes-Benz, no such thing was ever proven. As with the prior cases of death by auto, the men and women of the jury, being of sound mind, thought it both 'fanciful' and 'beyond proof' that the defendants might have taken control of another person's car, accelerated out of control and then braked only one wheel.

As for my role in destroying all records, memory and production processes of certain global corporations and their lawyers, it was easily established that I was unaware that my typed pages had been scanned, converted to a PDF and then contaminated. For the crime of expressing pleasure that my book would be available to future generations, I was judged not only immoral but also vain and preening, but no matter what ugly threats and slanders were issued by the corporate holders of the copyright, I have not as yet been charged with anything more weighty.

In the matter of her role in bringing Woody to meet her fugitive daughter, the court found Celine not guilty of 'aiding and abetting'.

Gabrielle Baillieux and Frederic Matovic were convicted of espionage and malicious damage caused by certain worms and viruses written by them in collaboration and contained, in many variations, within the first digital edition of my book. The charges, one hundred and fifteen in total, resulted in Australian life sentences. They each served three years in Barwon Prison until November of 2013 when an updated version of their Angel Worm was released by their 'supporters'. This alpha iteration invaded and multiplied inside the corporate defences of Global Supermax. At that time the angel of the lord by night opened the prison doors, and brought them forth. The present whereabouts of Gabrielle Baillieux and Frederic Matovic are unknown. It is said that an American grand jury is still empanelled.

Felix Moore is a writer living in Denison Street, Rozelle. His early novel Barbie and the Deadheads *is soon to be a major motion picture.*

The Chemistry of Tears

London, 2010. Catherine Gehrig, conservator at the Swinburne Museum, learns of the unexpected death of her colleague and lover of thirteen years – but as the mistress of a married man, she has to grieve in private. Her employer at the museum, aware of Catherine's grief, gives her a special project – to piece together both the mechanics and the story of an extraordinary automaton, commissioned in the nineteenth century by Henry Brandling to amuse his dying son. Linked by the mysterious automaton, Catherine and Henry's stories intertwine across time to explore the mysteries of life and death, the miracle and catastrophe of human invention and the body's astonishing chemistry for love and feeling.

'Alive with the vivid evocation of place and period that is always Carey's forte . . . *The Chemistry of Tears* isn't only about life and inventiveness: it overflows with them.' *Sunday Times*

'A unique combination of raw human passion and complicated puzzling about human ingenuity.' A. S. Byatt, *Financial Times*

'A portrait of grief, its violence and its inevitable place in the cycle of human life. . . At the beautiful heart of this novel lies wonder.' *Independent*

ff

His Illegal Self

Seven-year-old Che was abandoned by his radical Harvard-student parents during the upheaval of the 1960s, and since then has been raised in isolated privilege by his New York grandmother. He yearns to see or hear news of his famous outlaw parents, but his grandmother refuses to tell him anything and forbids him to watch television.

When a woman named Dial come to collect Che, it seems his wish has come true: his mother has come back for him. But soon Che and Dial have become outlaws as well, and Che is thrown into a world where nothing is what it seems.

'A wonderful novel, full of hard-won truths, which leaves you with a feeling of immense satisfaction.'
Evening Standard

'A richly absorbing novel which can be relished for the beauties of its prose and the pertinence of its themes.'
Sunday Telegraph

'Carey writes with beauty, audacity and wit about this lost generation of idealists and ideologues.' *Independent*

ff

Parrot and Olivier in America

Shortlisted for the Man Booker Prize 2010

From the two-time Booker Prize-winning author, an ir–
repressibly funny portrait of the impossible friendship between a master and servant. Olivier is a French aristocrat,
the traumatised child of survivors of the Revolution; Parrot, an Englishman who always wanted to be an artist but
has ended up a servant.

Through their picaresque travels in the New World – in
love an politics, prisons and the world of art – Peter Carey
explores the adventure of American democracy with dazzling wit and inventiveness.

'I finished it with unabated enjoyment . . . Dazzling.'
Guardian

'[Carey] is an extraordinary clever, able writer . . . and I think
this novel is right up there with the best of his books. It is an
amazingly ambitious, ingenious, clever, wonderful book.'
Andrew Motion, Chair of the Man Booker Prize, 2010

'A comic masterpiece.' *New Yorker*

ff

Oscar and Lucinda

Winner of the Booker Prize and Shortlisted for
the Best of the Booker

Peter Carey's novel of undeclared love between clergyman
Oscar Hopkins and the heiress Lucinda Leplastrier is both
a moving and beautiful love story and a historical tour de
force. Made for each other, the two are gamblers – one obsessive, the other compulsive – incapable of winning at the
game of love.

'A novel of extraordinary richness, complexity and strength
. . . it brings the past, in all its difference, bewilderingly into
our present. It fills me with wild, savage envy and no novelist could say fairer than that.' Angela Carter

'This remarkable novel has a Dickensian amplitude, and
the energy of its writing is also Dickensian.' *Spectator*

'Magnificent.' *Daily Telegraph*

ff

Jack Maggs

London, 1837. Jack Maggs, raised and deported as a criminal, has returned from Australia in secret and at great risk. What does he want after all these years, and why is he so interested in the comings and goings at a plush townhouse in Great Queen Sreet? And why is Jack himself an object of such interest to Tobias Oates, celebrated author, amateur hypnotist and fellow burglar – in this case of people's minds, of their histories and inner phantoms? A thrilling story of mesmerism and possession, of dangerous bargains and illicit love.

'Sensationally bold and brilliant.' A. S. Byatt, *Sunday Times*

'Carey, wonderful deviser of gnarled and twisted stories, reinterprets the moral and physical make-up of the Dickensian landscape . . . Not simply a pastiche, but a report by hellish half-light on one of the great dreamlands of human obsession.' Peter Porter, *Guardian* Books of the Year

'Bold, gripping and wonderful.' Hermione Lee, *Observer*

ff

True History of the Kelly Gang

Winner of the Man Booker Prize for Fiction

I lost my own father at 12 yr. of age and know what it is to be raised on lies and silence . . .

To the authorities in pursuit of him, Ned Kelly is a horse thief, bank robber and police-killer. But to his fellow ordinary Australians, Kelly is their own Robin Hood. In a dazzling act of ventriloquism, Peter Carey brings the famous bushranger wildly and passionately to life.

'Packed with incident, alive with comedy and pathos . . . Contains pretty much everything you could ask of a novel.' *New York Times Book Review*

'It is credit to Carey's extraordinary skill that he has created for Kelly a voice so mesmerising and moving. Carey has conjured up with vibrant immediacy the inner life of this legendary figure and the harsh, stunning landscape of the Australian bush.' *Mail on Sunday*

'Carey is without question the pre-eminent literary voice of post-colonial Australia.' *Guardian*